The
RayBright
Caper

ISBM : 978-1479270880

Interior design by Booknook.biz.

A KIRBI MACK NOVEL

The RayBright Caper

B.B. TEETER

For my parents, Marie and Bill

ONE

Harvey Grant stood for a moment at the curb outside 24 Hour Fitness. He'd just done his usual hour of weights and half hour of cardio. A chilly breeze was tossing the fronds of the palms that lined the street ahead. But this being subtropical Southern California, *chilly* was a relative term. Harvey had come out from northern Michigan thirty years before. He knew what a January breeze could be like there.

Looking off across the lot, he idly watched someone climbing into the back of a van. The kid. Over the last couple of weeks, Harvey had noticed him inside, usually on the stationary bike reading a book, or else shaving at the sink in the gym's men's room.

He'd also noticed the van. Just never put the two together, the kid with the van.

Both had caught his eye for some reason. The kid, a kind of tall, self-consciously good-looking specimen, but with something sly about him maybe. The van, an ancient rattletrap on its last legs, its faded lettering advertising some dry cleaners in Austin, Texas.

Setting his gym bag down beside him, Harvey thrust his hands into his trouser pockets. The kid had left the sliding side door open. After disappearing for a few seconds, he came back into view now, slouching comfortably on some pillows in the van's carpeted rear.

Was he down on his luck and *living* out of the van?

Harvey thought about this possibility, as well as his general feeling that the kid was bent somehow. Harvey had recently been presented with an intriguing business opportunity. Something doable, but which required help in the doing. However, the people he might normally have called on for that help were for various reasons unavailable.

So if he was going to take a run at the thing, he was also going to have to take a chance. He was going to have to find someone fresh. Someone untested. Someone from the outside. And he was going to have to do so soon—because the project had a deadline.

Had he as yet made any progress toward finding such a someone? No.

When was he going to get up off his procrastinating ass and make an effort to look? Another good question.

You'd think he might take the matter more seriously, given his current dire need for money. Yeah, you'd think so, Harvey told himself. He drew in a deep breath and blew it grimly out through pursed lips.

Intuition wasn't much. But in the absence of anything else, it was at least a place to start. Half minute and a short walk later, he knocked politely on the side of the van.

"Excuse me, is this a nineteen ninety?"

The kid glanced up, cigarette in hand, giving Harvey a careless once-over. "Ninety-one."

"The reason I'm asking is my nephew has a van something like this, and he's looking to buy another one for parts."

"Yeah. Well, I'm not interested in selling."

Harvey nodded his acceptance of this fact.

But then lingered, making a show of examining the vehicle's interior, taking in the rolled-up sleeping bag, propane stove, and clear-plastic containers of neatly folded clothes.

"I see you got it fixed up nice."

"Uh-huh," the kid said.

"You by yourself?"

When the kid shot him a puzzled look, Harvey went on, indicating with a glance the women's dresses hanging at the back. "I figured maybe you had a girlfriend."

"What fucking business would that be of yours?"

"Sorry. Just making conversation."

The kid studied him for a long moment. "I do a little drag karaoke sometimes, if that's any of your business either."

"Ah," Harvey said thoughtfully, as if he'd expected just such a commonplace explanation. "You have to be gay to do that?"

"Not necessarily—it matter to you if I was?"

"Not to me."

"You looking to have your dick sucked or something?"

Harvey wasn't sure how much of the question was taunt and how much serious invitation. He put on a solemn expression, as if giving the idea the careful consideration it deserved.

"No, I don't think so," he said at last. "But how about I buy you a cup of coffee?"

"Why would you want to do that?"

"What do you care?"

"What do *I* care?"

"Yeah, you got something better going?"

The kid didn't seem to like this. He took a long pull on his cigarette, scowled, and exhaled in a kind of smoky snort. But after a moment slid across and out the door. "What the fuck, old man."

"The name's Harvey."

"Yeah," the kid said, accepting Harvey's handshake.

"And you're?"

"Mark."

Up close and out in the light, Harvey couldn't help but notice the dinner-plate size of the kid's pupils. He was clearly amped on something. Maybe that's what made him so testy.

Harvey waited while he locked up the van. Then the two of them set off together across the lot toward the Starbucks on the corner. Along the way, Harvey stopped at Dorothy's Mercedes SL to toss his gym bag into the trunk.

"Nice car. Except for the color."

Harvey shrugged. He'd never thought much about its color, which happened to be beige. His focus was its accessories and the way it handled. "It's my wife's."

"My dad drives an SL."

"Good for him."

"*Black.*"

Harvey offered a bland smile, refusing to rise to the bait. It sounded like the kid came from money, which was good. Money gave a guy polish and confidence.

For his part, Harvey had grown up in a two-room shack without running water or electricity. His confidence came from usually being able to outwit and outfight other people. You played the cards you were dealt. And played to win.

Once he and the kid were in motion once more, he said, "I wonder if you'd satisfy my curiosity about something."

"And what would that be?"

"I was wondering if you'd ever been in jail."

The kid's boyish face morphed through several expressions. He forced a wry chuckle. "Have I ever been in *jail?*"

"That's right."

"You know, I can't say I have."

"Just curious. Sometimes I have a feeling about people."

"And you had a feeling I'd been in jail."

Harvey tipped his head to the side. "Weird, huh?"

"Yeah," the kid said. "Definitely."

Starbucks was packed with Sunday morning coffee drinkers. But amazingly they found no line at the counter. Harvey stepped up and asked for a small decaf. In turn, the kid—as Harvey could have predict-ed—ordered something expensive and elaborate which took two dozen words to describe.

A minute later, their respective beverages in hand, they made their way outside to sit at one of the umbrella-covered tables. Ahead in the street, a line of cars waited for the light. Music blasted from one of them, a vintage convertible, its top down despite the brisk weather.

Credence Clearwater's "Fortunate Son."

For Harvey, the song always brought to mind Vietnam. He'd served a year-long tour there, four decades before. He listened for long moment, lost in wartime memories.

Then took the lid off his decaf to let it cool, sat back in his chair, and looked across the table at the kid. He'd taken the lid off his own cup, but was busy spiking its already exotic contents with whatever was in a small flask. Going by color, Harvey suspected bourbon.

When the kid made an offering gesture with the flask, Harvey shook his head.

The kid shrugged. "To each his own."

"You got it," Harvey agreed amiably.

"I just need to take the edge off."

Harvey wondered if he meant take the edge off the coffee. Or off whatever chemical was running riot in his system. He watched the kid imbibe a series of gulping quaffs. Then set the cup down and grin over at him.

"Why'd you happen to think I'd been in jail, by the way?"

"I'm not sure," Harvey told him. "Maybe you look like a guy with larceny in his heart."

"What are you, a cop?"

"I *look* like a cop?"

"Not particularly. But if you are, you're a crooked one. Or maybe one who's been undercover so long he's lost track of which side he's supposed to be on."

Harvey laughed and the kid joined in.

"Actually, you look like an old biker."

"I had a Harley once," Harvey admitted.

"How about you—*you* ever been in jail?"

"Once upon a time."

"What for?"

"Smuggling marijuana."

"Federal?"

"Yup. Twenty-two months. Minimum security. I taught bridge and tennis."

The kid gave him an admiring leer. "I like it. That's what I call getting over."

"Sure. But you have, too, haven't you?"

"Have what?"

"Been in jail."

"I told you—no."

"Sorry, I forgot," Harvey said, frowning at his own carelessness. "I have a *hypothetical* question, then."

"What if there were no hypothetical questions?"

Harvey ignored the witticism. "If you *had* been in jail, what would it have been for? Just hypothetically."

"Let's say…computer fraud."

"Let's say."

"Yeah."

"So you're free and clear now?"

"More or less. I might have a little hypothetical paper out on me from Texas."

"*Mark* your real name?"

The kid said nothing, but his eyes had shifted for an instant.

"My point is," Harvey went on, "how bad would it be—this hypothetical paper that's out on you?"

"It's no big deal."

"It's *no big deal?*"

"Right."

Harvey chuckled, shaking his head.

The kid raked him with a hard look. "Anybody ever tell you the smug asshole act wears a little thin?"

"You know, I get that all the time."

"Gee, what a surprise."

Harvey took a blithe drink of decaf. The kid reminded him of a cat, all touchy dignity. Was this anybody it made sense to get involved with? A guy this deep into booze and drugs? And with outstanding warrants, to boot?

On the credit side of the ledger, though, the kid did seem smart, had a veneer of class, and sounded like he possessed some useful computer skills. Properly handled, maybe he could fit the bill. After all, it'd only be for a couple of weeks.

"Look," Harvey began, putting some apology in his voice. "I don't mean to give offense. My curiosity has a purpose."

"And what might that be?"

"Think of this as a job interview."

"A job interview."

"Does making some money interest you?"

"Making some money doing what?"

Harvey smiled and lowered his voice. "Helping me take something of value that belongs to somebody else."

"What's it involve, this help I give you?"

"This and that—it'd be kind of half con game, half smash-and-grab."

"I'd have to hear *way* more."

"Of course you would."

"So tell me way more."

"No. Not yet."

"Oh dear," the kid said, bringing his hands up in an exaggerated face palm. "You don't trust me."

"Whether I trust you is less important than that you trust me."

"Oh really?"

"It's a law of the universe," Harvey explained, leaning to one side to dig out his wallet. From it he counted five hundreds onto the metal tabletop, and placed the kid's cup atop them to hold them in the breeze. "You don't have to trust someone if you can get them to trust you. This is me getting you to trust me."

"But I don't."

"Sure you do, in a way."

The kid rolled his eyes in dismissal of the notion, but soon grabbed the bills and folded them into his pocket. "So this buys you what exactly?"

"Just shows you I'm for real."

"That you're for real."

"Here's the situation," Harvey said, summoning an earnest tone. "I'm not trying to be your new best friend. Let's just get to know each other. And later today, even if there's no meeting of the minds, I give you another five hundred and we can each choose to go our separate ways, no hard feelings.

"Another five hundred."

"Right. Also this job might include a place for you to stay. An apartment over my garage. That's got to beat sleeping in your van and having to go into the gym in the middle of the night to take a dump."

The kid sighed and took another drink from his beverage. Then looked away, thinking or pretending to.

"Well?" Harvey said.

"Whatever."

Which Harvey rightly interpreted as a greedy yes.

TWO

Mark Hatcher followed the old man home.

The only trouble was, home proved so remote, so far out in what San Diegans called the *back country*, that the needle on the van's gas gauge was grazing E by the time they got there. The vehicle's beat-to-shit engine got horrible mileage. He'd seen an Arco station a few miles back, and made a mental note to be sure to fill up there when he headed back. Whenever that was.

Because how long he'd be staying had yet to be settled.

This old redneck asshole seemed to have some sort of heist movie going, and Mark was being auditioned for a role in it. That didn't mean Mark was necessarily going to get the part. Or even that he'd accept the part, once he learned more about what playing it required.

But he'd be a fool not to at least check out what was being offered.

He needed to move on from the hand-to-mouth living he'd been doing. Ever since coming out to the West Coast, he'd been scuffling. And scuffling wasn't good enough.

Climbing out of the van, Mark watched an Australian shepherd come trotting across toward him, its tail wagging. He scratched the dog's head, taking in the property as he did so. He smelled horses, but something else as well.

Money.

Here in the middle of nowhere, like Shangri-La in the barren Himalayas, was some kind of country estate. A huge rambling adobe-brick house with adjoining four-car garage. Assorted outbuildings, barn, and, fencing—all painted to match. A greenhouse. No less than an acre of perfect asphalt. And no less than an additional acre of lovingly maintained landscaping.

Across at the garage, the old man was getting out of the Mercedes.

When he beckoned, Mark nodded and followed him to the side of the house.

"Dorothy?" the old man called as they came through a back door into a kitchen.

A tall white-haired woman appeared.

"Dorothy, this is Mark."

She stepped forward and offered her hand, eyes lit with welcome and interest. Older than Harvey maybe. Lithe and upright, stylishly dressed, confident in manner.

Right away, Mark knew she and the old man still fucked.

"So pleased to meet you," Mark said, holding her hand for an extended moment, giving her the full treatment.

In his head, he couldn't quite put her together with the old man. She seemed such a straight arrow. Could she not know what an utter thug the guy was?

"Mark might be doing a little work for me. If he does, what do you think about him staying up above the garage for a week or two?"

Dorothy spoke up in a concerned tone. "I don't know how clean it is up there."

"He'll be okay," the old man told her. "He's a young fella and used to roughing it."

"I'll be fine." Mark chimed in, offering a good-natured smile.

"Well, Lupita's here tomorrow," Dorothy said, and turned to Mark. "She's our cleaning lady. I'll have her give it a good going-over, first thing."

The old man had begun digging through the contents of a nearby cabinet drawer. "Here we go," he said, holding up a key on a tagged ring. "Let's take a look. See if the place works for you."

11

When he crossed toward the door they'd come in, Mark dogged along behind.

"Harvey, you guys going to be wanting lunch?" Dorothy asked.

The old man stopped, seemed to think for a moment, and looked at Mark. "You hungry?"

Mark shrugged. "Not ravenously. But sure, I could go for a snack."

"Okay," the old man said. "Give us five minutes."

Outside, the two of them climbed a flight of wooden steps alongside the garage. At the top, Mark waited on the landing while the old man fiddled with the lock.

"I'll have to hit this with some WD-40, later," he told Mark when he finally got the mechanism to yield and they were able to enter. "Nobody's been up here in a while. Dorothy's niece used to live here when she was going to art school. But that was two or three years ago at least."

The stuffy air smelled of dust and something else. Insecticide, maybe. When the old man hoisted open one of the dormer windows, Mark did the same with another.

Air circulation thus established, the old man moved on to plug in the refrigerator. Switch lights on and off. Check the sink taps. Then meaningfully touch the controls of a large boxy thing attached to the far wall.

"Heat and AC."

Mark nodded. The place was nice. Far better than camping out in his van, or scaring up a night in somebody's bed.

As he watched, the old man stepped through a darkened doorway. "And this of course, is the shitter."

When a light came on inside, Mark came forward, poking his head in.

Again, the old man moved about like a hotel concierge or real estate agent.

Water flow was checked in the shower and sink. The toilet got flushed. A small, high casement window was cranked open. The ventilation fan received a test.

"I like it," Mark told him.

"Well, I wanted you to have a look at it. Tour over. Let's grab some lunch, then we'll talk some more."

"I'll be right down. I'm going to hang back a minute and use the rest room."

The old man shrugged and headed out the door.

Mark stood in the middle of the room, listening to the retreat of footsteps down the stairs. He waited for the sound of the kitchen door being opened and closed. Heard it. Then strode into the still-lit bathroom.

His reflection in the mirror told him he looked as ragged as he felt. He'd been up all night and was starting to fade. He wasn't going to make it through the afternoon without some more help. Not just coffee, *real* help.

Reaching down into the elastic top of his sock, he pulled out a small plastic container of white powder. Opened it and tap-tap-tapped a tiny white heap out onto the edge of the sink. Pressed the pad of an index finger into the heap. Brought the finger up to his nostril. And vacuumed the finger clean with a savage intake of breath.

He repeated this procedure with the other nostril.

Within seconds a familiar taste arrived at the back of his throat. Sharp and bitter, but oh so welcome. Mark shivered, looking in the mirror.

Today he needed to step up, to present himself well, to be at his best.

Because whatever kind of movie this old body-building bozo had going, Mark wanted *in*.

Chance had at last dropped something into his lap. He needed to take advantage of it. Not drop the ball. Not come across as an incompetent fuck-up.

He remembered the old man's face when he'd seen the flask—that look of disapproval, even disappointment. Mark couldn't afford to disappoint. Not today.

He patted the wad of bills in the right front pocket of his jeans. Then nodded to his reflected image, switched off the light, and headed down to lunch.

* * *

Though he didn't eat much of it, Mark recognized the time and care that'd gone into the meal. Dorothy was a foodie. Chicken salad sandwiches, the chicken salad containing seedless grapes and walnuts. A platter of exotic cheeses. Some sort of Thai soup with a peanut flavor.

Dorothy and the old man drank iced tea. Mark had a micro-brew. It went down so easy he wanted to ask for another, but didn't dare.

The old man kept to himself during the meal. He smiled and nodded once in a while, but seemed content to let Mark and Dorothy get to know each other.

As they talked, Mark played her the sanitized version of his life. He stressed his accomplished parents and how he'd grown up comfortably in the Dallas area. There seemed nothing to be gained, however, in mentioning his year-long stay in the Texas prison system, or his recent, accidental release due to clerical error.

The safest tack was to change the topic of conversation. From *him* to something else. While Dorothy had manners and curiosity, like most people, it didn't take too much to get her talking about herself.

He soon learned she'd grown up on a nearby ranch. That her father, and grandfather before him, had bought and sold two things. Land and horses. And that, lifelong, she hadn't strayed far from the family tradition, herself. In fact, she told him, she still occasionally dabbled in the local real estate market, and almost every day took one of her horses out for a long ride.

Mark liked that she also made sure to mention she had a masters in English Lit. Likewise, that her now-deceased first husband had been a two-term U.S. Congressman.

14

"Did you care for Washington?" he asked.

"I did. I enjoyed the social life to an extent. The big city was a thrill for a country girl. Going to parties and meeting the wheeler dealers." She gave him a conspiratorial grin.

"A political wife."

She laughed. "Phil got elected the first time pretty easily. Some movers and shakers in the district put him up to it at the last minute. His predecessor had dropped out a month before the election. Caught in a scandal."

"Sex or money?"

"Sex," Dorothy said, savoring the word and showing a wicked smile.

"Oh-oh."

"Somebody on his staff."

"Male or female?" Mark asked.

Her eyes flashed in amusement, as for a moment she held him in suspense. "Female."

"What do they say—anything but a live boy or a dead girl."

Dorothy threw her head back and laughed, glancing at the old man. He showed her an amused grin, but Mark wondered if he got the reference. He was hard to read.

When Dorothy stood up and began bussing the dishes to the sink, Mark rose to help. Though she insisted she'd be fine doing it herself, she let him participate. Together they began rinsing everything and placing it in the dishwasher.

"I think my husband found politics tiresome the deeper he got into it," she said, picking up where they'd left off. "All the fund raising. As I said before, the first campaign—in money and effort—was easy. He got spoiled. By the second go round, though, the competition had had time to organize, and accumulate a war chest." She grimaced, stretching some clear plastic wrap over the top of the cheese platter. She handed the platter to Mark to put in the fridge. "I think that's why Phil had had enough. He got tired of spending such a big part of each day hounding people for contributions."

"Not very dignified," Mark said.

"Not at all."

Drying her hands, she smiled at him. "Thank you," she said, and closed the dishwasher door with finality. "You didn't need to, but I appreciate it."

He nodded, and after a moment asked in a throwaway tone, "So how'd you and *Harvey* meet, by the way?"

He caught the old man's eye to check his reaction to the question, but got nothing.

"Bridge," Dorothy said.

"Really," Mark said.

"We belonged to the same bridge club and played as partners sometimes."

Mark sat back down at the table. "I've never played. But I gather it can be a demanding game. Let me guess—I'll bet Harvey's competitive as hell."

The old man startled them both with a loud bark of laughter. Mark looked from one to the other, seeking understanding.

Dorothy, wearing a wide, lop-sided grin, explained. "Actually we have a disagreement on that point. Harvey tends to want to accuse *me* of being the overly competitive one."

"She's a fucking shark," Harvey said, as if stating a generally known fact.

"Oh, Harvey!" Dorothy said, but Mark couldn't tell if she was exasperated at his judgment of her, or at his use of the f-word.

* * *

16

A few minutes later, the old man got to his feet. Took a small leather knapsack off the nearby counter, and slung it over one shoulder. Then announced to Dorothy that he and Mark were going for a walk.

Mark, in need of some nicotine, thought this was a great idea.

Outside, on a flagstone patio behind the house, he lit a Marlboro and waited while the old man chained up the Australian shepherd. Apparently so it couldn't follow them on their walk.

The sun had come fully out, and the wind had died down. Mark had expected it be cooler inland, but it didn't seem to be. At least not today.

When the old man rejoined him, they set off, side by side, down across the sloping lawn. Ahead, Mark could only see what looked like a canyon. He wondered if this was their destination.

It was.

At the edge of the lawn, a long set of railroad-tie steps led down through lush, dark-green iceplant. The old man went first and Mark tagged along a moment later. The descent was steep and there was no railing.

At the bottom, iceplant gave way to tall grass, weeds, and brush. What Mark thought of as scrubland. Now civilization—or at least, irrigation—appeared to cease, and the way down was a zigzagging dirt trail.

He hadn't been out on foot in raw *nature* in a long time.

Everything seemed strange and slightly overwhelming. The strong plant odors. The noises of the birds and insects. The powdery slipperiness of the soil under the soles of his cross-trainers.

He felt overloaded with sensory input. A feeling magnified by how tired he was, and by the nerve-electrifying drug he'd put up his nose to fight that tiredness.

In front of him, he watched the old man plod down the trail. A broad-shouldered ape walking with determination. Mark had just begun wondering where they were going, and if this little jaunt were simply for exercise, when he saw the old man turn off to the right.

A cluster of large rocks protruded from the ground. When the old man picked out one and sat down on it, Mark did likewise. He smoked quietly for a few moments then, looking around, said, "So, Harve, this still your land down here?"

"Yeah, we own from the other side of the little road coming in, to the ridge there on the other hill."

Mark nodded. "How many acres is that?"

"A little over a hundred. Probably not much of a *ranch* by Texas standards."

"Still, your own little kingdom away from the problems of the world."

The old man made a wry face. "You can't escape everything. Sometimes things come to you. Like fire, for instance."

"What do you mean?"

"Well, a few years ago, this whole area burned. Just about as far as you can see in every direction."

Mark made his own wry face. "No kidding."

"Oh yeah. Wildfires. Tens of thousands of acres. We saved the house and most of the buildings, but just barely. Afterwards, everything down here looked like a lunar landscape, trees with no leaves or branches, everything all gray and white with ash."

"Hard to believe."

"It was all too real, let me tell you."

Mark wondered if he should put out his cigarette. But figured the old man would've spoken up if it was a problem. "Everything seems pretty green now."

"The operative word is *now*. In the late summer and fall everything dries out and turns all yellow and brown. That's when things get dangerous."

"The burn season."

"Right," the old man said. He stared across the canyon for a long moment. Then turned back to Mark, as if remembering something. "By the way, let me pay you that second five hundred."

Mark stretched to take the bills from him. "Thanks."

The old man gave an absent nod, but said nothing further, gazing off into the distance once more.

Mark folded the bills and slid them into his pocket with the other five. He appreciated the money but wished he knew what being given it meant. Had he failed the tryout or passed it? Was he being brushed off now, or was he still in the running for a part in the heist?

He felt he'd made a good impression on Dorothy. But wasn't sure if that counted for anything with the old man. With an inward shrug, he took a final drag from his Marlboro, then ground it out in the loose red dirt at his feet.

Beside him, the old man seemed oblivious now, wrapped up in his own thoughts. Self-contained, like some bald Buddha. Or rather—some bald *Mr. Potato Head* Buddha. Because that's what the old man's oblong noggin reminded Mark of.

Mr. Potato Head. The toy. He'd played with one as a kid.

Mark smiled to himself.

And for a silly, manic, methamphetamine-fueled instant, considered mentioning this amusing comparison to the old man. But caught himself in time.

Taking a breath, he instead said, "So, Harve, tell me more about this job."

"Like I said before, it's swiping something."

Mark was heartened by this reply. It seemed to suggest he was in the movie. Cool. "I get that. But *what* is it you're looking to swipe?"

"Let me put it this way: it's a valuable, one-of-a-kind piece of high-tech. More than that I don't want to say just yet. I'll let you in on things more as we go along."

"Okay. That sounds good."

"What's necessary, first off, is getting the details on where exactly the piece is being kept and how exactly it's being secured."

"So it's owned by an individual?"

The old man shook his head. "A company."

"Okay."

"The theft itself is the dangerous part. But the reconnaissance beforehand is what makes the actual rip-and-run possible."

"Reconnaissance."

"Yeah. By that I mean research. Sniffing around. Buddying up to the people in the organization."

"Well, all right then," Mark enthused, laughing, wanting to show his willing commitment to the project. "If it's about lying, cheating, and stealing, you've got yourself the right partner!"

"Except I'm not looking for a partner."

Mark caught something ominous in the old man's tone. "Okay."

"This isn't a partner thing."

"Got it," Mark said firmly. Not really getting it, but knowing when to backpedal. And seeing the old man's eyes now locked on his.

"I'm interested in hiring an *employee*. A well-paid employee. Because this is my job. Gotten by my reputation and my connections. Funded as we go along by my bread."

"Absolutely."

"There're a thousand ways this thing could go sideways. It may not even be able to be done. And if it can be, it might still turn out to be a bust, and I lose my investment. But whether the job turns sour or is a roaring success, you get paid. Well. In full. On time."

A vein had begun to stand out in the old man's wrinkled forehead.

"It's your movie," Mark insisted.

"I pay you in full, no matter what."

"Your money, your risk. I do what I'm told."

"We're clear on this?"

"We are."

"No room for misunderstanding."

"Not a bit."

"Good," the old man said, at last breaking off his stern scrutiny.

Then again lapsed into self-contained silence, peering off across the canyon.

To Mark, the old man was a type he'd encountered before—the white OG. Prison was full of them. They were usually hillbillies and cowboys. You could get along with them, you just had to be careful. Which was what he needed to be doing now, getting along.

At least for the time being.

Because he needed to keep those hundred dollar bills flowing. Later, who knew? Things might be different. Merely because some goddamn geriatric prick has the script written a certain way doesn't mean the movie has to turn out that way in the end. Not one bit.

Out of the corner of his eyes he noticed the old man getting slowly to his feet.

Mark generated a casual smile. "Back to the house?"

"Not yet," the old man said. "Let's head down the way a little farther. I want to show you something."

"Okay."

"And there're a few more things we need to discuss."

Mark shrugged. "Sure."

Returning to the trail, the old man once again led the way.

Soon Mark could see what must be the bottom of the canyon. The beeline distance didn't look that far. But the trail had to switchback more now as the descent grew steeper. So that it took several minutes to get there.

When they arrived, Mark lit another Marlboro and waited to see what was up.

Here the vegetation was thicker. There were even a few scraggly trees. Mark leaned patiently against the trunk of one, watching as the old man poked about here and there, kicking in the tall grass. He seemed to be searching for something.

At last, Mark saw him bend down and pick up what appeared to be a wad of weathered cardboard.

"What's that for?" Mark asked, when the old man joined him at the tree.

Up close he could now see it had once been a twelve-pack beer carton.

The old man shrugged, setting the thing down and ignoring the question.

Mark tried another. "So what was it you wanted to talk about?"

"Well," the old man began, "I thought maybe it was time we got around to discussing what I guess you'd call a *nondisclosure agreement.*"

"Okay."

"Something I will enforce if you ever reveal anything we do or say concerning my little...enterprise."

"Fair enough," Mark allowed.

"So the first thing I will mention is that I used to fight." This said, the old man presented the backs of two gnarly, age-spotted fists. "Golden Gloves, if you know what that is."

"Amateur boxing."

"Right. And I've always been a scrapper, I guess you'd say."

"Sure."

"That doesn't mean I take any pleasure in hurting people, but I've had a lot of practice doing it. And I know how. Note the scars and swollen knuckles."

22

"So noted," Mark said, not bothering to hide his annoyance.

"Good."

"Warning received."

"Good. All I'm saying is, I am not someone you want to want to double cross."

"So fucking stipulated."

The old man offered the tiniest of smiles at Mark's curt tone. Then picked up the wad of cardboard once more, and gestured with it. "See that big bush over there."

"Uh-huh," Mark said, looking in the direction indicated.

"Take this over there, if you would, and place it up in the branches about shoulder height. Face-out like a sign, so the word *Budweiser* shows. Alright?"

"Any particular reason?"

"Indulge me."

"Indulge you."

"If you would."

Mark studied the old man's lined face, looking for clues as to what was going on. Still baffled, he traipsed to the bush. A distance of maybe a hundred feet. Where with a deep sigh, he wedged the cardboard in between two springy branches.

"Like this?"

"Perfect," the old man called back, grinning and looking up. He was hunkered down now, his hands invisible inside his leather knapsack, which lay open on the ground beside him. "Okay, stay there, but take four steps to your left."

Mark grimaced, but went along.

He counted out each step aloud in a sarcastic voice, then halted. Sucked a bored drag from his cigarette. And turned to watch some crows flapping and cawing down the canyon behind him.

In the distance beyond, he could make out what seemed to be a dirt road. He wondered where it led to. When he turned back, he noticed the old man had something in his hand.

Just what that something was didn't register for a moment.

Until, with a shock, Mark realized it was a pistol.

A big, menacing-looking one. Pointed in his direction.

"Jesus H. Fuck," he muttered uncertainly, his heart beginning to race.

The old man was some kind of sick serial killer.

The heist had been just a ploy to lure Mark to this remote spot. Then shoot him. The money would be retrieved from his corpse before burial, down here in a shallow, unmarked grave. He'd been a fool.

But before he could move from these frantic thoughts to action—before he could run or shout or plead for his life—the pistol began bucking in the old man's hands. At the same time, a rapid succession of sharp pops sounded. And ejected shell casings arced and glinted in the sun.

Then the old man was stalking toward him.

"Not as loud as you'd expect, right?" He held the pistol out sideways for Mark to inspect. "This doohickey here on the barrel is a sound suppressor. Illegal in California—as well as tending to interfere with accuracy."

"Fuck you," Mark told him. In bringing his cigarette to his mouth, he realized his hand was shaking.

"Sure, fuck me."

"Yeah, fuck you and your pointless game playing."

The old man nodded, as if he found Mark's agitation perfectly understandable. Moved across to check his target. Came back. Nodded again. "Ten for ten."

"Aren't you wonderful."

"Just a demonstration, kiddo."

"Fine. I get it."

"Do you?"

"Yeah."

"Good."

"We done with the threats, then?"

"Almost," the old man said, undeterred. "Let me finish by spelling out what I mean by *never*. *Never*, in terms of our nondisclosure agreement, means no matter what. No matter how things turn out. Whether we succeed or fail."

"Got it."

"Not later, after the job, when you're drunk and bragging in some bar. And not, by the same token, if things go badly. Say, when you're under the hot lights in some police interrogation room, where you're tempted to rat me out for a lighter sentence."

"Got it," Mark repeated, this time between his teeth.

"Have you? Good, because I have a long memory and a major vindictive streak. Believe me when I say I will find you and get back at you. And if you think I can't reach out and find you from jail, then you don't know much about jail, or the world in general."

"Enough!"

The old man held his gaze for several more seconds. Then at last, his flushed, wrinkled features formed themselves into a sort of embarrassed grin. "Well, thanks for listening."

Mark considered saying, *Thanks for fucking sharing, Mr. Potato Head.*

But decided to keep the remark to himself.

THREE

The next morning, Mark felt good. Refreshed. It may have taken a mixture of Ambien, melatonin, and marijuana to do it, but for the first time in a long time he'd logged some solid sleep time. Today he had a sense of adventure. A sense he was involved in something cool and exciting.

The heist movie had begun.

He and the old man were sitting in Dorothy's Mercedes across the street from a block-long expanse of chain-link fencing topped with coiled razor wire. Down the hill was what seemed to be a big grey office building.

"So this is the company that has the thing you want."

The old man nodded. "RayBright."

Mark took in the elaborate sign on its little landscaped knoll. "Capital *B* in the middle. No space between the words."

"Correct."

"They seem to take their security seriously."

"That they do. Notice all the cameras?"

"Yeah."

"And that sliding gate, in front. It's closed and locked each night at ten."

"I assume there are guards."

"Watch," the old man said, directing Mark's gaze with his glance.

A car was approaching from the opposite direction. As they looked on, it slowed, turned in at the gate, and stopped at the entrance barrier.

Whereupon a uniformed guy with a pistol on his hip came out of a small structure the same gray color as the main building below. Checked the driver's ID. Then walked back inside to raise the barrier.

"How many guards are there?"

"Four during the day. Two at night."

"Are you thinking night?"

The old man made a face. "So far. But I'm willing to keep an open mind."

"Okay."

"We need to learn a lot more, though."

"Which is where I come in."

"Which is where you come in," the old man agreed, putting the car in gear and pulling away from the curb.

A hundred yards down the street was the strip mall where they'd left Mark's van a few minutes earlier. The old man turned in and parked in the slot next to it. He gestured ahead, out the windshield.

"The company's got a small cafeteria for those that don't bring their lunches from home. But a lot of them eat here. Or buy it here and take it back to RayBright."

Mark saw a deli, a taco shop, and a donut place. "How many work at the company?"

"Maybe seventy-five or eighty. The boss is Eric Van Horne. Heard of him?"

"Not really."

"Nobel Prize winner maybe ten years ago. Used to be a professor at one of the local colleges. I met him once at a charity thing Dorothy dragged me to."

"I don't know what that woman sees in you."

"As in what's her kind of class doing with my kind of crude?"

Mark stifled a laugh. "Your words."

"Well, maybe love's a mysterious thing."

"She know you're a convicted felon?"

"Of course."

"She know what you're up to?"

"What's that mean?"

"How about this, then—she know you're a thief?"

"Who says I'm a thief?"

"I do," Mark said with a grin.

The old man took a breath and turned in his seat. "I'll explain this once, then we'll drop it. Dorothy's old money. Respectable. Pays her taxes, obeys the traffic laws, volunteers for the Red Cross. She doesn't like trouble, so I do my best not to bring any into our relationship."

"Okay."

"She's rich and I'm not. But I think she likes that I pay my own way—and she knows enough not to look too hard into how I manage to do that."

"Hold on, I'm missing something. You're married right? I thought California was a community property state."

"I am, and it is."

"I don't get it then."

"It's simple. I signed a pre-nup."

"Ah. So there's her money and there's your money."

The old man shrugged. "It's slightly more complicated, but yeah."

"What would happen if she were to...have an accident?" Mark only realized how bad this sounded when he saw the old man's eyes narrow.

"She's not going to *have* an accident."

"Right," Mark said quickly. "Heaven forbid."

"Maybe you'd better watch that mouth of yours."

"I'm sorry. I apologize, Harve. That was out of line. I like Dorothy, and I didn't mean anything by it."

"I'll tell you one thing, she's been a good ol' gal to me."

"I don't doubt it."

"And I better *hope* nothing ever happens to her—or I might end up on death row."

Mark nodded, but the old man must have seen a lack of understanding in his face.

"None of her kids ever liked me from the get-go," he went on. "Or wanted her to marry me. The oldest as much as told me if anything ever happened to their mother, I'd be the chief suspect. And that they wouldn't stop looking into it until I was behind bars or dead. Not if they had to spend the rest of their lives and every cent they had."

"Jeez," Mark said in a sympathetic tone. Though it occurred to him that maybe Mr. Potato Head had met his match in the vengeful threat department. Regardless, he decided it might be best to change the subject. "So tell me more about RayBright Labs."

"What do you want to know?"

"What do they make? I mean aside from this particular valuable thing you still don't seem to want to mention."

The old man conceded a small smile. "They do research. Electronics, aircraft guidance systems, that kind of thing. You'd call them a defense contractor."

"And this guy, Van Horne, he owns the company."

"He has a partner. I think they own it together. This retired general by the name of Shellhammer. From what I've read up on the place, it's something like this: Van Horne is the brains and the general is the connections."

"Connections to what?"

"I guess you'd say, connections to government contracts."

"Ah."

"So, as we discussed, your job is snooping. Seeing what you can find out from RayBright employees without them realizing you're doing the finding out."

"Weaseling my way into confidences."

"That's it. To start, I suggest people stuff. Names. Some kind of org chart. Company phone directory...."

The old man's gaze slipped across Mark. The car's side windows were down. A young couple, the woman carrying a baby, had appeared on the passenger side, passing close on their way to the taco shop. When they were out of earshot, the old man completed his thought.

"...Work schedules, stuff like that. Anything you can get."

Mark nodded his understanding. "You know who I'm going to be?"

The old man just looked at him for several moments. "Who?" he said finally. Half annoyed, half puzzled, like Mark was forcing him to play along with some kind of lame knock-knock joke.

"I'm a *writer*."

"You're a writer."

Mark smiled, not caring what this senile dinosaur did or didn't get. "Check it out," he said. "I'm writing something on Nobel Prize winner, What's-his-name Van Horne." He shot his eyebrows. "A freelance magazine article. Maybe even a book on spec."

The old man stayed quiet again. Did he not like the idea outright, or merely not understand it? Finally he shrugged and said, "Well, kiddo, you're the college boy."

"Actually only a year and a half."

"Let me guess, you were thrown out."

Mark laughed at the accuracy of this, despite himself. "You've been checking on me?"

"How could I? I don't even know your real name."

Mark laughed again.

After a moment, the old man gave him an enquiring look. "We good then? I've got a couple of errands to run."

"We're good, except I might need a few tools of the trade."

"Tools of the trade."

"A good smartphone. All I've got right now is this cheap pay-as-you-go thing with no data plan. Also, a decent laptop would help. Seriously, you fucking watch what I do with a computer."

"This is stuff you want me to cover."

"If you wouldn't mind."

The old man blew out a breath and looked at his watch. "There's a Fry's not too far from here."

"Fry's will do."

"Do me a favor, okay? Just don't run off with the stuff I buy you, and make me have to hunt you down and kill you, okay?"

Mark laughed so hard the old man was forced to join in.

* * *

When the old man dropped him off back at the strip mall an hour later, Mark sat in his van for a few minutes. There he carefully took his new phone and laptop from their packaging. Placed the devices, their manuals, and their many accessories in his new, multi-compartment carrying case. Then got out of the van and chucked the bags and packaging in a nearby trash can.

Inside the donut shop, he chose an energy drink from the cooler and brought it to the register. A small, middle-aged Asian lady was behind the counter. After he'd paid and gotten his change, he asked her if she were Cambodian. She gave him an odd look, but said she was.

The old man had mentioned that morning that almost all Southern California donut shops were owned by Cambodians. It'd seemed preposterous. But Mark hadn't argued with him, suspecting the old man had simply been messing with him, testing his gullibility.

So once seated at a table with his energy drink, he used his new phone to Google the question. Only to learn that the old man had been more or less right. Cambodians *did* open donut shops. Just as Vietnamese were linked with nail places, Koreans with dry cleaners, and Indians with motels. Who knew?

Thirsty, Mark quickly finished his energy drink and bought another.

The place was almost empty. Just himself and two old duffers reading newspapers. He'd chosen a seat by the window so he could keep an eye out for the RayBright lunch crowd, but it was still a bit early. While he waited, he played with his new phone and laptop, and skimmed through both manuals.

At eleven, he switched to the deli.

There he bought an onion bagel with cream cheese, and a diet cola. At last, just after eleven-thirty, a forty-something man in a blue dress shirt and jeans entered. And, wait for it, he had a RayBright badge hanging from his neck on a green lanyard.

Mark got up, slid into line at the counter behind him, and managed to start what he hoped came off as a casual conversation.

This was the first of many such (hopefully) casual conversations. Some went better than others. In many he learned a lot. In others, nothing much more than the person's name.

But wherever there was a break in this process, he made notes. He felt a sense of purpose and engagement that'd been absent from his life for a long time. He'd always liked getting over on the straight world. Crime had always been fun for him.

Stolen watermelon just *tasted* better.

FOUR

The next night, up above the garage, the apartment door stood open.

Harvey climbed the steps, deciding to check in before he went to bed. It was almost midnight. He hadn't seen the kid all day.

All the lights were on, of course. And out through the propped-open door, heat and music poured into the cold night.

The kid sat hunched over at the desk, gaze fixed on the screen of his laptop. Fingers moving on the keyboard. Feet alternately tapping to the beat.

Harvey called out a greeting but it was lost in the pounding, swirling noise. When he strolled into the kid's peripheral vision, the kid gave a violent start. But then laughed, grabbing his chest like he'd had a heart attack.

"Hey, Harve," he shouted.

Harvey peered over the kid's shoulder at the screen. Some kind of message board maybe. But incomprehensible.

After a moment, the music getting on his nerves, Harvey reached in and flicked the knob on the speaker. In the sudden relative quiet, the kid glanced up. Shock on his face.

"I know," Harvey told him, "it *is* too loud and I *am* too old."

The kid cracked a tiny smile.

"Who is that, by the way?"

"The music? Skrillex. It's called dubstep."

Harvey tried to think of a suitable comment but gave up, just shrugging. "Tell me something else," he said. "What's all this?" He pointed to the jumble of numbers, letters, and symbols on the screen.

"Leetspeak." The kid paused, maybe thinking how to explain. "It's, like, a kind of secret code."

Harvey nodded. Okay.

"Hey, I made some great frozen margaritas," the kid said, picking up a half-filled glass from the desk and drinking from it. "Pitcher in the freezer if you want one."

Harvey wasn't much on alcohol, but decided to do the bonding thing. "Sounds good."

He found a glass in the cupboard and poured himself a small amount from the frosted pitcher. He wandered back to the desk. Forced himself to take a sip. Winced.

Very cold, very sweet, and very citrusy. And *incredibly* strong with tequila.

"What've you been up to, kiddo?"

The kid just smirked at him for a moment. Rolled back in his office chair, hands joined behind his head. Then spun himself around twice and stopped, grinning up at Harvey in self-satisfaction.

"I did tell you I was a demon hacker, didn't I?"

Harvey smiled and played it right back at him. "I never had any doubts."

"Not to mention, social engineer extraordinaire."

"Not to mention."

"Check that out," the kid said, making a gesture across the desk.

Harvey realized he meant the printer. An old clunky thing that had belonged to Dorothy's niece. He scooped up an inch-thick sheaf of papers from its tray, hefted them, and glanced at the kid, who gave him a small intense nod.

Harvey pulled his reading glasses from his shirt pocket and moved the papers over under the desk lamp. He did an unhurried scan of the first couple of pages. Followed by a random sampling of the rest of the stack.

"Employee records," he said, impressed and letting the kid know it.

"Everybody except Van Horne and Shellhammer."

Harvey chuckled in approval. "But how could you *get* this?"

"Their overall computer security's not bad. It has holes, but it's not bad. Their personnel, though?" The kid shook his head as if sadly. "They give it up like prom night."

Harvey was intrigued. "Tell me."

"It's all little puzzle pieces. I start with what I got from a couple of lunchtimes at the strip mall, then use that to go fishing for more, right? In conversation, but also on the phone. Putting the pieces together and parlaying them into more."

"Okay."

The kid rocked in the spring-loaded chair, excited. He worked the Groucho thing with his eyebrows. "For instance, who do I meet at the deli yesterday, but a cute girl named Gloria. Now, guess what Gloria was."

Harvey gave the required shake of his head.

"She's—get this—a *new hire*. So what do I do a little later? I make some gag calls to RayBright until I learn her extension. Then I phone RayBright Shipping Department and I say I'm trying to get through to Gloria in Special Projects. I tell them I was routed wrong or something. Can I just be transferred? I give them the number." He nodded to Harvey. "Get it? So, if the phones work like RayBright's do, the call to her seems to be coming from inside the system. Her call display shows me inside the building."

Harvey grinned, liking it.

"So, they transfer me and I say, Hi, Gloria, I'm Mark, from I.T. I'm down at Shipping and I just remembered I never called you. Welcome to RayBright. Are you up on RayBright's security policies? No matter, dear, it's my job to explain them. So I talk a lot of boring, common-sense stuff about logging off when you leave your desk, and on and on. Then I say, Oh, of course we all need to make sure our passwords are not of the 1-2-3-4 or birthday or social security number variety—because Ray-Bright handles top secret government contracts, don't you know. We all have to be extra careful with people trying to hack us." He rolled his eyes at the irony.

Harvey took another sip of frozen margarita and chuckled.

"So, eventually, I get to the point of the whole five-minute call. The make or break moment. I just slide the question in, in the same tone of voice I've been using so far. I say, What password are you using right now on your desktop?"

Harvey provided a proper expression of amazement and admiration.

"And she fucking *tells* me!" the kid said, flushing, eyes dancing. "I say, that seems good. Keep it for now. Then I chat about this and that for another little bit so she doesn't get suspicious, and I thank her and end the call."

"I love it," Harvey told him. And he did.

"Am I not slicker than weasel shit on a doorknob?"

Harvey nodded and laughed. "But you didn't get this stuff from her," he said, waving the sheaf of employee files.

The kid lit a cigarette. "Shit, no." He blew out a long plume of smoke, striking a triumphant pose. "You know what *root* is?"

"I'm not sure. Tell me."

"It's like getting *administrator* access." He watched Harvey's face for understanding. "Doesn't matter. But when you're in their system and you get *root* you fucking own their asses."

Harvey gave a shrug of happy ignorance.

"So did I do good, Daddy?" the kid asked, cocking his head.

On impulse, Harvey jumped in with both feet. The kid *had* done good. "Sonny boy, you're beautiful. You make me proud. You're the best."

The kid beamed almost shyly, lapping it up. For once, speechless.

He leaned back in his chair, set his mouth, and puffed out three slow smoke rings.

Then peered up at Harvey and said, "One more thing."

"What's that?"

"I want to tell you about somebody *else* interesting I met at the deli."

"Company employee?"

"Yup. Wearing his RayBright Security uniform and everything. Guy named Stanko. He's on the list you have there. Check this out, I strike up a conversation with him outside as he's getting into his big ol' honking pickup, right?"

Harvey nodded. "Right."

"So we're shooting the shit and what does he start doing but crying on my shoulder, Mr. Sympathetic Stranger, about how they're trying to repo the thing."

"Money troubles. Leverage."

"Exactly," the kid said in evil glee. "Great minds think alike."

Harvey bobbed his head at how smart the two of them were.

"Then," the kid went on, "I asked if he had a light." He swung his hands out in a gesture of wonder. "He said he might have some matches in the glove compartment. And starts pawing through stuff and laying it on the seat. Just the usual junk everybody has—except for one thing."

"What?"

"A fucking glass drug pipe."

Harvey couldn't help but smile. "Ah-ha."

"Ah-ha is right. Because I've been reading the RayBright Staff Handbook." The kid paused to give his head a mock-regretful shake. "And as I'm sure this guy knows, the company has a *zero-tolerance* drug policy. You have to pass a urine test when you're hired, and you're subject to random testing at any time. Evidence of illegal drug use means you lose your security clearance. And without that, you can't work there."

"Beautiful."

"But anyway, this guy definitely, definitely needs money. Lots of it and right away."

Harvey nodded. "I like it. A weak link in the chain."

"In-fucking-deed," the kid said, all ear-to-ear predatory grin.

Harvey stopped to think for a moment. "Listen, let me take a run at this guard guy, okay? You stay on the rest—you're doing great. I'll try dangling some money. If that doesn't work, maybe blackmail him with the drug policy."

The kid agreed.

They talked for a few more minutes. Then Harvey separated out Stanko's pages from the stack, and left with them to head down to bed.

Outside, under the stars, he poured the rest of his frozen margarita onto the lawn alongside the house. Above, the blaring music started up again. Harvey wondered when the kid slept, high as he seemed to be so much of the time.

The guy was clearly *out there*, but he was delivering—that was undeniable.

Harvey counted off the days in his head to the date the device would leave RayBright. Time was zipping by. If he decided to do the job, he had to start making things happen.

The buyer would be getting in touch the day after tomorrow.

FIVE

The landline in the house rang.

And he was foolish enough, make that *wrecked* enough, to answer it.

"Steven Stanko?" a strong male voice asked.

His face tightened in a grimace, but he said, "Yeah."

"My name is James Beresford Tipton."

"Uh-huh."

Stanko was poised to blow the guy off, whoever he was.

He had a Netflix movie going on the bigscreen. And he'd just smoked a nice old chunk of Humboldt bud. Why had he even picked up the phone? If he'd just waited, the answering machine would've kicked in.

Too late now. Could he just hang up?

"I work for the United States government in Washington, D.C. The Department of Homeland Security."

Wait. What? He looked away from the movie for the first time.

"Could you repeat that, please."

The guy on the other end did.

Stanko's pulse spiked. He fumbled for the remote to hit pause. "Uh, what's this about?"

"Mr. Stanko, I just need to verify something, okay?" The guy then proceeded to read off Stanko's Social Security number. And his date and place of birth. "Is all this correct?"

Stanko's first thought was identity theft. Like you heard about in the news. Some game to somehow get his information. But this didn't scan, because the guy wasn't *asking* for information. He *had* it.

"Yeah," Stanko said after a moment.

"Thank you, sir." A pause. "Something was dropped off at your home earlier today. I'd like you to take a look at it."

"I'm not sure what you mean," Stanko said. He felt a half step behind. The effects of the THC. "Uh, I don't think I got anything." His gaze swept to the coffee table where his father usually put the mail when he brought it in.

No, nothing.

But this was too early in the morning for *today's* mail. He squinted at the clock. It was only a little after nine a.m.

"It was left outside," the guy told him. "What I'd like you to do is take your phone with you and go outside your front door, okay? Check your mailbox. It's a small manila envelope with your name on it. It contains money."

Whoa. Again Stanko wondered if he was hearing right. Money?

This was major bizarreness here. But how could he not at least check? He sucked in a deep breath and lurched up off the couch toward the front door. A passing glance at the screen showed two commando types in a fist fight. But frozen eerily in mid-action. Unlikely expressions on their faces.

He opened the door, slipping outside. The cement stoop was cold under his bare feet. He saw no cars passing, no people walking. A quiet weekday morning. His day off.

He stepped close and peered into the mailbox. Yes, a yellow-brown envelope. Switching the phone to his left hand, he drew it up and out, scissored between the first two fingers of his right. It was the kind that closed with a piece of red string wrapped around a cardboard button.

His name was printed in capitals on the front in black marker. Block letters.

STEVEN STANKO.

His dope-clumsy fingers worked the flap open. With a start, he realized it did in fact contain money. Amazing. Just as the guy had said. He fanned the bills slightly with his thumb to get a count. Six fifties. Three hundred dollars.

This had to be some kind of joke. Like somebody was pranking him.

He surveyed the neighborhood for where anyone could hide and/or video him. At the same time, he ran through a list of friends or acquaintances who might play such a trick on him. He could think of no one. Certainly no one who thought toying with him was worth three hundred dollars.

He put the phone back to his ear.

"Hello?" he said.

"I'm here, Mr. Stanko."

"I found the envelope."

"Great."

"What is this…about?"

"Very good question," the guy said. Like he was pleased to be dealing with someone who didn't waste time. He sounded like maybe an older guy. Polite but with that in-charge attitude. "It's what we call here at Homeland Security an *attention getter.*"

You got my attention, Stanko thought. But what he said was, "Uh-huh."

"That envelope is just to show you we're straight up. That your Uncle Sam is willing to pay you for your time. If you're willing to listen further, I have another envelope for you. Are you interested in listening further, sir?"

Stanko blew out a big breath. Whoa. This was *so* weird.

He folded the currency down into one of the front pockets of his jeans. Then wadded the envelope into the other.

"Sure," Stanko agreed in a provisional tone, seeing that nothing bad could come of listening. His eyes roamed the yard and street once more

41

for where someone with a camera could be lurking. "I'll listen. I'm sorry, I forgot your name."

"Tipton. James Beresford Tipton."

"Go ahead, Mr. Tipton."

"We at Homeland Security do security audits of government, military, and private sites. Our aim is to protect this country's key assets from terrorist threat and from foreign espionage. Do you understand what I'm saying?"

In his mind Stanko saw a fifty-year old male with a brush cut and well-trimmed moustache. Wearing a dark suit and calling Stanko from behind a large government-issue desk. A lot of important papers in front of him. Corner office on an upper floor.

"Sure," Stanko said.

"Great. Sometimes we employ temporary contractors. You have a background in security, Mr. Stanko. I have your DD214 here in front of me. What makes you attractive is your MOS—that you were an MP—and your high achievement scores. Would you be interested in some temporary contract security work on a cash basis?"

"Uh…doing what?"

A flock of noisy birds had lighted in the big tree across the street. A bottled-water delivery truck rumbled by just then. Stanko didn't usually like going outside when he was this wrecked.

"Not anything much different from what you're doing right now at RayBright."

Stanko steeled himself and asked, "How long would I be doing this, when, and—" With the utmost sly nonchalance he dropped the most important question in at the number three slot "—*how much would I be getting paid?*"

Stanko hardly dared to think this might be the solution to his money problems. There had to be a catch. There had to be something his blown mind was missing.

"Well," Tipton said, "on a temporary basis only, if you can start right now, we can pay you two hundred dollars an hour."

Stanko was speechless. This went way beyond bizarre into preposterous. He found himself shuffling about back and forth on the stoop, nervous, trying to think. Lost in the friction of his bare, callused heels scuffing against the chilly cement of the stoop.

This all didn't feel right somehow. How did he know this guy was really Homeland Security? Why would some federal agency put an envelope of cash in his mailbox, then call him about it?

But unless the money was counterfeit—and it didn't look counterfeit—what did he care? What was he quibbling for? Opportunity was knocking. Not to answer was to be a fool. If things got too weird or scary or illegal, he'd tell them to take a hike.

"I'm your guy, Mr. Tipton," he heard himself announce.

"Are you really. That's wonderful. I guess now you're entitled to the second envelope."

Yes, Stanko thought. More money sounded wonderful. "Okay," he said, but business-like. Not too hungry.

"Along the front of your house is a hedge. Correct?"

What? "Yes, sir."

"Go to the end of the hedge at the southwest corner of the house. Got that?"

Stanko's head swam with the concept of direction for a moment, but he figured it out. He stepped down off the stoop to his left, down onto the bristly grass of the front lawn. He began moving along the hedge. Past the living room windows. Along to the corner.

"Look down. Look for a red golf tee in the dirt at the base of the hedge. Okay? A red golf tee. When you see it, pick it up."

Stanko saw it. He squatted and grasped it. A red string—the kind of string that held the flap of the other envelope—was knotted to the tee.

43

Stanko yanked on the tee and out of the loose dirt came a buried envelope. A yellow-brown envelope, just like the other one.

He set the phone down in the grass to open the envelope.

This one contained *twenty* fifty-dollar bills. Stanko's heart was racing. He caught himself glancing furtively around, like some small scavenger among larger scavengers out on the savanna. Lest his lucky find be snatched from him.

"Got it," he said into the phone. "Thank you, by the way."

"You're welcome, Mr. Stanko."

Feeling a sudden energy, Stanko loped across the lawn toward the front door. He went inside and locked the door behind him. The new bills went into the same pocket as the others. Both envelopes got tossed now on the coffee table.

Money. Not enough, but a start.

He'd see if the collection agency had an eight hundred number. If he got right on it maybe he could stop them trying to repo his truck. Right now it was hidden in the garage behind the house. Not much of a hiding place, though.

Flopping down onto the couch, Stanko remembered the phone in his hand. "You still there?" he asked, hoping he wasn't screwing it up by being rude to this guy.

"Yes, I am, Mr. Stanko."

"Okay, what do I have to do for this money?"

"The money you now have, thirteen hundred dollars, is a gift. Earnest money. Yours to keep whether you choose to proceed or not. If you'd like to start working for Homeland Security, there're some things we need to discuss."

"Okay."

"First, all of this is entirely confidential. When I say *entirely* I mean nobody gets to know. Not family, friends, or drinking buddies. Entirely nobody. Not other agencies of the federal government. Not state and local police. Not your employer. Is this going to be a problem for you?"

"Not at all," Stanko told him, summoning what he hoped was a compliant, can-do attitude.

"Good. Okay then. What I'll be doing is giving you assignments and then calling you to debrief you on the results. You'll be expected to keep accurate track of your own hours. We'll provide any equipment if necessary. I'll be communicating with you at this number."

Stanko immediately warmed to the idea of keeping track of his own hours. "That all sounds fine."

"I need you to be absolutely honest with me, Mr. Stanko. If you have any misgivings, tell me. If you encounter any trouble in carrying out the assignments, also tell me. We're paying you top dollar and we want your best efforts. I have to be able to justify the results to my bosses up the line. We understand each other?"

"Yes, sir," Stanko told him. Chain of command, like in the military.

"Okay," Tipton began, "I'm going to give you your first assignment. What I want you to do is this: Based on your experience as someone in the security field, I want an honest evaluation of security procedures at RayBright. Spend some time thinking about it, organize your thoughts, put your considerable intelligence into the evaluation, Mr. Stanko. Ray-Bright has several federal government contracts. We're interested in your take on how safe the place is from penetration by agents of a foreign country or by a terrorist organization."

"You talking about, uh, written down? Like a report?"

"Not necessarily. But if that seems like the best way to approach the process, sure."

Stanko was getting into it. This could be a cool challenge. "So what you're interested in is, like, are the alarms that are supposed to be set, actually set. Stuff like that."

"Right. Both an overall take on security, and a take on the details. How are things handled—or mishandled—in all areas. If things are being done properly, let's hear about it. But if things are *not* being handled in keeping with good security protocols, we want to hear that too. Any report you make to us will be under the radar. The confidentiality works in both directions. Nobody at RayBright will know what you tell us."

"Okay, Mr. Tipton. I'll start right in thinking about it today."

"Good," Tipton said. "Remember, total confidentiality. Keep track of the time you spend to the quarter hour. And I'll call you in exactly thirty-six hours. Tomorrow night at nine. Okay?"

"I'm on it."

"Welcome aboard, Mr. Stanko. Thank you for your service to your country. Goodbye."

Stanko replaced the phone in its stand.

He got up and went to his room to get some paper. Then, grabbing a pen from the kitchen counter on his way by, returned to the living room. He dropped onto the couch and grabbed the remote. A few minutes into the rest of his movie, he began making notes about RayBright.

When the movie ended, he'd completed both sides of two pages.

Later, after lunch, he hid the pages in his room. Put the money in his wallet. And tore the manila envelopes into tiny pieces, which he put in the trash under the kitchen sink.

His father would be home from work that afternoon. Stanko didn't want to have to answer any questions. He'd been dreading that he might eventually have to admit to his father what financial hot water he'd gotten himself into. Now, maybe that wouldn't be necessary.

SIX

Jane Bouchet headed for the bar to get a Diet Pepsi. She hadn't been in a place that served alcohol in four years. Not since the night of her DUI.

As she waited in line, a sufficient number of guys were checking her out to raise her spirits. Hey, she was a hot little chick. Still. At forty-five.

Vas smiled when Jane approached the table. She rose from her chair and stepped close to give Jane a warm hug. Jane still felt a little odd embracing people since getting her new boobs. She wondered if Vas had heard about the surgery or noticed. Did she feel them now when their chests met?

She could smell Vas' perfume and the woman's long braided hair touched Jane's cheek.

Truth be told, she really hadn't known Vas all that well, but it was a small company. And farewells seemed to draw people together somehow.

"When're you actually moving?" Jane said into her ear above the club's loud music.

Vas in turn put her mouth to Jane's ear. "Jim—" Meaning her husband, who Jane had never met " has got to be in Seattle on the fifteenth. So we've been packing, and shipping, and giving stuff away." Vas gave a little shrug. "It's crazy but exciting, too."

"I'll bet," Jane shouted.

Vas and her husband were both engineers. Brainiacs. He had a new job at Boeing. She'd lined up a teaching position at one of the local colleges up there.

Jane couldn't see the band from where she was. The music had been crescendoing to an end and now it came. With a sustained crashing of cymbals and rumbling of bass, the song died. The people on the dance floor broke into applause. The singer murmured something into the mike. Then silence.

But after a few seconds some canned dance music came on. Almost as loud.

Vas re-took her seat and gestured for Jane to join the table.

Jane smiled and held up an index finger, then pantomimed smoking a cigarette.

"I'll be back," she mouthed in silent exaggeration.

Vas nodded and smiled.

To smoke you had to go outside now. California had tightened up even more over the years when Jane had been a nonsmoker.

A long retaining wall seemed to be the informal smoking area. She joined two young guys already sitting there. She'd lived in San Diego long enough to be able to peg them as single, active-duty military.

They gave her simultaneous nods, then went back to an involved conversation. Fellow members of the smokers club.

Jane lit up a Pall Mall. That delicious first puff. Once she'd started smoking again, in six months she'd lost the twenty-plus pounds she'd put on after quitting years before.

Her father had been a heavy smoker, and died early of heart disease. But which was worse for your health? Being overweight or being a smoker? Well, she'd chosen. If smoking shortened her life, so be it. Quality over quantity. She liked the way guys looked at her new boobs and her cute little slimmed-down ass.

As if in tune with this kind of thinking, an attractive male manifested himself in her field of vision.

A tall, slim guy in the open doorway of the club. Getting his bearings. Lighting a cigarette. Then ambling farther outside, bottle of beer in his other hand.

Jane let her gaze drop as he neared. There were many places to stand and sit.

Nevertheless, a pair of black cowboy boots appeared in front of her. "Mind if I sit here?"

Jane peered up at him. She gave him a subdued shrug and a hint of a smile.

"I'm Mark," he told her as he sat down, and reached to take her hand.

He had very long fingers and soft skin. His grasp was gentle and unassuming, and he had friendly eyes. But, God, up close he was younger than she'd first thought.

"Jane," she said and took a drag on her smoke.

She was glad for the dim lighting outside.

Though she'd spent a long time putting on her makeup earlier in the evening, nothing truly concealed age. She hated being older and having a wrinkled face and neck. Her body she had more confidence in. Especially since taking off the weight.

"You like the band?" Mark asked.

"Decent cover band, I guess."

"But…" He looked at her, waiting, drawing her out.

She smiled. "If you came to dance."

He seemed to nod to himself, considering her answer.

"Do you like to dance?"

Jane regarded him for a moment. "I used to want to *be* a dancer."

"Ah. Like Swan Lake?"

"Not necessarily."

Jane watched him tip his head back and drink off at least half of his beer.

The conversation had taken a left turn. Which wasn't necessarily bad, just odd. Odd as in revealing. She found herself wanting to impress him.

Turning her head toward him, she leaned forward and put her forearms on her thighs.

"My mother taught dance when I was little. I took lessons from the time I was probably three. Ballerina stuff, but all kinds—jazz, modern, tap."

"But you gave it up at some point. Because you say *used to* want to be a dancer."

"Well, when I was nine or ten," Jane told him, "my mother re-evaluated." She shrugged, like it didn't matter after so long. "She decided I was too small. That I didn't have enough talent. And that was the end of that."

"Sounds painful."

"Yeah" she had to agree, and took a hungry pull on her Pall Mall. "It kind of was."

She wondered why she was getting into all this. When he'd asked about her dancing, he'd meant just dancing as in out on the dance floor.

"You dance much now?"

Jane looked at him. If she said yes, he might ask her to dance, and if she declined that might put him off. And she didn't want to put him off. He was fifteen years younger than she was, but she'd risk it. See where it went for a while.

"Just in the exercise class I take."

He gave her an appraising glance. "Well, you must be doing something right."

"Oh yeah?" she said coolly, liking the understated quality of the compliment.

"When was the last time you danced other than in exercise class?"

"Mmmm…maybe a Phish concert a few years ago?"

"Oh," he mocked, "you're one of *those*." He smiled and their eyes met.

This guy scared her. This guy could break her heart. So tall and young. So smart, so funny. She picked up her soda glass from next to her on the top of the little wall. She drank the rest of it.

Her plan hadn't included flirting with some tall, handsome stranger. Her plan—her rules for the night—were to stay for just a half hour or so. Say goodbye to Vas. And not to drink. Coming here tonight was a kind of test. Could she go to a bar and not drink?

Because sometimes—often—alcohol ended up being a problem in her life.

If only she could just drink a beer or two and stop there, like other people could.

She watched Mark finish the second half of his Corona. Then wipe his mouth with the back of his hand in satisfaction. She could imagine the frothy taste and texture of the stuff sliding across her tongue and down her throat.

"When was the last time you took a psychedelic?"

"That's a pretty fucking personal question?" she told him.

His face fell in embarrassment. "Sorry."

She liked that he cared what she thought, that she could manipulate him. She grinned. "I'm kidding." She took a final drag on her cigarette, and ground it out on the asphalt at her feet. "What exactly constitutes a psychedelic?"

"I don't know. Shrooms? Acid? Ecstasy?"

"Ecstasy's considered a psychedelic?" she asked in genuine curiosity.

"I guess."

"I've never done ecstasy. Have you?"

He laughed in a quiet way for several seconds.

She found herself laughing along. "Does that mean you're doing some right now?"

"Maybe. Does it bother you? Kind of invalidate me or something?"

"No. Not at all. I'm merely surprised."

"I took a half. Enough for a sort of mild buzz." He slowly stood up. "I know you're not supposed to bring drinks out here, but I'm going to get myself another beer. Can I bring you another of whatever that is?"

She thought about a beer and decided against it.

The words *Diet Pepsi, no ice* were on the tip of her tongue. But at the very last instant, she stunned herself by saying, "Rum and Coke."

Where did that come from?

As she followed his retreating figure with her eyes, she experienced a kind of dizziness. She could still get up and leave now. She didn't *have* to drink anything alcoholic. Or, when he got back, she could still politely decline, saying she'd changed her mind. And not drink it.

But of course Jane did neither of these things.

When Mark returned and placed her drink ceremoniously in her hand, she took a sip. The flavor of the rum brought back memories. Put her in a familiar frame of mind.

One that scared her, but one she missed.

Mark resumed his seat on the wall next to her. He winked at her. Actually winked. It was hokey and endearing at the same time. She watched him pick up his bottle of Corona.

"What's ecstasy like?" she asked him. "I mean, it's effects."

He rocked his head from side to side, trying to decide how to describe it. "Mmmmm, mellows you out, I guess you'd say."

She nodded.

He started laughing quietly. He leaned back and struggled to reach into the pocket of his jeans.

"Here," he said, putting a tiny, clear-plastic, zip-lock bag on the top of the wall between them. "In case you want to try it sometime." Maybe she frowned, because he added, "Now or later or throw it away. It didn't cost me anything. Somebody gave it to me." He shrugged and smiled.

More because she didn't want to leave it sitting out there, she pushed it into her purse. But she had no intention of taking it or anything like it.

She lit another cigarette and took a second sip from the drink. God, did nicotine and alcohol go together, or what?

"Where are you from, originally?"

"You askin' cuz my ac-cent?" he drawled in comic fashion.

She heard herself giggle. He was so funny. "That and your shit-kicking boots."

"I resemble that remark."

"You can't possibly be old enough to remember him." Did she want to confront the age difference between them at this point? She had crowsfeet. And, if she didn't touch it up, gray in her hair.

"Norm Crosby?"

"How do you know that?" she mock-demanded. "He was on his way out when *I* was a kid."

Well, she'd laid it out there. Let's see how he handled it, or if he chose to.

He drank some beer and smirked. "My uncle Fred used to always say that one. He was a big comedy fan and I sometimes look up people he liked on YouTube."

"Well, God bless YouTube," she said, getting to her feet. She carefully laid her burning Pall Mall on the top of the wall. Then touched his shoulder with her hand. "I'll be right back. Got to visit the rest room."

"I'll be here," he said.

And he was. A few minutes later, she sat back down next to him on the wall and picked up the cigarette she'd left.

He smiled at her. "What do you do for a living?"

"I'm kind of a bookkeeper, accountant, that kind of thing."

"Numbers. Were you always good with numbers?"

"I guess. How about you? What d'you do?"

"Me? I'm a word guy. A writer." He gave her a disarmingly vulnerable look and corrected himself. "Actually, I'm *taking a shot* at being a writer. I inherited some money from my grandfather. Enough to live on for a couple of years."

"Writing what, for instance?"

"I've always been attracted to non-fiction. Like essays, articles. Eventually a book, but you've got to start somewhere, right?"

Jane didn't know what she'd been expecting him to say, but not this. Being a writer sounded intriguing.

"What're you working on now?" she asked, putting some challenge in her tone. Wanting to engage him on some deep level, make him show her who he was.

"I was a business major, so I want to try a profile of a company or a successful CEO, something like that. I've only been in San Diego a couple of weeks, but there's a lot of high tech here."

"You ever heard of RayBright Laboratories?"

Mark puffed on his cigarette. Nodded in a vague way. "Defense contractor?"

"That's where I work."

"Really," he said in surprise and curiosity. "Tell me about it."

Jane looked into his large brown eyes. She hadn't foreseen anything like this. She'd come tonight as an experiment. And yet, here she'd gone and had a drink, seemed able to handle it, and had met this amazing guy who appeared interested in her.

Was fate weird or what?

SEVEN

Harvey followed the directions he'd been given.

He walked through the little touristy shops that made up Seaport Village. Continued out behind it onto the finger of park land that jutted into San Diego Bay. Then stopped halfway along, under the trees, even with one of the cast-concrete picnic tables. A particular cast-concrete picnic table.

After a careful glance around, he sat down.

Calm and quiet, senses attuned, he waited. He didn't bother checking his watch. He knew he had five or ten minutes to spare. He was reminded of hunting, the kind he'd done in backwoods Michigan growing up.

The number of people out and about here surprised him. A safe, pleasant place for some fresh air and mid-morning exercise, it seemed. Tourists from the big hotels, and downtown locals from the high-rise condos.

They walked and jogged, alone or in groups. They pushed their children in strollers and brought their dogs along on leashes. They chatted with each other or spoke into their phones. More than a few wore earbuds, listening to music.

Also present, he noticed a uniformed maintenance worker pruning some foliage down by the public bathrooms. Then a can-picker rooting through the trash barrels one by one along the walkway. And a couple of guys fishing off a skiff, a few dozen yards from shore.

Harvey suspected nobody and everybody. His eyes roamed the area in a continual, repetitive sweep.

The backside of Seaport Village. The looming arc of the Coronado Bridge. A nearby multi-storied hotel complex. A marina filled with rows of moored pleasure craft.

At nine o'clock exactly, Harvey called the number that he saw written in pencil on the concrete tabletop in front of him. He used one of several disposable phones he'd recently bought.

A man answered. "Thanks for being prompt."

"What other way is there," Harvey told him.

"Absolutely." A pause. "So, how's it been going? Can the thing be done?"

"The deadline makes it complicated. But I'm inside."

"*Inside?*"

"Yeah. Meaning, I've got some access to most of their computer system and I've got one employee I've corrupted, and another I'm… manipulating. So, things are moving forward."

"That sounds promising," the man said. "But details would help, if you don't mind."

Fair enough, Harvey supposed.

"Well," he began, trying to decide what and how much to say, "as you may or may not know, the place has armed guards. Twenty-four hours. At least two on at night. And there are biometric locks and alarms on all the labs, including the one I need to get into, which also has reinforced steel doors." Harvey turned his head as the can-picker appeared off to his left, close but still out of earshot. "And besides all that, the system requires an officer of the company to key in for access to that particular lab."

"What's your plan to overcome these, uh, difficulties?"

Harvey took a breath. "There are five company officers. The two owners, and three others. So either I trick or coerce one of these five into opening the door. Or I find a way to bypass that feature of the system."

"Okay."

"And I'll need to be able to do everything on a no-comeback basis. The two million dollars you're promising is nice. But it's not enough to drop the life I have and go on the run. I have to be able to steal this thing, then not get caught and prosecuted afterwards."

"Absolutely. I understand."

Right, but did he?

Harvey waited a moment, elbow propped on the table, phone to his ear. He looked out across the water, watching a single power boat race up middle to the bay. "So maybe we're at the point where a little commitment on your part would help my confidence."

"But you think you can *acquire* the thing."

"There are no guarantees in life, but, yes, I think so."

"Let's go ahead then."

"Maybe you're not hearing me," Harvey said, putting a little grit in his tone. "I don't know how you got together with Mario, but we wouldn't be having this conversation if he hadn't given you some hints about my past exploits and capabilities. As for you, so far I don't know squat about you, except that Mario vouches for you, and says you're not FBI or something."

"I'm not. I want that device and I'll pay you two million dollars for it."

"Fine, but I'm not risking life and freedom to swipe some exotic, maybe otherwise unsalable item, merely on a *promise* you'll buy it from me later. I looked into the matter, which required an investment of time and money. I told you it looks do-able. Now it's your move. Money talks and bullshit walks."

Silence for several seconds.

"Okay, how much commitment we talking about?"

"Mario said you agreed to a number."

Another silence. "Fifty thousand."

"There you go then," Harvey told him. "When I get the fifty, we're back in business. But not until."

A sigh at the other end. "Yeah. Okay. You have any objections to krugerrands?"

Harvey braked mentally to a halt. "You're talking about gold."

"Right, gold coins. They can be delivered to the same address I sent the instructions for this meet, and arrive tomorrow. We don't want any hold up. As we both know, there's a deadline."

Harvey felt a wary tingle up his spine. Was there a con involved here? He'd need to have the coins appraised to make sure they weren't fakes.

"Fine," he said, trying to keep suspicion out of his voice.

"So you'll get them tomorrow, and we're a go after that?"

"We are."

"And we talk again, using this same number, when you acquire the device."

"Right. But one more thing. When we get to the two million, it'll have to be cash. No coins, gems, bearer bonds, or anything else. Is that going to be a problem?"

"No. No problem. When we do the transaction, it'll be cash—all hundred-dollar bills."

Harvey said, "Perfect," and the conversation ended.

Before he got up, he made sure the number on the tabletop was in the disposable's memory. Then, just to be sure, he took a pen and small Moleskine notebook from his pocket and copied the number down.

As he made his way back along the walkway, he thought about his anonymous buyer.

He'd gotten onto him through a guy named Mario Flores.

In the early two thousands, Harvey and Mario had done a job together. An armored car containing one point six million dollars had gone missing one hot Friday afternoon in August. Mario had been its driver. Harvey, for thirty-five percent of the take, had done the planning and logistics. Which had included Mario's successful escape to Mexico and change of identity.

The unsolved theft was a favorite on true-crime TV. Ironically, he and Dorothy had once seen it discussed and re-enacted on a History Channel show called *Open Case*. She knew nothing about his involvement and he never said a word as they watched. It had been in a Las Vegas hotel room, late at night, both of them in bed, pillows propped behind them.

So it was a big surprise when, two weeks ago, Mario had phoned him.

Not saying much of anything about his life since their parting, years before. Merely mentioning a guy he knew who'd approached him with a big-money job proposition. One that tempted Mario. But one which would have required he return to the U.S., something he was unwilling to risk.

Was Harvey interested in the job?

Mario was asking a five percent finder's fee. Payable afterwards, only if everything worked out.

Harvey had thought about the whole thing for a day. Then, needing money badly, and sick of the chump change his legitimate investments were bringing in, said yes. Yes to trying to steal the RayBright device and yes to dealing with its mysterious buyer.

* * *

Ten minutes later, Harvey met up with the kid, inside the bookstore.

"Anything?"

"Hold on," the kid said. He was reading something in a book he had open in his hands.

Harvey had an impulse to throttle the kid, right then and there, but restrained himself. He glanced at the spine of the book when the kid at last re-shelved it. *The Varieties of Psychedelic Experience*. The kid was nothing if not predictable.

"You know, I like this cloak and dagger stuff."

"Yeah," Harvey said, blowing out an exasperated breath.

"What's wrong?"

"Nothing."

The kid eyed Harvey a moment longer, surprised at the tension in Harvey's manner. Then got out his phone. Poked and pawed at it. And turned to let Harvey look its screen. "As you can see, he was over by the boats."

Harvey examined the photo. A guy in his fifties or sixties. Upper middle class looking.

Still holding the phone, the kid began slowly swiping through a series of similar shots. All middle-distance. In the last few, the guy was holding binoculars.

The kid nodded at the screen. "When he has the binocs, he's looking in your direction."

"How about him making a call?"

The kid manipulated the phone again until he got the shot he wanted. "Bluetooth. There, look up at his left ear when he's turned the other way. His lips began moving at exactly nine o'clock."

"You noticed him, but did he notice you noticing."

"No way."

"You did good," Harvey told him.

The kid began once more tapping the screen. "Well if you liked those, you might like these."

Harvey looked.

A sequence of three partial shots of a silver BMW. Half of its front license plate readable in one of them.

"His?"

"It would seem so," the kid said. "That's what he drove away in."

Harvey smiled, shaking his head in amazement. He gave the kid a warm, grateful handshake. "Mark, my son, you're a bloody wonder. That's what you are."

"You're too easily impressed," the kid said, playing it off. But his feline eyes shone at the approval.

"I think I know somebody who can find the plate for me. I'd like to know a little bit more about who this guy is."

"Makes sense."

"Can you print those out for me when you get home?"

"You got it. And, listen, something else occurred to me."

They ambled through the store, past the coffee and snack counter.

"What?" Harvey said, once they were outside.

"Why does this guy want to meet you here? To get a peek at you, right?" He waited for Harvey's look of agreement before going on. "But why here? Because he's comfortable here. You see what I'm saying? He's got some connection to this place. He was over in the marina, right?"

"Okay."

The kid waggled his brows. "Might be he owns one of those nice boats over there. Rents a slip. We take the photos over there and see if anybody knows him."

Harvey stalled, not wanting to shoot the kid's idea down outright. "I like it," he said, putting on a thoughtful face and nodding slowly. "The thing is, though, we can't afford to spook him."

"You sure?"

"He doesn't know we saw him. If we go poking around, it might get back to him."

The kid said nothing for a moment, disappointment showing in his features.

"All right," he said at last.

When they were out in the lot, beside Dorothy's Mercedes, Harvey touched the kid's shoulder. "Listen, don't get me wrong, okay? I'm not discounting your behavioral analysis—I think you're dead-on about our boy and this place. I just want to be super careful. We good on that?"

The kid nodded, brightening. Then shrugged. "Hey, your movie."

EIGHT

L ater that same day, Mark drove back into San Diego by himself. To the Hillcrest area.

Sometimes when he went to gay bars, it would be with women who had no suspicion he also had a thing for guys. He'd be playing a kind of double game, like a spy in the movies. On the one hand pretending to be the sure-of-my-own-manhood sophisticate, while on the other, secretly ogling the gay men he saw there.

But it was a game he had to be in the mood for.

Just as he had to be in the right mood to do his drag karaoke act. It wasn't often, but once in a while he'd just feel like *performing*. Like dolling himself up and sashaying onstage to sing a soul-deep torch song. There was nothing like it.

Today though, Mark had come only to make a connection.

And he soon did.

Flush with his newfound Harvey wealth, he stepped to the bar. Indulged himself in a shot of Johnny Walker Black. Then in a friendly gesture, bought a shot of the same for the guy sitting two stools down.

As luck would have it, like Mark, the guy was new to the San Diego area. So there ensued a ten-minute chat about the peculiarities of Southern California climate and culture. After which the two men went to the back of Mark's van for some quick sex. And then Mark bought two hundred bucks worth of Ritalin, Xanax, and weed from him.

Dual-purpose connection.

By the time Mark returned to the ranch, it was the middle of the afternoon.

Up in the apartment, he fixed himself a bowl of Captain Crunch with milk. Which tasted so good when he ate it that he fixed another. It was only as he was consuming the second bowl that he realized the reason for his hunger—he hadn't eaten anything since lunch the day before.

He needed to watch his nutrition.

Having taken his empty bowl and spoon to the sink, he stopped off at the fridge. Got out a can of Lone Star and his bottle of multivitamins. Opened both. Shook out a multivitamin and washed it down with a slug of beer. Capped the multivitamin bottle and put it away. Then drank the rest of the Lone Star standing at the kitchen counter.

Feeling better, he lit a Marlboro and sat down in front of his laptop to check a couple of sites he liked to post on.

As he'd hoped, there were more welcome-back messages. Word was getting around that he'd flown the coop in Texas. He'd floated a vague story that he'd engineered his own escape, which made him look clever and resourceful. He liked this better than the all-too-tame truth that his getting out of prison had been a fluke.

He responded to a few of the messages.

Watched a couple of YouTube videos while smoking some of the weed he'd just purchased.

Then decided he'd better call his new girlfriend, Jane.

They talked for an hour or so. About the nature of love and relationships. About music, movies, and graphic novels. And at last, when he steered the conversation around to it, about RayBright.

When the call ended, Mark got up and went into the bathroom. He'd just learned something important he felt the old man would want to know, but decided a little freshening up was in order first.

Visine for his red-rimmed eyes. Mouthwash to hide his recent use of weed and alcohol. Some cold water splashed on the face to stimulate alertness. Followed by a clean shirt that didn't reek of perspiration and marijuana smoke.

Downstairs, Mark knocked at the kitchen door, and stepped inside calling, "Hello-hello."

When there was no response, he called again. Went inside to poke his head into the living room. Saw and heard nothing. Then went back outside through the kitchen to check the cars in the garage.

Both vehicles were present. Which strongly suggested the old man had to be somewhere on the property. Mark walked around to the patio and ambled out across the lawn, looking and listening as he went.

The sun was low in the sky and the day was cooling down.

He was halfway to the barn when it occurred to him that he should just *call* the old man. But in the next moment, realized he'd absent-mindedly left his phone upstairs. He looked back at the garage. Looked ahead at the barn. Sighed and continued toward the barn.

Once there, hearing voices, he circled around to the rear, where he found Dorothy and the old man sitting astride horses.

"Howdy," Mark said when he got near. "Just going or just coming back?"

"Just coming back," Dorothy told him. She gave him a broad smile. "We took a ride down to the orchard."

Mark smiled back. "Sounds like fun."

She and the old man then dismounted and led their horses in through the big door. Mark followed. The Australian shepherd had arrived at this point. Mark seated himself on a bale of straw and petted it, as he watched Dorothy and the old man unsaddle the big animals and brush them down.

Later, as they were all walking back to the house, Mark signaled to the old man that he wanted to talk. The old man nodded. And when they got to the patio, the two of them let Dorothy go on inside, and found a couple of chairs at the far end.

"We've got a problem."

"Okay," the old man said.

"Stanko got caught and fired. I told you about that woman I've been seeing from the Accounting department, right, Jane? I found out about it from her."

"Caught doing what?"

"I'm not sure exactly. But she said the story going around is that he was discovered somewhere he wasn't supposed to be. Then refused to speak when questioned."

The old man shrugged. "I'll call him tonight and see what he has to say."

"You don't think this puts them onto us?"

The old man shook his bald head, unfazed. "I think we stay alert for any further signs of trouble, but I'm not real worried."

"Okay," Mark said, adopting the same calm tone.

Hey, if the old man wasn't worried, why should *he* be worried?

Lighting a Marlboro, he looked out across the canyon. And remembered something else. Something he'd better blurt out and settle now, lest it come back to bite him worse later. He summoned his courage. "Oh, yeah, one more thing."

"What's that?"

"Well...."

After a moment, when Mark didn't go on, the old man shot him a look. "What?"

Mark shifted nervously in his seat. "I was in the house yesterday, by myself. And your maid came into the master bedroom and...caught me trying on one of Dorothy's dresses."

He wasn't so much concerned that his cross-dressing fetish had been revealed. The old man already knew that. He might've even told Dorothy.

But Mark was uneasy about the old man's reaction to hearing he'd been snooping around the house when nobody was home. Or at least when Mark *thought* nobody was home. He was afraid the old silverback might go ape on him.

And for an instant, Mark thought this might be the case.

He felt himself tense in anticipation as he watched the old man's face suddenly contort with strong emotion.

But that strong emotion turned out not to be rage, Mark soon saw.

It was amusement.

Eyes bright, Mr. Potato Head burst into prolonged laughter.

Mark grimaced. "Hey, fuck you."

"Kiddo," the old man said, gulping for air, "you made my day."

"I'm so glad."

"My week!"

Embarrassed and annoyed, Mark looked away.

When the old man finally seemed to have to laughed himself out, Mark went on. "I played it off with her in Spanish, like it was our little secret. But she still might tell Dorothy. I don't want Dorothy thinking I was stealing."

"If it comes up, I'll explain," the old man said, still grinning.

"Thanks. I think."

"Dorothy's cool."

Mark sighed. He decided to change the subject. "On the plus side of things, Jane told me something else. About her boss. A guy named Norman Gunderman. Keep in mind, he's one of the five company officers who can get us into the labs downstairs."

"The CFO."

"Right. Get this, Norman is a fifty-something, single guy who lives with his mother."

"So you're thinking he might be gay?"

Mark sometimes forgot how quick the old man could be. "Yeah. Jane's worked with him for years and she told me she's always wondered about him in that respect."

"Have you gotten a look at him?"

"Not yet."

"But you're going to," the old man said.

"Yeah. I'll get close to him and see what I can improvise."

"My son, you are a handsome and silver-tongued devil."

"Aren't I just."

"Only you have to make sure Jane never talks to Norman."

Mark nodded. Point taken. He took a long, unhurried pull on his cigarette.

"Just curious, you and Dorothy been together a long time?"

"Going on six years," the old man said, having to think. "How about you?"

"Me?"

"*You* ever been married?"

"Oh, yeah. I was nineteen."

"How'd that work out?"

Mark turned his head to look at the old man, acknowledging the implication. "'Bout like you'd 'spect, I reckon," he said, channeling his inner Texan.

The old man grinned.

They sat in silence for several seconds.

"Dorothy your first marriage?" Mark asked.

The old man rubbed the side of his face. "No, before I got busted for the dope, I was married. To somebody else. A woman named Evelyn."

"She leave you when you went inside?"

"No. I left *her*. It was after I got out—when I learned the house was in foreclosure, both our cars had been sold, and the hundred ninety-some thousand dollars I had in the bank the day they put the cuffs on me was gone."

"What'd she say when you asked what'd happened?"

"She said it'd all gone to the lawyers."

"But you didn't believe her."

The old man shrugged philosophically. "I didn't know what to believe."

Mark gazed off at the rocky crests in the distance. Some wispy clouds hung in the sky beyond, turned pink by the setting sun. "I remember the day they put the cuffs on *me*."

After a moment, the old man said, "Oh yeah?"

"It was a hacking thing. The prosecutors called it credit card fraud, but it wasn't."

"What was it then?"

"Actually, at the time, there weren't really any laws on the books for what I did." Mark frowned. "So they just *lied* and said I did something else. And the judge let them."

"Well, life's not always fair, I guess."

Mark gave a bitter chuckle. "Hold on. Let me write that one down, Harve."

NINE

It wasn't until two nights later that Mark and the old man talked again. They hadn't seen each other much. Not only had each been separately busy, the two kept *very* different hours. So when Mark called him and explained where he was and who he was with, the old man agreed to drive out for a meet-up.

But it would be an hour or two before he got there—would that be a problem?

No, Mark told him.

Then rejoined Norman on his slow tour of the casino's table games.

Over the course of the evening so far, Mark had mostly just looked on, a non-participant, while Norman played. Mark found gambling boring. He didn't see the point.

So to tolerate the situation, he did what he often did in such circumstances. He diverted himself with drink and/or drugs. Tonight he'd been relying on Ritalin. A lot of Ritalin.

So much in fact, that by the time the old man at last came sidling quietly up next to him and murmured, "Is that him?" Mark almost jumped out of his skin.

"Jesus!" he said under his breath. "You fucking startled me."

"Sorry, kiddo. The brown shirt?"

Mark sighed and gave a tiny nod, still looking straight ahead.

But out of the corner of his eye, watched the old man drift off to the right, seeking a better view of the game and its players.

Mark stayed where was.

Ahead at the table, when the hand ended, he stepped forward. Leaning in close, he laid his palms gently on Norman's shoulders from behind. "Hey, I'm going to go get something to drink. Can I bring you anything?"

Norman craned around and smiled. "Thanks. I'm good."

"You're *doing* good," Mark told him. He indicted with a glance Norman's stacks of high-value chips. "I'll be back in ten minutes or so."

That said, Mark turned and walked past the old man.

He bore left down the wide aisle between the rows of felted tables. Bore left again at the far end, near the cashier's cage. Then drew up near an ATM kiosk to wait for the old man to catch up.

"First things first," Mark said when he arrived, "I need a goddamn beer."

"Okay."

"There's a place around the corner here."

The old man nodded. "Lead the way."

"Where's Dorothy?" Mark asked as they set off.

"She's playing the nickel slots."

"You guys staying over?"

"Yeah. We got a room in the hotel. How about you two?"

"They *comped* Norman a whole suite, if you can believe it. You should fucking see the place."

"Nice?"

"The taste is questionable, but pimped-out like you wouldn't believe. Seriously, they *know* this guy here."

"Oh yeah?"

"Which is why I've got an idea for some leverage on him," Mark said distractedly.

They'd reached the entrance of a restaurant. Some of the casino's restaurants served alcohol, some didn't. This one did. Inside, he turned toward the bar, where the service would be quickest. But it being Saturday night, all of the stools were occupied.

Frustrated, he made for a small table against the wall, the old man in tow. When they'd seated themselves, Mark peered around for the server, at last catching her eye with an impatient arm wave. She nodded at him.

"So, go on with what you were telling me," the old man prompted.

Mark took a calming breath, his nerves raw from the Ritalin. "Like I said, they *know* Norman here. And they treat him like fucking royalty. Which can't be because he's a good tipper—because he tips for shit."

"Okay."

"Earlier, while he was busy playing poker, I was talking to somebody at the Players Club desk. Norman has an Ultra card. You know how many points you have to earn in a six month period to get Ultra status. Guess."

"How many?"

"A fucking *million*. To state the obvious, casinos make their money on the percentages. So if you're playing long enough and often enough, you're going to be losing. Period. The percentages are going to kill you. And he's been playing regularly for years."

"So you're thinking we blackmail him with the gambling problem."

"Will you just listen until I'm finished telling the story!"

A silence seemed to followed this outburst, Mark's words hanging in the air.

His gaze flicked around the room, taking in the faces now turned toward him. From the bar, from nearby tables. He could feel his cheeks flushed hot.

Meanwhile, the old man had slipped into Buddha mode, and was just calmly eyeing him.

Mark fumbled out his Marlboros and lit one.

But had no sooner inhaled the first soothing lungful than a female voice stated, "I'm afraid you can't smoke in here, sir."

The server had at last shown up. Though her head was cocked in sympathy, her tone told him no slack was being offered.

Scowling, he looked around for an ashtray. Saw there were none. Understood the futility of such a search in an establishment that didn't allow smoking. And grimly licked his forefinger and thumb to pinch out the offending cigarette's fiery tip.

He shot the woman a look that said, *Satisfied?*

But she just waited him out, eyebrows raised. Finally he asked for beer, any kind, in the bottle. After which the old man said he'd have an orange juice.

Once she left, the old man leaned forward in his chair.

Mark was sure he was about to hear some condescending remark. Like, *Jeez kid, you okay?* But he was wrong.

"Sorry. Go on with what you were saying."

Mark hid his surprise. He gave the extinguished Marlboro a final longing glance, and slid it back into the pack. He forced a slow breath. He tried to ignore the manic energy he felt surging through him.

"He's the deal. What I'm saying is, he's living—make that gambling—beyond his means. So I ask myself, Where's this extra scratch coming from? Does he have family money, like an inheritance or trust fund? Nope. Far as I can tell, Norman's the only one in his family with a pot to piss in.

"So how about investments or retirement savings? Again, no. Remember I've got his payroll records. He's never taken advantage of the company IRA, which with a three percent employer match is free money. And he's never exercised his option to buy RayBright stock."

"That's strange. When the new IPO goes through, the stock will skyrocket."

"Case in point," Mark said, his fingers half-consciously straying to his Marlboros. He picked up the pack, stared into its open top, then set it back down. "Anyway, I think he's basically broke. I wouldn't be surprised if his house is mortgaged to the hilt. Normie's *deep* into this gambling thing."

The old man nodded, and seemed about to speak, when Mark saw his eyes dart right.

The server had arrived with their beverages. She set a glass of OJ in front of the old man. Then a Tecate in front of Mark.

Mark immediately picked up the bottle, drained it in a rapid series of full-throated gulps, and handed it back. "One more, please."

Her eyes flashed wide for a moment, maybe in astonishment. But she accepted the empty and left.

After a sip of OJ, the old man said, "Let's keep in mind that our steal-by date is fast approaching."

"I'll be ready," Mark told him.

"Okay, then. Good."

"Hey, I fucking *own* the guy."

"Good. Good."

"You don't believe me?"

The old man regarded him evenly. "Kiddo, I didn't say I didn't believe you."

"Look," Mark insisted. "Normie's *in love* with me, okay? I don't think he's ever gotten his rocks off regular before. I give him a little sex and a little coke, and he's bouncing off the fucking ceiling."

"That's fine. Just be careful, alright?"

"Be careful?"

"Like giving him the coke. We can't have him self-destruct on us ahead of time."

"I'm watching him."

The old man gave a slow nod. "Watch yourself, too. Okay?"

"Myself?"

"All I'm saying is…be careful."

74

"Be careful?" Mark repeated incredulously, an abrupt anger rising in him.

"Look…"

"You don't like the way I'm handling things? You don't like the results I'm getting?"

"Kiddo, I'm—"

"I should *watch myself?* The implication being that I don't have it together? The implication being that I'm some kind of fuck-up who can't be trusted—is that it?!"

Mark's gaze strayed to the un-cleared table next to theirs.

A steak knife lay across a greasy plate. For an instant Mark imagined himself grabbing it up and stabbing Mr. Potato Head in the chest. Pictured the old man's shocked expression as it plunged in. Felt himself twist the blade.

But then, simultaneous with return of the server bringing his second Tecate, the wave of violent ill will in him seemed to break.

And again, it came to him that he'd drawn attention to himself.

He'd lost control. He'd been loud and crazy.

People at the bar were rubbernecking, their expressions ranging from curiosity to pity to contempt. He'd allowed himself to become *that guy*—the one nobody wanted to be. The loudmouth. The fool. The jerk making a spectacle of himself.

Mark watched the server warily place his beer in front of him and depart.

He picked up the bottle and, as before, drank it empty in a few seconds.

"Kiddo, listen to me, I want to tell you something."

Mark felt a gassy belch rise in him. It escaped through his parted lips. He peered numbly across at the old man.

"You're right," the old man went on in an earnest tone. "Results *are* what matter, and you get them. Period. I should butt the hell out. I didn't mean to give you a hard time. I'm sorry. Okay? It's obvious you're aces at what you do—with the research and with the people. Your handling of Norman is fine. Forget my little-old-lady hand wringing, alright?"

Mark, surprised at what he was hearing, tried to gather himself. To focus.

The old man was looking at him, maybe expecting some sort of reply.

"Alright," Mark managed at last.

Then saw the old man produce an envelope and slide it across the tabletop.

"I was going to give this to you anyway. Another bonus for extraordinary results."

After a long moment, Mark's fingers, as if of their own volition, opened the envelope. It held a thick wad of hundreds. What had to be a couple of thousand dollars. He pushed the envelope into his pocket.

"You know what I'd really like to do," he said.

"What?"

"Get the fuck out of here so I can smoke a cigarette."

The old man bobbed his head. He pulled a twenty from his wallet and slipped it under his OJ glass. And half a minute later, the two of them were back out on the casino floor, where Mark wasted no time in relighting his pinched-out Marlboro.

It tasted like everything he'd ever wanted in life.

He drew the smoke in deep, held it, then let it seep slowly out through his mouth and nose.

He noticed the old man watching him.

"I'm sorry I got a little tense there, Harve."

The old man shrugged. "Don't let things stress you out."

"No, it's perfectly reasonable to have your doubts. I shouldn't get so goddamn fucking wound up."

"All within acceptable bounds."

"Thanks. And thanks for the cash."

"No thanks necessary, kiddo—you earned it."

"Sometimes I'm a little too much…*me*."

The old man laughed. "Don't worry about it. Just stay close to lover boy and see what kind of angle you can work."

"I'm on it. In fact I'd better get back."

"Go ahead. I'm going to go see how Dorothy's doing."

* * *

The next morning, Harvey's cell phone rang.

He opened his eyes, remembered where he was—in the hotel that adjoined the casino—and reached across to the bedside table. Squinting at the screen, he cleared his throat. Beside him, Dorothy stirred then rolled over.

"What's up, kiddo?" he said quietly.

"You want to play some golf?"

"Golf?"

"You told me you play. So do I. We can rent clubs. Come on, it's a nice morning."

Harvey looked at the time display. He scrunched the pillow up behind him and sat up. "You even been to sleep?"

The kid gave a buoyant chuckle. "Normally, that would've been guilty as charged. But last night I actually got a few hours. But we need to talk some more. A little problem has come up, or should I say *challenge*."

Harvey almost asked if this could wait. Instead he said, "I need fifteen minutes for a shower and shave. Where you going to be?"

"There's a little snack bar off the pro shop. I'll buy you breakfast."

Harvey sighed and swung his feet out from under the covers and onto the floor. "Okay. I'll be there. Fifteen."

"I'm going to kick your ass at golf, old man."

"Don't hold your breath," Harvey told him and cut the connection.

After a moment, Dorothy asked in a drowsy voice, "Mark?"

"Yeah. You go back to sleep. I'll be back in couple of hours."

* * *

The kid had already eaten and drunk all he wanted. But they sat in the snack bar until Harvey had his coffee and consumed an order of wheat toast. The kid—in typical stubborn-jerk fashion—refused to discuss whatever it was he wanted to discuss until they were out on the course.

Harvey was getting used to him being moody. Youth, substance abuse, and a sociopathic personality. The kid was the complete package.

When at last they'd each hit their first drive, Harvey said, "So tell me what's going on?"

"Normie and I had a little heart to heart last night."

"Okay."

"He's had something worrying him for the last few days. I asked him to tell me. To let me help if I could."

"Good," Harvey encouraged.

He and the kid put their drivers away and climbed into the cart, the kid at the wheel.

"Anyway, last night he was telling me about this conference he's supposed to attend in Vegas this week. Like a convention for CFOs or something. He doesn't want to go, but Van Horne is insisting, and he can't seem to get out of it."

"Okay."

"So I ask him *why* he doesn't want to go."

The kid put the cart in gear and they rolled silently ahead, the only sound the thrum of its wheels on the cement path. The morning air was brisk and still. Harvey was glad now he'd agreed to play. He savored the scent of fresh-cut grass and the general visual tidiness of a well-kept private course. Ahead, where the hills rose in the distance, he saw a hawk circling high above.

"I tell him I just want to help," the kid went on. "Maybe I can do something."

"Good."

"But all he'll say is that he can't go and leave his ailing mother."

"Is she truly ailing?"

The kid made a skeptical face, and waved a dismissive hand. Then pulled the cart over off the path to the left. "Okay, she's old, and she walks slow. But she doesn't seem all that sick or helpless to me."

The two of them got out and shouldered their clubs. Then set off across the fairway. They went to the kid's lie first. Harvey watched him choose a club, set up, and make his shot. He wasn't bad. He had an unorthodox swing, but he connected well and had definitely played before.

They strolled on to Harvey's lie.

As Harvey was taking some practice swings, the kid said, "So I keep asking myself, Why wouldn't a rabid casino junkie want to go on a company-paid trip to Las Vegas? I mean, we're talking about the gambling Mecca, right?"

Harvey addressed the ball now, making an effort to focus. Though it'd been a while since he'd played, he hit it solidly. Nice and straight and lots of distance.

"But you figured it out."

The kid presented Harvey with a triumphant grin. He hesitated for a long moment, milking the drama, then leaned in close. "Damn straight I did. He's reluctant to go because he doesn't want anyone else getting a look at the books while he's gone."

"Ah," Harvey said, thinking about this. Liking its logic.

"I told you my theory he'd been embezzling to pay the freight for his gambling. But the more I turned it over in my mind, the more it made sense this wasn't just a recent thing. I think he's been siphoning off Ray-Bright money for years."

"Robbing Peter to pay Paul. The classic trick of shoveling current revenues into the hole of missing, past revenues."

The kid looked a bit crestfallen at Harvey's unexpected knowledge, but he nodded. "Yeah."

They carried their clubs back to the cart, stowed them, and got in.

"But there's yet another twist in the story," the kid said. "Guess who'd be in charge of things if Norman were to go away?"

"Who?"

"My good friend Jane," the kid said with a smirk, putting the cart in gear and pulling back onto the path. "I already know this from Janie, but I don't let on to Norman I do. I get him to tell me."

"Those two must never compare notes."

"You fucking got that right. So then I ask Norman, all naïve-like, like I just stumbled on a brilliant idea, What would happen if whoever runs the show while you're gone didn't come to work the day you're supposed to leave? Failed to call in? A no-show?"

"Go on," Harvey said.

"This is where I think Norman's beginning to suspect that maybe ol' Mark Hatcher isn't what he at first seems."

"He's got an MBA from Stanford. That's got indicate he has *something* going on upstairs." Harvey had noticed the kid tended to underestimate everybody's intelligence except his own.

"You're probably right. Anyway, he gets all flustered. He doesn't want anything *bad* to happen to her. I tell him of course not." The kid touched his fingertips to his chest in a gesture of heartfelt honesty. "But what if I could just delay her somehow? Would he be capable of playing along? You know, trying to contact her, calling around, acting real worried—then oh-so-reluctantly canceling the trip?"

Harvey turned in his seat. "Kid, I love you. And I mean that in the most heterosexual of ways."

A broad smile blossomed on the kid's face. He looked about five years old.

"Check this out, Harve. The guy hasn't taken a sick leave or vacation day since he started at RayBright, ten years ago. Not a single day off. Shit, that ought to raise red flags right there. Guy handles your money and never wants to take time off!?"

"If he lets you do this for him, he's crossed the line. He's corrupted himself. Aside from anything to do with the embezzlement."

"Exactly."

A maintenance cart passed them. Trash cans in the back. Older Mexican guy driving, wearing a light brown uniform and matching pith helmet.

"So what's your plan with Jane?"

The kid pulled a wry face. "Well, to start with, if I do anything, it's gotta be tonight."

"*Tonight?*"

"Yeah, today's Sunday. This Vegas thing starts Tuesday. Norman flies out early tomorrow afternoon."

"You going to be able to manage it on such short notice?"

"As luck would have it, Jane and I have a date tonight—to go to a concert. I'm thinking something in her drink. Enough to hopefully keep her out of it for the rest of the night and into the next day."

"You'd better be careful with the dose," Harvey said with a frown.

"I know. I don't need a murder charge."

"And if she dies, he'd never forgive you. He might freak and run to the law."

The kid gave a thoughtful nod. "Yeah, Normie's a sensitive soul, all right. There's no denying that."

He pulled over once more. The two of them got out, grabbed their bags, and headed across the fairway. Both had landed second shots close to the green. And without much ado, both now chipped onto the green in three.

"Let me tell you one more story about this guy," the kid said, a minute later as the two got out their putters. "I mentioned how Norman has this reputation for being the hard-working type, right?"

"Yeah."

"But everybody also talks about how tight he is with a dollar. Check this out. The other day I got him to invite me home for lunch. Just him, me, and his poor sick mom, who he lives with. Now remember, this at a three-bedroom house in exclusive Del Mar and my host is an officer at a hundred-million-dollar company. Guess what I was served?"

"I give up," Harvey said. By this time he was taking small practice strokes over top of his ball.

"Baloney sandwiches on white bread. Mustard and mayo. Potato salad that you buy pre-made at the store in the two-pound tub. Stale potato chips. And to top it off—are you ready?—*under-sweetened cherry Kool-Aid!*"

Still chuckling a half minute later, Harvey flubbed what should have been an easy putt.

TEN

Mark arrived at Jane's condo about seven-thirty.

He wore some of the new clothes he'd bought with the old man's bonus cash. A charcoal sports coat. A black silk shirt with a large pink flamingo on the front. Some light-grey slacks with pleats. And a pair of black moccasin loafers with Mercury dimes in the slots instead of pennies.

He'd also gotten his hair cut and styled.

Which she noticed right away.

"I love it," she told him, reaching up to run an affectionate finger along his sideburn.

As he'd hoped, she preferred to take *her* car, instead of his van. He knew she saw his vehicle as both unsafe and infra dig.

"I'm so glad you're not one of those guys bothered when the lady drives," she teased, breaking into a little laugh.

Mark shrugged and laughed along.

Downtown, they had to search out the place where the concert was happening. The King Club. Near the trolley tracks off C Street. But after going round the one-way blocks several times in frustration, they gave up trying for a parking spot close by.

Jane chose a multi-story commercial garage over near the main Post Office. Mark thought this was a long way to walk, but wasn't about to say anything.

She looked sharp for her age tonight. A tidily wrapped little gift package.

All made up. Striking blonde hair. Heels. Cute black toreador-like suit, tailored flatteringly at the waist. He offered her his arm and she leaned against him as they strolled out of the garage and up the sidewalk.

This was a Sunday, and downtown seemed quiet. Except for a few street people, they met no one until they got to Fourth Avenue, where they cut over.

Mark hadn't seen all that much of San Diego yet, but he liked the town. He suspected, though, that once he and the old man made their grab for the Merman thing, it would be goodbye time. "Mark Hatcher" had had to *show* himself—to Jane and to Norman. So they'd be able to describe him, maybe even provide something with his fingerprints or DNA. Not good.

The old man, meanwhile, had managed to stay behind the scenes. The crafty old fuck.

Still, Mark knew he shouldn't complain. All this was better than jail. Better than camping out in his van. Better than eating ramen cooked on his camp stove.

Right now he had a fat wallet and the promise of a far fatter one.

"I haven't been to see a concert in years," Jane told him as they entered the venue. She grinned with excitement. "I think the last one I saw was the Chili Peppers in L.A."

"I love the Chili Peppers," Mark said. He checked the time on his phone. Just shy of eight, the supposed starting time.

They shuffled in through the milling people and found a place to stand over near the bar. It was a slightly raised area that would allow small-in-stature Jane to see the stage better.

"I'm getting a beer," he announced after a few minutes. "How about you? Rum and Coke?"

"You're not trying to get me drunk and then have your way with me, are you?"

Mark put his face close to hers. "My intentions are strictly honorable."

"I hope not," she said back to him in the same low voice, and they kissed.

Mark bellied up to the bar, waiting to be served. An older female bartender approached him. Mark figured her for management, having watched the way she carried herself and how she dealt with the waitresses.

He ordered and paid. A minute later, she placed two cups of beer, and a rum and Coke, on the polished bartop in front of him. He gave her a wink.

The house lights went down.

A few moments later spotlights caught the band as they came onstage.

A wave of murmured excitement swept through the room. Suspense built. At last, the drummer struck his sticks together, counting off the first song. And amplified music blared forth, followed by a collective howl of recognition from the crowd.

Mark stayed at the bar in the dimness. His back was to Jane, some twenty feet behind him. Earlier in the evening, he'd jacked himself up with a little crank. Now, feeling parched, he lifted the first beer to his lips and drank off two-thirds of it.

Yes, his body said. Thank you.

Sighing, he dug a hand into the pocket of his slacks and brought out a tiny plastic container. Opened it. Let his gaze wander about for anyone watching him. Then shook out the powdered contents of the container into Jane's drink and lowered a pinkie to stir with.

After a count of thirty seconds, he bent his face close, inspecting the liquid and the cup. Was there any discernable trace of the powder? Not that he could see.

A waitress crowded up against him in her eagerness to give her order to the bartender.

"Sorry," she told him with an appraising look.

Mark shrugged. "Don't worry about it, sweetie."

He gulped down the remains of the first beer, left the empty cup on the bar, and brought the second beer with him.

When he got back to Jane she was bouncing happily in place to the music. He handed her the rum and Coke, and watched her take a large sip. Nervous, he half expected some grimace at its taste, but she shot him a smile and sipped again.

Good. But had he calibrated the right dose?

She was so *small.*

Too little, and the stuff might have no effect.

But too much and—as the old man had reminded him—he might end up doing her in.

Though no stranger to Xanax, himself, he knew different people had different reactions to particular drugs. He'd slipped her a pretty potent blast. He'd need to watch her closely.

The first song ended and the audience broke into wild applause.

Mark found he could take or leave the band. He'd only gotten the tickets because Jane had mentioned she was a fan. What did it matter? He was high and drinking beer, wasn't he?

After about the fourth or fifth song, Mark saw Jane stop a passing waitress.

Then turn to him with a knowing smile. "I'm going to have another rum and Coke. It goes without saying you want another beer, right?"

He returned the smile and nodded.

Onstage the lighting changed, and the band broke into a slow ballad. Mark put his arm around Jane, pulling her close. She snuggled against him. They swayed together until the waitress returned with their drinks.

"This one and no more," Jane said with a chuckle, sampling hers.

"Famous last words."

"No, I mean it. Besides—*some* of us have to get up for work tomorrow."

He chuckled along. "Okay, Cinderella. Home by midnight."

A few songs later, the two of them talked about the common need for a bathroom break. As well as the idea of smoking a quick cigarette outside on the street. This settled, they wended their way through the crowd toward the lobby, and the restrooms beyond.

"I'll meet you right here," Mark told her when they reached their mutual destination.

She nodded. Then stepped into the women's room, and he, the men's.

The men's side was crowded. He had to wait his turn for a urinal. Likewise, for a sink to wash his hands afterward. Back out in the lobby, when Jane didn't immediately join him, Mark figured she'd been delayed for the same reasons he had.

However, after a while, he began to worry.

Females were coming and going, but none of them was a small blonde in a toreador suit. Could she have passed out in a stall or something? Pacing back and forth, he wondered if he should ask one of the young women entering to check for Jane's presence. Maybe she'd already come out and he'd missed her.

He'd just gotten out his phone to text her when she appeared.

"Hey, you," he called out.

About to walk obliviously by, she hesitated and peered up at him. Her eyes had an unfocused look. "Hey, yourself."

"How you doing?"

"I feel ghastly tired all of a sudden."

"Oh yeah?"

She scowled at the absurdity of it, shaking her head. "Yeah, I'm beat."

"Let's go then," Mark said, shrugging. "We saw them. We had a good time. It was fun."

"You sure?"

Mark gave her a nod, put his arm through hers, and guided her gallantly toward the doors leading to the street. Then outside, steered her around the corner in the direction of the parking garage. The stuff had come on fast. He could feel her unsteadiness.

They walked a full block at a maddeningly slow rate of progress.

Once they'd crossed the street to the next, he stopped her.

The heels weren't helping, he decided. Squatting in front of her, he placed her hands on his shoulders for support. And feeling like a farrier with a horse, persuaded her to raise one foot at a time so he could remove her shoes. He wedged them into the flap pockets of his sports coat.

While they were still stopped, he lit a Marlboro, and held it so Jane could have a puff. She mumbled something that might have been a thanks. After which he put his arm supportively through hers once more, and they set off.

She still lurched a bit but, barefoot, her pace improved. Mark was glad. Having to fireman's carry her would only draw unwanted attention to her condition. And he wasn't even sure he could physically manage the maneuver.

As it turned out, she stayed conscious all the way to the garage.

Then all the way to the second floor where the Lexus was parked.

But it was there, as he fumbled in her purse for the keys, that her lights finally went out. Half propped against the passenger door, she didn't stay propped. But instead slipped from his one-handed grasp. And slid in slo-mo down the side of the vehicle to the floor.

Shit.

Mark cast a few casual glances around. He could hear noises coming from elsewhere in the structure, but saw no one on their level. He at last found the keys and opened the passenger door. Then paused to appraise the situation.

The next step, he suspected, wasn't going to be easy. And it wasn't. Sure, Jane was a tiny girl. But handling an *unconscious* Jane was not much different than handling an unwieldy hundred-pound bag of potatoes. He remembered just such bags from his job in the prison kitchen.

Nevertheless, he somehow got her inside.

And having seat-belted her upright, put her shoes back on.

At the kiosk a minute later, he paid the ticket. Pulled out onto a deserted street. And made for the entrance to the 163, a few blocks north and east, where traffic stayed sparse through Balboa Park. When he finally exited onto the I-8 East, he dug out his phone and called the old man.

"Everything's a go," Mark told him.

"Good. Where are you?"

"Mission Valley. I'll call you again in twenty minutes."

"I'll be waiting," the old man responded and ended the call.

The plan was for Mark to drive Jane and her Lexus a few hours out into the desert. Where, at a remote spot he'd chosen, he'd puncture one of the tires, take her shoes, purse, cell phone, and keys, and leave her. Maybe even see if he could pour a little more alcohol into her.

Then the old man, who'd have been following behind in Dorothy's SL, would pick Mark up and they'd drive back.

All that was necessary was that Jane be hindered enough not to show up for work the next day. She'd wake up hung over and confused. Stranded and shoeless. A couple of hundred miles away from her job at Ray-Bright.

And, hopefully, she'd be way hazy in her recollections.

In any case, Mark had worked out a story and would have it ready.

He glanced over at her now. The shoulder harness was holding her up. He reached for her wrist to check her pulse. She was out of it, but was she *too* out of it? No, she was okay.

When he was passing El Cajon on the 8, Mark pulled off at the Second Avenue exit. The drive to the desert was going to be a long one. He needed a fresh pack of cigarettes. And maybe a six of beer to help pass the time.

He stopped at the signal at the bottom of the ramp. Though he saw a Shell station to the right, he liked neither how brightly lit it looked, nor the large number of people already there gassing up. When the signal turned green, he instead cut left under the highway. If he remembered right, there was a 7-Eleven up the street a few blocks.

Mark fumbled with his phone to check the time.

But moving his gaze back to the road—was shocked to see a small white pickup accelerating out from a side street. A moment later, it was suddenly and unavoidably in front of him. He slammed on the brakes but it was too late.

At thirty-fives miles per hour Jane's heavy powerful Lexus T-boned the pickup.

The sound of the collision was tremendous. The pickup was skidded sideways several yards. Mark saw a haze in the air. White powder from the deployment of the airbags.

He sat for a moment.

Paralyzed in time. Stunned.

He checked his mirrors. No one was coming behind. He opened the door and climbed out to stand in the empty four-lane street. As if moving in a dream, he stepped to the pickup and peered in. A fat guy in a sweatshirt was slumped over the steering wheel.

All Mark could think of was not going back to jail.

His fake ID was not going to hold up to record-checking police scrutiny. He was driving without a license. There were warrants out on him from Texas. And any blood test they gave him would show the crank he'd taken earlier in the evening.

He stumbled about in a kind of helpless, nervous dance, his mind racing.

There were still no cars coming from either direction, but this couldn't last. Time was passing. To stay was to tempt fate.

Without even having thought it fully through, Mark bolted to the Lexus.

He jumped back into the driver seat. Undid Jane's seatbelt. Dragged her up and hugged her to him. Then scrambled awkwardly backwards out the open door, yanking her limp body over the console into the driver seat as he went.

Ahead in the distance, approaching headlights appeared.

Fuck!

After straightening Jane's legs in the foot well, he leaned over her to latch the seat belt. But try as he might, he couldn't get it to work. Finally, giving up, he instead got out his flask and emptied what was left in it down the front of her outfit.

Heart racing, nerves screaming, he butt-bumped the door closed behind him. Ran in a crouch around the back of the car. And three seconds later, was gone into the darkness down the side street from which the pickup had emerged.

And just in time.

Over his shoulder he caught sight of the car he'd seen coming. It was slowing to a stop next to the accident.

Mark took a big gulp of air and continued jogging away through the shadows. It was a residential area. There were lights still on here and there, but he encountered no one for several blocks.

By the time he got to the Vons supermarket, maybe a mile away, his shirt was soaked with sweat and he could smell himself. He flopped down on a wooden bench in front of the store and let his heartbeat slow. After a short while, he lit a Marlboro. He needed to think things through.

Calmly and logically.

When he felt ready, he got out his phone.

As soon as the old man answered, Mark said, "Harve, there's been a change of plan."

ELEVEN

It came to Jane that she was in a strange bed. Flat on her back, she stared at the shadowy ceiling and opposite wall through slitted eyes, trying to make sense of her circumstances. Why did she feel so *horrible*?

She wished she could go back to oblivious sleep, but it wouldn't happen.

There was something hurting her left forearm. The pain was precise in location, accompanied by a slight weight. Was she being bitten by an insect?

The arm lay beside her. Jane lifted it and brought it slowly up across her body, feeling a trailing resistance as she did so. Wait, it was a tube. She could just make it out, silhouetted against the light from the open door ahead.

Jane thought about this.

Was she in a hospital? An IV suggested something serious, like a bad illness or injury.

In a kind of numbed alarm, she made to lift her head to get a better look at her surroundings. But before she'd risen an inch from the pillow, a fierce stabbing pain in her head froze her. She lay back, ever so carefully.

Straining to hold herself still, she closed her eyes and waited for the throbbing waves to subside. Their intensity frightened her. She blew a slow breath out through dry lips. Her mouth tasted sour.

This was all wrong, she thought. I'm not supposed to be here.

Then, what seemed like a moment later, she heard something next to her.

"You're awake. How're you feeling?"

It surprised Jane that her eyes were already open.

Around her, the room was now bright with natural light. It was day. She shifted her gaze and saw a small plump woman in light blue peering down at her.

A nurse. She was in a hospital and this was a nurse.

"You were in a car accident," the nurse said. "Do you remember?"

Without thinking, Jane moved her head to indicate no. But was pleased when the pain was minimal, at least compared to earlier.

The nurse touched her own brow. "You got a bump on the head."

Jane gave the slightest of nods, and made an effort to speak a single raspy word. "Thirsty."

The nurse smiled and disappeared.

When she came back she pressed a button to mechanically raise the top half of Jane's bed. Waited until Jane reached a sitting position. Leaned across to put a small cup to Jane's lips. And tipped it to send a small amount of crushed ice into Jane's grateful mouth.

An hour later, Jane had graduated to water. Followed by juice and some too-salty chicken broth. Not to mention a mild painkiller for her aching head.

So that by the time a doctor came by to see her on his rounds, she was beginning to feel much better. He asked her some questions. She answered them. She was even ready when he asked her about her head.

"It still hurts," she told him. "But I think this might be partly due to a lack of my usual morning caffeine. Would it be possible to get some tea or coffee or diet cola?"

The doctor, a goofy-looking forty year old with frizzy red hair, seemed to need a moment to consider the request. But nodded. At which point Jane was almost tempted to then ask for a cigarette. But decided not to press her luck.

The doctor went on to discuss her prognosis, which he said was good. He told her that she'd been given a CAT scan. That her head injury seemed minor. But that it was important to watch how things developed to make sure there was no concussion or brain injury.

When she inquired about the accident itself, he told her he knew nothing. He did say that the hospital had done routine blood work on her, however. Which had come up positive for alcohol—but only marginally so—and for benzodiazepine.

"What's that?" she asked.

"Benzodiazepine? An example would be Xanax."

Jane frowned.

She mentioned that she had no recollection of taking Xanax or anything else. Further, that she had no recollection whatsoever of the night before. None. Was this cause for worry?

He gave a reassuring double shake of his frizzy head. "No."

Then went on to explain, rather long-windedly, that both benzodiazepines and blows to the head could result in just this sort of amnesia. In which case, memory might eventually come back. Or it might never.

He was just striding out the door when she had a thought. She called out after him. "Excuse me, doctor, but could I ask you what day of the week this is?"

He hesitated mid-stride. "Uh, Monday."

"Monday?"

"Yeah."

High voltage panic lit up Jane's circuitry. Her eyes swept the room for a clock. She finally found one on the wall to her left.

Eleven fifteen.

God, she was supposed to be at work! Her boss was supposed to leave for Las Vegas today. At this moment she was supposed to be in his office, going over the stuff she needed to know to replace him for a week. This couldn't be happening to her.

A landline phone sat on the table next to her bed. She snatched up its receiver.

94

"Norman," she said a few moments later.

"Jane, where are you?" There was both annoyance and concern in his voice. It made sense. He'd relied on her and she'd stood him up. "I've been trying to call you."

"I'm sorry, Norman. I just woke up in the hospital. I was in an auto accident last night."

There was a brief pause on the other end while what she'd said sunk in. "Oh, my God, Jane. Are you all right?"

"I think so. They'll let me out later today or tomorrow morning. I'm sorry to mess you up with your trip. Can Maria take over?"

"I don't know," he said. "Maybe. Probably not. Anyway, look, don't worry about things here. You take care of yourself, okay? Get better."

"Thanks, Norman."

"Can I do anything or get you anything? What hospital are you at?"

"I'm at Grossmont," she told him.

She read him off the number on the phone, ended the call, and flopped back on the pillow. She blew out a long breath, staring at the wall opposite. She tried to cast her mind back to the night before, but couldn't seem to do it.

What about this supposed accident? Where then was her car?

This had to be what it was like when Alzheimer's set in. You called up files on your mental computer, only to find them empty.

Jane asked one of the attendants where her cell phone might be. It and her other possessions—clothes, purse, watch, shoes—turned out to be right there under her hospital bed. In a big, clear-plastic bag.

She made a call to her friend Patti. "It's me."

"Jan-ie," Patti said, playfully stretching the word out.

Patti in casual mode. Jane glanced at the wall clock. Going by the time, and the chatter in the background, she made a guess that Patti was on an early lunch break.

95

"You won't believe this, but I'm in the hospital. I was in a car accident."

"Oh no!"

"I'm going to be okay," Jane assured her, touched by the concern in her friend's voice. "I got a bump on the head, but apparently nothing too serious. I'm hoping to go home later today."

"Still, Janie. Oh my God."

"I know. It's so weird."

"What happened?"

"That's what's so weird—I can't *remember*."

"Okay, sorry. So who was driving?"

"What do you mean?" Jane asked, suddenly getting an odd feeling.

"You went to that concert with what's-his-name, right?"

Jane said nothing for several seconds, at a loss. Concert. What's-his-name.

"Jane, are you there?"

"Mark? Did I tell you I was going out with Mark?"

"Yeah," Patti said in a hesitant tone. "You seemed up for it. And for him."

All Jane could reply was, "Wow."

"Listen, I get off work at four-thirty. I'm coming over. Where you at?"

"Grossmont. But they may be discharging me. Call me first, okay?"

"Okay? But you're gonna need a ride anyway, right? You didn't *drive* yourself there last night, did you?" Patti laughed at her own joke.

Jane hadn't even considered this. People did sometimes drive themselves to the emergency room, she supposed. Had she? She tried to think. No, from the way the doctor and nurse had talked, she'd come by ambulance. Which brought up the question, Where *was* her car?

"Yeah, at some point I will need a ride. But maybe not today. I appreciate the offer, though. Let's see how it shakes out."

* * *

They did not release her that day.

But did let her have a lunch and even some coffee. She made some more phone calls. And took a nap.

Still dozing lightly at four, she was awakened by a knock at the door.

Deborah Rosen. An attorney specializing in DUI. And in person, a heavy woman in her late forties, who wore expensive clothes that didn't seem to fit her very well. She told Jane to call her Deb.

"Here's what I was able to find out," she began, once she'd jockeyed a chair around next Jane's bed and settled into it. She had an open notebook in her lap, and glanced from Jane to the page, and back. "The other driver died at the scene. Francis Prouty, 26, of Boulevard. Apprentice welder. Married with a young child."

Jane felt her stomach drop. She'd *killed* someone?

Deb paused, registered her reaction, then went on.

"The police haven't filed charges yet. They're still investigating. But if they do, it could be vehicular manslaughter or worse."

"Oh my God," Jane said, the words sticking in her throat.

"What you have working against you is the benzodiazepine in your blood."

"As I told you on the phone, I don't remember anything about the accident."

Deb nodded, but forged on.

"Your blood alcohol was point oh-two, which is nothing. And being charged with DUID—Driving Under the Influence of Drugs—is actually better than DUI alcohol. Because it's much harder to prove. You were apparently unconscious, or nearly so, at the scene, so there's no way for the responding officers to gauge your behavior or administer a field sobriety test."

"What's going to happen?" Jane asked.

"You'll get a letter from the police regarding your case. I work regularly with everybody involved—so they'll tell me as well."

"Let's say they do file homicide charges. What's the worst that can happen to me? Jail time?"

Deb winced. "Possible, but not likely."

Jane briefly closed her eyes, shaking her head as if wishing it all away.

"Let me get some more information," Deb said.

"Sure."

"This guy you went out with—I'll need to talk with him. Also the name of the place where you saw the concert."

Jane talked with her for another ten minutes, providing information, asking questions, signing a legal representation contract. But all the while fighting a feeling of despair. A feeling her tidily woven life had begun to unravel.

At work, they'd been counting on her to take over, so Norman could make that conference in Las Vegas. And she'd let them down. The excuse of a car accident sounded good until you heard the Driving Under the Influence part. That in itself might lose her, her security clearance, and therefore her job.

Years before, she'd managed to beat the charges, but she might not be so lucky this time.

She thought about her crashed car, her possibly *totaled* car. Thought about the hassle of getting the thing fixed or replaced. And about the likelihood her insurance company might raise her rates.

Then there was going to court, where it was it going to take a fortune in legal fees to fight this thing. Court, where she might lose her license, or be sentenced to jail time. Court, where the details of the accident would become public knowledge. That Jane Bouchet, behind the wheel while high on unprescribed medication, had taken the life of another human being.

The phrase Deb had used, *with a young child*, haunted Jane. A young child was now alone. Alone like ten-year-old Jane had been when her father had left her mother.

Jane felt a yearning to talk to Mark. To learn what had happened, but also to be comforted by him. She'd called him twice, leaving messages, but he hadn't called or texted back.

What was going on?

(TWELVE)

Tuesday morning, Kirbi Mack saw the RayBright sign and wheeled in through the outer gate. A young uniformed brother about her age emerged from the guard shack. He gave her an appreciative smile.

"I'm here to see John Shellhammer," she told him, handing him her California driver's license.

He nodded, took a photo of it with the device he had with him, and handed it back. Kirbi noticed a security camera mounted low alongside the barrier post. And another under the eaves of the guard shack.

"Visitors parking is down there on the left," he told her and pointed.

"This a good place to work?"

A question she always asked, a way of taking a read on the person and the place.

He didn't have to think long about an answer. "Good benefits. Good people."

"Cool. Have a great day."

"You too," he called, as he stepped back into the shack to raise the barrier for her.

Kirbi found a slot where he'd indicated, and parked. She was driving her undercover vehicle. A scraped-up, fifteen-year-old Volvo station wagon.

As she strolled to the entrance, she admired the row of queen palms along the front. The building itself was three-stories. Some kind of grey composite, the mirrored windows framed in dark metallic blue. Everything said taste and prosperity.

Inside, a woman in the same uniform as the gate guard looked up from behind the counter.

"I'm Kirbi Mack. I have a nine o'clock appointment with John Shellhammer." She had her ID ready once more, and passed it over.

The woman smiled and said, "Hold on just a moment."

Then tapped some keys, eyes now on her computer screen.

Kirbi turned for a look around. The reception area was high-ceilinged and spacious. The grey-and-dark-blue exterior theme was continued here in wallpaper and paint. This also met with her approval.

When Kirbi turned back a few moments later, the woman's face had just the slightest crease between the eyebrows. "I'm still looking," she said, and went on tapping keys.

Kirbi gave a half shrug, smiled, and glanced at her watch. Six minutes before nine.

She'd driven like crazy to make it on time.

The woman behind the counter gave a little sigh. "I don't see anything here." She shook her head once, to herself. The crease between the eyebrows had become more pronounced. "Let me phone upstairs."

Kirbi nodded, leaning on the counter. "He just called me."

Shellhammer had reached her on her cell, an hour before. He'd introduced himself as a co-owner of RayBright Laboratories and asked if she could possibly, despite the short notice, come in that very morning to discuss doing some work for them.

Though always interested in fresh clientele, she'd at first tried to beg off. She explained to Shellhammer that she'd just come off an all-nighter, staking out a warehouse in downtown San Diego. Not only was she currently dead on her feet, she was still dressed in her disguise as a homeless person.

He'd said it didn't matter. He emphasized she'd be doing them a big favor just by showing up and giving their problem a listen. And that RayBright would be glad to pay her for her time meeting with them.

101

Won over by his earnestness, she'd reluctantly agreed. As long it was understood the person they'd be meeting would be red-eyed and funky-looking. Shellhammer had laughed and told her that wouldn't be a problem.

The woman behind the counter caught Kirbi's attention.

"I can't seem to get anyone up there to answer my calls," she said in an apologetic tone.

Kirbi stole another look at the time and paced over to the windows.

When she'd paced back, a big Latino guy in a dark suit had joined the uniformed woman behind the counter. He stood with Kirbi's driver's license in his hand.

"What's the problem?" he asked.

"This lady has an appointment with the general," the woman told him. "But it isn't listed, and I can't get hold of anybody up there to confirm."

Waiting at traffic lights on the drive over, Kirbi had Googled both Shellhammer and RayBright on her phone. Otherwise she wouldn't have picked up on the reference. Shellhammer was retired army.

Kirbi got her phone out and called back on the number Shellhammer had used earlier. It rang four times and went to voice mail. She left a message saying she was downstairs. That there was some problem.

"He phoned me a short while ago," Kirbi told the Latino guy. She read off the number aloud to prove it.

This didn't seem to help. His face conveyed skepticism, if not downright suspicion.

"Make one more attempt," he told the uniformed woman.

She did. "I tried everybody in the office there. Maybe they're all in a meeting or something."

The Latino guy moved his shoulders in a minimal shrug.

"Is it possible for somebody to run up and check?" Kirbi asked.

He shot her a my-hands-are-tied look. "What was the nature of your appointment with Shellhammer?"

Kirbi's fatigue brought her emotions close to the surface. His attitude was getting to her. She had to make a big effort not to respond in kind.

"I'm a consultant," she told him. "He wanted to discuss my doing some work for RayBright."

"What kind of consulting is it you do?"

Kirbi gave him a tight smile. She considered telling him, The kind where clients expect me to be discreet when discussing the nature of my work. Especially with nosy macho assholes. Instead, she said, "Security."

"Security," he repeated, as if making sure he'd heard right. He squared his shoulders, returning her tight smile. "I'm Head of Security here."

As if that clinched it. As if anything to do with security he would definitely know about.

"Maybe they wanted to interview me as your replacement," Kirbi heard herself say, the dig just slipping out.

"Gee, that's pretty funny."

Kirbi sighed and folded her arms. Her gaze dropped to her baggy sweat clothes. Her homeless get-up wasn't helping her credibility here. Not one bit.

Nor probably were her gender and race.

To *this* schmuck's way of thinking, she was some badly dressed sales person running a cold-call hustle on his boss. She peeked at her watch. Nine straight up.

Kirbi picked up her license from the countertop where he'd put it down. She stepped over to one of several padded reception chairs and seated herself. She'd decided to give things a few minutes. But only a few. She was tired and didn't need the aggravation.

It'd been a mistake to come as is. As she ought to know by now, appearances mattered. What she wore—with its artful red wine stains down

103

the front—worked for who she needed to be on Fourteenth and J. But here, what worked was a business suit and heels.

At ten after nine, Kirbi approached the counter and raised her eyebrows to the woman in the uniform. The big Latino guy in the suit was nowhere to be seen.

The woman showed her a concerned wince. "Sorry. I've tried several more times, but I can't get anybody."

"Not your fault," Kirbi told her. "Thanks for trying."

That said, Kirbi headed out to the parking lot.

She got into her car and drove up the incline toward the gate. Just as she drew even with the guard shack, though, she caught movement out of the corner of her eye.

The brother on gate duty had come jogging out, waving his arm. Not a goodbye wave but the hold-on kind. The lane barrier was up. Was she required to log out before leaving?

Kirbi rolled down her window.

"I just got a call from inside," he told her. "You're supposed to wait."

A moment later, when his gaze moved down the hill toward the building, she used her side mirror to look in the same direction. Her wonderful new friend, the big Latino guy in the suit, was now dashing laboriously up the grade.

"Hey," he gasped when he arrived at her open window. He was winded and gulping air. "I got a call. From General Shellhammer. He said he's. Been trying. To call you back."

She just looked at him.

He went on. "He wants to. Have you. Come up to the meeting."

She continued to just look at him, the engine idling, the car in gear, her foot on the brake.

He seemed confused. He began tucking in his white shirt, which had pulled out in the course of his scramble up the hill. But his eyes stayed on Kirbi's impassive face.

"First," she prompted, "I think maybe you wanted to apologize."

He regarded her for a long moment. "You're... right. I'm sorry."

"And what was it you're sorry for?"

Kirbi saw anger rise in him, but also saw him master it.

"I'm just sorry," he told her again, either meaning it this time, or at least trying to sound like he did. "Please, they're waiting for you upstairs."

"You're not very good at your job, are you?"

She could think of no worse insult, especially to a guy. But she meant it. Meant it factually and meant it as an insult. She saw its sting register in his eyes.

Kirbi rolled up her window. Shifted into reverse. Then backed down the slope to find the parking slot she'd pulled out of a minute before.

The big Latino guy, who'd followed on foot, met her at the front door and held it for her.

Inside, the woman from behind the reception counter came forward with something in her hand. It proved to be a visitor's badge on a green lanyard. She slipped it gently over Kirbi's head.

In the elevator, Kirbi bent forward, peering at the name on the Latino guy's badge.

"David Martinez," she read aloud. As though making a mental note.

When the doors opened on the top floor, a tall wiry man with short grey hair stood waiting. "Ms. Mack," he said in a warm tone. "I'm John Shellhammer."

And approached to take her hand in his, his manner almost courtly.

"Very nice to meet you, sir," she told him in turn. "Again, please excuse my lack of business attire."

He gave a dismissive shake of the head. "It's not a concern. And I'm sorry about the mix up downstairs."

"I'm here now. Let's talk."

Shellhammer nodded, as if at the good sense of her statement. Gestured to indicate she should accompany him down the thickly carpeted corridor. Then after a few steps, looked back over his shoulder.

"Oh and, David," he said, "why don't you join us."

Halfway down on the right, Kirbi followed Shellhammer into a suite of offices.

She took in the rich brown woodwork, and elegantly matching desks and chairs. There was a faint, pleasant citrus odor in the air, which she guessed might be from lemon-oil furniture polish. She also smelled coffee.

An older woman, an admin, was behind a central desk, murmuring into a phone. A younger woman nearby was busy at a copier. Both were dressed the way Kirbi wished at the moment *she* were.

Ahead, Shellhammer was disappearing into what looked like a conference room. When she stepped in after him, the first thing she saw was a long table, at one end of which sat a small, plump man with a bow tie. Noticing her entrance, he at once stood and pulled out the chair next to him, gesturing for her to join him there.

"I'm Eric Van Horne," he told her, briefly shaking her hand.

Shellhammer sat across from Kirbi, at that same end of the table but on the other side. Martinez, Head of Security, who it seemed hadn't known about the meeting, took a chair next to her.

The older woman from the outer office entered now.

She asked Kirbi and Martinez if they wanted anything to drink. Martinez chose orange soda. Kirbi, after a long night, asked for coffee.

Once Kirbi had been served her coffee, Van Horne said, "Thanks for coming in on the fly, so to speak."

He had a deep voice for someone so small, and he spoke in a thick New-York-area accent. From the Wikipedia article on RayBright, she knew Van Horne was co-founder of the company with Shellhammer. And had a Nobel Prize in Physics.

106

"Sure," Kirbi told him.

Shellhammer spoke now. "We'd like to present a situation and get your take on it."

She nodded, took a sip of the excellent coffee, and he went on.

"The other day, one of our guards was found in a restricted part of the building. Also, while the guards all carry *company* phones and radios while on duty, they are forbidden to have *personal* phones with them. He had his personal phone with him. And on it were a collection of photos taken on the premises here, including of restricted areas and sensitive projects."

Shellhammer paused to glance at Martinez.

"David was the one who caught him."

Martinez saw that he'd been passed the ball. He cleared his throat. "There were a couple of odd things about what happened," he began. "One, he wouldn't say a single word. Just clammed up when I confronted him." His expression suggested he'd been impressed with this, in spite of himself. "And two, he had fifty-six hundred dollars in his locker."

"Which might suggest he was being paid to take his pictures," Kirbi suggested.

"Yes," Van Horne said, "that's what we thought, too."

Shellhammer drew a breath. "RayBright Labs has several contracts with the federal government. Security is a big concern of theirs and, as result, of ours. Big concern."

"Also, we're just about to do an Initial Public Offering," Van Horne added.

She looked from Shellhammer to Van Horne and back. "And you don't want anything …scandalous to occur at this point."

Shellhammer shook his head. "We can't afford trouble right now."

"So," Kirbi summarized, "you're looking for somebody to find out what this guard was up to."

She sipped some more coffee. If this was all the job entailed, maybe she could just work it into her schedule. Doing so might give her a foot in the door for future RayBright business.

"Correct," Van Horne said.

"It could be something," Shellhammer said. "It could be nothing."

Van Horne made a face. "But we want to know which—and we want to know as soon as possible."

After a suitable pause, Kirbi said, "I think I could do that for you. But before I commit, I'd like to discuss a few things first. Just to save misunderstandings later." She looked at Shellhammer and Van Horne who both nodded. "First and foremost, I do things my own way and I don't always tell my clients how I get my results."

"We'd be perfectly satisfied with just results," Van Horne said.

This settled, Kirbi continued, giving them her rates, how she billed, and how much she liked to get up front. Neither man showed any reluctance about any of it. When she finished, she watched Van Horne pick up a phone and tap its screen.

"That all sounds fine," he told her. Then began speaking quietly into the device.

She turned to Shellhammer. "I'm going to need everything you have on this guard, sir." He glanced at Martinez. "David will make that happen for you."

Martinez nodded.

Van Horne put his hand over the phone for a moment. "They're cutting you a check now, downstairs."

THIRTEEN

Ten minutes later, Kirbi sat across from Martinez at his desk in the Security office on the first floor. As she looked on, he called up something on his computer, then printed it out. This done, he handed the copy to her. A single sheet of paper.

"Confidentiality agreement," he said.

She scanned its half dozen paragraphs. The thing seemed standard. She used her own pen to scrawl a signature at the bottom and date it.

When she returned the paper to him, Martinez passed her an unsealed envelope that bore the RayBright logo. She pulled its flap back to glance at the check amount. Then folded the whole thing into her shoulder bag.

She'd been amused earlier to see a stunned look flash across Martinez's face when she'd mentioned her rates. She, the little five-foot-nothing black gal in raggedy-ass sweat clothes. What's with that, huh?

She looked across the desk at him now, smiling at the thought.

He tried to smile back but couldn't quite manage it. Instead, he now passed her a nine by twelve manila envelope. "What we have on Steven Stanko."

Inside was a sheaf of photocopies.

Kirbi began shuffling through them for a quick look-see.

Stanko's four-page job application, dated three years before. Paper-clipped to the top, a small color photo. Blond-haired guy in his late twenties.

This was followed by his security clearance. A fingerprint page. Six pages of results from a background check. A copy of his army DD214.

Firearms certification. Results of a medical check-up. And finally, some letters of reference.

"RayBright doesn't mess around," she said. "This is thorough."

Martinez nodded, leaning back in his chair, eyes hooded.

She continued through the paperwork.

A ninety-day probationary review from his supervisor, followed by three yearly reviews. A copy of his attendance and schedule going back to hire date. Certificates showing he went to OSHA, firearms safety, CPR, and other classes provided by RayBright. Even results of two drug screens.

Finished for the time being, she squared up the photocopies and slid them back into the manila envelope. She took a deep breath and blew it out. And lifted her gaze to meet Martinez's.

She'd enjoyed herself taking a little petty revenge on him. The opportunity had come and she'd jumped on it, but it wasn't the way she usually did things. And it had to end.

"I'd like to ask you a personal question, David."

He eyed her with a hint of suspicion, but said nothing.

"I know you've only just met me, but what would you say annoys you most about me as person? The fact that I'm black and female and a midget?"

After a long moment, he said, "I'm not sure you're exactly a *midget*, are you?"

"How about the fact that I can be an arrogant bitch? Do you think that could be annoying?"

"To some people, maybe."

"You been at RayBright a long time?"

"I started a month ago."

"FNG."

Martinez gave a slow nod. "That's me."

"They didn't tell you they'd called me in. That bother you?"

Martinez forced a shrug. He had big shoulders. He was carrying too much fat, but looked like he worked out. "Hey, I go with the flow."

"Okay."

"I *need* this job."

"I can respect that," Kirbi said. "Do you think we can get along?"

He gave another slow nod. "I don't see why not. We got off on the wrong foot—which was my fault. Let's work together. You need something—tell me, okay?"

She stood up, reached across the desk, and the two of them shook hands.

When she sat back down, Martinez asked, "So how you thinking of getting Stanko to talk?"

"You wouldn't believe me."

"Try me?"

"I'm sorry. I wasn't trying to mess with you."

"Yes, you were."

Kirbi thought about this and allowed a guilty smile. "Maybe a little."

"So what's your plan?"

"He heterosexual, by the way?"

"That matter?" Martinez said, messing back with her.

"Might."

"Well, far as I know, he's straight."

"Good, cause I'm thinking of trying to *fuck* it out of him?"

His facial muscles betrayed him, but he made a quick recovery. "Oh," he said, almost managing to make it sound casual.

"Not *personally* fuck it out of him."

"I see."

Though Kirbi didn't think he did see, it was time to shut up.

At least until she got to know him better.

111

Legal issues over her methods sometimes came up. But also, Kirbi liked having a professional mystique. Liked being someone who did magic and didn't reveal how the tricks were done.

"So tell me about Stanko," she said. "He worked for you for a month, right?"

Martinez pursed his lips for a moment. "Yeah. I talked to him some, but I wouldn't say I knew him well. He seemed to be a, you know, solid employee. Always had his uniform squared away. Showed up on time, didn't miss a lot of days. Did his job."

"So this was all a big surprise."

"To me, yeah."

"I assume," Kirbi said, "it was also a big surprise to his fellow guards."

"As far as I can tell."

"You saw the pictures Stanko had on his phone?"

Martinez nodded.

"Was there any pattern to them? What did *you* make of them? What do you think their purpose was?"

"I know what you mean," Martinez told her. He rubbed the side of a thumbnail along his lower lip, thinking. "There was nothing that seemed to be the focus of his attention more than anything else. But it was a sightseeing tour of secured areas of the building. Maybe thirty pictures."

"Did you keep them?"

He shook his head in regret.

"I probably should have downloaded them off his phone. It's just that it all happened so fast. We searched his car and person and locker because we had a waiver he'd signed when he was hired. Like everybody signs. But the phone thing worried me. Like being more of a gray area, if he got a lawyer and made trouble." He made a wry face. "My first big crisis. All eyes on me. Fucking New Guy didn't want to screw up."

He laughed but there wasn't much humor in it.

Kirbi asked, "How about the place where he wasn't supposed to be?"

"What do you mean?"

"Where was he when you caught him?"

"Uh, the labs area on the first level."

"What's there?"

"Lots of things," he said with a frustrated shrug. "That's the problem."

"Give me some for-instances. What's down there?"

Martinez's eyebrows rose and his lips parted. He exhaled. "Maybe a half dozen projects. Specifically, what the projects are, I don't know. But, the people who work on them are computer and electronic engineers. Half of the people who work here have a Ph.D.—so that should tell you something."

"If you had to guess, what would you say is the most valuable, the most desirable of the projects? To someone doing industrial espionage?"

"I don't know. You'd have to ask Eric something like that?"

She let him see that she accepted his answer. That she understood. "Okay, then, what has the reputation for being the most top secret—the most hush-hush—project down there?"

"Project Sixteen," he said without hesitation.

"What's Project Sixteen?"

He smiled, then broke into an ironic chuckle, and she knew what he was going to say before he said it: "I don't know."

* * *

Kirbi drove home to Normal Heights. She lived in a classic three-bedroom Mission Style stucco, built in 1927. As she pulled up to park on the side street next to it, she did what she often did. Marveled that such a wonderful thing belonged to her.

Inside, she quickly got out of her homeless disguise. Took a shower and brushed her teeth. And put on clean jeans, a pocket tee, and sandals.

A new woman, she headed down the hall to her office.

There, seated at her desk, she took out the photocopied material Martinez had given her on Stanko. After staring at his RayBright ID photo for a long moment, she moved on to the next page and began reading. Who was he?

Half an hour later, she made the first of three calls. To Roy Baines, who among other things did computer research for her.

"Roy, it's Kirbi," she told his voice mail, "I need a rundown on a Steven J. Stanko." She spelled out the name, then read off the DOB and SSN. "I've already got quite a bit on him, but I'd be particularly interested in anything you can find in the areas of money problems, high tech connections other than where he works, and foreign travel. Give me a call or text me when you get a chance."

This said, Kirbi switched off, but immediately tapped in another number.

It rang three times. "Hello."

"Steven Stanko, please."

"Speaking."

"Hi, Steven, this is Diane Di Giorgio from Sunscape Vacations. How would *you* like to take a twelve-day, eleven-night Mexican Rivera cruise?"

Diane Di Giorgio was an invented character Kirbi used for phone work. Only the truly clueless and lonely listened to Diane's sorry pitches. So it was no surprise when Stanko cut the conversation short, saying, "I'm not interested," and broke the connection.

Which was okay with Kirbi.

Her purpose had been to verify his address and she had. He'd just answered the landline registered in his father's name, the father with whom he lived. Also, she'd wanted to learn if he was at home. Which he was, at least for the time being.

Now came the third call, to Vanessa Aparicio.

"Vanessa? Kirbi. Glad I caught you."

114

"What's up, baby doll?"

"I could use you on something," Kirbi told her. "What's your schedule like?"

"Let me guess—it's a hurry-up thing."

"You know me too well."

"Well, I'm afraid I'm pretty busy," Vanessa drawled, negotiating.

"You know I'm always willing to pay for inconvenience. You're the best, and I need the best."

Vanessa's muffled chuckle was audible on the other end. "You think that flattery shit works on me, huh?"

"What do they say? Sometimes one is flattered by the effort to flatter."

"Double rate?"

"You got it," Kirbi told her.

Though it wouldn't be smart to state it explicitly—to Vanessa or any of her other subcontractors—money was hardly ever at issue. Almost always, time and results were bigger priorities than cost. So while Kirbi's ethics would never allow her to *squander* her clients' money, she'd learned not to be counterproductively cheap.

"All right then," Vanessa agreed happily. "When and for how long?"

"A day or two at most. But I'd like to *try* to get it started this afternoon. Any chance of that?"

"Wow. Hmm. Okay. You want to come pick me up, or you want to meet?"

"How about I stop over at your place about—" Kirbi checked the time "—one?"

"Done deal. I'm out and about, but I'll be back home by then. See you at one."

Having ended the call, Kirbi at last put the phone down and opened her laptop.

115

While it booted up she stared absently out the window, thinking.

Then opened Word and began typing. It went well. Forty minutes later she had a four-page document. A media survey on behalf of her favorite fictitious company, Global Services.

Global Services was a wonderfully vague and versatile enterprise. Its address was that of a commercial mail place where Kirbi rented a box. Its phone number, that of an automated answering service.

She printed out a dozen copies of the survey on GS letterhead.

* * *

A little after noon, Kirbi drove to the nearest Office Depot where she bought one of those aluminum pre-printed-form boxes. The kind delivery and trades people carried for their orders. Also, a package of clear plastic self-laminating luggage tags, and a badge lanyard.

This accomplished, she hit a nearby chain supermarket, where she paid cash for an assortment of twenty-five-dollar gift cards. Restaurants. Movie theaters. A day spa. A local amusement park.

And finally, headed for Little Italy.

Vanessa's building was four stories of concrete, colorfully painted in pastels. She lived on the top floor. Kirbi got a buzz in at the entrance, climbed the stairs, and was met at the door. The two women embraced, then Vanessa led Kirbi inside.

Once they were seated together on the couch in the main room, Kirbi went straight to business. She handed Vanessa Stanko's ID photo. "This is our target. A recently fired security guard."

Vanessa shrugged. "Could be worse."

"He got bounced for taking pictures with his phone of top secret areas at the place where he used to work. And when they caught him, he had a big wad of cash on him. Like maybe he was spying for somebody on the outside."

"Got it."

"So we want to know why he was taking those photos, and where the money came from."

"And anything else I can get," Vanessa noted, still looking at the photo.

"Yes."

"You have a plan?"

Kirbi nodded, passing Vanessa the aluminum forms case. "This is your game."

Vanessa popped the lid and examined the uppermost copy of the survey. Then smiling, began reading aloud. *"How much television do you estimate you watch per day? Do you pay for cable, or satellite dish?"*

"I bought some gift cards that you can offer people for participating."

"Door to door."

"Yeah. I want to try him this afternoon. He lives in El Cajon. When we get out there, I'll try another pretext call and make sure he's still home. Then you start down the street a ways, warm up with a few surveys, and when you get to his house hopefully *meet cute*."

"I like it," Vanessa told her, getting up. "I've got an idea. I'll be right back." When she was about to disappear into the bedroom, she called over her shoulder, "Refreshing beverages in the kitchen, babe. You know the way."

Kirbi thought about whether it was time for more caffeine. She'd been up all night. No, she decided, not yet.

She instead busied herself unloading some things from her shoulder bag.

On the coffee table in front of the couch she laid them out, side by side. The gift cards. The luggage tags. The lanyard. Her phone. A small portable printer. Scissors. A glue stick. And the piece of cardstock bearing the Global Services logo and the name *Vanessa Aparicio*.

Kirbi had just finished this preparation when her friend came prancing back into the room, eager to model her new look. Instead of the chic sweater and jeans of a few minutes before, she now wore a plain white button-up blouse with rounded collar, and blue and white plaid Capri pants.

Vanessa touched her usually stylish hair, now clumsily pinned up. "What do you think? Midcentury modern—in a mousy, down-market, nondescript kind of way."

Kirbi smiled. "Only *he* notices your underlying beauty and desirability. "

The two women burst into laughter.

"How about the glasses?"

"Oh my," Kirbi said. They looked like drug store reading glasses. The lenses were clunky ovals with orange-metallic rims. "The only way I can put it is *delightfully unflattering.*"

Giggling, Vanessa collapsed onto the couch. "Yessss!"

When the two of them had settled down after a few moments, Kirbi turned, picked up her phone, and said, "ID photo time. Ready? Turn toward me and say, *Cheesy.*"

Vanessa grinned into the lens and said just that.

"I forgot to ask about things on the acting front," Kirbi noted as she checked the picture she'd just taken. She'd attended several of Vanessa's local theater productions.

"I'm in *Our Town* next month. Also, I'm auditioning for a couple of commercials."

"Cool."

"Girl's gotta dream."

Kirbi, nodding, plugged her phone into the printer. "Always."

When the printed photo emerged, she used scissors to crop it to fit the cardstock that was to become Vanessa's company badge. Glued it on. Laminated the result between the sticky sides of the clear-plastic luggage tag. Then clipped badge to lanyard.

Satisfied, she caught Vanessa's eye and leaned forward to loop the lanyard around her neck. After which she leaned back and spoke in a tone of mock-solemnity. "I'd like to welcome you to the Global Marketing Research family."

* * *

Out in El Cajon, the block of Fawcett Street they wanted was down near Washington.

"We're coming up on it," Kirbi announced, having already Google Earthed the address. "There on the left. The orangey stucco one with the hedge along the front."

Vanessa craned to see. "Got it."

Kirbi drove two blocks past and U-turned. Immediately parked at the curb on the same side of the street as the Stanko house. Then got out her phone.

"Let's make sure," she said, tapping in the number. As before, it was the one for the home landline. Not the fired guard's cell. When the call was answered, she made her voice deep and plummy. "Steven Stanko?"

"Yeah," Stanko said.

"This is Mary McVickers. I'm calling from Southland Insurance. You recently stopped working for RayBright Laboratories, am I right?"

"…Yeah."

119

"I'm calling to verify your mailing address. You have a refund check coming." She rattled off house number, street, city, and zip. "Is that correct?"

"What's this—?"

"We have you listed as having a group life insurance policy through RayBright. We have a check we'd like to get to you. For the pro-rated remainder of your yearly premium."

There was a pause in which Kirbi imagined Stanko scratching his head.

"How much is it?" he asked.

"The check? Forty-four dollars even."

"Great. I can use it."

"We'll put it in the mail today. Thank you, Mr. Stanko. Good-bye."

Kirbi closed the phone and looked at Vanessa who was frowning.

"You going to actually send him a check?"

"Yeah," Kirbi told her. "It's best to follow through. So there're no suspicions. We don't know how much this dude will be in the picture later. I don't want to burn him down until we know." She grinned. "I used the forty-four-even figure so I can remember the amount later."

"Seems like a waste of forty-four dollars."

"Probably is. Anyway, you ready?"

Vanessa laid her fingers on the door handle. "Born ready."

"Good girl. I'll be at the Starbucks we passed on the way in, catching up on my reading." Kirbi opened her handbag and hefted a thick paperback.

"*A History of the Jews*," Vanessa read aloud.

"My mother was Jewish."

Vanessa gave her an astonished look.

120

"What?" Kirbi went on. "I don't look Jewish?"

Vanessa made a comic face, chuckling. "I thought you were a light-skinned black lady from Mississippi."

"I am. That's where my Jewish schoolteacher mama met the handsome, smooth-talking brother who was my father."

"You're full of surprises."

"That's me," Kirbi agreed. "So, listen, call me when you're done, or if you have any problems. And the trouble code is *Sorry to bother you at home.* Okay?"

Vanessa nodded and climbed out.

Kirbi watched her saunter up the nearest front walk and knock at the door.

A white-haired woman answered. She and Vanessa spoke for half a minute. Their body language said it was a relaxed and friendly conversation. The woman made a parting comment and shut the screen.

Nondescript Vanessa moved on. Aluminum case in the crook of her arm. Shoulder bag swinging jauntily with each stride. A push on the doorbell. A long pause. No answer?

But at the next house Kirbi saw her invited in.

Confident Vanessa had things under control, Kirbi started the car.

* * *

It was just shy of two hours later when Kirbi looked up to see someone drop into the padded chair next to hers. Vanessa's red-rimmed eyes had a slightly glassy look. She carried a clear plastic Starbucks cup filled with a beige liquid.

"I decided to walk," Vanessa said.

"Sure. Everything okay?"

121

"I had to get stoned with him—I probably stink of the stuff."

Kirbi sniffed the air. "If so, I can't tell. All I smell in here is *coffee*."

Vanessa raised her cup. "That's exactly what I'm about to flood my system with. Iced. I'm hoping it'll wake me up." That said, she brought the cup's straw to her mouth and took a long, thirsty drink.

Kirbi waited. She dog-eared the page she was reading, and closed the book. Glancing up, she saw Vanessa watching her.

"How're the Israelites doing?"

"Not too well," Kirbi said. "They ran into something called the Holocaust. But now they're in the process of taking the Promised Land away from the Palestinians."

"Well, God bless them, every one."

"Did we succeed in our mission, by the way?"

Vanessa gave her a loopy smile. "You ready for this—it all has to do with something from a Chinese submarine."

FOURTEEN

The previous evening Kirbi had left a message on Shellhammer's voice mail, telling him she had some news. But he'd never called back. So she'd tried him twice more earlier this morning—once by voice mail, once by text. Again without response.

Oh well, clients were all different. This one apparently didn't answer or check his messages very often. Be that as it may.

Once off the freeway and on surface streets, Kirbi put her windows down. She let the cool morning air wake her up. Though she'd gotten some much needed sleep the night before, she still didn't feel fully rested somehow. Her body clock was out of adjustment.

As arranged the night before, this morning Roy Baines was waiting for her at the strip mall. His vintage yellow Corvette was hard to miss.

She backed her Jaguar in next to him so their driver side windows matched up, cop style.

"How's Cheryl?" she said. "I forgot to ask when I was on the phone." His wife had been fighting breast cancer, on and off, for the past year.

Baines gave a tiny nod. "Good for now. She starts chemo again tomorrow."

"What fun."

"Lots of yuks," he agreed with equal irony. "Hey, I'm not supposed to be wearing a suit or something, am I?"

"What?"

"It's just that you're looking particularly well-groomed and attired."

Kirbi grinned. "Yesterday I showed up dressed as a homeless person. Today I thought I'd reframe myself as someone a little more upscale."

She had on a gray tweed jacket, off-white silk blouse, black slacks, and heels. Even a hint of perfume and makeup.

"Well, I hope you can excuse my usual jeans and souvenir concert tee."

"Do you even own a suit?" she said.

Baines chuckled, shook his head, and started the Corvette's engine.

Down the street at RayBright, the same young brother was at the gate as the day before.

He gave Kirbi a flirtatious smile of recognition. When he handed back her ID, she explained that the person in the yellow car behind would be accompanying her. He nodded and waved her through.

Down at the visitors parking, she waited for Baines.

Then the two of them walked together to the building's entrance.

Through the big front windows, Kirbi could see Martinez and a pink-faced older guard behind the counter. They seemed deep in discussion. Martinez looked up when Kirbi and Baines came through the doors. He shot her a surprised look.

"I've been trying to get the general on the phone," Kirbi explained. "I've got some information I think he needs to hear."

"What's that?" he asked with interest.

"I'd like to wait, and tell you and the big guys at the same time, if that's alright."

"Sure, sure. Let's go find them."

Kirbi turned to Baines and said, "David, this is my associate, Roy Baines." As the two men shook hands, she added, "Roy, David here is Head of RayBright Security."

Introductions over, Martinez typed in their names at the keyboard and handed them visitor badges. He then picked up his phone and tried a four-digit extension. When this seemed to get him nowhere, he reached for a black Motorola radio.

"Terrell Berry," he said, holding a button down. "Are you outside Bay Two?"

"Yes, sir," a voice replied after a moment.

"Eric and the general still there with the television people?"

"That's a ten four."

"Thanks," Martinez said, releasing the button and clipping the radio back to his belt. "Let's all go down there."

Kirbi nodded. They followed Martinez along a corridor and out a side door.

"This is probably the quickest way," he told them, throwing his considerable bulk behind the wheel of what looked like a four-seater dune buggy. Kirbi got in alongside him. Baines folded himself into the seat behind.

Kirbi had been expecting the sound of a gas engine, but the thing appeared to be electric. Martinez merely turned a key, popped the brake, and they were in motion. Down the sloping asphalt next to the big building. Then left at the corner, to continue along its backside.

Tall eucalyptus trees lined the chain-link fencing on their right.

Ahead, there was a truck parked at the far end. The name of a local television station and its network affiliation were colorfully displayed on its side. A broadcast mast had been raised.

A guard stood next to the big open rollup door across from the truck. He turned at the approach of the cart. Gave his boss, Martinez, an alert look. Then glanced curiously at Kirbi and Baines as they walked past him a few moments later.

Inside, at the rear of the bay, a live interview seemed to be taking place. Three people sat in canvas high chairs. Van Horne, Shellhammer, and a young woman in dark maroon. There was a lot of portable lighting and a camera on a tripod.

125

Van Horne held one of those oversized display checks mounted on foam board. The symbolic, presented-on-camera kind. He and the newswoman chatted animatedly.

Kirbi felt the faint brush of Baines' beard at her neck. He'd leaned close from behind to say in a low voice, "That's Andrea Yamaguchi."

His infatuated tone amused her. She looked back and gave him a condescending eye roll. An intense-looking guy, hovering next to the cameraman, turned to survey the new arrivals. He put an insistent finger to his lips. Kirbi noticed he wore a RayBright badge. Their PR guy maybe.

She held her hands together in namaste and met his gaze. He turned back to the proceedings.

The thing seemed to be coming to an end. The woman in the dark maroon was thanking Van Horne and Shellhammer. Kirbi thought they presented themselves well. Both wore tieless white dress shirts, sleeves rolled back on their forearms. Just two hard-working multimillionaires, glad to be able to help out.

The newswoman now looked into the camera and recited a sign off.

A few moments later, Shellhammer stood up, put his hand in his pocket, and got out his phone. As he held up it in front of him, Kirbi saw his gaze stray past its screen to her. Then his eyes widen in curiosity. Phone still in hand, he came striding over.

"I'm sorry," he told her. "I haven't returned your calls yet." He heaved a sigh. "My usual crazy schedule." His eyes searched her face. "Your message said you'd discovered something important."

Kirbi took a breath. "I have. But let's wait a moment and get Eric in on this."

Shellhammer impatiently waved his partner over.

When he arrived, Kirbi gave him a nod of greeting. Then with Baines at her side, and the others—Shellhammer, Van Horne, and Martinez—gathered in a semicircle, she began.

126

"Stanko was hired over the telephone by a guy he never met in person. Someone representing himself as an agent of the federal government. Whether that's true or not, I don't know. But saying it, along with a pile of cash money, was enough to get Stanko to do whatever the guy wanted."

"Like what?" Van Horne asked.

"Like giving this alleged fed a rundown of RayBright's security set up and procedures. Right down to a list of guards, their names and addresses, and schedules. He even gave him the makes and models of all your locks—"

Martinez murmured, "Jesus."

"—safes, and biometric devices. *And*, provided a sample of the badges you wear. Stanko said that the guy sounded particularly interested in a project called Merman. Which I guess is something to do with a Chinese submarine?"

Van Horne wore a stricken expression. Shellhammer, one of cold anger.

"I'm afraid there's more," Kirbi went on. "This is Roy Baines. I brought him along because I want him to have a look at some things, if it's okay with you. Stanko said he installed something on at least two computers here. A keystroke device."

Maybe seeing baffled expressions, Baines explained. "It's a way for someone to record everything that's typed on the keyboard of that computer. By no means the latest and most sophisticated way to do so, but an effective one."

"What should we do about this?" Van Horne asked.

Baines shrugged. "If you'll let me, I'd like to talk to your IT department. Maybe have a look at the whole system. And once I do that, if necessary, we can talk strategy."

"Stanko doesn't know we're onto him yet," Kirbi added. "At least I don't *think* so. One of my people got him to talk, kind of brag about his exploits working for this 'fed.' For now, the hope is, he isn't suspicious that she was anything but a chance acquaintance."

Martinez shot her a look, probably remembering their talk in his office the day before.

"So if there are in fact such devices in place," Baines said, "removing them might alert him, and his employer, that we're onto them. Which we may or may not want to do."

Shellhammer frowned and folded his arms, but said nothing.

Van Horne was making a sequence of faint popping sounds with his lips. A child's unconscious mannerism. "Whose computers?" he asked finally.

"The first one is named Jane," Kirbi said. "Last name something French-sounding."

"Bouchet," Martinez suggested.

Kirbi nodded. "What's her role here?"

"Accounting," Shellhammer said. "How about the second one?"

Kirbi turned back to Martinez, knowing he wasn't going to like it. "The second one is on the computer in *your* office."

His eyes snapped to hers. "Oh, man."

"This has the feel of a nightmare," Van Horne noted, almost to himself. He exhaled a fierce breath through his nose. He glanced at Shellhammer, then got out his phone and entered a number. He looked off into the middle distance for a few seconds. "Mickey? This is Eric. We've got a problem. I'm going to need for you to drop pretty much everything you're doing and get on something for me. Okay? Are you in your office? Good. I'm bringing some people up in a minute. I'll explain then. Thanks, Mickey."

Everyone followed Van Horne through a nearby door.

They entered a long corridor. But before they'd gone very far, Kirbi called out in an insistent voice, "Eric?"

128

Plump little Van Horne was in full stride. He, Shellhammer, and Martinez were already a half dozen steps ahead. They halted and looked back.

"Roy's got a bad leg," she explained.

She'd noticed the awkwardness in Baines' gait and his grimace. Though of course he would never mention it, let alone complain. He'd had a motorcycle accident years before.

"John and I are going on ahead to talk with Mickey," Van Horne announced. Then said to Martinez, "David, why don't you stay with our visitors and show them the way."

This settled, Van Horne hurtled off once more up the corridor in high gear. Shellhammer gave them a fleeting glance over his shoulder as he followed his partner.

Martinez fell back with the slower-moving Kirbi and Baines. "They're a little freaked by this," he explained. "Especially Eric."

"It's understandable," Kirbi said.

When they arrived at the IT offices, Van Horne, Shellhammer, and a man with a white moustache could be seen conferring in a room off to the right. Van Horne noticed them and beckoned. He opened the door, then shut it behind them. He motioned toward the chairs around a small table.

Everyone seated themselves, while Van Horne remained standing.

He introduced Kirbi and Mickey Walters.

But turning to Baines, had to apologize, having forgotten his name.

"Roy Baines," Baines told him.

Something subtly changed in Walters' face. "*Roy Baines?*" As if maybe he was being put on. Or had happened upon a curious coincidence. "As in *the* Roy Baines?"

Baines bobbed his head. "In another incarnation."

Though Baines almost always played it off, Kirbi knew he found the attention gratifying.

"Who's *the* Roy Baines?" Van Horne asked, not liking being left out. He looked to Shellhammer, who gave him a small negative head movement, apparently equally ignorant.

"Kind of a famous old-school hacker," Walters said, gazing across at Baines. "I hope I'm not being insulting with the word *hacker*."

Baines moved his right shoulder half an uninsulted inch.

Van Horne nodded and showed Baines a toothy smile. "Well, we're glad to have your expertise, Roy," he said. Then took a breath and addressed all at the table as a group. "Until we get a handle on what's going on, I think it'd be best if we keep the whole Stanko thing quiet and compartmentalized. Okay? Right now, unfortunately, John and I've got a meeting with some money people having to do with the rollout of the stock offering. It's something we can't get out of. So, do what you can now, and we'll meet up later."

That said, he and Shellhammer hurried from the room.

When the door clicked shut behind them, Walters said, "Why don't you guys explain the situation and tell me what you want. Eric said you're to have full co-operation."

FIFTEEN

Later that same day, Jane sat out on the balcony of her condo, thinking about her future. For almost half an hour she'd been scribbling numbers on paper. More or less the same numbers. Her savings divided by her monthly expenses.

The truth wasn't pretty—without any money coming in, Jane figured she'd last five months.

And this figuring didn't take into account her possible legal bills.

Or that she might be in jail in five months.

When the doorbell rang downstairs, she wrenched herself upright, and peered down over the outer wall of the balcony to her front door area. Two people were standing there. But from almost directly overhead, it was difficult to see who they were.

Two guys. No, a man and a woman. A guy with a buzz cut, big and bulky in a dark pinstripe suit. And a woman with a tight afro, much smaller in gray tweed.

Not salespeople. Not Jehovah's Witnesses. Cops? Lawyers?

Wait.

David from RayBright, the new Head of Security.

Jane sighed and strode inside. Her purse was on the counter. She rifled it for a brush, found one, and ran it through her hair a few times. Then, having shoved it back into the purse, bounced down the carpeted stairs to open the front door.

"David," she said.

He wore a serious expression. "Hi, Jane. This is Kirbi Mack. She's doing some security-related consulting for the company. Would you be able to spare us a few minutes?"

Jane had a sudden impulse to mention that he could have called first, but let it pass. What was crankiness going to get her?

"Sure," she managed, trying for a friendly tone. "Come on in."

"Thanks for making time for us," Kirbi told her, smiling as she stepped in. She reached to clasp Jane's hand.

She looked thirtyish and carried herself like an athlete. Jane liked her taste in clothes.

"That's a nice jacket," Jane said as the three of them ascended the steps.

"You like it?"

"I do," Jane told her, stopping at the top to appraise it on the other woman. "We're about the same size. Your shoulders are a little broader, maybe."

Grinning, Kirbi slipped the jacket off and handed it to her. "Try it on."

Jane hesitated, a little embarrassed, about to say no. But for some reason, maybe Kirbi's infectious grin, Jane instead took it. She shrugged into it. And ducked around the corner into the bathroom and flicked on the light.

Kirbi followed her in, a moment later. "Not bad," she said, standing next to Jane at the mirror. "Sets off your blonde hair nicely."

Jane nodded her agreement. She preened, turning left, then right. "I've always liked tweed."

"Me, too. So wonderfully British or something."

"It looks expensive."

Kirbi shook her head. "I got it cheap—a sale at Nordstrom."

When the two women emerged from the bathroom, David was in the TV area. He stood, arms crossed, glancing around in a self-consciously patient way. As if perplexed at this delay in the business at hand.

Jane stepped to the kitchen nook. "I was going to have some tea. How about you guys? Or, I have soda, juice, milk...?"

"Tea's good," Kirbi said and turned to David, who managed a reluctant nod.

"Just give me a sec, then," Jane told them. She made a gesture toward the sliding glass doors. "Why don't we have it out on the balcony so I can smoke."

They then walked outside, and Jane joined them there a few minutes later, bringing with her the promised tea. She set a tray down on the table. Poured three cups from the pot and distributed them. And pointed to an assortment of napkins, spoons, lemon wedges, and sweeteners on the tray.

"Lapsang Souchong?" Kirbi asked, bringing her cup to her nose.

Jane grinned and nodded, impressed.

Across the table, impatient David cleared his throat. "We needed to ask you some questions about work."

"Sure," Jane told him, adding a daub of honey to her tea and stirring it with a spoon. "Shoot."

She thought back to the previous Head of Security, Johnny Ryder. He'd retired a month or two before. Much smoother than David. Subtler. Easier to get along with.

"What do you know about Steve Stanko?"

Jane felt her eyebrows rise and forehead wrinkle. "The guard? The one who got canned?"

"Did you hear what he got canned *for*?" David asked.

"I heard a couple of stories." She paused to offer a philosophical shrug. "As I'm sure you're learning, there are no secrets at RayBright. Rumor Control might not get it right at first, but everything comes out eventually."

She glanced at Kirbi but found her engrossed in her tea. Listening maybe, but not participating yet. Jane wondered what exactly *security-related consulting* meant.

David again cleared his throat. "Just tell us what you heard?"

133

"Let's see, my impression was he got caught taking pictures of Ray-Bright stuff with his cell phone. Is that right?"

"Who is it you heard this from?"

Jane reached for her Pall Malls and lighter. "Suspect nervously fumbles for a cigarette," Jane said in an aside to Kirbi. "A futile attempt to stall for time." She lit up, inhaling and holding a deep first drag.

Kirbi looked up and chuckled.

David seemed to be suppressing a scowl.

"Look, David," Jane began, letting the smoke come out as she spoke. "I'd really rather not say who told me about Stanko. I feel weird sicking you on somebody who just passed on a little gossip to me. Okay?"

Kirbi shot Jane a sympathetic look, but said nothing.

"How well did you know Stanko?" David went on.

"Not well. RayBright's a small place. So we said hi, and I talked to him once in a while. But he worked mostly nights. So we didn't run into each other much. He seemed like an okay guy, though."

David's expression suggested he was waiting for more.

Jane refused to play.

"Was what happened to him a surprise to you?" he asked at last.

Jane took a pull on her cigarette. "I guess." She looked from David to Kirbi and back to David. "What's going on? You think I was in on what he was doing?"

"What's going on," David said, annoyed, "is that you're coming across as uncooperative."

"Well, maybe I don't like being treated like a hostile witness."

"You got something to hide, Jane?"

"I'm not hiding anything. I may be currently suspended without pay, and about to lose my job, but I'm still at heart a loyal RayBright employee. I've been one for eight years. Here's the straight story: I don't know anything about what Stanko was up to. I'd tell you if I did. Okay? We cool?"

David, who did not look cool, took a breath. As if about to respond. But Kirbi seemed to catch his eye and he hesitated.

"Let's try something different here," she suggested. "How about I lay out for Jane what I know about the situation. And you can correct me if I have any of the details wrong."

"Okay," he said, but not before giving Jane a distrustful glance.

Jane ignored him. She laid her cigarette in the ashtray and picked up her tea.

Kirbi appeared to take a moment to organize her thoughts, then began.

"Stanko seems to have been paid big money to take those pictures. Somebody hired him to, I guess you'd say, *size up* the security at Ray-Bright."

"Like industrial espionage," Jane said, wanting to show she wasn't stupid.

"Exactly. So what would they be after? We don't know. Proprietary secrets? Money? Maybe they're planning to break in and swipe expensive scientific equipment, which I gather RayBright has a lot of."

Jane brought her tea cup to her lips and sipped. "Okay."

"But Stanko did something else," Kirbi went on. "Which is why we're here. He installed a device on two company computers. A thing that records whatever's typed on that particular keyboard. One of them was on David's." She paused to look in his direction. "Which makes perfect sense—where better to learn about RayBright security, right? But the second one was on *your* computer."

Jane felt her heart jump in her chest. "Mine?"

Kirbi made a face, showing she shared Jane's surprise. "Which begs the question why? Why your computer? Alright, let's game it. Let's imagine *we're* the thieves and try to figure it out."

Jane's gaze flicked to David, silent across from her. He was leaning back in his chair. One elbow propped on the armrest, hand in front of his mouth. Tea untouched before him. Watching and listening.

She wondered what their relationship was. He seemed to have deferred to Kirbi.

"Okay," Jane said.

"So what can we—the creeps, the thieves—learn from the work you do on your computer? What will move us toward getting something of value? You're Accounting, so you handle money. Do you do banking? Transfer funds? Use authorization or account codes? You see where I'm going."

"I do," Jane told her, taking it seriously, trying get into the spirit of the thing. "But there's something you should know. Even through I've been at the company for a long time, and make really good money, I'm going to tell you a secret. I'm pretty much just a glorified clerk. There are only four of us in the department, including Norman."

"Go on."

"Now *Norman's* computer—*that* would be the gold mine." Jane paused to drink some more tea. "You see, Norman does all the important stuff himself. He does the banking. The contracts. Makes international transfers. Authorizes payment for expensive purchases." She heard her voice amp up as she tried to convey her point. "That's why it seems strange that they would bother with *my* computer."

"How about security codes? Is anything like that on your computer. The codes you have to punch in when you use your finger on the biometric things to get into the labs?"

Jane gave her head a helpless shake.

"You're doing fine," Kirbi told her, reaching across to lay a hand gently on hers for a moment. "I have some more questions, though. Is that okay?"

Jane indicated it was.

"Let's start with, What unusual happened at work recently?"

Jane sighed. "You mean other than I got suspended?"

"Other than that," Kirbi said. "For instance, did anybody at work, or outside of work, ask you any odd questions? About RayBright, or about anything?"

Jane tried to think. She gave her head a tentative shake no.

"How about strange phone calls? Package deliveries? Unusual visitors to the office. Repair work being done at the company? Any of your co-workers acting out of character in any way?"

At each query, Jane made a conscious effort to open her mind to any such recollection, but nothing occurred to her. She felt she was being a disappointment.

Kirbi seemed to read her frustration, offering a kindly shrug.

The three of them sat in silence for long moment.

Jane picked up her tea, finished it, and poured herself another cup. "Anybody else?" she asked, still holding the pot aloft.

David, though he had yet to taste his, put his hand over his cup to indicate no. Kirbi held hers out for a refill.

A car passed by below. The sound of its engine and music echoed in the cul-de-sac. Had to be the guy from the end unit. "Everybody Wants to Rule the World." Tears for Fears. He seemed to play a lot of eighties stuff.

"Anything I missed, David?" Kirbi asked.

He shook his head, his expression unreadable.

"I'd like to switch the talk to something else, then," she said.

Jane picked up her Pall Mall from the ashtray. She took a long drag from it. "Sure."

Kirbi slouched back thoughtfully in her chair. She braced both elbows on the armrests and put her spread fingertips together, five on five. "In what I do, Jane, I find it's best not to ignore coincidences." She paused. "So I'm going to ask you to bear with me, alright? I need to switch to another topic."

Jane wondered where this was going. She dipped her head once, acquiescing.

"This may have nothing to do with anything. But it's something that's there."

Jane moved her head again.

"I need to ask you about your accident," Kirbi said.

"My accident?"

"Yes."

Jane had a sudden notion that she'd been maneuvered into a trap. That David had been playing bad cop, so good cop Kirbi could get in close for the kill. Charming little sister-girl Kirbi.

"I promised my lawyer I wouldn't discuss the case with anyone," Jane stated evenly.

Kirbi nodded. "Tell me then about the DUI you had four years ago."

Jane met her eyes. "I drank and decided to try to drive home. Pretty simple and pretty stupid. Cop stopped me. I got a lawyer, paid a lot of money, and my lawyer beat it in court. I was lucky."

"Do you have a problem with alcohol?"

"Do I have a problem with alcohol?"

"Yeah."

Jane took a hungry drag on her cigarette, then tapped the ash off into the ashtray. "Alcohol interferes with my judgment," she said finally. "I know *that.*"

Kirbi nodded again. "I want to respect your privacy. And your promise to your lawyer." She pulled her clasped hands earnestly to her chest. "What I'd like to know though is this—Is there anything *funny* about what happened to you the other night? By *funny*, I mean unusual."

Images flashed through Jane's mind. Images tinged with guilt and shame.

"You think my accident had something to do with what's going on at RayBright?"

"Probably not," Kirbi admitted. "But it's a coincidence."

"I don't see how it could."

"On the surface, I don't either. But I have to know if there's anything about it that's not right. That's out of the ordinary. Please forgive my prying."

Jane looked into her eyes, seeing honest emotion.

There were several things that bothered Jane about the night of her accident. One was her blood screen at the hospital. Well below the legal limit for alcohol. But showing Xanax, or something like it.

The second was blacking out. She'd *never* awoken with no memory of what had happened the night before. Never. Not even in the Phish years.

She recalled Mark's phone conversation.

How he'd said she'd acted toward him. Though he wouldn't tell her what exactly she'd said or done, it had apparently been bad enough to turn him off to her for good.

This saddened her. Their relationship seemed to have so much potential.

Looking at Kirbi, and David, Jane could see that her own pregnant pause, and likely her face, told them that indeed something unusual had happened.

Jane licked her lips.

"Listen," she explained, focusing mostly at Kirbi as she spoke, "there *are* some funny things, okay? But I can't see how they could have anything to do with RayBright." She stopped, wincing in apology. "And I made a promise to my lawyer."

Kirbi looked disappointed, but seemed to force a shrug. "It's okay."

"But let me call her. If she'll let me, I'll..."

"Would you? That'd be great," Kirbi said. "Thanks."

David just looked at her.

SIXTEEN

"**H**ow about giving me a hand here?" Harvey said.

The packaging wasn't so much heavy, as wide and cumbersome. Harvey gripped it and pulled, sliding it partway off the back of the pickup bed. Then waited until the kid reluctantly shuffled forward to take the other end.

Inside the shed, they laid it on the cement floor next to the newly purchased box truck.

The kid frowned. "Why don't we do it outside in the sun?"

"Because I want to do it in here," Harvey insisted, stepping across to a pile of scaffolding parts against the far wall.

"It's awfully fucking dark inside."

"So what."

"It's not like anybody's going to see us out there. Way the hell out here in the boonies."

Harvey's jaw clenched for a moment in frustration. "Look, the warmer the vinyl gets, the more it stretches, which makes it hard to put the letters on straight. I'm not taking any chances doing it in the sun. Okay?"

The kid shrugged, conceding nothing.

Harvey picked up one of the wheeled scaffolding pieces and stood it against the shed wall. Picked up the other, and glanced at the kid. "Can you come over and hold this thing upright for me."

"You should've hired somebody to do the signs *for* you."

"Maybe. But I'm trying to keep this all on the down low."

"Then you could've hired it done out of town—in L.A. Or in Mexico."

"Yes, I could have. But as I've been saying, the trick on this job will be in the getaway. In not leaving a trail of breadcrumbs behind us for the cops to follow. The more we do ourselves, the safer."

The kid shook his head. But finally deigned to come forward and grasp the item as requested. "What about the place you bought the vinyl? Aren't they going to remember *Creighton Specialized Maintenance*. And won't they have a record of your address and phone number?"

For a moment Harvey had to fight an urge to grab him by the throat, if only to shut him up. Instead he met the kid's smartass eyes and said, "Let me answer that question by posing another."

"Okay."

"When we get through putting the lettering on both sides of the truck, why are we going to throw away more than ninety percent of what I bought?"

The kid's expression grew wary. As if maybe Harvey had set some trap he was determined not to fall into. He looked off across the shed, thinking it through.

In the meantime, Harvey quickly attached one of the side supports to the wheeled piece that stood against the wall, then connected its other end to the wheeled piece the kid was holding up. Next he fetched the other side support. Attached it. And set the floor section on the frame.

This done, he stepped away from the assembled whole, and turned to the kid.

"Well?"

"Because you didn't buy the words as words," the kid said, wearing a proud smirk now. "You bought enough letters to *make* the words."

"And how did I pay for it?"

"That's *two* questions. But the answer is, in cash."

Harvey turned his hands out, palms up. "There you go. Can we just fucking do some work now?"

"Of course. What's the holdup?"

141

Harvey took a calming breath.

He rolled the scaffolding over next to the box truck. Loaded some tools aboard, climbed aboard it himself, and waved for the kid to accompany him.

In total, the process of attaching the signage to the truck's flat-sided compartment took just short of three hours. Half an hour to measure and snap chalk lines on each side. Then almost another full hour per side to apply the vinyl lettering.

Harvey liked the results.

He checked his watch and decided it was time for lunch. Which consisted of some ground-sirloin burgers and fresh asparagus that he grilled out on the patio. Both came out perfect. He had water with his meal and the kid, two cans of Fosters.

Afterwards, he and the kid reclined on chaises, digesting their food and looking out across the canyon.

"How're things going with Norman?" Harvey asked after a while.

"I'm going over to see him tonight."

"He still cool? I mean, in general."

The kid gave a thoughtful nod and took a pull on his after-lunch cigarette. "He hasn't said much about what happened to Janie, but I think he's a little shocked by the whole thing."

Harvey shrugged. "It was what he wanted."

"Yeah. But that other driver getting killed bothers him. He's tender-hearted, Normie is. It freaked him. He thinks I somehow staged the whole thing, but I'm sure he can't figure how."

"Did he ask you that?"

"No."

"He's still going to be ripe for the picking, though, right? Come Thursday?"

"You mean the night we execute the 'RayBright Caper?'" the kid said, waggling his eyebrows.

142

"This is serious. Either he is or he isn't."

"He is."

"You're sure."

The kid airily waved a hand. "I'll just start by asking him, like it's a favor. Then if he balks, I blackmail him with the Jane thing. And if that doesn't work, I use his embezzlement from the company."

"But you *can* handle him?" Harvey said. He tried to keep his tone light, not wanting to antagonize the kid, but he needed to know.

"If I have to, I've got some emergency back-up ideas."

"Like what?"

"Well, I've been looking into the fingerprint recognition thing, on-line. What RayBright has isn't that sophisticated. I'm thinking of bringing something with me that day when I go see him, something I can use to create a cast of his finger. They say the stuff they make gummi bears out of works."

"So are you and him headed to the casino again tonight?"

"No. We'll probably just go out for dinner."

"And I'll bet I can guess who usually pays when you do?"

The kid allowed a crafty smile. "That's one of the things cheapskate Normie likes about me."

Harvey returned the smile and nodded. "Why I bring it up is this— things like that are business expenses. Okay?"

The kid looked confused. But then seeing Harvey taking out his wallet, said, "Harve, that's not at all necessary. I'm serious."

"Kiddo, humor me."

"You sure?"

"I insist," Harvey told him, thumbing out ten hundreds and passing them across.

"Well, I've always depended on the kindness of strangers."

"Just don't stick it all up your nose and get busted before Thursday."

The kid laughed. "I'll have the car home by midnight, Daddy."

For an instant Harvey feared he was talking about borrowing Dorothy's SL. Then laughed, realizing the kid was making a joke. "Have a good time then."

"I will. Everything going okay on your end?"

"As well as can be expected. I have to make some RayBright badges for the cleaning guys. And we'll need a couple of pairs of white coveralls."

Beer belching, the kid stubbed his cigarette out on the flagstone next to the chaise. Then, as if eager to point out that he remembered his own responsibilities, said, "I'm going up to buy the masks tomorrow. I got a line on a place in L.A. I'll buy the two most common ones they make—the ones they sell the most of—and I'll pay in cash."

"Good. And you'll wear a hat and dark glasses when you go in."

"And I'll wear a hat and dark glasses when I go in," the kid parroted, grinning as he got to his feet.

"See you when I see you."

The kid nodded. "Later."

Harvey watched him amble away toward the garage. He was glad he hadn't let his temper get the better of him in the shed, when the kid had been giving him a hard time.

So far, Harvey hadn't laid hands on him. As long as the carrot worked, he'd hold back on using the stick. But the kid's childish, drug-fueled mood swings sometimes got to him.

After a short while, Harvey rose, gathered up the paper plates and other refuse from the meal, and carried it all in to the kitchen to throw away. Then stood at the sink for a moment, absently looking out the back window. The days had been hectic lately. He hadn't been getting to the gym.

Impulsively stepping back, he took a breath and bent from the waist until his fingertips touched his toes. Held the position for a ten count.

144

Then dropped to the floor and knocked out a hundred push-ups, hands flat on the cool tile.

It felt good. Just what he needed.

His chest and arms tingled, and his heartrate was up.

Determined not to lose his momentum, he strode to his office at the other end of the house, and there threw himself into more calisthenics for another twenty minutes.

A hundred slow, strict-form sit-ups on the carpet, toes tucked under his desk. Ten handstand pushups against the wall. A hundred Hindu squats in the open area by the big window. And finally, twenty-five pull-ups on the chin bar that hung from the closet doorframe.

Yes. Now a lot more of him tingled, and his heartrate was really up.

He flopped down into the chair behind his desk. Atop it, in front of him, sat the empty packaging from the delivery of the krugerrands. They'd been messengered out to the farm the previous week as promised. He'd been a little worried on two counts.

First, that the mysterious man in the silver BMW might not come through. That his promise of earnest money would prove empty. In which case Harvey would have wasted a lot of time and expense setting up something that wasn't going to happen.

Second, that there wouldn't be enough of the shiny gold coins to cover the cost of unloading them. Something he and Mr. Silver BMW hadn't gotten around to talking about in their brief phone call. Since even selling them to a legitimate dealer—which Harvey wasn't about to do, as it would leave a paper trail—would net him only three quarters of their market value, at best.

So he was glad when the number of coins sent had been *more* than sufficient. Even when sold under the table at an even worse rate. He took this as a good sign. The guy had bought himself some credibility.

Which was a relief, of course. Because Harvey needed the RayBright thing. *Needed* it.

Over the past two years, he'd been foolishly trying to do something he swore he'd never try again. To go legit. To earn an honest buck, like other people seemed to be able to do.

But just as it hadn't worked in the past, it hadn't worked this time.

Not even close. He simply didn't have the knack. Not matter how hard he worked or how smart he thought he was playing things, he'd consistently come up short.

So despite how nerve-racking and crazy-making it could be, here he was, once more having to resort to criminal enterprise to shore himself up.

The crux of the problem was lifestyle. The expensive one to which Harvey had grown all too accustomed.

He liked living with a woman like Dorothy. He liked dining in expensive restaurants. He liked touring the U.S. and Canada in a top-of-the-line motorhome. He liked flying first class to Europe and the Caribbean.

He'd come too far from his dirt-poor Michigan childhood to go back now.

No way.

Moving his hand in almost absent fashion, he fished his keys from his pocket and unlocked the desk's center drawer. Inside was a rubber-banded roll of currency. He took it out and brought it near his nose, inhaling the grubby, unmistakable odor of paper money.

He thought about something his armored-car-driving buddy Mario used to say.

No risk-it, no biscuit.

SEVENTEEN

K irbi had been keeping track of the ascending numbers on the roadside mailboxes.

She slowed and signaled when she saw the one she wanted. Just beyond it, a sign attached to some chain-link fencing read *The Edna Graham Shelter*. Kirbi turned in and parked in the paved lot.

At some point the building must have been a three-bedroom ranch house. But that had been many remodels ago. From the interior sills of large windows along the front, cats watched her arrival with curiosity.

Jane Bouchet's lawyer did volunteer work at the place. If Kirbi wanted any sort of immediate meeting with her and her client, it had to be here and this afternoon. Kirbi stood beside her car and checked the display on her phone. Ten minutes early. Good.

She ambled up the walk to the front door.

Her nose tingled with the acrid tang of litter boxes as soon as she stepped inside.

Behind a beige metal desk, a heavyset woman in her mid-forties was on the phone. She nodded a welcome but continued with her call.

"That's right," she went on. "We keep our cats until they're adopted out. We don't euthanize."

Kirbi wandered the room as she waited. She stopped at some framed photos on one of the walls. The organization through the decades. Pictures of people and of cats. Some of the oldest photos showed a tall, intense-looking woman with wire-rimmed glasses. Their captions indicated this was Edna Graham.

Do-gooder cat fanatics.

Kirbi was reminded of the internet. How you encountered subcultures you would never have guessed existed.

She only half listened to the woman on the phone. An explanation of fees and procedures. Directions to the shelter. Finally a goodbye, and the click of the receiver set back in its cradle.

Then from behind her, she heard, "Kirbi Mack?"

Kirbi turned and nodded.

"I'm Deb Rosen," the woman at the desk said, hoisting herself from her chair.

Kirbi stepped over to clasp the offered hand. "Nice to meet you in person."

"Jane's in the back, playing with the cats. I'll get her and we can get started."

"Sounds good," Kirbi told her.

A few moments later, Jane appeared, holding an orange tabby over her shoulder, stroking its back. She gave Kirbi a warm smile and lowered herself onto a vinyl couch. Rosen followed soon after, and went back to her seat at the desk.

Kirbi sat down on the couch with Jane. She adjusted herself so as to face both Jane and the lawyer. She got out a pen and notebook from her shoulder bag.

Rosen gestured for her to begin.

Kirbi nodded and said, "How about we start with the night of the accident."

Jane took a breath, held it, and exhaled. "Well, I went out to hear some music with a guy named Mark."

Kirbi asked his last name, then for its spelling. She wrote it down: H-a-t-c-h-e-r.

"We met at my place and drove in my car. It was downtown San Diego, the King Club. Like a nightclub, I guess you'd say." She named the band that played.

Kirbi knew the King Club but didn't recognize the band. More subcultures.

"What'd you have to drink that night?" she asked in a careful tone.

It had taken quite a bit of wheedling to get Rosen to agree to the meeting. At first she'd seen no upside in legally exposing her client. The point being that no attorney-client privilege existed for Kirbi, who could be called to testify as to anything Jane said.

But somehow Kirbi had persuaded Rosen to trust her. So far.

"I remember drinking two rum and Cokes," Jane said, but not before giving Rosen, her lawyer, a glance. "I knew the next day at work was an important one, so I didn't want to get sloshed or anything. And that ties in with my blood alcohol later at the hospital."

"Point oh two," Rosen put in. Low in her chair, elbows on the chair arms, index fingers steepled in front of her lips. A big woman in jeans and a sweatshirt, but putting out a professional vibe. Used to being taken seriously. "Well within the legal limit."

Kirbi furrowed her brow as she turned back to Jane. "But you're sounding like you don't remember it very well…."

"That's just it—I don't." Jane shook her head in regret. "Not leaving the concert. Not anything between then and waking up in the hospital the next day." She sighed. "And I don't remember taking any Xanax. The doctor said my memory loss could be connected with that, or with my hitting my head in the accident."

Kirbi wrote the word *Xanax* in her notebook. "You have a prescription?"

"No. And I've never tried it or anything like it."

Kirbi keyed on the word *tried*, assuming this implied that Jane *tried* other things. She'd come back to that.

"So you don't know how it got in your system."

"No."

Kirbi looked at Rosen. She assumed Rosen's work doing DUI defense gave her an acquaintance with this sort of thing. "They test at the hospital for stuff like Xanax as a matter of course?"

Rosen gave a small shrug. "I don't know. You wouldn't think so. But maybe she was unresponsive and they were trying to determine why. I know they sometimes do blanket screens for certain common drugs."

Kirbi nodded. "Tell me about this guy Mark," she said to Jane. "When and where did you first meet him?"

Jane continued petting the cat. "I met him a week or so ago. He was at this Mission Valley bar where we were having a going-away get together for somebody from RayBright. We got talking."

"He work at RayBright?"

Jane shook her head.

"Tell me as much as you can about him."

"Well," Jane began, thinking, "six feet, maybe a little more. Kind of boyish—thin, long eyelashes, full lips. Cute. Kind of a clothes horse."

Kirbi was nodding along. "What does he do for a living?"

"Some kind of writer, I think."

"Do you have an address and phone number for him? I'd like to talk with him."

Jane got out her phone and read a number off it for Kirbi to copy down. "I don't know where he lives," Jane added. "He told me he had an apartment out in the back country somewhere. He came home with me, that first night. The second time—the night of the concert—we agreed to meet at my place and go together from there. So I never saw where he lived."

"I've tried to reach him myself," Rosen added. "I left several messages, but so far he hasn't called back."

"That's not a good sign," Kirbi said and pursed her lips. She looked back at Jane. "Okay, go on."

"Well, we took my car."

Kirbi interrupted. "Why *your* car?"

"I didn't like his beat up old van. Plus, I don't know, it didn't look safe."

"Can you describe it?"

"The van? Let's see, black, I think, or a very dark grey. Older. Like at least ten years, maybe more. I'm not good on models or years. And it had the name of some dry cleaning business on the side. You know, all faded. From somewhere in Texas. Did I mention he was from Texas?"

Listening to the nuances of how Jane spoke about him, Kirbi concluded that though the romance was apparently over, it wasn't over because *Jane* wanted it over.

"Okay," Kirbi told her, scribbling away. She glanced over at Rosen. She'd been prepared for more legal wariness from her. More balking. "Now you're at the concert."

"Right," Jane said. She started slowly, seeming to reconstruct things in her memory. "The place was full. The band came on."

"And you had a rum and Coke."

"Right."

"But normally, until recently, you told me you hadn't been drinking."

Jane winced. "That's true."

Kirbi let that go for the moment. "How about Mark? Did he drink?"

"Yeah. But he always held it well. The night we first met, he must have drunk six or seven beers, but didn't seem to show any effects."

"He use drugs that you know of?" Kirbi asked.

"That same night, he told me he'd taken some ecstasy. Half a tab. He gave me some, but I didn't take it."

"You ever do ecstasy before?"

Behind the desk, Rosen stirred.

151

Having caught the movement, Jane's gaze flicked to her. Kirbi wasn't sure what passed between them, but after a long moment, Jane continued.

"No."

"How about other things?"

Jane stole another glance at Rosen, but went on. "Back in my younger days, I guess you'd say. But nothing in the last ten years or so. Both for my own sanity and for the fact that RayBright has a random drug testing program. In the past, sure. Me and my ex-husband liked the Grateful Dead and Phish. We went to a lot of concerts in those days, and sometimes we tripped out when we went."

"But never Xanax."

"My mom was addicted to prescription drugs," Jane said, her face creasing in a mixture of disgust and sadness. "I know it doesn't make any sense that I'd take street drugs but not stuff from a pharmacy, but…." She shrugged.

"But this toxicology report, or whatever you'd call it," Kirbi said, "did indicate you had Xanax in your system."

Rosen interrupted at this point to clarify. "Not necessarily Xanax. Benzodiazepine."

Kirbi got her to spell the word. Then asked her a few questions about dosages and the effects of the drug. As a lawyer specializing in DUI, this was her world.

Kirbi went back to Jane. "*Mark* ever talk about Xanax?"

Jane shook her head. "No, I would have remembered."

"You think he might have put it in your drink for some reason?"

"I've thought about that, but I can't imagine why. It's not like he wasn't going to get in my pants that night."

Jane gave a nervous chuckle and Kirbi smiled along.

Rosen's expression remained a detached one.

Kirbi looked down at her notes. "You talked to Mark since that night?"

"Yeah. Once. I had a hard time getting him. And when I finally did, he acted all weird."

"Weird how?"

"Like he's mad at me," Jane said. "Offended or something." She paused, as though deciding how best to put it. "I told him I kind of blacked out and didn't remember the details of that night. He said, Oh that's real convenient." Her eyes flashed in anger at the memory. "But what I finally dragged out of him is that as we drove home I supposedly went all Mr. Hyde on him, like some kind of *mean drunk*—his words. Getting on his case. All bitchy and in his face for no reason. He said he just shut up after that and when we got to my place, he got out and drove away."

Kirbi flipped the page in her notebook and scrawled a few more lines. "What else?"

"He also said that on the way home I'd been talking about going to meet somebody in El Cajon. A guy. Like I was trying to make him jealous or something."

"You remember any of that?"

"Not really."

"Why *were* you in El Cajon at that hour, do you think?" Kirbi asked.

Jane's lips formed a wry smile. "That's just it. You asked yesterday if there was anything funny about my accident. There's nothing *but* funny."

"Any witnesses to the accident?"

Rosen answered this. "Nobody saw it, as far as we know."

Kirbi bobbed her head. Then, looking from Jane to Rosen and back, said, "I'm sorry to have to ask this next one, but aside from the Xanax and alcohol, and whatever—" She groped for the right words "—*legal* bearing they have on what happened, who would you say was at fault in this accident? You?"

Jane's expression was a pained one.

Rosen sat up straighter in her chair. "That hasn't been determined. There were skid marks, so it would seem Jane applied the brakes. And... for all we know, this guy driving the pickup just blindly barreled out in front of her."

"Or was I so blasted I didn't even notice him until the last minute?" Jane said.

Rosen shot Jane a look. Then started to say something, but seemed to change her mind.

No one spoke for several seconds. Kirbi could hear the cat purring on Jane's shoulder.

The phone rang and Rosen answered it. A quick call, the subject of which seemed to be how late the place stayed open that day.

Out the glass front door, something moving caught Kirbi's attention. It proved to be a bird, hopping into view across the front walk. Only to be gone a moment later.

Something bothered her about this Mark guy.

An idea came to her.

Rosen finished the call and turned to Kirbi in expectation.

Kirbi smiled at her, then at Jane.

"I'd like run something unusual by you guys," she said. "Just a possibility. About the accident."

She saw she had their attention.

"We'll leave motivation out of it for now, okay? And just deal with how things *could* have happened. Not *why* someone would do a particular thing. Alright?"

Jane gave a little shrug. Rosen just looked, waiting.

"Suppose, just suppose," Kirbi began, "*Mark* was driving your car on the way home from the concert. Because you were zonked out on the Xanax Mark put in your drink." She paused. "Why he's in El Cajon—I don't know. But let's also suppose, it's *Mark* who has the accident. Maybe he's on Xanax too. Maybe he's drunk. Or maybe, it's just that this other guy causes the crash, like Deb said. But for whatever reason *Mark's* at the wheel when it happens."

Rosen leaned forward now, planting an elbow on the desktop. Fist in front of her mouth. Eyes alert. Listening hard.

Kirbi went on. "But he panics—"

"And drags Jane behind the wheel," Rosen said.

"Exactly," Kirbi said with an emphatic nod. "And bolts."

Jane wore a stunned expression.

Rosen turned to her. "Did you," she asked in an unhurried tone, "or do you still, have any bruising on your chest or shoulders?"

Jane considered this and shook her head.

"Like from the shoulder harness," Rosen explained, glancing at Kirbi.

"Wait," Jane said after a moment. "You know, it's not on my shoulder or chest, but after the accident I did have this place like on my neck. Like a burn."

"Show me," Rosen said, getting to her feet and angling in close to see. "Which side?"

Jane gently pulled the cat down into her lap. And tipped her head to the left, so as to display the right side of her neck. "Here," she said, indicating a spot with her fingertips.

Kirbi craned to see also.

An abrasion.

Now suddenly Rosen's logic was clear to Kirbi. "If you'd been in the driver's seat," she told Jane, running her hand diagonally across her own chest, "the angle of the belt would be one way. In the passenger's seat, the other way."

"It's not conclusive," Rosen warned.

"So if the belt scraped me on my right side," Jane said, growing animated, "up high like this, maybe I was in the passenger seat. With the belt coming down, right to left across me."

Rosen and Kirbi nodded at the same time.

Jane gaped at them in amazement.

Rosen re-took her seat at the desk.

Kirbi gazed over at her. "Is there anything else, any physical evidence we can look for to show where Jane might have been sitting at the moment of the crash?"

"The police report might be a place to look," Rosen said. She tapped her fingers on the desktop, thinking. "I haven't read it myself yet, but I'll be getting it. Hopefully, the responding officers will have taken note of the position of the driver's seat."

Kirbi said, "Whether it was back, like for a six foot-plus Mark Hatcher, or forward for someone Jane's size."

"Right."

"How about checking to see if maybe both air bags deployed."

"Yes—that might show two people were in the car."

Jane was grinning at them both.

"Of course, a witness would be a big help," Kirbi mused aloud.

"Well, there's a gas station and a 7-Eleven somewhat nearby," Rosen said. She gave a doubtful shrug.

Kirbi took a breath. "Couldn't hurt to check. You give me the details and I'll take a run at it. And I have another idea. If Mark bolted from the scene, he'd be on foot. This might mean he'd need a ride out to Jane's place to get his van. And that would take extra time. Maybe one of Jane's neighbors noticed what time the van left. That might be useful to know."

Jane startled Kirbi by blurting, "I could do that part myself. I could start asking around when I get home."

"Okay," Kirbi told her, enjoying her excitement. "Go ahead. I like it."

"And," Jane added, with a look from Kirbi to Rosen, "maybe that parking garage downtown has surveillance video. I remember seeing cameras."

Kirbi nodded at her, pleased. "If they do, it might show just how intoxicated you were coming out of the concert."

"And whether I was even behind the wheel at that point."

The conversation came to a stop.

A car had pulled up outside in the lot. A young man and woman came through the front door and Rosen greeted them. She answered some questions and guided them into the back to look at the cats.

"I feel so much better, somehow," Jane told Kirbi in a heartfelt voice, her eyes moist. "Maybe I didn't kill that guy."

"Well," Kirbi said, not wanting to burst her bubble, but wanting to be truthful, "we haven't *proved* anything yet. But it's looking better, isn't it?"

Jane gave a slow double nod. "Yes." She peered straight ahead out the window, still idly petting the cat. Then after a moment asked, "You think Mark has something to do with what's going on at RayBright?"

"Seems like a stretch. But I definitely want to talk to him. Call me if you get in touch, okay?

Jane nodded again. "I sure would like not to lose my job over all this."

"Yeah."

"This parking garage thing—let me go there and see what I can find out, okay? I'm off work and going stir-crazy. I need something productive to do."

Kirbi thought about this. "Sure," she said, "give it a shot."

Not only did Kirbi already have a lot on her own plate, she wasn't sure her deal with RayBright included billing them for trying to get one of their employees out of a DUI.

EIGHTEEN

Thursday night, Kirbi was at home and getting ready to turn in early when she got a call from Martinez. He told her he was with Van Horne, about to drive to the home of Norman Gunderman. Could she meet them there?

Kirbi said she could. Martinez then gave her the address and ended the call.

A little bewildered, she quickly got dressed once more and hit the road. She was in a strange frame of mind. While one part of her hoped nothing was amiss, another part almost nursed a hope something *was*—if only for sake of vindication.

Because earlier in the day, she and Baines had gotten a sorry surprise.

The two of them had given a tag-team presentation before a full assembly of RayBright staff, even those who worked other shifts or had the day off. For almost an hour they reviewed basic security procedures. Described some of the methods bad guys used to gain information and access. And suggested ways to combat deception, intrusion, and outright theft.

They even shared stories of how the two of them had been hired to red-team companies in penetration tests.

All in all, the talk was well received. Lots of nods during, and enthusiastic applause after. Then a smaller presentation was made upstairs in the executive conference room. A presentation attended only by Van Horne, Shellhammer, Martinez, and a few others.

There Kirbi and Baines had handed out copies of a detailed security analysis they'd worked up for RayBright. It outlined weaknesses, and offered possible solutions. Kirbi briefly made note of the document's main points, read aloud through its summary, then asked for questions.

To her shock, there *were* no questions.

Instead, Shellhammer took the floor, and began praising their work. RayBright was so fortunate in having the benefit of Kirbi's and Baines' expertise. The two of them were so insightful. So professional. After which Van Horne took up the tune for a chorus, and so on around the table.

Kirbi remembered catching Baines' eye in the middle of all this. Despite the flattering way it was being done, it was clear they were being *shined on*. When Shellhammer asked her to present them with a bill as soon as possible—even hinted at a bonus—she bit down on her frustration, and offered a gracious smile.

RayBright management felt the situation was now under control.

An attempt to do harm to the company had been uncovered, and thwarted.

It was time to move on.

Except that she and Baines feared the attempt might not be over. It was possible things were still in play. Sooner or later, a major attack might very well be coming RayBright's way.

Downstairs afterward, Martinez, who had been subdued during the meeting, walked them to their cars.

"What's wrong, David?" Kirbi asked with mild irony.

"You know what's wrong," he said, shaking his head.

"Yeah, but beyond a certain point, what can we do?"

"Nothing, I guess. You tried to wise them up but they don't want to be wised up. They think the crisis is over. Especially the general."

Kirbi sighed. "They're sheep who've never met any wolves yet."

"Right," Martinez said, "but you watch who gets blamed when the wolves show up. Me. The company sheepdog."

For a long moment, Kirbi could think of nothing to say to this. She felt bad for him. Eventually she laid a sympathetic hand on his upper arm.

159

"Listen, bud. Baines and I'll backstop you if necessary. If things get sticky, you've got both of our numbers. We're ready to offer advice, or help, or whatever you need, okay?"

To which Martinez gave a glum nod and said, "Okay. Thanks."

Then everyone shook hands, and she and Baines drove away.

And now, as Kirbi barreled up the 5, but a few hours later—the evening of the same day—she wondered what could have happened.

Something off-site apparently. But what?

It was a little before nine when she took the Del Mar exit indicated by her GPS.

At the address Martinez had given her, she parked across the street and got out. The coastal air felt damp in her nostrils. She stood next to her car for a moment, trying to orient herself.

"Over here," she heard Martinez call out in the foggy darkness.

Then the dome light came on in a vehicle on the other side. Inside it, she made out Martinez behind the wheel, holding his door ajar so she could see him. Van Horne sat next to him in the passenger seat.

She crossed to them. The driver window was down.

Kirbi bent her knees to look at them, giving a nod of greeting.

"This is probably nothing," Van Horne said. "But let's go see what's going on."

Kirbi and Martinez flanked Van Horne as the three of them trekked up the wet asphalt drive. It was a large, single-story house from the nineteen fifties or sixties, dug into the hillside on the high side of the street. There were tall lush plants along the front. And a light above the front door.

Van Horn pushed the bell button and looked at Kirbi.

"I'm not sure how much David told you on the phone," he said as they waited. "Norman lives with his mother. She's not well. She called me because she's alarmed he's not answering the door to his room. For some reason, David's got a bad feeling about this."

Martinez gave her a look. Kirbi nodded, not knowing what to say.

Was Van Horne such a close friend that the mother thought to call him instead of someone else? Instead of the police, or a neighbor?

The latch clicked and the door swept inward.

A small, lean, elderly woman peered out at them. Brown house robe. Matching fuzzy slippers. Eyes wide above a forced smile.

"Eric, thank you for coming," Mrs. Gunderman said, shuffling back to let them in.

Kirbi, last to enter, closed the door behind herself.

"I didn't know what to do," the woman went on, grasping Van Horne's upper arm as the two of them made their slow way across the living room. "He won't answer me and he won't come out. Plus, he's locked his door, and he *never* locks his door. You know him, Eric, he's a creature of habit." She paused. Then, her voice breaking, added, "Something's wrong."

"Let's have a look, Emily," Van Horne said.

Kirbi and Martinez trailed behind. The snail-like pace was excruciating.

They made a right turn and progressed along a hallway.

At the end, Van Horne stopped at a closed door and knocked. "Norman?" he said in a loud voice, and knocked again. "Norman, it's Eric Van Horne. You all right?"

Mrs. Gunderman stood to one side, wringing her hands. Her throat tightened and relaxed several times, as if she were trying to swallow.

"Do we have a key to this door, Emily?" Van Horne asked.

It seemed to take her a long time to work through the question. "No," she managed at last, shaking her head.

"How about the sliding glass doors in the back?"

"Locked—I went around and checked before I called you. I knocked and called out some more, but there was still no answer. I tried to look in, but the drapes were drawn."

161

Van Horne bobbed his head, as if in approval of these actions. "We're going to have to break in, then."

"Please. Whatever you need to do."

"Would you be willing to do the honors?" Van Horne asked, turning to Martinez. When Martinez nodded, he moved out of the way, herding Mrs. Gunderman along with him.

Martinez examined the door. Stepped back. Pressed his back and the palms of his hands flat against opposite wall. Took a breath. Then kicked out with his right foot.

Hard rubber heel met door and door crashed inward, bouncing off something and coming back to rest lightly against the jamb, which was now badly splintered.

Kirbi gave him an impressed nod.

The room was dark, but Martinez found the light switch. He took one step, glancing about, and froze. He looked back over his shoulder, his face contorted.

"We need to call the police," he said in a taut voice.

"What's wrong?" Mrs. Gunderman said, alarmed, grappling with Van Horne and struggling to get around him.

Martinez wore a sick expression.

"You don't want to go in there, ma'am. Norman's dead. I'm very sorry."

"I want to see my son," she squawked, scrambling to get into the room, almost falling in her haste.

Martinez made a half-hearted attempt to block her, not knowing what to do.

But half a minute later, all four of them stood in the room.

Looking at the dead Norman.

It was a scene you couldn't unsee. Aware of the shock to her own nervous system, Kirbi felt bad for the old woman. But strangely, of those present, Mrs. Gunderman seemed least affected. For the moment, anyway.

Kirbi remembered meeting Norman once before at RayBright. An encounter of maybe ten seconds. He seemed smaller now without his clothes. And older. She felt a sadness, both for Norman and for the human race.

She saw why Martinez had been so instantly sure the man was dead. The face above the ligature was such an unlikely color.

She'd heard about this. You choked yourself at the moment of orgasm. A trick that supposedly intensified pleasure.

Van Horne was on his phone, making a nine-one-one call.

Keeping his voice down, but speaking clearly, he explained to the dispatcher what had happened, and gave the address.

In the meantime, Mrs. Gunderman seemed to be trying to come to terms with something outside her experience. "…This is something he did to himself?"

Martinez gave a reluctant nod.

"I think it's called *autoerotic asphyxiation*," Kirbi put in.

But even as she said it, something caught her attention. She leaned forward. Then dropped into a crouch for a closer look. What the hell?

"Probably best not to touch anything," Martinez warned.

She offered a murmured word of acknowledgement, but pointed to the dead man's right hand. "Look here."

He leaned in to make his own inspection. And having done so, shot Kirbi a stunned look.

"Now why would someone cut off his own index finger?" she asked in a rhetorical tone.

He gave his head two small shakes, perplexed, not following.

"Or," Kirbi went on, "maybe it wasn't him who cut it off." She locked eyes with Martinez. "Maybe somebody else did—somebody who needed it for a biometric reader back at RayBright."

163

Martinez looked at her blankly for a moment, then his eyes widened.

"They'd need the badge, along with the weekly code. But even so, you think it would even work?"

She shrugged. "It does in the movies."

Van Horne and Mrs. Gunderman had gone out into the hall.

Kirbi and Martinez joined them there, Martinez closing the door behind him.

"Mrs. Gunderman," Kirbi said, "I have something I'd like to ask you."

The old woman glanced instinctively at Van Horne, who nodded, then back at Kirbi. "Go ahead."

"This could be important. Did Norman have any visitors today or tonight?"

"I don't think so. I don't know. Why?"

"How about this—has he made any new friends lately?"

Kirbi didn't know what she was expecting, but it wasn't what she heard next.

"Just Mark."

"Mark Hatcher?" Kirbi asked, trying her best to make the question sound casual.

"Uh-huh."

Kirbi gave a slow nod, taking one of the old woman's hands in hers. It was tiny and thin-boned. Kirbi was reminded of holding a bird. "Thank you, for your help, dear. And I just want to say how truly sorry I am about the loss of your son."

"This is all so..."

"I know," Kirbi told her. Then stepped forward to gently embrace her.

Ahead, over Mrs. Gunderman's shoulder, she saw Martinez hurriedly pulling out his phone.

"I'm calling the guard shift at RayBright," he said.

"What's going on?" Van Horne inquired, picking up on Martinez's tone and haste.

Kirbi gave Mrs. Gunderman a final tender squeeze, then disengaged from her.

"Willingly or unwillingly," she explained to him, "before or after, somebody—" She moved her eyes twice in the direction of the dead man's room "—gave up an index finger. Also maybe a badge and this week's access code."

Van Horne's eyes popped in disbelief.

"I think David wants to make sure nothing's going on over there," Kirbi went on. "But even if nothing is, to be *ready*."

Van Horne's face had gone strangely slack. "This is all getting scary."

"Yes."

Martinez stopped talking and put his phone away. He wore a baffled expression. "They say everything's normal." He shrugged. "I told them to stay extra alert."

"Good," Van Horne said. He turned to Mrs. Gunderman and put an arm around her shoulders. "Emily, let's go out to the living room and sit down, okay? We'll wait for the police."

She acquiesced in this. She and Van Horne turned and began shuffling away down the hall.

Kirbi and Martinez looked at each other.

"I think you and me ought to get the fuck over to RayBright," Martinez whispered.

Kirbi whispered back. "You got that right."

NINETEEN

"**H**ere we go," Mark said in a quiet voice as they pulled up to the gate.

The guard was a rangy, middle-aged guy with a watch cap pulled low over his ears. He came out of the little guard building and walked to the driver window. Mark lowered it and handed over their badges.

"Evening. You guys new?"

"Yeah, the boss changes things around every once in a while," Mark told him.

Earlier in the day, the old man had called Creighton on behalf of Raybright and cancelled that night's scheduled cleaning. Thus allowing he and Mark to show up instead.

"And a different truck."

Mark nodded. "They gave us the goddamn *old* one."

The guard examined the badges, took a picture of them, and passed them back.

Then, after just standing there for a long moment, said, "So you guys always work swing?"

Mark eyed him evenly, fighting down a rush of alarm. Why was this guy questioning them? Had he noticed their silicone masks? Even in this dim light?

No, maybe he was just bored. Wanted to talk.

"Yeah," Mark said. He felt the side of the old man's knee bump impatiently against his. "How about you?"

"It varies. But yeah, mostly."

"The trouble with nights is staying the hell awake."

"You're not lying."

"Well, we better get going," Mark told him, and shifted into gear.

"Sure. You guys have a good one, okay?"

Mark nodded. "We will."

"Thanks," the old man chimed in.

An instant after the guard stepped back into the guard building, the barrier began rising.

Mark eased the truck forward. And leaving it in low gear, began chugging slowly down the slope alongside the main building. At the bottom, he cut left in a wide arc. The door they wanted was the first one from the corner. He nosed in just to the right of it, shut off the engine and headlights, and glanced at the old man.

"Good work, Ron," the old man said, using the name on Mark's badge.

"Thanks, Sam," Mark replied.

When they climbed out, Mark walked to the appointed door, while the old man headed around to the rear of the truck to lower its lift gate. A few seconds later, the soft whirr of the gate's motor could be heard on the cool night air.

Mark sighed, shifting nervously from foot to foot. He'd prepared himself for tonight's adventure by snorting a boatload of crank. He hoped he hadn't overdone it. Because he could feel the high still building in his circuitry.

At last there came a metallic noise, and the door he'd been staring at swung outward.

The young Latino guard's eyes widened in surprise.

"What happened to Tony and Felipe?"

Mark shrugged. "They got sent to LA for some sort of training."

"I'll need to see both badges," the guard said.

"Not a problem. Hey, Sammy—bring yourself and your badge over here for a minute, will you."

An answering grunt sounded from behind the truck. Then the old man came into view, lugging a canvas tool duffel. Ambling forward, he set the duffel down and gave his badge to Mark, who passed it and his own to the guard.

The guard scrutinized each badge in turn, glancing up to compare photo to face.

"It's just that I've never seen you guys before," he said, his tone apologetic. He handed the badges back.

Mark shook his head. "No worries, man. You're just doing your job."

He and the old man put their badges back on.

Then Mark produced a yellow rubber doorstop and wedged it under the door. This allowed the guard to remove his foot, which had been holding the door open against the pressure of the automatic closer. Stanko had mentioned this propping open of the door.

It was of course a security violation. But other cleaning crews did it for sake of convenience. So even though Mark and the old man wouldn't be making the usual repeated trips to the truck for supplies, they thought it best to do what the others did. No point in arousing suspicion.

"Hey, you know what, Sam," Mark said, grinning, as if he'd just had an idea. "You should show our friend here what we found on that can of dusting product. He'll get a laugh out of it."

The old man now broke into a wide grin of his own. As he approached, he pulled a small aerosol canister from the back pocket of his coveralls. Peered down at its label. And seeming to find what he wanted, marked the place with a thumbnail, and held the canister out before him.

"Read what it says here under Warnings," the old man suggested, chuckling.

The guard wore a reluctant-but-game smile.

He took a step, leaning slightly forward to see what was supposed to be so amusing. And just as he did so, the old man blasted pepper spray up into his face.

The guard's reaction wasn't pretty. Or dignified. He lurched back, whimpering and pawing blindly at the air. Mark danced out of his way, and turned to watch him slam against the doorframe and tumble to the floor inside, rolling and thrashing.

Mark and the old man hurried to don latex gloves.

After which, the old man muscled the guard into submission while Mark bound his wrists and ankles with zip ties.

Two guards covered the four-to-midnight shift. The one at the gate and this one. If this one didn't happen to answer his radio for a short while, so be it. Because if things went as planned, Mark and the old man didn't expect to be on the premises for very long. So it didn't matter.

The old man went to fetch the tools from outside.

Alone for a moment, Mark put his hand over his heart, feeling it pounding hard against his ribcage. He was both scared out of his mind and ecstatically exhilarated. Just be cool, he told himself. Like Brad Pitt or George Clooney in *Ocean's Eleven*.

When the old man returned, they set off.

Several yards ahead was another door. On the other side of it, as expected, they found the main corridor and bore right. Brightly lit, it ran the length of the building.

Offices and labs lined both sides, each with its own boxy metallic access panel.

The right side of the corridor seemed to be mostly offices. Single doors with mesh-reinforced windows. While on the left side, labs predominated, these accessed by double doors without windows.

Project 16 was a lab, and all the way at the other end.

When they got there, Mark pulled Norman's badge out of the chest pocket of his coveralls. Followed by something rolled up in clear plastic. A little sausage-like item.

He glanced at the old man.

Indoors, under the fluorescent lighting of the corridor, the masks looked just a tiny bit less realistic. They were good. Mark liked the detail in them. The faces even had pores and zits. But there was something just slightly wrong about the eye and mouth openings. Just slightly.

Taking a breath, Mark slid the RayBright badge through the slot on the reader.

The first of the three lights stayed red.

Okay, he slid it again. Nope. Still red.

He took another breath, and tried bringing the badge up through the slot from the bottom.

Bingo. Green light.

Mark punched in the four digits: eight, six, four, one.

Which turned the second of the three red lights green.

Now came the potentially trickiest part.

Tricky because Mark hadn't been able to blackmail Norman into accompanying them in person tonight. It wasn't that Mark hadn't been expecting the confrontation to be a hard one. A nasty one. He'd been ready for rage, or tears, or both. Ready even for hysteria.

He just hadn't been ready for what he got—Norman's sudden withdrawal into a kind of shocked silence. A silence Mark had found no way to break, despite repeated tries over the course of an hour. Finally, he'd snuck out the patio door to go for a drink, leaving Norman staring despondently at the floor.

But when he'd snuck back in a while later, Mark got something else he wasn't ready for. A dead Norman. Intentionally or accidentally, using one of the very tricks Mark had taught him, the guy had *offed* himself.

So Mark had had to improvise.

With time running short, he'd had to abandon the gummi bear idea, and resort to a pair of pruning shears scrounged from the Gunderman garden shed. And luckily he'd known where Norman kept the weekly code and his RayBright badge.

Mark shook his head to himself now.

Banishing the ugly memory of the dead Norman. Safely compartmentalizing it.

He needed to focus on the task before him.

Taking a deep breath, he pinched the little sausage by the cut end, wanting to plump out the opposite end—the part with the fingerprint—to its life-like maximum. Then laid it gently in the designated slot. Nothing happened.

The third light stayed red.

Next to him the old man stirred restlessly.

They had a sledgehammer, saws, even a torch. But not only might these take a lot of time, they might not work at all. The doors looked sturdy, to say the least.

Mark pulled the little sausage out and reinserted it, this time giving it a wiggle as he did so. The third light went green. And simultaneous with that, a loud *whonk* sounded from the lock mechanism, and the old man was able to wrench the door handle to the open position.

Elated, Mark hurried inside and flipped on the lights.

It was a large room. He saw work benches, electronic instruments, some industrial hoisting devices, and a lot of stainless-steel cabinetry. But no Merman device.

The buyer had provided a rough description of it. Grey, very heavy, and proportioned roughly like a coffin. If it was here, it had to be in one of the bigger of the locker-like cabinets.

The old man appeared to have come to the same conclusion. He dropped the duffle, unzipped it, and brought out a long wrecking bar.

Then, as Mark looked on, began hurriedly prying open the first of the stainless-steel doors at floor level.

It opened with a bang. But held only an array of small tools and clamps.

The old man popped another. Nope. More useless junk.

Popped a third, a fourth, and a fifth—all with the same result.

The sixth and last, however, contained the device.

The old man sank to a crouch and started wrestling with the thing, which rested on a wooden shipping pallet. "Get the dollies," he growled. Meaning the ones in the duffle.

But Mark suddenly had a better idea.

Across the room was a *pallet jack*. Just like the ones he'd used in the prison kitchen when shipments of food were delivered. A moment later, he had it by the handle and was wheeling it around to where the old man struggled with the pallet.

"Watch yourself," Mark said.

The old man peered back over his shoulder, registered what Mark had, and crabbed himself out of the way.

Mark angled the jack into alignment. Jammed its long prongs forward under the pallet. And after several pumps of the handle to hydraulically raise the heavy device off the floor, rolled it out of the locker into the light.

It did indeed look like a coffin.

He backed and filled a few times, wanting to position himself in front so he could pull the jack behind him. In his experience, this made for easier steering. When he looked up, ready to go, he saw the old man already at the doorway, bracing one door open with his back, and holding the other with an outstretched arm.

Mark grinned.

With a yank on the handle, he dragged his burden forward.

172

At the doorway, he ducked under the old man's arm. Then wheeled left, gaining speed. He felt buoyant, hurtling along like a little kid with a brand new toy wagon.

This buoyancy lasted about two seconds.

It ceased when a loud male voice at the other end of the corridor shouted, "Hey! What the fuck are you doing?"

Mark's heart jumped. His steps faltered. Ahead, he saw the rangy guard with the watch cap, hand menacingly on his holstered weapon.

In a flash, the old man was beside Mark. "Keep going," he urged.

And to Mark's astonishment, drew his own weapon and began firing at the guard.

In the confines of the corridor, the noise was deafening.

Wham. Wham. Wham.

By the second of the three shots, wide-eyed and open-mouthed, the guard ducked back out of sight. The old man then tossed the duffle atop the Merman device. And joined Mark on the jack, pulling with one hand and firing the occasional shot with the other.

When they neared the door leading outside, Mark's gaze stayed glued to the doorway opposite. The one through which the guard had retreated. Mark's stomach was tight. He half expected to see the man reappear and at last—and at close range—return fire.

It didn't happen.

In the side corridor, they found the other guard where they'd left him. Still zip-tied and face down against the wall. As they raced past him and out into the night, the old man deftly bent down and grabbed up the doorstop.

"Start the truck," he growled.

Mark nodded, released his own grip on the jack handle, and veered off toward the vehicle's cab. At which point, the old man and the Merman device continued in a beeline toward its box-like rear compartment.

A moment later, Mark was behind the wheel. Having pulled the driver door shut, he leaned over and shoved open the passenger door. Then brought the engine to life, and flicked on the headlights.

Soon, through the truck's frame, he could feel the vibration of the lift gate hauling the heavy device up to the level of the compartment bed. This was followed by a series of jerks as the old man wheeled the pallet jack inside.

Mark glanced left and right. He checked behind, using his side mirror. He undid the top of his coveralls, groped out his Marlboros, and nervously lit one. Time seemed to have slowed down. Puffing on his cigarette, he clenched and unclenched the steering wheel with his other hand.

Finally, just when the strain of waiting seemed unbearable, he heard the clank of the lift gate being locked upright into place. After which the old man came bounding into the cab and slammed the door.

"Go!"

Mark didn't need to be told twice.

He stuck his cigarette in the corner of his mouth, shifted into reverse, and accelerated back in an arc. Braked to a sudden stop to shift into low. And made a wide right at the corner of the building to head up the hill.

Above, the guard in the watch cap was back at his post. He'd closed the outer gate, and stood on the far side of the guard building, weapon at the ready.

"Now listen," the old man said in even tone. "Everything's cool. I deal with him. You just drive. So don't stop and don't slow down. We clear?"

Mark bobbed his head, touched the clutch, and popped the transmission into second.

Slowly depressing the gas pedal, he willed the truck forward. But inertia and the slope of the hill were working against any immediate speed.

Glancing down, he saw the needle only just passing ten miles per hour. Damn.

Beside him, the old man was now rolling down the passenger window. Then, having twisted around and climbed up on the seat, he poked his upper body out the opening and over the top of the cab.

They'd almost reached the vehicle barrier. Which was of course down across the exit lane. Amazingly, the truck was now doing almost twenty.

Mark didn't worry about the flimsy barrier, but he did worry about the chain-link gate. And he did *very* much worry about the guard, who was by now edging forward, pointing his weapon in their direction. As before in the corridor, Mark could feel his entire body tensing in anticipation of a bullet.

But then once again the old man's pistol began barking.

And in quick succession, one of the big plate-glass windows in the guard building turned white and collapsed into nothingness. Followed by a second window. While a third shot took out the flood light mounted atop the building's roof.

Was the guard going to fire back?

No, he wanted none of this.

The last Mark saw of him, he'd turned, panic-stricken, and was stumbling through some low shrubbery into the shadows.

A second later the truck snapped the exit lane barrier.

And a second after that, smashed the chain-link gate off its track and flattened it.

Mark fought the wheel to make the turn onto the street without reducing speed.

Once on the straightaway, he glanced at the old man, who'd climbed back inside. "Fuck, Harve, I thought you said nobody was going to get hurt."

"Wait," the old man said, hand up, shushing him. His eyes were bright with excitement and he was studying his side-view mirror. "Here we go. Listen. Listen…"

Mark grimaced, not understanding what was supposed to be happening.

But just as he shifted into third, above the noise of the engine, he heard it.

Four sharp pops from behind.

The last one simultaneous with a twang from the back of the truck.

"Fuck," Mark gasped.

The twang, he realized, had been the sound of a bullet striking the steel of the tipped-up lift platform. It wasn't hard to imagine another bullet penetrating the flimsy metal of the rear compartment. Then ripping through the seatback into his spine.

He peered back by means of his own side mirror, but could see nothing in the dimness.

The old man let out a guffaw. "Oh right, now the guy returns fires."

"Yeah, at fucking *us*."

"Relax, kiddo. Nobody got shot. Not them, not us."

"Not for want of trying," Mark said.

"Them I can't speak for. But look, you've seen *me* shoot, right? Do you seriously think I couldn't have hit that guy if I wanted to, both times I drew down on him?"

Mark hadn't considered this. Grimacing, he let the subject drop.

He put his attention back on his driving.

He had to resist an impulse to tromp down further on the gas. They'd pulled off the big heist. It was no time to get cop-stopped for something stupid, like speeding.

Four minutes and two point three miles later, Mark slowed and made a right onto Pinion Court. Followed by an almost immediate left into a little industrial park consisting of four tall bays with roll-up steel doors. An auto-electric shop. A weld shop. A place that did spray-on truck bed linings. And the vacant bay on the near end that the old man had rented, two days before.

Everything was quiet, as it had been less than an hour ago when they'd changed vehicles there.

Mark braked to a stop and waited, the truck in neutral, his foot on the brake. The old man got out and walked across to the bay's pedestrian-access door. Opened it with a key. Stepped inside. Then began raising the larger roll-up vehicle door.

After a few moments, the old man's red Toyota pickup nosed out.

As soon as it was safely parked out of the way, Mark put the "Creighton" truck in reverse and carefully backed into the bay. Everything according to plan. Now it was hide-the-signage time. Mark killed the engine and lights and climbed out.

The old man was already unfolding a monster blue-plastic utility tarp. The kind you buy at Home Depot or Lowe's, but larger than any Mark had ever seen. Mark helped him lay it out next to the truck.

When this was done, the old man clambered swiftly up onto its hood like an ape. Raced up the windshield to the cab roof. And leapt onto the top of the box compartment.

Watching, Mark wondered if he'd ever be as spry at sixty, himself. Or if he should even expect to make it to sixty.

The old man waved his arm and Mark tossed up one of the ropes attached to the tarp's grommets.

In another five minutes, they had the sides of the box covered.

And in five more, and they had their masks, gloves, and coveralls off, and stowed in the back of the truck. After which they rolled down the big bay door and locked it.

Mark felt exultant. The night had been a thrill ride to end all thrill rides.

When they walked across to the pickup, the old man quickly slid in behind the wheel, eager to go. However, Mark had something he wanted to do first. So, opening the passenger door, he leaned in and unlatched the glove compartment to find something he'd put there earlier.

The old man wore a puzzled look. But then seeing what was clutched in Mark's hand, sagged back in his seat and rolled his eyes in mock exasperation. Mark grinned at the performance.

"Celebratory pipe," he explained. "I'll hurry."

"Please," the old man said.

Nodding, Mark leaned back out of the vehicle and stood beside it.

A few hours before, he'd readied the pipe for just this moment. It contained a small rock of crack cocaine and some synthetic weed. Just the mixture he hoped would allow him to bravely go where no man had gone before.

It seemed to.

When he finished, he heaved the pipe as far as he could out into the darkness. And heard it land with a distant clink among the tall weeds of the vacant lot next door.

"Good arm," the old man said as Mark climbed in and shut the door.

"I didn't want to be in possession of anything that could get us in trouble."

The old man started the pickup. "Kiddo, I'm thinking, at any given time, just your *bloodstream* is probably a felony."

Mark gave a giddy chuckle.

It was a good line.

TWENTY

Martinez drove off only a few moments before Kirbi. But either he knew a quicker route or drove a lot faster. Because when she got to RayBright his car was already parked up on the street outside the gate. And she could see him down at the building's front entrance with his guards.

She left her Jaguar behind Martinez's Honda and hurried across a section of downed chain-link fencing. What she assumed had been the sliding gate. She also noted pieces of the out-lane barrier, strewn across the asphalt. Then piles of glass on the ground in front of the guard shack, apparently the remains of its windows.

When she got to the entrance, she saw one guard dribbling something from a little squeeze bottle into the eyes of the other. The second man's upturned face looked taut and pained.

"Chuey got pepper sprayed," Martinez explained.

"Robbery?" Kirbi asked.

Martinez nodded. "Two guys in a truck from a maintenance company called Creighton. They come every four weeks. At night. Tonight was that night."

"How long ago?"

"Five minutes. The maintenance guys were here when I called." Martinez winced at the irony. "Kenny didn't report it as unusual, because it wasn't. They've been coming here once a month since this place was built."

"Doing what?" she asked, trying to understand.

"They have a contract to maintain certain air systems. They also deal with our hazardous waste chemicals and metals."

179

"So the guards knew these guys?"

The guard who was administering the eye drops interjected.

"No," he said. "These were two guys I'd never seen before. White guys. And the truck was different." His gaze moved to Martinez, his boss. "But they *had* RayBright badges."

"One of them kind of tall and thin?" Kirbi asked.

The guard nodded. "Yeah. Ron Something. The other one was Samuel. I logged their IDs and surveillance coverage will have the truck plate."

She didn't have much faith in either proving useful, but kept her mouth shut.

Leaving the guards there, she and Martinez headed inside.

"They pepper sprayed Chuey and tied him up when he opened the back for them," Martinez said, as they got into the elevator. "And guess what their target was?"

She glanced over at him. His mouth was a tight mirthless smile.

"Project Sixteen," she said.

He nodded.

Downstairs, the corridor stank of gun smoke. Kirbi pointed to shell casings on the floor. Martinez acknowledged them with a glance.

He walked a few steps to the left, stopped, and touched something on the wall.

Kirbi joined him.

It was a small gouge. The shiny off-white paint missing, and the gray cement block beneath exposed. The result of a glancing blow by a bullet.

"Kenny said they opened fire on him when he came down to confront them. He couldn't get Chuey on the radio, so he'd accessed the surveillance system from the guard shack. Then saw Chuey on the floor by the back door. And that somebody was inside Sixteen."

"Worst fears realized," Kirbi noted grimly.

"Yeah."

"You called Eric?"

"Just before you got here," he said. He grimaced, giving his head a small, regretful shake. "I love being the messenger with the bad news."

Kirbi touched the gouge in the wall with her finger, wondering idly where the ricocheting slug had gone.

Some loud static came from the radio on Martinez's belt. Then, "David?"

"Go ahead," he answered.

"Cops are here."

"Ten four." Martinez shrugged and turned on his heel toward the elevator.

Kirbi followed.

Upstairs, out the front widows, they could see a City of San Diego cruiser parked up at the gate. Angled carelessly to the curb. Light bar flashing crazily.

While below in front of the building, two uniformed policemen were talking with a tall lean civilian, who Kirbi didn't immediately recognize. Crew cut grey hair. White windbreaker over black polo shirt. Dark slacks. Erect posture.

Wait, *Shellhammer.*

Summoned no doubt by a phone call from Van Horne. He'd gotten here fast.

"Whoever they were, they seem to be long gone," Shellhammer was saying as she and Martinez came out through the front doors. He seemed to be in full take-charge mode. The general. "We've already given the building and grounds a thorough walk-through, just to be sure. And we'll be fixing the front gate tonight."

"Okay," the older of the two policemen said.

"So what we'll do is run an inventory tonight and see what, if anything, is missing. Talk to the cleaning company and see who these people were. Then come downtown tomorrow and make a more complete report."

"If you're satisfied, sir, we're satisfied."

"Thank you, sergeant," Shellhammer told him. "Your response time was outstanding, by the way."

Kirbi glanced up at Martinez.

It seemed Shellhammer was shutting things down. Playing it off. Minimizing interest.

One of Martinez's eyebrows rose a fraction of an inch, independent of the other. She'd never been able to manage the gesture. She wondered if it was genetic, like rolling your tongue or wiggling your ears.

"Well, good night, sir," the older of the two cops said now, and he and his partner headed back up the hill to their cruiser.

After watching them for a moment, Shellhammer turned to Chuey, who with Kenny, the other guard, had been quietly looking on. "Do you want medical attention, son? Shall we call an ambulance?"

Chuey shook his head.

"Your eyes are important. We can also get somebody to drive you to the emergency room."

"I'm good for now," Chuey told him.

To which Shellhammer nodded.

Then swung around to address Kirbi and Martinez. "Quite the night, eh?" He looked from one to the other. "How about we go to the Security office and have a look at surveillance."

They did just that.

And once there, David immediately plopped into a chair behind the desk and began tapping at a keyboard. Above him on the wall was an array of screens, each displaying a different RayBright interior or exterior location. Soon some of the screens began changing. Kirbi and Shellhammer stood looking on for a few moments, then likewise seated themselves.

182

"So I take it," he said to her, "we have a pretty good idea who did this now."

Kirbi nodded. Apparently Van Horne had conveyed to Shellhammer what had been discovered at the Gunderman house. "Yeah. The one who goes by *Mark Hatcher*. I've called Baines already, and he's working on the name. But it may or may not get us anywhere. My feeling is these guys are too good for it to be real."

"I see."

"Hatcher's the same one we suspect of drugging Jane Bouchet the night of her accident. He may even have been driving when *she* supposedly was. When that guy in the other vehicle was killed."

Shellhammer's expression clouded. "That part doesn't make any sense to me."

"To me either," Kirbi acknowledged. "But that aside, it looks like he's one of the two that broke in here tonight."

"And used Norman's finger and badge to get into Project Sixteen."

"Right."

"Eric said they might have made off with something."

Martinez, listening, glanced over his shoulder. "They did. Here's them coming out of the Project Sixteen lab now. I'll put it on the central screen."

As Kirbi and Shellhammer watched, two white-suited figures came into view in a hallway. One was carrying what looked like a canvas bag. While the other was dragging something behind him on a pallet jack.

After a few seconds, David froze the action and switched to another view. This one from behind. Now the object on the pallet jack was more clearly visible. A long, gray, boxy item.

"Is that Merman?" Kirbi asked when she saw Shellhammer give a slight start.

He sighed. "I'm afraid so."

183

David again froze the action on the screen and turned in his chair. "They knew right where to go to get it."

Shellhammer gave a slow nod. After which he turned to meet Kirbi's eyes. "You were right, by the way. We should have listened to you about the threat."

Though she enjoyed hearing him admit it, Kirbi forced a politic shrug. "I only wish I'd pushed harder to make the situation clear to you, sir."

"Well, we are where we are. However we got here."

"Yeah," she agreed in the same grim tone.

"Do you think there's any hope of getting it back at this point?"

Kirbi hesitated, not wanting to promise anything she couldn't deliver. "The truth? It's not very likely. These guys are pros. Look at all the trouble and planning it took to get in here tonight and snatch the thing."

Kirbi let her gaze drift to Martinez but he had nothing to add.

Shellhammer crossed his arms. "But we can *try* to get it back."

"Of course," Kirbi said. "Unlikely doesn't mean impossible."

"Then give it everything you've got until the end of the month, alright? That's when RayBright's contract with the federal government is up, and the thing's scheduled to be picked up."

"I'm on it then."

"You need more money?"

She shook her head. "Not yet. But I could maybe use something else," she said. "I know the matter is classified, but it might help to know a little more about what exactly Merman is. If I'm going to be hunting for it—and the people who grabbed it—some details and background might aid me in my search."

Shellhammer pursed his lips in thought, but said nothing.

She waited.

At last he showed her a vague nod and got out his phone.

"Eric, this is John…No, the police were here when I got here… Right…Listen, before we get into that, I'd like to run something by you if I may. It's about Merman…."

As they eavesdropped, Kirbi and Martinez exchanged a look.

"I'm here talking with Kirbi Mack…Right. She says she's willing to stay on and take a shot at getting the thing back, though she's told me the chances of doing so are probably slim…True, yes. Anyway, she's asking me to put her a little further into the picture on the Merman device. So as to increase our chances of recovery. Myself, I'm inclined to do so, but I wanted to hear your thoughts on the subject first."

This said, Shellhammer, pinching the bridge of his nose, listened for several seconds. Kirbi could hear Van Horne's voice, but could not make out the words.

Then Shellhammer spoke again. "Okay. Thanks, Eric. I'll bring you up to speed on the rest in a short while…Yes. I'll impress that on her." And when he ended the call, he shot Kirbi a small smile.

Seeing this, Martinez made to get up. Maybe figuring that a conversation was about to take place that didn't include him. But she caught his eye and held up a forefinger, then turned back to Shellhammer.

"If it's acceptable to you, sir," she said, "I think David should be in on the secret, too. He's a smart guy and we've been working well together from the start."

Again Shellhammer didn't directly answer her. But picked up his phone.

He called Van Horne back, presented Kirbi's request, and appeared to get the go-ahead.

When he switched off, he said, "Nothing personal, David. The basis of my partnership with Eric has been that we don't make unilateral decisions. I just needed to check."

Martinez assured him no explanation was necessary.

185

Shellhammer then drew a deep breath and fixed both Kirbi and Martinez with a severe look. "Both for RayBright's sake, and for national security reasons," he began, "I'm trusting you two to keep what I'm about to tell you confidential." That said, he paused for their affirming nods before going on:

"Two years ago off the Philippines, a Chinese submarine went down in deep waters. This wasn't in the news because China never made the loss public. However, the U.S. had not only been tracking the sub—and so knew what'd happened—but it was later able to retrieve things from it. One of which was Merman.

"So the Chinese are, we hope, still in the dark about the whole matter. Not aware that we know about the sub sinking, or that we're technologically capable of operating at those depths. Or that we now have something they don't know we have. Merman. Which is the navigation system of their latest cruise missile. RayBright has been studying and reverse engineering it for a full year. Part of the secrecy is that the longer the Chinese don't know we're onto their latest gadgetry, the more advantage we keep."

Kirbi sat back in her chair. "So what was this Hatcher guy's purpose in taking the thing?"

Shellhammer made a face. "It's difficult to say."

"Terrorism?" she suggested.

"That's a possibility."

"But you're not going to bring the CIA or military, or whoever, in on the theft."

He shook his head. "Not at this point. Not yet."

Kirbi had more questions, but just then Shellhammer's phone sounded. He glanced at its screen and got to his feet. "I'm sorry, I've got to take this," he said, and stepped out the door toward the lobby.

As he walked away, she listened to his voice as he answered the call. His serious and decisive tone of a moment before, was now gentle and intimate. He seemed to be talking to his wife. Telling he'd probably be staying at RayBright all night.

Kirbi and Martinez looked at each other.

"I'm trying to think what I should do next," he said.

She blew out a long breath. "I'm not sure it can be done at this time of night, but it would certainly be nice to find out what Creighton knows about this whole thing. Did the thieves hijack a Creighton truck, or corrupt Creighton employees, or what?"

Martinez gave an enthusiastic nod. "I'll see who I can wake up," he said. But then, having picked up the landline receiver from its cradle on his desk, stopped. "Hey, thanks for sticking up for me, by the way."

"They shouldn't be leaving you out of this."

"Still, thanks."

"You got it," Kirbi told him.

TWENTY-ONE

The excitement over, Harvey was glad to be headed home to the ranch.

Taking the 8, he kept the pickup in the right lane and stayed within the speed limit.

For the first time in a long time, he let himself relax. The device hadn't been transferred to the buyer yet, so no, he didn't yet have all that wonderful money in his clutches. But things were moving in the right direction. And if everything went according to plan—and so far it had—a lot of the financial pressure would soon be off him.

Over on the passenger side, the kid had his earbuds in. He was lost in his music, rocking back and forth and taking periodic slugs from his flask. Harvey marveled at the sheer quantity and variety of substances the guy seemed to be continually putting into his body. Ah, the stamina of youth.

He'd told Harvey he'd found Norman already dead from suicide and *then* cut off the finger. Harvey hoped this was the case. Because the addition of a murder charge might mean more heat.

In any event, the kid was coming to the end of his usefulness, as far as Harvey was concerned. He was a clever guy and had been a big help. But it was time to cut him loose. When they got back to the ranch tonight, Harvey had in mind to pay him generously off and send him on his way.

They'd successfully snatched the device. Tomorrow he'd be making that important call to set up the meet. His instincts told him it would be unwise to have the kid anywhere near the actual exchange.

"So now you'll be phoning the guy in the silver BMW, right?"

Though startled, Harvey kept his face blank. It was as if the kid had been reading his thoughts. "Yeah," he said, forcing a causal tone. "Probably tomorrow."

"To sell the thing."

"Right."

"You know, you might want to be on your guard with this fucker. You never know—he might just try to take the thing and stiff you for the cash."

Harvey nodded, pulling a face, as if he hadn't considered this possibility. "You may be right."

"Anyway, if you want me there for back up, I'm in," the kid noted, grinning and rubbing his hands together in a parody of greed. "We can't have anything going wrong. I need to get *paid*."

A car had come zipping up behind, and was now tailgating. Harvey waited to see if this move was a prelude to something else. Something he should be worried about. But after a few seconds it signaled, pulled out, and raced by. Simply another driver in a big hurry.

"Speaking of getting paid, kiddo, if you want, we can settle up tonight."

"Tonight?"

"Absolutely." Harvey said. "Plus, I'll be giving you a large bonus. You *more* than held up your end of the deal, and I appreciate it."

"You serious?"

Harvey shrugged. "Of course. I can pay you when we get back to the ranch."

"You don't need to wait until you make the handoff?"

"No. In fact, I've got your money right here in the truck."

"You're kidding."

"Nope."

"Harve," the kid said, his lips slowly forming themselves into a loopy grin, "that's so, so cool."

Harvey returned the grin.

Then shifted his focus back to driving.

There wasn't much traffic on the road. As the minutes and miles passed, he found his thoughts drifting to what he needed to do tomorrow. The job wasn't over. Aside from meeting the buyer, there was still a lot of running around and tidying up to do. He sorted through a mental checklist of those tasks, fixing their order in his mind.

The pickup had just whizzed by the Lake Jennings exit, when Harvey was drawn out of these thoughts by motion in the corner of his eye.

Turning to look, he got a surprise.

The kid was holding Harvey's pistol. Pointing it at him.

Harvey sighed and shook his head.

He recalled stashing the weapon under the front seat of the box truck. Not giving the action a second thought. Stupidly, not imagining the kid might pull just this sort of stunt.

"You did check to see if there're any bullets left in that thing, right?"

"As a matter of fact I did," the kid said with a sly giggle.

"Got a new plan, have you?"

"Could be."

"You don't even know who the buyer is?"

The kid gave a nonchalant shrug. "So what. If I can't find him, maybe I can get RayBright to buy it back. You ever think of that?"

Again Harvey sighed.

Then eased gently down on the accelerator.

He kept his expression neutral and his eyes on the road. But allowed his forward-looking gaze to also take in the illuminated dashboard display. And there watched the vehicle's speed begin a slow climb. From seventy to seventy-five. Then seventy-five to eighty....

It was only when the pickup was edging past ninety-five that the kid finally noticed.

"Hey, what the fuck do you think you're doing!?"

Harvey laughed. "Might be my question to you, Markie boy."

"Pull off at the next exit," the kid told him, curling sideways in his seat now. Leaning back against the door behind him, pistol extended in both hands. "This one."

Like he expected Harvey to do exactly what he said.

"I don't think so," Harvey replied.

The pickup was now hitting a hundred. Eight years old and just a work truck for the ranch, but still peppy. Harvey saw the kid's eyes register their speed on the display.

A moment later they raced past the turnoff for the ramp.

"I'll fucking kill you, old man."

"Will you really," Harvey said, putting on his evilest smile. "Let me first bring a couple of things into perspective for you, kiddo. Just to be sure we're both on the same page. You shoot me or try to wrestle the wheel away from me, there's going to be one hell of a crash. You might survive, you might not. But if I continue at this speed, there's a chance the cops will notice and pull us over. You ready for that?"

"Are you?"

"Sure. But if it happens, are you ready to kill both me *and* the cop? Remember, he'll have called the plate in before he even gets out of the cruiser. Or, if we somehow escape CHP notice, and I keep driving at a hundred miles an hour—we've got almost a full tank—we're going to be out in East Bumfuck by the time this thing eventually putt-putts to a stop. And then what are you going to do, out there a couple hundred miles? Kill me there? Okay, but then what? Call for help? Okay, from who? And what about cellphone coverage out there? Course there're those roadside emergency phones."

Harvey paused, pretending to evaluate all this. "Might work," he went on. Then gave his scalp an exaggerated comical scratch with his right forefinger.

"Fuck you, you demented geriatric asshole."

Harvey shook his head, as if in disappointment. "When they start calling you names, you know they've run out of ideas."

"I ought to blow your fucking brains out," the kid screeched in a hoarse voice.

He was wound tight now. The face grotesquely distorted. The tendons standing out in the hands that clutched the pistol.

Harvey knew he should be afraid, but had made a conscious decision not to be.

"Put the fucking gun away and we'll talk," he suggested.

The kid said nothing for thirty seconds or so, still staring at him with fiery eyes.

Harvey kept the accelerator depressed and the speed up over ninety-five. He checked the mirrors. There was a car way back but nothing nearby. They'd just began the ascent to Alpine.

The kid exhaled violently and scowled. The pistol's aim wavered, then dipped.

The kid still had his game face on, but Harvey could see that he was clearly struggling with what to do. After a while, he lowered the weapon. Then pushed it into the right pocket of his jacket.

Harvey glanced in the mirror once more. He pulled his foot off the accelerator. Then, as he'd been mentally rehearsing since first seeing the gun pointed at him, he reached out and used the back of his right fist as a club.

With everything he could muster, however awkwardly, he swung at the kid's midsection.

The pickup wove a bit as Harvey was forced to glance between the road and the kid. But he delivered three more such punches. Two of the four—the first and the last—were the solid punishing shots he was trying for.

The kid slumped forward. For a time at least, neutralized.

Harvey stepped on the brake, pulling off the freeway onto the shoulder.

As soon as he had the transmission in park, he leaned over and clawed the pistol from the kid's pocket.

A car whooshed by. The one he'd seen way behind. But it was neither any sort of law enforcement, nor someone stopping to see if he needed help. Just somebody in a ten-year-old blue minivan, straining to maintain speed up the long grade.

Good.

Harvey climbed out of the pickup and searched behind the seat. Then got down on his haunches to peer under it. He needed something to restrain the kid with. But found nothing suitable.

He grabbed the keys from the ignition and unlocked the toolbox behind the cab.

Inside, on top, he saw the bag of money he'd been going to pay the kid off with. It had been a mistake to have mentioned having it with him. Live and learn, he told himself.

Taking a breath, he rooted through the box's contents. Various tools, supplies, and odds and ends he kept handy for work around the ranch. Lots of stuff. But among it no wire, no rope, no zip ties. The best he could come up with was a roll of masking tape and a single plastic grocery bag.

Frowning, he chose the tape.

Another vehicle hurtled past in the time it took to truss the kid up. But only one. And it neither stopped nor slowed.

While paper masking tape wasn't particularly strong, twenty or thirty layers of it were. He tied the kid's wrists behind him. Then did his ankles.

He even wrapped the kid's mouth. Might as well have a quiet ride, he told himself. What could the kid say that would have any relevance now, anyway?

Once more behind the wheel, Harvey accelerated up to speed, then pulled back onto the roadway. Though pleased to have settled the kid-with-a-gun problem, he now faced another. What to *do* with this trussed-up package slumped on the seat next to him.

Because from here on, the package simply couldn't be trusted.

Even if Harvey paid him off and let him go, the kid could cause all sorts of trouble. He could try to blackmail Harvey. Or rob him once he got the money from the buyer. Or even turn him in to the authorities, out of spite.

Pulling that gun had been a foolish step from which there was no going back.

Which was too bad.

Harvey liked the kid and was saddened by his treachery.

But if the kid couldn't be trusted, he would have to be *disposed of* in some way.

There was always the desert, Harvey thought. He had no doubt there were a lot of treacherous people buried out there. In fact, he had a folding camp shovel behind the pickup's seat.

But was killing and burying him the best choice?

He'd killed before. He didn't like doing it, but he'd done it. However, based on his own experience and on what he saw others do, it was usually a chump move. Most of the time, rather than really solving the problem, killing only further complicated things.

Maybe the solution was to somehow just *strand* the kid?

Temporarily. Like the kid had been planning to do with his little girl-friend. Except in this instance—for somewhat longer. Say for couple of days until Harvey could do his deal with the buyer.

But where and how?

Harvey turned the notion over in his mind as he drove on.

Then something occurred to him. A possibility.

Several miles ahead, Dorothy's family owned a piece of property. An old farm, long abandoned. The house had burned down in the seventies, and most of the out buildings had collapsed from age and inattention.

Harvey hadn't been to the place in at least five years. Searching his memory, he tried to recollect exactly where it was. He considered calling Dorothy for directions, but decided it would be a mistake to involve her. Could he find it on his own, in dark? He thought he could.

However, forty minutes later, after more than a few wrong turns, he was ready to give up.

Which was when he saw the sign.

A homemade thing done on plywood in faded white paint. *Kaltman Well Digging*, and a phone number. He recalled he and Dorothy joking about the fact that *kalt* was German for cold—as in the old line *colder than a well digger's ass.*

So he knew he had to be on the correct road.

Slowing down, he started scanning the left side. If memory served, the entrance had been on the left. But how far had it been from the sign? A quarter mile? A half?

The area's population hadn't grown any, as far as he could see. There were very few lights visible in any direction. And he'd passed only a couple of mailboxes.

But then, he wasn't looking for mailboxes. Unless the property had been sold and Dorothy had failed to mention this fact to him, the place he was looking for wouldn't have one. Because nobody would be living there and getting mail. It was an abandoned farm from another era.

Also, he needed to remember that the drive leading in would likely be overgrown.

Even more so than it was last time.

Which is what he found.

What had once been a dirt drive was barely that now. Tall grass and weeds were growing up through its humped center. And from the sides, more tall grass and weeds arched inward to almost fully conceal access.

Harvey turned off the two-lane and rolled in. The dry foliage scratched loudly against the pickup's sides and undercarriage. He wanted to turn his headlights off, so as to not draw attention to himself. But he also wanted to see where he was going.

Beside him, the kid—who'd been slouched down in the passenger seat, probably to ease the pressure on his bound hands—sat up. He knew something was about to happen. He just didn't know what.

Harvey glanced over at him, amused to see him staring straight ahead, defiant like a sulking cat, refusing to look in Harvey's direction.

Still smiling, Harvey rolled down the window, and breathed in the brisk night air. On it he caught the faint familiar scent of wood smoke. Somewhere in the vicinity, one or more households had the fireplace going in this chilly winter weather.

Soon the pickup's headlights revealed clusters of dark trees. One where the house had once stood. And another, surrounding the remnants of the barn and other structures.

When he got there, Harvey cut left a tight circle between the two clusters, leaving the pickup pointed back toward the road. Having stopped, he turned off the engine and lights, pulled the keys from the ignition, and got out.

His pistol and three-battery Mag-lite were behind the seat. He extracted both. Put the pistol down the waistband of his pants and transferred the Mag-lite to his left hand. Then leaned forward into the cab, to stick his free right hand behind the kid's back.

Was the tape on his wrists still tight? It was.

That settled, Harvey clicked on the Mag-lite and trudged off into the darkness to check something. His possibility.

He was gone five minutes.

When he got back, he found the passenger door open and the kid outside on the ground.

He was in a sitting position. Harvey put the Mag-lite's beam on him and stepped forward to once again examine the tape on his wrists. It was almost sawn through. He'd been scraping it on the outer edge of the door.

"Very resourceful," Harvey told him, impressed.

Then he rewound the wrists with fresh tape from the roll.

(TWENTY-TWO)

orty minutes after Kirbi phoned her, awakening her from a deep sleep, Jane pulled in at the Raybright entrance. She'd been given no details, but it seemed evident something big had happened. Two maintenance day-shifters were wrestling what looked like the gate itself down the hill. And she noticed there was no barrier bar on the out-traffic side.

Stopping opposite the gate shack, she expected having to explain that she no longer had a badge. But the guard didn't even come out. Instead, apparently recognizing her, he shot her a thumbs up, raised the in-traffic barrier, and waved her on.

Jane had been off work for several days. It felt good to be back on site, though a little strange to be showing up in the middle of the night. Her throat clenched with emotion as she parked in her usual spot. She hadn't realized how important her job was to her until it had been taken away.

The lobby lights were on. As she'd been instructed, she rode the elevator up to the executive offices. There the lights were also on, and she followed the sound of voices to the conference room.

Standing in the open doorway, Jane had a feeling she was late to a party.

Present were Kirbi, Eric, the general, David Martinez, and some pony-tailed guy in his late forties she'd never seen before. The table was littered with coffee cups, soda and water bottles, and wadded up paper napkins. And in the middle sat a couple of almost-empty containers of cheese spread, and a platter containing some stray crackers and half of a toasted bagel.

Kirbi was the first to notice her.

198

"Jane!" she called out, patting the back of the chair next to her.

Hearing this, the other four looked up and smiled. To Jane, it felt like being welcomed back into the family. She seated herself beside Kirbi. Laid her large, string-handled shopping bag sideways on the table. Then slid from it two clear-plastic pouches.

"I thought about what you asked," she said. "And at first I couldn't come up with anything. Then I remembered these."

Kirbi examined the pouches, each of which contained a glazed ceramic mask. "Comedy and Tragedy."

"Right. The first night he came to my condo, I remember Mark handling them. The day before I'd done some cleaning, and I remembered hitting them both with Windex. So any fingerprints on them would have to be his, because nobody else had touched them since. And when I picked them up a half hour ago, I did it by the edges."

"I *love* it," Kirbi told her, squeezing Jane's shoulder.

Next Jane opened her purse and took out a wad of printed-out photos. "I also brought these. From the parking garage."

Moments later, Kirbi's eyes lit up as she leafed through them. "The night of the accident. You and you-know-who."

"Exactly."

"Hey, everybody," Kirbi announced, holding the photos meaningfully aloft. "Jane managed to get us some pictures of Mark Hatcher. Still shots from security footage in a downtown parking garage."

Eric was scribbling away on a pad of paper. The general had a phone to his ear. And David and the pony-tailed guy were absorbed in an intense murmured conversation.

But again, each stopped what he'd been doing for a moment to acknowledge with a nod or grin Jane's contribution.

"Did you show these photos to Deb?" Kirbi asked.

"Not yet. But I called and told her."

"Proof."

"Yeah."

"You did good."

Jane shrugged. "The woman from the parking company wouldn't help me at first." She gave a weak, embarrassed chuckle. "But then I broke down and started weeping right there in her office, and she had to take pity on me, I guess."

Kirbi chuckled along. "However you got them, they're going to help a lot."

On the other side of the table, David leaned across to take one of the photos Kirbi was passing to him. He studied it for a long moment. "That's him, huh, the guy driving?"

"Yeah," Jane said.

"And there you are in the passenger seat. Man, you look *out of it*."

"Apparently I was."

David shook his head. "This Mark dude is a piece of work."

"Let's see if we can't find out more about him," Kirbi suggested, pushing the masks across the table to him. "If we can lift prints from these, Baines can get his friend to run them through NCIC."

Picking up the pouches, David stood.

The pony-tailed guy sitting next to him rose also. He addressed Kirbi. "David and I are already set up downstairs in his office."

Kirbi nodded, then turned to Jane. "I'm sorry. I don't think I introduced Roy Baines. He and I work together."

"Nice to meet you, Roy," Jane said.

"Likewise," Roy told her, leaning across the table to bump fists.

As the two men headed out the door together, Kirbi called after them, "Thanks, guys."

Eric got up now. He moved down a couple chairs and slipped into the one directly opposite Jane's. Then peered across at her for a few seconds, as if gathering his thoughts.

"We're kind of on emergency status here," he began. "I know it's the middle of the night and short notice, but we could use your help."

"Not a problem," Jane said, mirroring his quiet, formal manner.

"I'm afraid there's some bad news. Norman died yesterday at his home. So what we'd like you to do for now is keep things running in your department. Until we can decide what we want to do going forward."

Norman was dead?

"All right," she said, feeling numb. Then added, "I guess I should mention that I don't have my badge or keys anymore."

He gave a dismissive wave of the hand. "We'll fix that."

Jane didn't know exactly what she'd expected when Kirbi had called. But it wasn't all this. Why was the gate messed up and everybody here in the wee hours? And how did finding out who Mark was fit in?

When Eric left the room, she turned to Kirbi and asked in a low voice, "What's going on?"

"Two guys broke into RayBright earlier tonight and stole something important."

"You think Mark was one of them?"

"We aren't positive yet, but we think so. Did you know anything about Mark being friends with Norman?"

Before Jane could answer, the general said, "So *this* is the guy," as if thinking aloud. He'd finished his phone call and was now sifting through the photos Jane had brought. He looked up at Kirbi. "He doesn't really look much like either of the two in the surveillance though, does he?"

"The tall thin one has a similar build," Kirbi said. "Let's have Jane look at the surveillance coverage and see if the way he moves tells us anything. Roy's theory is that they were wearing disguises."

"That's worth trying," he said. Then stood, looked idly at what was left of the crackers and cheese spreads for several seconds, and wandered out of the room.

"Why did you want to know if Mark was friends with Norman?" Jane asked Kirbi.

"Norman's mother said they were."

"Really. I didn't even know they'd met."

Jane wasn't sure what she should feel. Mark appeared to have had a plan. Maybe even a list of people he needed to get next to. Did this make her less of a fool or more of a fool?

She didn't know.

A few minutes later, she and Kirbi took the elevator downstairs to the Security office.

David swung around in his chair when they came in. "Roy got some good prints off them," he said in a pleased way, indicating with a glance her ceramic masks.

"Good," Jane told him.

"And Eric called and told me to get you a badge and set of Accounting keys."

Jane shrugged. "Thanks."

Pony-tailed Roy was working at a laptop. He turned, caught Jane's eye, and said, "You got a minute to take a look here?"

She joined him, peeking over his shoulder.

"I think these are the two masks they wore," he said. It was a commercial website display of several rubber faces. He gently touched one image with his fingertip, then another. "If I'm right, we might be able to track them through recent purchases from this company."

He then clicked on one of the site's demonstration videos. As Jane looked on, a young guy in a black T-shirt pulled one of the masks over his head and modeled it. It struck her as surprisingly realistic.

"So lifelike," she said.

"Yeah. Now that you've seen what they were probably wearing, let's play some surveillance for you. See if you recognize anybody."

"Over here," David said. He was seated at the counter in front the wall of screens. "Ready?"

Jane nodded.

And the show began on the large screen in the middle.

A man in white coveralls was standing next to a building. Waiting at a door. Tallish and slender. Wearing a mask like what she'd just seen. Then the door opened and Chuey Orozco, one of the RayBright guards, came into view.

Jane focused on the man in the white coveralls. She watched his mannerisms and how he carried himself as he spoke with the guard.

"That's Mark," she said. It just burst from her.

The giveaway was the way the guy tilted his head. It was the way Mark did when he was trying to portray earnestness. She'd first noticed it that night at the bar in Mission Valley. I'm for real, the gesture said.

Except, of course, he wasn't.

Jane felt a slight nausea at the thought of how Mark had deceived her. At how gullible she'd been. How eager for love and authenticity. But she also felt a rage, a desire to get back at him, to make him pay for what he'd done—to her and to the company.

Kirbi was standing beside her. "You're sure?"

Jane nodded. "Definitely."

"How about the other guy?" David asked.

The action was still going. Jane put her attention back on the screen.

She watched the shorter, heavier guy appear carrying a long canvas bag. Then spray Chuey in the face with something. However, so far nothing about the second guy seemed familiar.

Then the scene changed. And Jane was intrigued to see the two men emerge from one of the labs. The taller one was pulling something on one of those wheeled warehouse thingies. While the other was wielding a handgun, from which fire flashed several times.

"Wow," Jane said when it ended. "The Wild West, right here at Ray-Bright."

Kirbi nodded. "Yeah. But do you recognize the second guy at all?"

"Oh, sorry. No. As far as I can tell, I've never seen him before."

A while later, she and Eric and Roy took the elevator to Accounting on the third floor. And there, using her new set of keys, she opened not only the outer door to her own office, but the one to Norman's as well.

Roy's expertise, Eric explained, was computers.

She watched Roy sit comfortably down at Norman's desk. Switch on Norman's computer. And while it loaded, fumble through the contents of the desk drawers.

"Listen, I'm really burnt," Eric said, almost in embarrassment. "I'm going to try to catch a cat nap in my office. I'll have my phone on. Call me if you need anything."

"We'll be fine," Roy assured him. "Mickey showed me around the system the other day."

Eric nodded, gave a bleak smile, and left.

"Okay, let's see what we've got," Roy muttered to himself, tapping some keys.

Jane liked his air of understated competence. And his very pale blue eyes. Unfortunately he was wearing a wedding ring.

She watched the screen over his shoulder.

He moved fast. She noticed he was on as administrator, but couldn't follow what he was doing. After a while, he began asking her questions about the how the department handled things. Sometimes she had the answers, sometimes she didn't.

Soon Jane dragged another chair around behind the desk and sat next to him.

As he worked through various files and programs, he made notes on a yellow legal pad.

"You're going to need these passwords," he said at one point. He showed her a list he was compiling on one side of the page. "When we're done, the two of us will go back over it a couple of times. To make sure you've got it."

"Sounds good," Jane told him. She appreciated his help. But was a little frightened of what might be expected of her in the coming days.

"First though, I want to see if I can get the big picture."

"You studied accounting?"

He shook his head in an absent way. "No. But I understand the general idea. And as we go along, I'll count on you to tell me if you notice anything that doesn't seem to make sense, okay?"

"Like what?"

"Did anybody tell you how your boss died?"

"No."

"Well, it hasn't been determined exactly what happened. But things were suspicious."

"Suspicious how?"

"He might have died accidentally. But there are also more sinister *interpretations* of the event." He took a deep breath and blew it out. "He might have been killed. Or he might have killed himself."

"Jeez," Jane said, trying to get a mental handle on this.

"To put it simply," he told her in an ominous tone, "we want to find out if there's any money missing."

Jane's breath caught. "Money missing?"

"Under such circumstances, it's just wise to check. This doesn't mean we're going to find anything."

Jane wasn't sure what to say to this.

But forty-five minutes later, they did find something. Something that didn't make sense. Or rather, Roy found it and Jane watched him find it. But they went over the logic of it together. Several times.

And agreed it was indeed a problem.

Then they began finding more things that didn't make sense. More problems.

"Should we wake Van Horne?" he asked her finally.

Jane shrugged. "He'd want to know. And John too. It's their company."

Roy made a call, but it was to Kirbi, telling her they'd discovered some pretty serious accounting anomalies. Did she want to see if she could briefly assemble everyone up on the third floor to have a look? It seemed she did. Roy switched off and pocketed his phone.

He gave Jane a grim smile.

Five minutes later, John, Kirbi, and David arrived in a group. Then a minute after that, Eric followed, trudging in alone, rubbing his eyes.

Everyone now present, Jane scooted out of the way so the others could see the screen.

"Here's the deal," Roy began, addressing especially John and Eric. "I'm was no business major. But what it looks like to me is this—over the course of the last six years, money has been disappearing from your Bank of San Diego operating account. Right here, see?"

He pointed at something on the screen, touched the keyboard, and pointed again.

He did this several times. Eric sat fidgeting in the chair next to Roy. He'd always reminded Jane of a little kid. A *very smart* little kid, but a little kid, nonetheless.

Then Roy slid his chair to the left and let Eric work the keyboard.

"The total," Roy said, looking up and over his shoulder at John standing behind him, "looks to be about a million eight. So far."

John had his arms crossed. He looked away from the screen and into the middle distance, an expression of shock on his features.

(TWENTY-THREE)

It took some prolonged blind groping, but Mark at last found what he needed. Just the right hard sharp fragment of wood. And using it, he set about awkwardly poking, cutting, and sawing at the tape that bound him.

The process was a painstaking one, and seemed to take an eternity.

But finally freeing himself, he arose from the hard cement floor and staggered about for a few moments, arms across his chest, rubbing his bare, goosed-pimpled upper arms. He was naked and shivering. That fucking old man had cut his clothes off with a knife. Then taken the fragments with him when he left.

Aside from being cold, sore, and pissed off, Mark was also somewhat disoriented.

For one thing he was still high and drunk. For another, it was dark and he couldn't see.

And for a third, he didn't know where he was, and had lost track of how long it'd been since the old man had dumped him off.

He did know, however, that he was being confined in what amounted to a large steel cylinder. He'd learned this fact in the course of rolling and crawling around in search of a means of breaking his bonds. Now though, it was time for some *real* exploration. He wanted out of this nightmare situation—and fast.

So, teeth chattering and hands tentatively out before him in the blackness, he began shuffling forward through the debris that littered the floor. Dry leaves, small branches, and what smelled like bird and animal shit.

The cylinder, he soon estimated, had a diameter of about twelve feet. And didn't appear to have a roof. Because some dozen feet above him, he could discern a circular expanse that looked just *slightly* less black than the rest of his environment.

The sky? He hoped so. Maybe he could somehow climb out of the thing.

First, however, it made sense to check out the small square door through which he'd been dragged in. He searched for it by touch and found it at floor level. And found as well, a series of identical doors extending upward in a vertical line.

All were constructed of the same steel as the walls.

All were locked from the outside.

For several minutes, Mark manically pried and shook and banged on these doors. But to no avail. Though there was some minor play in them, he could by no means get any of them open. Stepping back, he hugged himself once more against the chilly night air, trying to think.

He knew he was in danger.

If he was going to live through the night, he would need to generate metabolic heat. In other words, to stay in motion. The choices were keep moving or die of hypothermia.

Mark started moving. Walking.

Setting off clockwise, he swung his arms as he went, letting the fingers of his outer hand brush the curving sides of the structure. But after doing a couple of laps this way, he stopped. Some of the woody branches underfoot hurt his bare soles. He spent several minutes brushing the floor debris out of his path, inward toward the center.

Then resumed his circular journey.

After a while, if only to fight the boredom, he fell into *counting* the laps. It passed the time. When he'd reach a hundred, he'd reverse course and count out a hundred more in the opposite direction. After which he'd repeat the whole cycle. A hundred and a hundred.

But even that soon grew stale.

So he resorted to singing songs in rhythm with his steps. He sang rock songs, pop songs, nursery songs, patriotic songs, hymns, and Christmas carols. He might have done this for an hour. At least it seemed like an hour.

After this, Mark went through a period, perhaps of equal length, during which he lost himself in muttered cursing. Curses directed at himself for being an idiot. At the old man for being an asshole. At people from his past for wronging him or letting him down.

All Mark knew was that he had to keep walking. And so he did.

Overall, he felt physically horrible. He was weary and chilled and his chest was sore from where the old man had slugged him. If there was any upside to this nightmare, it was the residual crank still buzzing in his system, which not only helped keep him awake, but nervously drove his muscles onward in their boring repetitive effort.

But, he wondered, for how long could he really keep this up?

Because a part of him wanted to simply lie down, curl up in a ball, and give up.

Mark tried not to listen to this part.

And as if fleeing weakness and self-defeat, he abruptly lurched forward, picking up his pace and calling out for help. He shouted at the top of his lungs, then paused to listen. Shouted, then listened. Over and over and over, until his voice went hoarse.

At times during this phase—again, he couldn't have said how long it lasted—he thought he might be hearing the faint barking of dogs in the distance. Their ears were better than human ears. Were they hearing him and responding? He didn't know. In fact, he might be simply imagining the dogs.

Because by this point he no longer felt he was thinking rationally.

Though he was still plodding along, one foot in front of the other, he occasionally caught himself drifting away. Little snippets of dream were slipping into waking consciousness. Brief fantastical stories, flashing before him. He tried to stop them, but couldn't.

In one particularly vivid dream he was a fairytale giant, striding around the darkened globe. Ahead he kept seeing the setting sun. He was in pursuit of it for some reason, but it continually sank out of sight behind the horizon, just out of reach. This seemed to go on and on... until Mark realized he was at last catching up.

Because the sky was brightening.

And then Mark realized something else—he was in a *silo*. One of those big can-shaped things farmers stored chopped corn or grass in. Or maybe even grain. He hadn't noticed many in Southern California.

This particular version, he could now see, was maybe twenty feet high. And had been constructed from curving rectangular pieces of steel, probably bolted or welded together on the outside. Which, except for the access doors, made for a more or less featureless interior surface.

In the light from the pinkish-grey sky above, he counted them. Eight.

He had an idea.

After gathering up a wad of twigs, he stepped to the bottommost door. The one the old man had dragged him in through. It was of course locked from the other side. But there was enough give in the locking mechanism to allow him to pry it open half an inch on the side opposite the hinges.

Could he somehow use this small gap, and the gap in each successive door, to climb up the interior of the silo as if on the rungs of a ladder?

Mark knelt on the cold cement. Broke the thickest and driest of the twigs into small pieces. Pulled at the door with his fingertips. And wedged a couple of the pieces into the resultant gap.

This done, he stood and likewise wedged the second door open.

Followed by the third and fourth, which was the limit of his reach.

Each of the four doors now had a triangular opening along its top edge. A half inch in width on the right side, diminishing to zero inches on the left, hinged side.

Now came the hard part.

He gripped top edge of the third door with his fingertips. Then laid the side of one bare foot atop the protruding upper edge of the first door. Put weight on the foot. And at the same, pushed off with the other foot and pulled with his arms.

Rung one. Success. Except his foot hurt like fuck.

He wanted to jump down, but didn't.

Instead, he took a deep breath and reached up to the top of the fourth door with one hand. Gripped it. Reached up to grip it with the other. Brought his free foot up to rest sideways atop the second door. Then as before, simultaneously pushed off and pulled himself up.

Okay, rung two.

But now his other foot hurt like fuck, as did both sets of fingertips.

Besides, how was he going to climb any higher without more wedges? He had none with him. Having no clothes meant having no pockets. He could put the wedges in his mouth, he supposed. But even so, it was going to be difficult, if not impossible, to insert them one-handedly while clinging to the doors below.

Defeated, Mark tried for a graceful dismount but ended up falling in a painful heap on the floor. The *ladder* thing wasn't going to happen. Facts had to be faced. He wasn't strong enough.

He needed a new plan.

After a few minutes rubbing himself for warmth, he scrambled to the center and searched through the available twigs and small branches. Blown in, or brought in by animals? He didn't know. Most were dry and brittle, but a few were still green.

Bringing the most flexible pieces with him, he adopted a hands-and-knees pose at the bottommost door. Cheek flat against the rusty metal, he squinted down, one-eyed, through the thin gap at its top. His objective now was the door's latch. That was the puzzle to be solved.

To find a way to lift the door's lever-like latch out of the U-shaped thing holding it.

What was required was a loop of rope.

So Mark set about trying to *make* rope. He stripped the greenest branches of leaves. He experimented with sections as is. Then moved on to splitting sections and braiding the strands together.

The process was mind-numbing trial and error. His back grew cramped and his knees hurt. Though the birds were now chirping outside, the air temperature was still in the refrigerator range.

But as with the freeing of his hands, then the walking to keep warm, he persevered.

Until at last, on what felt like his billionth attempt, one of the loops of braided green wood dropped over the lever just right. Held tight. And didn't break or slip off when he exerted upward pressure.

Mark held his breath. He gave it an even firmer tug. He felt the lever resist but then slowly move. *Move.*

His heart leapt.

He jostled the door with his shoulder as, at the same time, he drew carefully upward on the loop. Yes. He could both see and feel the lever moving. It was rising in an arc, rotating out of its U-shaped restraint.

When it finally slid free, and the door popped inward toward him, Mark exhaled in an explosion of emotion. He sobbed for several moments in joy. In relief. It had been a miracle.

The Lord helps those who help themselves, his great aunt in Texas had liked to say.

He was no longer imprisoned.

Dropping to his belly, Mark slithered through the two-by-two aperture.

Then struggled to his feet, gazing around. A barn had once stood attached to the silo, which made sense. But that must have been long ago, because now all that was left were some rotting planks and beams, barely visible among the tall, thick clumps of brush and saplings.

Be wary of nails, he reminded himself as he stepped forward on bare feet.

To his right, on the silo's corrosion-brown exterior, he saw graffiti. Scrawled names, initials, dates, and phrases, many indecipherable. *Class of 1994. I love Alice. J.R.*

And as he picked his way through the tall weeds, he encountered other indications that the spot, however remote, did not lack for the occasional visitor or visitors. Old beer and soda cans. Bottles, both broken and unbroken. An ancient avocado-green refrigerator with bullet holes in it. Two weather-eaten automobile tires.

While none of this junk interested him, when he reached the rutted, overgrown track that led in from the road, his gaze lighted on something that did. A black plastic trash bag. It was snagged on a bush.

Mark carefully pulled it free and tore it open along the seams. Then wrapped and folded the plastic around his nakedness. The simple black loincloth. An elegant, essential piece of fashion attire, welcome anywhere.

He smiled grimly to himself and resumed his slow, tentative, tip-toeing progress.

The dry, bent stalks of vegetation hurt his feet. And the gravelly shoulder of the road was no better when he got there. He chose instead the asphalt itself. He walked right, remembering how the night before the old man had made a *left* coming in.

The night before seemed like weeks ago. Mark hadn't slept in thirty-six hours, and hadn't eaten anything since lunch the previous day. He felt horrible.

Nevertheless, he knew he would need a story, and so set to work on one.

Because no frazzled-looking guy without clothes, shoes, money, or ID was likely to get help from a stranger without one.

* * *

"You sure you don't want me to come in with you?"

Mark pulled his thoughtfully puckered lips to one side. Considering the offer. Like he wasn't sure, like he hated to impose.

"How about as witness," he suggested. "If you're along, he can't really jump me." He met the other man's eyes. "I'm just looking to get my stuff and go, but he may not see it that way."

"I'll go with you," Patrick said, a decisive set to his jaw. He had his hand on the ignition key. "You want me to pull up closer?"

Mark shook his head. "Here's good. Let's just quietly walk up the drive. With any luck he won't even notice. I'm not into any more threats, shouting matches, or late-night drives at gunpoint."

Patrick turned off the big truck. The two of them climbed down and headed up the drive. One in a black plastic loincloth. The other in Wranglers, pullover sweatshirt, and work boots.

The Australian shepherd came trotting across from the house, tail wagging. Mark petted it but didn't break stride. He liked that the animal wasn't a barker.

When they got to the garage, Mark peered in the windows of the first door. Dorothy's car was there. But since the red pickup was gone, the old man was gone, because Dorothy never drove the pickup.

Mark darted in through the side door of the garage and emerged with a big screwdriver. Then he and Patrick climbed the stairs to the overhead apartment. The door was locked. But it gave easily when Mark inserted the screwdriver blade at the bolt and pried.

Inside, nothing seemed disturbed. The old man hadn't messed with any of his stuff.

Marked checked the bedroom just to be sure, and found his money stash untouched. He sighed aloud in relief. Then peeled two hundreds from the roll and turned back to his companion. "Let me thank you for your help," he said, hand extended, offering the money.

Patrick pushed the bills aside and stepped back. "Don't insult me, bro."

"Goddamnit, you helped me out of a tough spot."

Patrick shook his head.

Mark frowned, thinking, and pulled back one of the hundreds. "Look, if you hadn't happened along and stopped, I would've have been up shit creek. Take a hundred. For the gas you used to get me here and the food you bought me. Please."

Patrick regarded the offered bill for several seconds before reluctantly taking it.

Then the two men clasped crossed hands.

"Partner, you saved my life."

"I know you'd do the same for me," Patrick told him.

"Get to work. I'm making you late."

Patrick shrugged, turning toward the door. But swung back to point an accusing finger. "You better learn to keep it in your pants."

Mark adopted a properly chastened expression and nodded. He'd concocted a tale of being caught in bed with the old man's daughter, home for the weekend from bible college.

As he listened to Patrick's footsteps receding down the stairs, Mark looked longingly across at the bed. What he needed was sleep, of course. But he didn't have time for it right now. From the top drawer of the dresser, he instead got some pharmaceutical assistance.

Then popped a Lone Star from the fridge and drank the whole can.

A couple of minutes later, he was just stepping out of the black trash bag when a sudden noise and vibration from below startled him. The garage door opener was working, directly beneath. Had the old man come home in the pickup?

Rushing to one of the dormer windows on that side, Mark relaxed when he saw Dorothy's SL roll out of the garage and across to the drive. That didn't mean the old man *couldn't* be here. But with both vehicles now gone, the odds were greatly diminished.

Mark grabbed up some clothes and stepped into the bathroom. After a moment's examination of his bruised torso in the mirror, he hurriedly dressed. He was glad to be wearing clothes and shoes again.

You took things for granted until you had to do without them.

Back out in the main room, he pocketed his roll of bills and his spare van key. Then reached under the bed for the old hardwood axe handle he usually carried for protection in the van. He hefted the thing. Against a pistol, it wasn't much. Even against the old man, barehanded, it might not be enough.

But it was *something*.

Carrying it at the ready, he crept down the stairs and across the drive to where the van was parked. It started, first try. But not without its usual six-cylinder, high-mileage roar.

Idling, he spent the next full minute watching the doors and windows of the house, alert for any sign of the old man. But finally, seeing nothing, brought the van over in front of the garage and left it running.

Back upstairs—axe handle still in hand—he did a quick gather-up of his laptop, most of his clothes, and his toiletries. Ferried them down to the van. Went back for the printer and two more cans of Lone Star from the fridge. And climbed back into his waiting vehicle.

Again he warily eyed the house.

More than anything, he wanted to break in and look for the old man's cash. The cash the old man goddamn *owed* him. The alarm was no doubt set. However, Mark *knew* two things.

First, he knew the code to the house alarm system.

This the result of a shoulder-surfing peek one afternoon when coming in behind the old man. Years before, Mark had invested several hours in laboriously teaching himself how to read the placement of fingers on keypads. An investment that had paid off more than once since.

Sure the old man could've changed the code when he got home last night.

But Mark considered this unlikely. He also doubted the old man had told Dorothy what'd gone down.

The second thing Mark knew was where the old man's safe was.

He didn't know the combination to it, but maybe he could manhandle the thing out of the cabinet it was mounted in. There was a sledgehammer and a pry bar in the garage.

Did it make sense to break into the house and try?

No, his best course of action was to just bolt.

That's what he *should* do.

However, nobody told Mark what to do. Often, not even Mark.

So flipping open the driver door, he jumped out and raced around the back of the house to the kitchen door. It was locked. He tried the sliding glass doors to the living room. They were also locked, and held fast by a broomstick-thick dowel wedged in the track.

Shit.

The dog was following along with him now, tail up, tongue lolling. Not knowing or caring what Mark was up to, but having picked up on his excitement.

Mark continued, checking the status of the sliding doors on the other three rooms. But they were also locked, and held fast by more dowels. He continued around the structure, arriving once more at the front door.

Frustrated and conflicted, he brooded there for a long moment, then did an about-face and strode to the van.

The dog just looked at him as he tore off down the drive.

Ten minutes later he was barreling west down the 8. Open can of Lone Star beer on the seat between his legs. Phone plugged into the van's speaker system. Volume cranked to the max.

Lyle Lovett and Al Green dueting on "Funny How Time Slips Away."

TWENTY-FOUR

After stranding Mark in the silo, Harvey had driven back to the ranch.

There he awakened Dorothy, explained to her that he'd be away for a couple of days, and mentioned that he'd had a falling out with Mark. Dorothy took it all in stride, which is what he liked about her. Following this brief chat, they made very satisfying love.

Very.

Then once Dorothy dozed off, Harvey took a shower, put on fresh clothes, and went outside to load some necessary tools and supplies into the pickup. He was headed back to the little industrial park where Merman was stashed. What'd happened earlier with the kid had rattled him.

He was pretty sure he wasn't going to be able to sleep, himself, unless he was in close proximity to the newly stolen Merman. The device was his future. The means by which he hoped to get back on sound financial footing. The basket into which he'd put all his eggs.

However, almost an hour later, when he got there and tried to settle in, surprisingly, sleep wouldn't come. First the padded bench seat in the box truck's cab proved too small to stretch out in. Then, when he dragged his sleeping bag into the back, he found the metal floor of the compartment too hard on his joints, no matter what position he adopted.

It was maddening.

Slumber did finally overtake him at some point. But when he was awakened by the nine a.m. alarm he'd set on his phone, he didn't by any means feel rested.

Oh well.

Sitting up, he spent a while thinking through what he needed to get done that day. After which he put on his shoes and climbed down from the truck. Shuffled across the bay's concrete floor to its scuzzy corner restroom. Relieved himself, washed his hands, and splashed cold water on his face.

Back at the truck, he dug out one of his disposable, pay-as-you-go phones and called the buyer. There was no answer. When it went to message, he spoke briefly. *Got what you want. I'll call back.*

That done, Harvey used his own—more versatile—smartphone to locate a place that rented trucks and vans. Then locked up both box truck and pickup. Locked up the bay itself. And walked quietly across the parking lot to the street.

Two of the other three bay doors were open. Behind him, he could hear voices and noises from within these businesses, but he saw no one and believed no one saw him. Which was the way he wanted it.

It took a quarter of an hour to hike to a nearby McDonald's.

Inside, he called for a cab and sipped at an orange juice while he waited. When the cab came he rode to the rental place. And once there, picked out a van, signed the necessary paperwork, and drove it back to the industrial park.

By this time it was well after ten.

All three bays were open, and there were more cars parked in the lot. Things were picking up. Harvey unlocked and raised the door to his own bay. Then after quickly jockeying the van inside with the other two vehicles, rolled down the door once more.

Now, in the privacy of the closed bay, he transferred the Merman device from the box truck to the back of the rental van.

And moved on to the job of sanitizing of the box truck.

This began with the removal of the blue plastic tarp that hid the words *Creighton Specialized Maintenance.* Followed by the removal of the vinyl lettering itself using a stepladder, hot soapy water, and a broad-bladed drywall knife.

Next, Harvey moved on to the front bumper and grill area.

Here there were two kinds of damage to minimize. The yellow paint from when the truck crashed through the RayBright traffic barrier, which he scrubbed off with a nylon pad, rags, and isopropyl alcohol. As well as the major scrapes and scratches made when the vehicle crashed through the chain-link gate, which required more work. These he touched up as best he could with a can of aerosol enamel that was close to the same hue of white.

The exterior of the vehicle done, he moved on to the cab and the rear compartment.

Both deserved a thorough wipe-down for fingerprints. Instead, he settled for merely checking these areas for any incriminating personal items he or the kid might have left behind. He couldn't dally. The day was flying by. He had things to do. It was almost noon.

Harvey tried the buyer's number once more, but got no answer. He declined to leave another message.

He put his pistol, his cash, and a few other things in a shoe box. Stowed the box under the van's front seat. Eased the van outside. Then rolled down the bay door and locked up.

There were a couple of customers outside the auto electric shop, next door, but they paid him no mind.

On his way back from the rental place, he'd seen a nearby shopping center. He drove there and parked the van, at the far edge of its busy lot. He was nervous about leaving Merman and his cash, but felt it was better than leaving them at the industrial park. The kid knew about the industrial park, which meant the location was *potentially* insecure. Who knew who the kid might have mentioned it to.

Harvey got out, obsessive-compulsively double checked the van's doors to make sure they were locked, then set off on foot toward the industrial park.

On the way, he stopped at a 7-Eleven and bought a pre-made turkey sandwich on wheat. Which he ate a short while later, sitting in the box truck's cab as he listened to oldies on the radio. Jim Morrison. Donovan. The Kinks.

When he finished the sandwich, he used the rest room, and hit the road.

He was leaving the pickup behind in the bay, and the rental van in the nearby shopping center parking lot.

Out on the freeway, driving the box truck, Harvey had to make an effort to shake a feeling of vulnerability. There was no telling how Ray-Bright had reacted to the theft. No telling how what he'd done might be viewed. Was this a federal crime, which meant the FBI? Was there a local law enforcement BOLO out for the vehicle he was driving?

Whatever the case, half an hour later, Harvey was at the border.

And as soon as he crossed, he noticed the usual change in road manners. A lot of the local Mexicans didn't have a problem cutting recklessly in and out of traffic. While he couldn't care less about damage to the box truck, he didn't want to be involved an accident. An accident that might draw Mexican cops.

Soon, picking up on the presence of yellow taxis, he began looking for a good spot. He found one on a side street. And though it wasn't quite big enough to accommodate the box truck's length, he backed untidily in at an angle, slipped the transmission into neutral, and pulled on the parking brake.

As he stepped down from the cab a moment later, Harvey grinned. To consciously leave the keys in the ignition and the engine running felt so wrong. A violation of lifelong habit. Walking away up the street, he looked back over his shoulder. It would be amusing to stick around and watch from a distance, to see how long it took for the truck to be stolen, but he didn't have the time.

"Taxi, sir?" a voice yelled to him two blocks later.

"La linea," Harvey told the guy, getting into the front seat.

They didn't say, *la frontera*, which to him was border. In TJ they said the line.

A quick drive later, Harvey gave the driver a five for the fare and two bucks tip.

As he'd expected, the pedestrian queue was something like fifty yards long down the sidewalk. Par for the course.

Prepared, he pulled a paperback of Sudokus and pencil from his leather knapsack and began working one. Ahead of him was an extremely fat woman in a purple T-shirt. Whenever in his peripheral vision he saw her wide shape move forward, he shuffled to close the gap.

And actually, the queue moved pretty fast. Past all the little shops and trinket displays. Through the gate. Into the customs building.

The agent who checked him through was a middle-aged Filipino. He ran Harvey's passport and asked, "Purpose of your visit?"

Harvey had an insane impulse to say, *Drop off a getaway vehicle*, but restrained himself. "Sightseeing."

The agent accepted Harvey's answer, gave him a jaded nod, and handed back the passport.

Harvey walked outside to look for a cab.

In other circumstances, he might have considered it an extravagance to be taking expensive cab rides. But a big job had a lot in common with a vacation. You went with the flow. You did what needed to be done.

Meaning, you spent money like water, and on things you never would have otherwise.

Not long after the cab pulled onto the freeway heading north, Harvey found his head tending to loll against the side window. He let it happen. He needed whatever sleep he could get. He closed his eyes and didn't open them again until he felt the cab decelerating on an exit ramp, twenty minutes later.

Harvey gave the driver directions to the shopping center, and once there, thanked him, paid him off, and got out. But then pretended to window-shop in front of a discount clothing store until the cab left the lot. Only then did he wander over to the rental van.

He knew it was silly, but when he got back to the vehicle, he found himself rushing to make sure the device was still there in the back. It was. Then hurriedly checking under the seat for the shoe box. It too was there, as well as its contents.

Exhaling in a grateful sigh, he smiled to himself. Or maybe *at* himself.

In the van once more, he drew out his disposable phone and again tapped the buyer's number. This time it was answered after three rings.

"Hello."

"I've got something for you," Harvey said.

There was a pause. "That's exactly what I was hoping to hear."

"Both our dreams come true."

"Yes."

"I'd like to deliver it. Today if possible."

Another pause. Harvey didn't like these pauses. But also knew he was in a suspicious frame of mind. Tired and a little stressed maybe.

"Okay. Do you know where we met last time?"

"Yeah." Seaport Village. Harvey was sure now the guy had a boat docked in the adjacent marina, just as the kid had suggested.

"How about the parking lot there. Someplace public, where nobody's tempted to cause a violent ruckus."

"Well we don't want any *violent ruckuses*," Harvey agreed. "When?"

Yet another pause. "You have any problem with seven tonight?"

"Seven tonight. You bring the money, I bring the device."

"Yes. What'll you be driving?"

224

Harvey gave him the name of the rental chain and described the van.

"Park dead center in the big lot out front," the man said.

"You're bringing cash, right? Hundreds?"

"Yes."

"How will I recognize you?" Harvey forced himself to say, not wanting to indicate he knew what the buyer looked like. Or that by now he'd learned the buyer's name.

"I'll know *you*," the man said, and cut the connection.

Harvey put the phone in his shirt pocket. He turned on the van's radio, fiddling with the tuner until he found an AM talk show about money. He listened to a discussion of interest rates for several minutes. Then shut it off, not wanting to wear the van's battery down.

Sliding, the seat back, he slouched as best he could, and let his eyes close.

A jingling woke him.

He'd set its alarm for six, but this wasn't the alarm.

He struggled to sit up, for a moment disoriented. Again the jingling. No, not the throwaway—his own phone.

Harvey cleared his throat. "Yeah," he said fumbling to answer the call, failing to check the display.

"I want my motherfucking money, Harve."

Harvey laughed, despite himself. "Well if it isn't my favorite person. My former partner in crime."

"That was the problem," the kid said. "We were never partners. You just wanted a cheap-ass assistant."

"So you decided to promote yourself."

Silence for a long moment.

"You owe me some money. If I don't get it, I'm going to be sending some trouble your way. Trouble with a capital T."

"Okay," Harvey said simply.

"Okay?"

"You got a hearing problem or something?"

"Fuck you. I want the twenty-five K you promised me. And I want a further cut."

"How much you figure I owe you—half?"

Again, silence. "Why not?"

"Because you don't deserve it."

"Okay, how much do I deserve?"

Harvey sighed, weighing the kid's potential for trouble. And made an immense effort to detach himself from his resentment at being blackmailed. He ran some numbers in his head.

"I'd consider dealing you in for a *third*," he said finally.

"A third of what?"

"A third of the transaction price. But if I go that far, I'm going expect you to put a little skin in the game."

"What the fuck does that mean?"

"Like we talked about. You backing my play when it comes down to making the actual exchange. I'll even bet you've got yourself some kind of firearm by now."

"You got that right, old man" the kid told him, an edge in his voice.

Harvey shook his head to himself. "Listen, kiddo, let me tell you something. If I'd wanted you dead, you'd already be dead. I'm not planning to shoot you, so don't be planning to shoot me. All right? We we're friends until you got all jacked up on your recreational drugs and pulled a gun on me. I'm able to forgive and forget. Are you?"

The question went unanswered for a long moment. Then the kid said, "Okay. You're still an asshole, but okay."

Harvey laughed. Looking at his watch, he saw it was almost five. "You know where the Star of India is docked?"

"The clipper ship?"

"Yeah. Downtown on the water."

"Sort of. I can find it."

"Can you be there by six?"

"I'll be there," the kid stated flatly.

Harvey ended the call and put the phone away. He drank some bottled water. Then started the van, put it in gear, and rolled toward the street.

Twenty minutes later, he was taking the Kettner Boulevard exit off the 5. Eventually he made a right, went two blocks, and made a left onto Harbor Drive. Then followed Harbor Drive all the way to Seaport Village, surveying the area as he went.

It was fully dark now, and growing cold. He switched the van's heater on. For a Friday night, traffic seemed minimal.

At Seaport Village he turned around and headed back.

But took an indirect route, scouting for a suitable parking spot. He saw places along the water, but they made him nervous. He'd told the buyer what brand of rental van he was driving and didn't want the guy making off with the vehicle if Harvey left it temporarily unattended.

After a few minutes, though, he found what he was looking for, a sparsely filled lot not directly visible from Harbor. He slipped into a slot in the back, turned off the engine, and glanced at his watch. Twenty minutes to six.

Harvey pulled the shoebox from under the front seat.

From it he took the stack of cash from his safe at home. Counted out twenty-five thousand dollars. Put the twenty-five in a paper bag he'd brought for just this purpose. Stowed the bag in his leather knapsack. Then stuffed the rest of the money, a little over ten thousand more, into the pocket of his coat.

Next he took out his pistol and its suppressor, screwed the latter onto the former, and slid the assembled weapon into the knapsack alongside the paper bag of money.

The night before at RayBright, he'd wanted maximum *noise*, and the fear and alarm it produced. Tonight, however, if he had to use the weapon—and he hoped it wouldn't come to that—*quiet* was the desired end. The quieter one was, the less attention one drew.

For a long moment Harvey stared ahead out the van's windshield, wondering if he'd overlooked anything.

Not that he could think of, but then there were a lot of variables in the equation. Variables he couldn't control. Variables like the kid.

With a grimace he climbed out of the van, locked up, and crossed the lot to the Pacific Highway side. There he set off up the sidewalk into the darkness. At Ash Street he cut left. A block ahead and across Harbor Drive, he could soon make out his destination.

Encountering two strolling couples in overcoats going in the direction he wanted, Harvey slowed his pace to slipstream close behind them. When the group reached the corner, he hung back a moment. Then edged left off the pavement into a shadowy area of landscaping.

Even at a distance, the kid wasn't hard to pick out.

He was attired in quasi-military costume. Black hooded sweatshirt, black cargo pants, and what looked like spit-shined black jump boots. And while everyone else in the area was absorbed in taking photos and peering at the big sailing ship, he was pacing back and forth, head swiveling expectantly.

Harvey studied him and the situation for a short while, then got out his phone.

"I'm nearby," he said as soon as the kid answered.

"Okay."

"See that hotel, catty-corner across the street?"

"Yeah, I see it."

"Let's meet inside."

"I'll be there," the kid announced and ended the call.

Harvey was pleased to see him immediately put the phone away. That is, as opposed to doing any texting, or making another call. Such as to a confederate.

He watched the kid's eye movements and body language, looking for any sort of nonverbal signaling. And examined others in the area for any undue attention to the kid's movements.

Had the kid come alone? He hoped so.

Continuing his recon as the kid crossed the street and passed by on his way to the hotel entrance, Harvey thought of something Lyndon Johnson was supposed to have said. And how it applied to his own situation with the kid.

Better to have the guy inside the tent pissing out, than outside pissing in.

In the hotel's lobby a few minutes later, Harvey found the kid slouched comfortably in an armchair.

"Hey, kiddo?"

The kid leaned forward, offering a fist bump. "Hey, Harve."

Harvey sat in the adjoining chair. He swung his knapsack off his shoulder and took out the paper bag of money. He handed the kid the bag.

The kid glanced coyly inside. Reclosed it.

"What we agreed on at the beginning," Harvey said.

"Twenty-five."

"Right."

"But now we have a new arrangement."

"Apparently we do."

The kid flashed him a hard grin. "Now we're talking about a third."

"Correct."

"A third of what, though?"

"Of two million."

The kid's eyebrows went up. "Six hundred sixty-six thousand, six hundred sixty-six dollars and sixty-seven cents."

"Right, but we may have to round off a little more than to the penny. It's going to be in hundreds."

"It's not half, though, is it?"

Harvey had resolved not to let the kid get to him. He fought down an urge now to make a *manual* adjustment to that annoying wiseass manner. He took a breath.

"My job. My expense money."

"I was just playing with you," the kid said suddenly, holding up his palms in surrender.

"The box truck alone cost me fifteen thousand."

"Okay. Okay."

"Either the third is acceptable or it's not," Harvey told him, locking eyes.

"A third is fine."

"If you're not going to be satisfied, now is the time to say so."

"Like I said, a third is fine. It's generous."

"Then quit bullshitting around."

"I'm sorry," the kid insisted earnestly. "I'm satisfied. Okay? I'm satisfied. Now let's do this thing. Let's go get it all over our faces."

TWENTY-FIVE

"This is our boy, here" Baines said, showing her his phone screen.

Kirbi studied the face. "Martin Russell McGarrity," she read aloud. A color arrest photo of a boyish-looking Mark Hatcher holding a sign with a number from Houston, Texas, two years before.

"Prison escapee."

Kirbi's eyebrows went up. "What's his record like?"

"Possession of methamphetamine. Receiving stolen merchandise. DUI. Driving with a revoked license. And—" Baines paused to catch her eye "—*computer fraud.*"

"Ah."

"I texted a friend in Texas. He's going to do some checking for me."

"Love it," Kirbi told him with smile. "Thanks."

They were sitting in Kirbi's living room. This was still the day after the robbery, but evening now. She'd come home and grabbed a five-hour nap. Then a long wonderful shower, some clean clothes, and a cup of tea. But *herbal* tea—she didn't need any more caffeine in her system right now.

She cringed inwardly as she watched Baines comfortably throw a leg over the arm of her Stickney chair. She tried to keep her expression bland. He wasn't *hurting* the chair, but all she could think of was how much she'd paid for it.

"It'd be better if we could get law enforcement looking for him," he said. He shook his head. "I'm not sure keeping things a secret is the way to go."

Kirbi frowned, agreeing. "I know."

231

"They're hoping you'll find him on your own. Steal the item back on the QT and save their bacon." Baines chuckled to himself at the absurdity of the notion.

"Doesn't mean I'm not going to try."

"And I'll help. But these guys were slick. Picking up their trail won't be easy. Besides, the thing might even be out of the country by now."

Five days until Wednesday, the thirty-first. But really, that was the day the Department of Defense or CIA—or whoever had lent RayBright the thing to study—would be stopping by to reclaim it. So really just four days.

Even though Kirbi was trying to relax this evening, she couldn't. Under the surface, the tension wouldn't go away. Couldn't be turned off. The deadline loomed and she had to do something.

She didn't second guess herself on what she'd done so far for RayBright. She'd done her all-out best, based on what she knew going along. But she still felt she'd let them down somehow. They'd hired her and the situation had nevertheless turned to poop.

Baines had been looking off into space. He turned to her now. "You know, losing it is bad enough. But not telling the authorities might come back to bite them."

Kirbi nodded. She made a grim face. "They're in a tight spot."

"They're in trouble with Uncle Sammy. Not to mention how it looks to the stock-buying public with their IPO coming up."

"And, they're out well over a million bucks, thanks to Norman," she said.

She crossed her legs at the ankles out in front of her. Finishing her tea, she placed the cool Art Deco cup on its cool Art Deco saucer.

She loved her 1920s house and everything she'd collected to furnish it. *Things* made her feel good, but they weren't enough. They were just a by-product of what she did and who she tried to be.

She heaved a sigh. "What could we do right now, right this minute, to find those guys?"

Sometimes, Kirbi brainstormed problems by posing questions to herself.

Baines looked over at her. The lines in his face sharpened as he considered what she'd asked. Maybe taking it as a challenge.

"What leads do we have?" Kirbi went on.

"Well, there's his van. Jane gave us a description. The Texas plates. The name of the cleaners. I can run with that. Maybe get the plate number that way. Then give it to the cops."

"We could leave the RayBright robbery out of it. Call Janie and have her file a complaint on Mark, say for drugging her, putting her behind the wheel, leaving the scene. Maybe even for vehicular manslaughter, or some kind of homicide. It's possible that the guy was alive in the other vehicle when Mark ran off."

"Tells us a lot about who we're dealing with," Baines noted. "What a schmuck."

Kirbi nodded her agreement.

Neither spoke for a short while. The tick of the big clock sounded from the kitchen. A car rolled by outside, a rap bass beat audible for a few seconds.

"We could talk to Stanko again, I suppose."

Baines frowned. "The security guard?"

Kirbi got to her feet and left the room. When she came back she had her phone. She checked the time. Six-forty-six.

She found Stanko's name in the phone's memory and called it.

"Steve," she said in a cheery voice when he answered. She exchanged smiles with Baines regarding her manner. "My name is Kirbi Mack. Eric Van Horne and John Shellhammer asked me to call you. We realize your separation from the company was not a pleasant thing. Not for you, not for RayBright. However, John and Eric asked me to offer you—" She struggled for a split-second with whether she should name an amount or keep it vague "—cash money if you'd talk to us about who hired you and what they hired you to do."

Kirbi paused. She thought for a moment Stanko was going to hang up.

"You already learned all you need to know from Vanessa," he taunted bitterly.

Kirbi was jammed up for a moment.

"I see," she said, adopting a tone that conveyed an admission that she'd underestimated him. "But hey," she added, "at least you got laid out the deal, right?"

Silence from Stanko. Kirbi couldn't lose him. She took a breath, psyching herself up.

"So what about this free money?" she asked. "You want some or you got all you need from Homeland Security?" She forced herself not to hurry it. "This is cash money in your hand. No charges filed. No shouting. No hard feelings. You there, Steve-o?"

"Yeah, I'm here."

"Well? This thing is too big for petty grudges, okay. RayBright's willing to pay you to learn what's going on. Maybe that's not much more than what you told Vanessa. We'll find out."

"How much we talking about?" he said in the suspicious voice of the hard bargainer.

"Minimum of one thousand," she told him. She had some cash in the house, but could stop at an ATM if she had to. "I hand you one thousand before we even talk. After that we *negotiate*. But it's going to have to be the straight-up truth. We can buy bullshit anywhere."

Stanko cleared his throat. "Fine," he said, all honorable and straightforward now.

"Okay then. Good."

"And who are you again, by the way?"

"Kirbi Mack," she told him, always having that slightly queasy feeling when she was forced to give personal information to sleaze-balls. "I'm a security consultant. Working for RayBright on contract."

"Okay, Kirbi Mack, when do you want to do this?"

Kirbi put her hand over the phone for a moment. "You able to go with me out to El Cajon for an hour or so?"

Baines nodded. Why not.

Into the phone, Kirbi said, "You game tonight? Say, seven thirty at your house?"

Stanko's turn to pause. "I get the money tonight. This isn't some scam you run on me."

"Nope. This is straight-up business. Minimum one thousand. Possibility of more. You down for it, bro?"

"Seven thirty. Bring the green stuff."

Kirbi chuckled for his benefit. "Seven-thirty."

Baines tipped his head back and laughed.

* * *

She came on time. Stanko had washed his face, brushed his teeth, and put on a clean pocket tee. On the phone she'd sounded young and cute. She was.

"Hi, Steve," a small black chick said when he opened the door. An edge to the chumminess. "I'm Kirbi Mack."

"Come on in," he told her.

A pony-tailed, older dude followed her inside. Stanko noticed he walked with a slight limp.

"This is Roy Baines. He works with me."

"Have a seat," Stanko said, waving his hand toward the couch.

235

The black chick's face wrinkled up. "How about we sit down out in the kitchen? I'm tired as hell. I'm afraid if I get too comfortable, I'll fall out."

"You got my thousand bucks?"

That'd been the come-on. If they couldn't deliver on that, then there was no point in even talking.

"Oh, yeah," she said, all shocked and apologetic. "Sorry. Pay the man, would you, Roy?"

The dude with the pony tail pulled a fat wad of bills out of his jacket pocket. He peeled ten off and handed them to Stanko. Hundreds. Beautiful.

"There you go," Stanko said. "You passed the test."

"Great," the black chick said, wandering toward the door to the kitchen.

She'd already plopped herself down at the table, all relaxed, by the time Stanko caught up with her. Pushy. Playing a power game maybe.

He watched her get out a little notebook and pen, giving him a raised-eyebrow look and modest little smile.

Stanko sat down next to her. He figured her for maybe twenty-eight or thirty. Nice butt. Hard to tell about the rack with the jacket on, though.

Mr. Pony Tail slid into a chair on the other side of her. He gave Stanko a carefully blank look.

"Well?" Stanko said.

"Right." She nodded to herself, putting on a show of thinking real hard about what she wanted to say. "Was it you who told *Homeland Security* about the Creighton crew coming once a month? How that would be a good time to rob the place?"

She'd made little double quotation marks in the air when she said Homeland Security. Then held her pen ready above the notebook page to take down his answer.

Stanko caught himself starting to squirm in his chair and stopped himself. Fuck that.

He put a fake, you're-so-amusing smile on his face and just looked at her.

When he hadn't spoken for maybe five seconds, she said, "Like I said on the phone, Eric and John aren't interested in prosecution. Or lawsuits. Or retribution. RayBright wants info. So simple question—hundred dollar question. Did you mention Creighton to this supposed fed?"

The words were hardly out of her mouth before Pony Tail laid a fan of five twenties on the table.

"Yeah," Stanko, picking them up and putting them with the rest in the pocket of his tee-shirt. "The answer is yes." Then he had a revelation. He caught the black chick's attention and gave her the fake smile again. "Ah. You asking means somebody did it, doesn't it? Robbed the place by coming in when the Creighton guys did."

She nodded at him, then shrugged. Like it was no big deal. Of course.

"You ever meet this *Homeland Security* guy in person?" In like a skeptical tone.

Stanko shook his head.

"What did his voice sound like on the phone?" He must have looked lost about what she meant, because she went on without waiting for him to say anything. "Did he sound old? Young? Educated? Deep voice? High voice? Any kind of accent?"

This was interesting. She saw he was taking the question seriously and she gave him a little smile of encouragement. Stanko tried to think back to his conversations with the guy.

"Older dude," he told her, folding his arms across his chest. "Maybe in his fifties or sixties." He shrugged. "I pictured him in a suit, calling from some office in Washington. So, he was believable. You know what I'm saying?"

She nodded.

237

Stanko had never gone out with a black chick. She was hot. He pictured himself being seen with her, walking on the street or in the lobby of a movie theater.

"As far as accent," he said, making a face, trying to think, "I don't know. Nothing obvious. He wasn't from Boston or New York or from the South. Just sounded like a normal guy, I guess."

"Deep voice? High voice?"

Stanko could hear the call in his memory. "He had a low voice. Oh, and sometimes in the later calls he got kind of grouchy."

A look flashed between her and Pony Tail, and he dealt Stanko another five twenties, face up on the tabletop. Stanko lazily picked them up.

"How many times you talk with him?"

Stanko had to count. "Four."

"He always called you."

"Yup. I never called him."

"Did you save his number when he called?"

Stanko grinned and showed her an exaggerated nod at this. Impressed with her.

"I didn't think about it at first," he said. "Then the second time I looked at the number and saw the area code was local. So I knew he wasn't calling from Washington."

She stopped him. "Did he say he was calling from there?"

"No, but he kind of implied it."

"But you *do* have that number for me," the black chick asked him now. He liked that he had something she wanted.

He didn't catch the signal this time—maybe she kicked him under the table—but Pony Tail came across with another hundred.

Stanko didn't touch the bills.

"Ought to be worth more than that," Stanko told her, seeing his moment and pushing it. It was like poker. When you got the big hand, you bet that pot up as much as you could. Who could fault a guy for that?

She waved her little manicured hand, blowing off this idea of more money. "Could just be a 7-Eleven pay phone. Or one of those throwaway phones. So then it doesn't do us any good at all."

She looked at him all doe-eyed, waiting. His move.

Pony Tail added another five twenties, making two hundred. But then the black chick put her hand on the pile and pulled it toward her a few inches.

"You do have the number?" she asked.

It was Stanko's turn for a little drama. Not allowing himself any sort of smile, he reached past where her hand was holding down the currency. She flinched just a tiny bit, like he was maybe making a grab for the money. Or for her.

Now he couldn't help himself. He felt a grin creeping onto his face.

Picking the pen from her hand, he wrote ten numbers in her notebook. He did this upside down and backwards, showing off a bit. He hoped he got the fours right.

"You looked it up and memorized it before we came?"

Stanko refused to answer but guessed she could see from his eyes that she was right.

She gave this cute little to-die-for chuckle. "Steve, you're a piece work, you are."

"Am I?"

She pushed the money toward him across the table.

Pony Tail tried to stay out of things, like he was just along for the ride. But Stanko could tell the dude didn't like or approve of him. And especially the cutesy way he was getting along with the black chick.

Like maybe he wanted something going with her, himself, but wasn't getting anywhere.

From her jacket now she took some photos and handed them to Stanko.

He flipped through them. "That's Janie from Accounting."

"Recognize the guy with her?"

He went through the whole bunch. "You know what?" he said, surprised he remembered. "I think I met this one outside the donut shop down the street from RayBright. Couple weeks ago. If it's the same guy."

"Important question," the black chick said, tipping her head for emphasis. "Thinking about his voice. Could he be the guy who called you on the phone?"

"Nope," Stanko said. He knew this idea was wrong immediately. He tapped the top photo. "*This* guy had an accent. From the South somewhere."

She nodded, as if it all made sense. She must have kicked her buddy under the table again, because another hundred bucks came his way. Stanko added it to the bulging wad already straining his pocket.

TWENTY-SIX

Mark didn't really trust the old man.

All he knew was, that if the roles had been reversed the night before, things would have been different. Way different. Because if the old man had drawn down on *him* and tried to rip *him* off, Mark would've simply doornailed the old doofus, right then and there. Just left him by the side of the road without a second thought.

So okay, the old man had now acquiesced in Mark extorting himself back into the game. And had even generously agreed to a sort of partnership where Mark got a share of the profits.

But was this slippery, wrinkled-up Mr. Potato Head really going to come through in the end? Or was he just saying what he had say to lull Mark? Would Mark's reward for his help be a large chunk of money—or a sudden bullet to the head?

Earlier in the day, Mark had purchased a handgun of his own. Something to defend himself with. Just in case.

As he and the old man now left the hotel and headed across the street to the Embarcadero, he toyed with it in the baggy pouch-pocket of his hoodie. But if he'd been hoping for reassurance from the thing, he was disappointed.

First of all, he knew it wasn't much of a weapon. Nothing more than a shabby little popgun acquired in a last-minute, street-corner transaction. Even he could see that.

Second came the problem that Mark was by no means a shooter. In fact, he'd never fired this or any other firearm. The closest he'd come to *shooting* at anyone or anything was spending a few hundred hours playing geeky games like World of Warcraft.

And third, he knew that just bringing a gun into a situation put more at stake. Doing so upped the ante. It increased the likelihood that he might himself be hurt or killed.

Because bringing a gun implied that the bringer intended to use it. Therefore others felt perfectly entitled to use their own weapons on the bringer. Maybe even if they hadn't considered doing so beforehand.

Would he pull it out and use it, if push came to shove—either on the old man, or on this guy who was supposed to buy the Merman thing? Mark didn't know.

He and the old man were currently walking south, leaving the Star of India behind. A cold damp breeze was coming in off the bay. Mark was glad he'd dressed warm.

"Let's go over how we're going to work this, okay?"

Mark nodded. "Okay."

"What I'd like you to do is count and verify the money, while I handle security." A threesome of college-age girls were approaching, walking arm in arm. The old man waited until they passed by before making a pistol by extending his right thumb and forefinger. "If necessary, I protect our interests."

"Is that why we're down here—Seaport Village again?"

"Yeah."

"The guy I shot pictures of last time," Mark said.

"Correct. He told me on the phone he wanted a public place to do the deal. So nobody got ideas. Hopefully he hasn't gotten any ideas, himself."

"You think he has in mind to get devious on us?"

The old man pulled a beats-me face and shrugged his muscular shoulders. He wore a bulky pea coat, watch cap, and jeans. It made him look kind of nautical.

Mark blew out a breath. "What I'm saying is, how afraid of this guy should we be?"

242

The old man pondered the question. "I don't underestimate him. I don't put anything past him either—including maybe trying to rip us off or kill us. But *afraid of him*? No."

Mark believed him. The old man was Original Gangster all the way. Someone who'd relied all his life on his streetsies, and who backed things up by putting the hurt on those who gave him problems.

Mark didn't consider himself a coward. But he'd never dealt in physical violence. Early in life, as a tall, gangly kid in the schoolyard, he'd quickly decided violence was not his arena. His gifts and strengths were best expressed elsewhere.

Nevertheless, here he was, striding along in the chilly darkness toward physical danger. Maybe it was best to think of it as just another drug deal. He'd participated in enough of *those*. He tried to reassure himself with this comparison.

"Where's the, uh, item we're selling?"

"Funny you should mention it," the old man said.

Then gave a little jerk of the head and veered left across the wide walkway. Mark followed. Wordlessly, he and the old man jaywalked across the main thoroughfare, then headed up a side street to a parking lot.

Mark looked for the box truck, but didn't see it. "What are you driving?"

"The white truck was too hot. I dumped it. I'm the van there on the end."

Ahead, over near one of the lot's overhead lights, Mark made out a small, national-chain rental vehicle. "How'd you get it up and in?"

"The device?"

"Yeah."

"The van has a slide-out loading ramp."

"We going to offload it for the buyer?"

243

The old man stopped next to the driver door, put his hands in his pockets, and sighed. "Don't know. If it comes down to it, I can always let him take the van with the thing in it—then report it stolen tomorrow."

Mark gave a vague nod to this, glancing around.

Earlier, he'd roamed the waterfront, nervously passing time before the six o'clock meeting. Maybe it was his lack of sleep, maybe it was the Ritalin he'd taken, but now, even more than then, he was struck by the weirdness of it all.

He felt he was on some tripped-out movie set.

The looming downtown skyscrapers. The city's bright lights reflecting off a low, hazy cloud cover. The incongruity of the Star of India, a wooden clipper ship, and the Midway, a huge steel aircraft carrier—both permanently docked nearby as tourist attractions. The funky smell of the bay. The strange honking bark of what proved to be an actual seal.

Mark lit a cigarette, looking to regain his focus and shake off this sense of eeriness.

As he exhaled a long first drag, he watched the old man drift back to the rear of the van. Then beckon for Mark to follow. It suddenly came to Mark that if the old man were going to kill him, it might be now, in this remote, deserted spot.

He hesitated a moment, fingering his revolver, wondering what to do. Of course *he* could just as easily use the opportunity to shoot the old man. The situation cut both ways.

Could he do it—pull the weapon out and fire it at the old geezer?

Taking another puff on his Marlboro, and adopting a casualness he didn't feel, he rounded the corner of the van. The old man was seated on the vehicle's platform bumper. Mark sat down next to him.

Neither spoke for several seconds, and when Mark could take it no longer, he said, "So, let's talk about what you want me to do. Specifically."

"First let me see your gun."

Mark turned his head, startled by the suggestion. But then met the old man's eyes in the dimness. "My gun?"

"Yeah, show it to me."

Was this an attempt to disarm him?

"Here?" Mark said, miming a wary glance around.

The old man was grinning. "Just slide it out enough for me to get a quick peek. Shield it with your body if you want."

The moment was electric with mojo. Mark's heart was pounding in his chest now. He was tempted to draw and shoot first, to protect himself, to eliminate the threat he faced.

Hell, what did he need the old man for anyway? Couldn't he simply go down to Seaport Village on his lonesome and make his own deal with the buyer? Or if that felt too dicey a proposition, there was always selling the device back to RayBright.

"Something wrong?"

Mark felt paralyzed. He swallowed. "No."

"I just want to see it, okay?"

Mark nodded. Grasping the weapon lightly by the handle, he slowly brought it out from the front pouch of his hoodie. "Thirty-two caliber," he said, then numbly handed it over. "Holds five bullets, but I only have three." He laughed at absurdity of what he was saying.

The old man laughed along. "You fire it at all?"

Mark shook his head.

The old man shrugged, turning the gun as he examined it. "Here's some advice then," he said in a quiet voice, passing it back to Mark. "That's a *very* short barrel. In order to have any chance of hitting something you're going to have to be *very* close. Okay?"

"How close we talking about?"

"Four or five feet."

Mark winced. "Jeez," he said, getting a sudden sick feeling.

"Seriously, kiddo, your best bet, if it comes down to it, is to put the thing right up *against* the guy before you pull the trigger. Okay?"

Again, the old man made a pistol shape with his hand. Then brought it up to Mark's belly. The image was too vivid. Only by a supreme act of will was Mark able to overcome an impulse to jump back from this blunt, gnarly forefinger of a barrel so close to him.

"Anyway," the old man went on, "back to the handover. You know anything about bulk cash?"

"In what respect?"

"As in, two million dollars in hundreds is twenty thousand bills. And if it's from a bank, banks do a hundred bills to the stack. Which means—"

"Two hundred stacks," Mark said, always enjoying the chance to show off his head for figures.

"Right."

"So how close a count you want me to do when I do it?"

"Just rough."

"Okay."

"Now this guy's already fronted me some earnest money. But that doesn't mean he's for real to the tune of two million bucks. And it doesn't mean he wouldn't just as soon drive away from this little meeting with both the two million *and* the device."

"So how do we handle that?"

The old man frowned. "It could be he's looking to off us right there—soon as he's sure we brought the thing he wants. Or, he could try to bamboozle us with some jive about paying all or part of the money later. Or, try to make a bogus pay off in some way—make us *think* he's giving us the two million but really not be."

"Let's not let him do any of that."

"Let's not," the old man agreed.

"So we need to be ready for anything."

"Yeah. It's even possible this whole thing is a set up, and as soon as we show the FBI swoops in to bust us. But that doesn't seem likely. They could have popped us last night at RayBright if that was the case."

"If we end up cell mates, you could teach me bridge," Mark said.

The old man grinned at the joke. "Sure."

"So what specifically do you want me to do when we get there?"

"Job one for you is to do a down-and-dirty paw through the cash. Look for anything hinky, okay?"

Mark took a pull on his cigarette, held it, and blew out a thoughtful plume of smoke. "No counterfeit bills with all the same serial number. No all-sequential numbers. No cut up newspaper that's not really money."

"Kiddo, I knew you were the right man for the job."

"What's our plan if it turns out to be a burn?"

"Good point. We better have a code."

"Okay," Mark told him, but in a tone that said he didn't understand. A code?

"First of all, you don't let on if you see it is a burn. The instant he or they see that *we* see, they might decide it's time to try to kill us. Instead, we play dumb for as long as possible. How's this: If either of us says the word *copacetic*, that means *count* or *cash*. Two *c*'s. Okay?"

"Okay."

"*Copacetic* means *count* or *cash*. You find out something's wrong with the cash, you put on a big smile, and say, 'Seems copacetic, Harve.' That's not much of an edge, but it might buy us a few seconds. You following me here?"

"Yeah, I like it. I got another one."

The old man gave him an intrigued look.

"*Right on* means *run*," Mark said. "Means bolt the fuck out of there. Save ourselves."

"Works for me," the old man replied with a shrug.

But Mark had a feeling he was just saying this. He wondered if someone the old man's age and build could run very far or fast. Besides, the old bastard's instinct was probably to stand and fight it out. Not run.

"So how does it happen? There by the same picnic table?"

The old man shook his head. He pulled back the sleeve of his pea coat to get a look at his watch. "Out in the main lot. Forty-one minutes from now."

"Okay."

"He said not to worry about recognizing him, because he'll recognize me."

"'Cept we know what he looks like," Mark said.

"That's another edge."

"So we both go in the truck?"

"No, you walk over ahead of time. Do some snooping around. You see anything you don't like, you call me. I do likewise, if I see anything. At seven, be ready and just kind of happen over to where I'm parked when you see him show up."

Mark nodded but had a thought. "You don't think he might try to jerk us around. Meet there but want to go somewhere else." Like some dope deals.

"He can try, but I'm not putting up with much."

"Good."

"We all set then?"

"Yeah," Mark said, getting to his feet.

The old man remained seated on the bumper. He and Mark exchanged thumbs ups, then Mark turned and strode away, back toward the water. Once he crossed the street and reached the Embarcadero, he bore left along the walkway, heading south.

Seaport Village wasn't far.

But when he got there, he was surprised to find a ghost town. Because, although all the stores appeared lit and open, he saw little human activity. And there couldn't have been more than twenty cars parked out in front.

Was the reason for this lack of business the brisk temperature? The fact that the holidays were over? The time of night?

Mark didn't know.

When he'd first arrived from Texas, he'd hooked up with a guy with a funny name. Rex, that was it. Guy with a skull and crossbones tattooed on his groin.

They'd binged through a couple of days of rough sex and drugs. Driving around, doing touristy things. And one of the places they'd visited had been Seaport Village. But that had been Christmastime and the place had been rocking then.

Not so now.

Mark ambled along the empty sidewalks, marveling at this odd absence of people in a place usually so bustling. He eyed the little shops, but kept going until he got to the bookstore. Inside, he stepped to the snack bar and ordered their largest mocha latte.

The barista was a cute little dark-haired girl in a baggy red sweater. While she made his beverage, he tried to chat her up, but she was having none of it. Undeterred, he tipped her a dollar. Then carried his latte to the sidebar, where he stirred in six packets of sugar, an inch of half and half, and two airplane mini bottles of Southern Comfort.

It tasted just as good as he hoped it would.

Outside was a small wooden deck area that overlooked the front parking lot.

There, striking a bored pose, he sipped some more of his latte and gazed around. Just a harmless bystander. Maybe somebody waiting on a spouse who was still shopping.

The lot wasn't very well lit. Was this good or bad? Mark wasn't sure.

He methodically examined it, section by section, looking for tall, lean males and for silver BMWs. He saw neither. He descended to the sidewalk and dawdled along to his right, as if just aimlessly killing time.

Soon the sidewalk was interrupted by a street. On the other side, there seemed to be a second lot which he'd never noticed before. He crossed and followed along its edge, curving around left with the sidewalk. And when the sidewalk ended, continuing leftward in a circle along this smaller lot's perimeter.

Eventually meeting the cross street once more, he stopped to check his phone. It was still twenty-two minutes before seven. Letting his eyes roam the area as he did so, he took his time lighting a Marlboro.

Next he meandered the perimeter of the larger lot. He stayed in the shadows as best he could, trying to be both inconspicuous and observant. It wasn't long, however, before he'd done a complete circuit and was back at his starting point. In front of the bookstore where he'd gotten the latte.

He stood there for a few moments, feeling uneasy. He put out his cigarette and thrust his right hand back into the pouch of his hoodie, grasping and ungrasping the handle of his revolver.

Ahead, a massive hotel complex dominated his field of vision. What if he, the supposed watcher, was the one being watched? It made sense. Any of the darkened windows in the huge dual towers could very well conceal a man holding binoculars—or even a rifle with a scope.

Mark again checked the time on his phone.

Deciding to stay in motion, he reversed course and headed around in the opposite direction now. Ignore the danger and focus on the payday, he told himself. Play your part. Hit your marks.

By five minutes to seven, he'd finished his second circuit and was partway through a third when he caught sight of the distinctively painted rental van. It'd stopped to take a time-stamped ticket from the machine at one of the lot entrances. In the dimness, Mark could just make out the old man at the wheel.

A few moments later, the van came forward. The lot had at least a hundred empty spaces. The van eased down one aisle, reached the end, and turned back up the next.

Mark slipped up onto one of the curbed landscape islands. Into the shadows beneath one of its ornamental trees. One that didn't have any lights on it.

For the thousandth time, his eyes flicked about, surveying his environment, near and far.

The van reached the halfway point on the aisle and swung into a slot. Its headlights went off.

His phone vibrated in his pocket.

The old man said, "Anything going on?"

"Not as far as I can tell," Mark told him in a murmur.

"Okay, stay alert."

"Right."

Five minutes passed. Mark began to get a craving for another cigarette but restrained himself. He took a deep breath and shifted his position. He leaned the other hip now against the smooth trunk of the tree, hunching his shoulders against the chilly air.

Then the brake lights on an SUV blossomed bright red at the far end of the next row. One of four vehicles in a cluster there. Mark moved his attention to it.

Was this their guy?

He heard the sound of an engine starting. Then saw its headlights and taillights come on.

As if on their own, Mark felt his fingers grip the revolver in his hoodie pocket. His nerves were wound tight. He could feel his pulse increasing.

He watched the SUV's white backup lights come on, and it drift back out of the slot. However, once out into the aisle, it turned and headed toward the exit at that end.

False alarm.

Mark looked away and returned to scanning the area as a whole.

A full minute passed.

Then he caught sight of a male figure in dark clothing crossing from the other lot. Trundling a large, wheeled suitcase ahead of him. Staying away from the lights.

And there was something funny about his face, but what?

Wait—he was wearing a *ski mask*.

Mark was in motion.

By the time he got to the rental van, the old man was out and pulling open its rear doors. The van's dome light popped on inside. Its low-wattage illumination revealed the boxy gray shape of the Merman device.

The ski-masked buyer turned when he heard Mark come tooling up out of the darkness.

"My buddy's going to check the money," the old man explained.

The tall, lean man in the ski mask stepped back from the suitcase and said, "Let's get it done, then."

He had his hands in the pockets of a dark jacket.

Mark saw that the old man had his silenced pistol out, held down at his side.

But neither he nor the guy in the ski mask seemed tense. Two cool characters doing a multi-million-dollar illegal arms deal. Mark imagined himself telling the story at some indistinct point in the future.

He took a breath and stepped in. He squatted and set down the latte cup he still had with him.

The suitcase was one of the soft-sided kind. Tipping it down on its back, Mark zipped it open. In the faint light, banded stacks of currency were visible. He could make out Benjamin Franklin's face and the number 100 at each corner. He picked up one of the stacks and riffled it with the edge of his thumb.

Behind him he heard the old man ask, "You want to check what I have in the van here?"

"That's it," the buyer said with a glance in the open doors. "I trust you. Let's get this over with and go."

Mark put the stack back in its place. He picked up a couple more at random. Benjamin Franklin, Benjamin Franklin. He burrowed his hand down, feeling, counting the layers.

"All hundreds, right?" Mark asked the buyer over his shoulder.

"All hundreds. Two million bucks."

Mark didn't like the guy's brusque tone.

He multiplied the layers by the rough number of stacks. Got a number acceptably close to two million.

Then fished down for one of the lower-layer bundles, and brought it up. He broke the paper band with his thumb, and cut the stack like a deck of cards. George Washington's face surprised him. The inside bills were ones.

Not hundreds. Only the top bill was a hundred.

"How's it looking?" the old man asked. His tone nonchalant, acknowledging the buyer's impatience, but also letting Mark know to take as long as he needed to take.

Mark didn't answer yet.

Shielding the action with his body, he realigned the broken-banded stack and fitted it carefully into place. His mind racing, he tidied the array and laid the nylon-fabric top of the case back across the money. As he zipped it closed, he spoke without turning.

"Everything's copacetic, Harve."

"Good," the old man said, not missing a beat. "I like being rich."

253

Mark turned and picked up his coffee. He worked at keeping his expression and body language casual. He got slowly to his feet.

The buyer gave a kind of concluding nod. "Let's all get out of here then." He had a strong confident voice. A voice used to telling other people what to do.

The kind of voice Mark hated.

That was the second last thing Mark thought before things went crazy.

The *last* thing he thought was that the buyer, or his buddy with the automatic weapon, must have picked up on something. Must have somehow seen that Mark knew the money wasn't real. Or maybe the two of them had planned to open fire at this point anyway.

Because there were some noises and flashes off to the right. And simultaneous with that, something hammered the sheet metal of the van's left rear door, which was standing obliquely open.

An instant later, out of the corner of his eye, Mark saw the old man stagger back and fall. He hadn't even got off a shot.

The buyer had a pistol out himself now, bringing it up to point at Mark.

Mark had been pulling the lid off his coffee cup, as if about to take a drink.

Instead he threw about eight ounces of tepid sugary mess into the buyer's face. He'd been preparing to do this even before he saw the buyer's weapon come out of the jacket pocket.

Mark had to admit, the guy had good reflexes. He leapt well back in alarm.

However Mark had good reflexes too, and had splashed him good. The dark front of his ski mask was now dripping and glistening with liquid. And some of the liquid must have gone through the eye holes. Because even in the scant light, Mark could see him blinking furiously. The buyer continued backpedaling. The pistol waved in his hand, but still pointed vaguely in Mark's direction. The other hand was at his masked face, fingers rubbing at one eye, as though trying to clear his vision.

Mark took a panicked step and skidded somehow in the spilled coffee. He ended up on the ground, where he felt glad to be as more shots came now. These directed at him.

On instinct, he scrambled across the rough asphalt on his hands and knees. Then, dropping fully flat to his stomach, slid under the rental van. He banged his head in the process, but continued forward, wriggling and scrunching up, his hands pushing and flailing for purchase.

The undercarriage blocked him. He scraped his back on it and banged his head again.

Bullets were being fired under the vehicle now. Following him, angled to hit him as he struggled toward the front. Ricocheting off the pavement, inches from him and slamming noisily into the metal undercarriage.

In his fright, Mark ceased to be a self-aware human being.

Because it was a crazed and terrified beast that, an indeterminate period of time later, found itself on its feet and running down the sidewalk in front of the San Diego Convention Center. No longer at Seaport Village. But several blocks away now.

As if awakening from a nightmare, he slowed his headlong flight and bent from the waist. His chest was heaving, and his heart hammering. He realized he'd pissed his pants. He could smell it, as well as the strong stink of his own sweat.

What to do?

His van, what he'd driven downtown in, was parked in a pay lot almost half a mile away. Was it safe to try to make for it on foot? Or were the shooters out driving around looking for him? Him, the loose end, the witness?

Mark didn't know. He couldn't separate paranoia from sensible caution.

But, if he left the van where it was now, he knew it might well be towed in the morning, and probably impounded. He tried to think. His cache of drugs were in it, as well as his clothes and laptop. Important things.

But that didn't mean, if necessary, they couldn't all be replaced. He patted the right cargo pocket of his pants, bulging with the sack of cash the old man had given him an hour before. He still had that.

Ahead a short distance, he saw a cab pulled up to a red light. Yes.

Feeling like a prey animal, Mark did a desperate visual sweep of the area as best he could. Then raced out to the street, one arm held high as he ran.

TWENTY-SEVEN

Harvey was down on his back next to the rental van.

He'd been hit by a bullet in the lower belly, and it hurt like hell. The old-school Kevlar vest he had on under his pea coat seemed to have stopped it. But he felt like he'd been kicked by a horse. He could barely breathe.

The shot that had nailed him had come, not from the buyer, but from another shooter firing from somewhere to Harvey's right. It'd been a single burst of automatic weapon fire. And it sounded like the weapon had a suppressor, as most of the noise had come from the bullets puncturing one of the van's back doors.

The buyer seemed to be blasting away at the kid under the van.

Wild shots with a small-caliber pistol, it sounded like. Harvey turned his head to the left to see the kid slithering by like a frantic snake toward the front bumper, bent on escape. It looked like he made it. Because the shooting stopped and Harvey saw the buyer's feet come into view at the back.

Then a dark rectangular shape appeared and rose up. This had to be the suitcase with the money being wheeled to the back of the van and lifted in. When Harvey heard the rear doors slam shut, he knew he had to move. The buyer was likely getting ready to jump in and drive away.

The pistol was still clutched in Harvey's hand. He raised it and aimed as best he could, knowing he'd only get one chance. And sure enough, a few instants later, a shadowy figure came striding around the back corner of the van.

Harvey fired once, then again.

The first shot appeared to go wide, but the second looked like it struck the buyer in the leg. Because he seemed to crumple to one side before stumbling back out of sight.

Aware his life depended on it, Harvey summoned every bit of energy he had and willed himself to a sitting position. He couldn't stay where he was. He had to move.

If the buyer didn't get him, the other shooter with the automatic weapon soon would.

Pistol at the ready in his right hand, using his left, he reached up for the driver door handle. It was a stretch, and the pain, searing. But, getting a grip, he was able to heave himself up along the side of the van to a more or less standing position.

This done, he leaned back and let his weight draw him toward the van's front. His left shoulder bearing him, he skidded it along the dusty metal surface about four feet off the ground in a series of tiny backward steps. It was awkward. He tried to cover his retreat with the pistol, but the thing shook crazily in his hand.

At last, around in front of the vehicle, he crouched. He wanted to drop all the way to the ground once more to look for feet, but wasn't sure he'd be able to get back up again if he did.

He set his mind to ignore the pain in his belly. That would be for later.

He stole a quick look left down the other side of the van. Then ducked back. Nothing.

He took a shuddering breath and trotted clumsily down along that side.

The automatic fire had come from the west. Probably from the small cluster of the cars parked at the end of the lot. At the rear of the van, Harvey peeked around the corner.

The buyer was nowhere in sight. But not too far away, a young man was visible, walking nonchalantly toward the van from just the direction the shots had come.

A couple of other cars were parked down the lot beyond the van, behind Harvey.

This guy could simply be a tourist or shop clerk heading for one of them.

No, Harvey thought not.

He forced himself to wait, letting the young man get closer and giving himself a better look. Broad shoulders. Dark hair. Relaxed gait.

But then the tell—the right arm looked just a bit less mobile than the left. Both swung slightly as the young man ambled along, but the right one less so.

Harvey stepped out, his own weapon hanging out of sight at his side.

He waited, watching the young man approach. He saw no detectable flinch or start when the young man caught sight of him. Then the young man's arm began to rise, coming up in a smooth arc. Some sort of machine pistol was visible now.

But Harvey had already put two bullets into him before the weapon's thick barrel reached horizontal.

As the young man collapsed, Harvey's gaze swept the area several times, looking to see if anyone else was present. Either the buyer with the small caliber pistol. Or some looky-loo witness of a bystander, attracted by the sound of shots.

He saw no one.

Where had the buyer gone? Had he bailed? Or was he lying in wait somewhere to get in a quick pot shot when Harvey turned his back?

Harvey glanced down at the pavement to his right. Three casings glinted in the dim light. He stooped to pocket them and searched for the fourth, finding it just under the van.

259

The night before, he'd left brass in the corridor at RayBright. By policing up what was here tonight, he was hopefully removing any obvious forensic connection between the two events, but the pistol had to go. He pocketed it now with a sense of regret. Though it'd been a reliable friend for a long time, he'd have to dispose of it.

Ballistically matchable bullets fired from it were now probably lodged in the young man—and maybe even in the leg of the buyer.

He couldn't take the chance.

Opening the back doors of the van, Harvey checked quickly to see that the suitcase was there. It was. He wondered what it was the kid had noticed wrong about the money. Why he'd given the Hey Rube.

But there was no time to determine that now.

He needed to go. A siren was audible in the distance. That didn't necessarily mean it was a police car or ambulance headed to Seaport Village, but why wait to find out?

Behind the wheel a few moments later, Harvey pulled out his wallet and phone. Took the parking ticket out of the wallet, as well as a wad of singles and fives. Swapped his knit watch cap for a Padres cap with a bill, a bill he could pull down low over his face. Then sought to further disguise himself with the addition of his reading glasses.

At the lot's exit booth, the young female parking attendant peered up from what seemed to be a textbook. She gave him a distracted look. Good.

Harvey hadn't seen any cameras, but people had memories. As he stretched to pass her the ticket with his right hand, he kept his head tipped forward and his phone up to his left ear, pretending to be preoccupied with a call. Out of the corner of his eye he watched her run the ticket. Then heard her tell him the amount.

Nodding, he picked out the exact amount from his lap, and handed it over. But still never looking at the attendant, nor allowing her a good look at him.

When she raised the barrier, phone still to his ear, Harvey rolled forward and out.

A few blocks ahead on Pacific Highway, he continued to hear sirens. He needed to put distance between himself and the scene he'd left behind. Continually checking his mirrors, he headed for the freeway.

By the time he pulled into his favorite little industrial park, the adrenaline in his system had worn off. His midsection throbbed. The hyper-alertness and tension had abated, leaving him with a sense of anti-climax.

Once the bay door was unlocked and raised, Harvey transferred the suitcase to the red pickup. Wheeled the pickup out and the rental van in. Then hid the van under the blue tarp.

Outside, sitting in the pickup, he sipped at a bottle of water and tried calling the kid. But got only an *unavailable* recording from the service provider. He hit redial with the same result. Sighing, he capped the water and put the phone away.

Later at the ranch, he half expected to find the kid's van parked in its usual spot. It wasn't. Dorothy's Mercedes was missing also, but he remembered she was visiting her sister in Riverside. Good. He didn't want to answer any questions. Not tonight, not in his current state.

In his office, he hoisted the suitcase onto his desk with a grunt of pain.

Any anesthetizing effects of adrenalin were long gone.

In the bathroom, he took off his pea coat and shirt and the Kevlar vest. Shirt and coat had tiny punctures in a similar place. The vest had a corresponding ragged hole a few inches from the bottom edge. On its inside, a protrusion in the lining indicated where the slug had been deformed and caught in the dense fibers, not quite passing through.

Harvey beheld himself in the mirror. Small blotches of blood were visible on his undershirt, just to the right of his navel. And when he pulled up the shirt's bottom, there was an ugly, swollen, crater-like depression. A second belly button, puckered, red all around, though not actually bleeding too bad.

Harvey got a couple of painkillers from an old prescription and downed them with some water slurped from the tap. Then stepped into the shower, hoping the medicine would take effect quickly.

His whole torso seemed to hurt.

He stayed under the hot water until it ran out. Dried off. Put a large adhesive bandage over the wound. Slipped into a robe. And walked out to the kitchen to snag a bottle of tomato juice from the fridge.

Down the hall in his office, he seated himself behind the desk. But immediately got back up, wincing with pain at the abrupt movement, and closed the room's drapes. It was no time to be careless in any way.

Once more at his desk, he took a first sip of tomato juice, and unzipped the suitcase.

A short while later, using pad and paper, he arrived at an approximate amount.

Just shy of sixty thousand dollars.

Yes, there were two hundred bundles. But not all the bundles contained the full hundred hundred-dollar bills. If that were so, the total would have added up to the promised two million. Instead, most of the bundles contained only *two* hundred-dollar bills—one on the top, one on the bottom, and in between, ninety-eight one-dollar bills.

Each of the deceptive bundles, in other words, contained only two hundred ninety-eight dollars. Not the expected ten thousand.

This is what the kid must have noticed.

Despite the way things had gone, Harvey felt a sense of gratitude. At least he'd gotten sixty K out of the deal. He'd pay the kid his third, twenty K, and use the rest to selectively shore up his own shaky money situation as best he could, ASAP. It wasn't enough to set things right, but it was better than a poke in the eye with a sharp stick.

The device? Like the kid had noted the night before in the pickup, there was always RayBright. Who else would even know what it was? What was he supposed to do, run an ad on E-Bay or Craigslist?

Top Secret Chinese Missile Guidance Hardware. Serious inquiries only.

If he in fact ransomed it back to RayBright, the transaction would have to be handled carefully. Ransom was a very difficult crime to get away with.

Harvey put the money back in the suitcase and rolled it into his closet, out of sight.

His belly was starting to feel better. It appeared the years-old painkillers had retained at least some of their potency. He wandered out into the living room and turned on the TV, wanting to see if there was any news coverage of what'd happened at Seaport Village. He could find no mention of it on any of the local channels.

Eventually, tipped back in the recliner, he fell asleep....

Only to be awakened a short time later by his ringing landline.

Without thinking, he pulled the recliner's handle and leaned forward to sitting position. The pain was instantaneous. Grimacing and groaning, he shuffled his way across the room and picked up.

"Hello," he said, interrupting Dorothy's recorded message. He looked at the time display on the phone. One nineteen a.m.

"How you doing, Harve?" The kid, sounding drunk.

"I'm good. Where are you?"

"Downtown, staying with a new friend, you could say."

"Glad to hear you're okay."

"I wasn't sure *you* were."

Harvey leaned on the kitchen counter, closing his eyes, focusing. "I'm good. But let's be careful what we say, alright?"

Several moments of silence followed. Then, "The walls might have ears?"

"You never know. Let's meet and talk in person. Say, day after tomorrow?"

"Okay."

"You cool till then?" Harvey asked.

Another silence. "Yeah. I'm cool."

"So, Sunday then. You know where we first met?"

"Uh-huh."

"How about there, out front, seven at night."

"All right," the kid agreed. Then, with a laugh, went on. "Tonight was quite the *adventure*, though, wasn't it?"

"You got that right."

Again, laughter. "Okay. See you Sunday night."

"One last thing, kiddo. I just wanted to say, I liked the way you handled yourself tonight."

"Did you really? Well, thanks, Harve."

(TWENTY-EIGHT)

"Counter offer," Kirbi said.

It was Sunday. She was talking into a borrowed landline at the cashier's desk of an Olive Garden. She forced an index finger into her other ear, trying to block out the lunchtime noise around her.

The male voice went on, "I'm listening."

Not Mark Hatcher—or rather, Martin McGarrity—she'd decided.

Somebody who sounded older. The shorter, brawnier of the two robbers. The one who'd pretended to be from Homeland Security when manipulating Stanko.

"I was thinking," Kirbi said, "of something more in the neighborhood of *one* hundred thousand." A moment before, he'd asked for five times that.

A silence stretched on the other end. "That's a pretty low-rent neighborhood. I'm afraid I had in mind something a little more *upscale*."

"Let me add something to the bargain, then. A no-comeback rider to the contract. Meaning, RayBright will sign a paper in which they agree that no crime was ever committed. Therefore, no prosecution. You take the money and walk away. Everybody's happy."

"That's not much of a sweetener."

"It's not?"

"No, because as of now, I'm not looking over my shoulder. I'm not worried about being prosecuted."

"Maybe you should be," Kirbi said, throwing his breezy tone back at him. "You guys are good. I'm professionally impressed." And she was, and let him hear it in her voice. "But nobody's perfect. Everybody leaves a trail. I stay on it long enough, your ass is mine."

"You haven't done so good so far."

"Well, as far as you, sir, I don't know much about you yet. But your buddy, Mark, I'm *all over* him. Him I find first because I get the feeling he's not wrapped too tight. An hour after we have him, I bet he gives you up, right down to address, shoe size, and favorite color."

"Maybe."

Kirbi wasn't sure how this was going. The last thing she wanted to do was overplay it and lose him. But then, *he'd* called *her*. He was the one who'd arranged for her to be at Olive Garden to take the call.

Which had to suggest need on his part.

Though she had to wonder if this was a real offer. Had the robbers really stolen Merman just to try to ransom it back to RayBright? Her instincts said no.

So maybe Merman had already been sold somewhere else, and the guy was just trying for a little extra on the side by selling RayBright a big load of nothing? An hour before, she, Van Horne, and the general had hashed all this out in a conference call. The consensus had been that she go ahead and explore the ransom offer on behalf of the company.

They had to try to get it back, even if they had to pay big money for it. RayBright's reputation was at stake. But deep down, what her two employers *really* wanted was for Kirbi to get it back for free. Hit the thieves over the head, handcuff 'em, and wheel the device back into RayBright.

Right. Well, people in hell *really* wanted ice water.

Free wasn't likely to happen. Sure, she'd jump on the opportunity if it presented itself, but were the robbers going to oblige by being stupid and careless in ways they hadn't shown themselves to be so far? Kirbi didn't think so.

She suppressed a sigh. All this could have been avoided if RayBright had just listened to her in the first place. If only they hadn't been complacent. She felt like the Trojan princess the gods had given the gift of prophecy—but with the proviso that she never be believed.

Regardless, Kirbi would do her best to get the thing back.

"So this no-prosecution thing is of no interest to you," she said, pressing on.

"Well, as of now, there *is no* prosecution, anyway, right?" His tone was lazy and baiting.

"What do you mean?"

"RayBright's not letting it out that anything's missing," he said and paused. Then, with an easy laugh, added, "Or am I wrong?"

Kirbi wondered where he got his information. It was scarily right.

"That may or may not be an accurate statement—"

"Come on."

"—but you do know there's a deadline." Kirbi struggled to decide how much to give away. "The item is due to be returned in three days. If RayBright can't come up with it by then, the matter will be turned over to the feds. And when the feds are after you on something connected with national security—time, money, and manpower are infinite. So you could save yourself a lot of trouble by dealing with us *before* the deadline."

"Really?" he said, playing it off. But she thought she might've heard the minutest of changes in the timbre of his voice.

"Yeah."

"What's their final, no-bullshit offer, Kirbi Mack? Tell me. We'll see if we can get this thing done."

"You're not going to like it."

"Beat me, hurt me, make me write bad checks."

"One hundred thousand and the non-prosecution, no-lawsuit guarantee."

She heard an audible exhalation of breath on the other end. She forced herself to say nothing.

Kirbi noticed the young female cashier eyeing her. Maybe picking up on Kirbi's tension. She'd given the woman twenty bucks for the imposition of taking the call and tying up the phone.

"Okay," the guy said. He sounded reluctant, but not as though he held a grudge about it.

Was he giving in too easily? Did this suggest it was all a scam? That he was just trying to get what he could get, having already sold it? Just going for the sucker play?

Kirbi hoped the hell not. "How and when are we going to do this, then?"

"You can forget the no-comeback paperwork. Just have the money ready by tomorrow afternoon. In cash. No tricks, no marked bills, no dye packs, no radio transmitters."

"I'm straight up if you're straight up."

"Good. I'll get in touch with you tomorrow at three."

"How?"

"I'll call you on the RayBright Security extension," he said, and cut the connection.

"Thank you," Kirbi told the cashier, handing the receiver back. "I appreciate it."

Maybe intrigued by what she'd overheard, the woman gave Kirbi an inquiring look.

But Kirbi only smiled and walked out the front door to her car.

She put in a call to Van Horne on her cell, and told him about the money and the arrangements.

Then punched in David Martinez's number and caught him up also. She wasn't sure she was supposed to include him in the circle of information. However, they'd been playing on the same team. And before this whole thing was over, she might very well need his help.

This done, Kirbi sat back in the seat for several minutes and tapped her hands on the bottom of the steering wheel, thinking.

TWENTY-NINE

In Jane's dream there were wind chimes.

Which *meant* something.

But this was all déjà vu, somehow, this whole thought pattern about wind chimes meaning something. Yes, but meaning what?

Meaning, wait…her phone. Her phone ringing. Chiming.

Jane rolled into a sitting position and listened more carefully. Where had she left her phone? It turned out to be on the chair nearby.

"Hello," she answered in an even voice.

"Jane, it's Ornetta Brown."

"Uh-huh."

"From Universal Parking. I got you those surveillance photos."

Jane sighed into the phone, embarrassed, annoyed at her memory. "Sorry, Ornetta. I was drawing a blank there for a second. Sometimes I've got a memory like a steel sieve. Yes, thank you for those. They helped a lot."

"The reason I'm calling you on a Sunday is I think I saw your boy."

Again, Jane drew a blank. But then—with an electric jolt—got it. "The guy with me in the surveillance."

"I wouldn't have noticed except for the shirt. It was the same black shirt with the single big, pink flamingo on the front."

In her mind now, Jane pictured it, and Mark wearing it.

"You saw him," she prompted.

"Yeah. In a bar downtown in the Gaslamp. Called The Pub. I was in there yesterday with my girlfriend. He was sitting at the bar, talking with the bartender. Same shirt, same curly hair. Tall skinny guy, just like in the pictures."

269

"Wow. I'm floored. I told you what this guy did to me."

"Yes. I thought you'd want to know."

"Ornetta, I love you. Thanks."

"You got it. Good luck. Oh, one more thing—he was barefoot."

"That's weird," Jane told her, examining the idea.

"Maybe he lives real close by."

Jane wasn't sure this logic followed, but put some enthusiasm in her voice. "I like it. Thanks again, Ornetta."

Jane switched off and lit a cigarette. It tasted like anger. Or maybe revenge.

Putting on her robe, she went into the kitchen to make coffee. Which, when it was done, she took out to the balcony with her. And cross-legged in her Adirondack chair, toes tucked up under the robe for warmth, she then turned the matter over in her mind. What to do?

Despite it being the weekend, she and Deb had arranged a meeting at one o'clock to go over some things about her case.

Jane checked her phone for the time: nine thirty-seven.

She thought about what time she'd gone to bed the night before. She'd slept almost ten hours, which was unlike her. Her body must have really needed the rest.

The morning sun illuminated the front of the condo across the street. The sky above was a pale, cloudless blue.

She lit another Pall Mall, picked up her phone once more, and looked in her call logs for Kirbi Mack's number. Kirbi impressed Jane. Very smart. Very present. The kind of person who made you want to come off as no less than smart and present yourself.

Jane thought through what she'd learned from Ornetta. Thought how best to coherently convey it. Then made the call and waited.

Unanswered, after four rings the call went to voice mail.

Jane held the phone poised for a long moment, sucking her teeth, but switched off without leaving a message. She considered texting the information, but decided no.

Ten minutes later, cigarettes smoked and coffee drunk, she went back inside. Put the empty cup in the sink. Padded barefoot down the short hall to her bedroom. Then flopped down on her still unmade bed, gazing at the ceiling, arms folded across her chest.

What she felt about Mark was complicated. It was as if she could not let herself feel humiliation, turning it instead to anger. He'd told her everything she wanted to hear. He'd taken her dreams and sold them back to her.

Jane could hardly face in her mind what had happened.

And what she hated most was that she still hoped against hope in some sick way that he would apologize. She still had feelings for him. He had some kind of power over her from their one night together. In that very bed.

She jerked her head abruptly and got up.

Forty minutes later, Jane was parking her rental Ford in the same Universal Parking garage as she had the night of the concert. Weird. She thought of Ornetta seeing today's surveillance video and noticing her. She had a whimsical impulse to wave up at one of the cameras.

But then realized Ornetta had only checked the video because Jane had asked her to. Otherwise the woman likely had better things to do. Besides, if Ornetta happened to check, would she even recognize Jane?

Today she'd dressed in a loose cotton shift and floppy straw beach hat. Her trademark whitish-blonde hair was concealed in a dark silk kerchief. And instead of her usual contacts, today she had on an old pair of prescription sunglasses.

Jane bought a newspaper on the way. She already had directions from her phone, and found *The Pub* easily, five or six blocks from the garage. It had a brightly painted Union Jack above the entrance.

Approaching the wide, varnished-wood door, she was all confidence. However, hand out to take hold of the handle a moment later, it was a different story. She was suddenly overcome by panic. She froze.

Finally, putting a forefinger to her lips as if remembering something, she turned back the way she'd come.

Slowing her pace at the corner, she lit up a Pall Mall and turned left. Then briskly circled the block, smoking and mentally revving herself up. Until she arrived once more at wide, varnished-wood door.

Was Jane now ready?

She was.

Entering, she paused just inside to let her eyes adjust.

The place was about half full, maybe two dozen people present. Her gaze flicked over them, looking for Mark. He wasn't there.

The bartender in a crisp white shirt glanced up as she stepped over to the bar.

"Diet cola," she told him. "No ice."

He nodded. Young with a square jaw and blond crew-cut hair.

When she'd gotten her drink and paid for it, she put her back against the bar and surveyed the place once more. Dark wood panels everywhere. High, stamped-tin ceiling. Tables and chairs but also some nook-like booths.

Jane picked up her glass and wended her way to an empty booth in the far corner.

Once seated, she opened her newspaper in front of her.

After a few minutes, she got out her phone and tried Kirbi's number again. Again got only voice mail. And again, left no message. Nor sent any text.

Next Jane called Deb, begging off on their one o'clock meeting. She gave no reason, but made an elaborate apology for the inconvenience. Deb sounded a little miffed, but went along.

Jane broke the connection, feeling out of sorts.

She wondered if it'd been wise to come.

She supposed she just wanted to *see* Mark. To tell him what she felt. How insulted she was and how much of an asshole he was, leaving her in the car that night. And for screwing up her life in general.

But just what did she expect back? What?

Ideally, he'd look stunned and contrite. He'd tell her how deeply sorry he was. Tell her he was ready to go to the police with her and straighten things out. Then maybe…

Then maybe what?

God, he'd hooked her good. She'd given him her heart that night. You did that and you never got it back—not for the rest of your life.

Jane snorted out a breath. She was forty-five years old. She'd been married and had had long-term lovers. By now she should know female psychology, and should know her own idiosyncratic quirks.

The guy was fifteen years younger than she was.

You get a modest boob job, lose twenty pounds, and suddenly you're thinking somebody's *the one.*

How must she look to others—say, Patti or the people at work? Like some deluded cougar with a taste for young flesh?

It was all so insane and humiliating. Look, here she was, waiting at the watering hole. Hoping he'd show up.

But, come on, what was the likelihood of that?

Had Ornetta even seen him? Yes, she believed Ornetta. Because of the shirt, and because Ornetta had looked at the photos with her that day.

Jane nursed her diet cola for almost an hour. When it was done, she placed the empty glass on the bar and stepped outside for a smoke.

Over the next several hours a pattern formed itself.

She'd finish a soda every hour or so. Visit the ladies room. Circle the block another time or two while enjoying a Pall Mall. Then return to her favorite booth or, if it'd become occupied in her absence, another.

For a while, she passed the time with her phone. She organized all of her photos and music. Played ten games of Klondike solitaire. Texted catch-up messages to several friends and relatives she hadn't communicated with in a while. Visited her social media pages.

She'd been tempted to post *Staking out Gaslamp bar for guy who tried to ruin my life*, but thought better.

Eventually, Jane turned to the newspaper she'd brought. For the first time in her life, she read every single item. Even the Sports section and all the editorials. Even the masthead, advertisements, and classifieds.

For almost four hours, people came and went, but Jane remained.

There'd been something of a lunch crowd—the place almost filling up—but it'd dissipated about one-thirty. She spoke to no one and no one spoke to her. The weird little woman in the floppy hat and bandana, the one wearing sunglasses indoors.

By two-thirty, the place was back down to half full once more.

Bored, she re-examined them.

A lot of nondescript middle-aged tourists. A few deeply tanned locals and a few European backpacker types. Two guys sitting at a table, one lethargically trying to convince the other of something—salesman and prospect maybe. A solitary bearded guy drinking shots and looking off into space. And a tall young woman in front at the bar.

Of all present, the woman at the bar was the most animated. Jane couldn't hear what she was saying but, going by body language, she seemed to be flirting with the square-jawed bartender. Then, as the woman leaned forward to emphasize something she was saying, her top rode up in the back.

At which point, Jane felt the floor drop away beneath her.

In the gap that opened between long yellow skirt and short white blouse, a small tattoo was briefly visible.

Jane found herself becoming very still. She raised her newspaper in front of her, slouching down in her seat behind it. Then stole little peeks over the top, watching the woman and waiting for her to lean forward again to reveal the tattoo. A tattoo Jane was pretty sure she'd seen before.

With each secret glance, she tried to analyze the woman's physical being, aside from the clothes.

If it was a wig, it was a good one.

Jane wanted to see the face in profile, and the breasts. But the woman never seemed to turn.

Clearly, she had something going with the bartender. The way she leaned forward when she made a point. The way she touched his fore-arm. The way she tossed her head every once in a while.

Could this be Mark?

The idea seemed so preposterous, it staggered her. If she hadn't been *expecting* Mark to show up here, would she even give this woman a second look? No.

But the tattoo. Jane had to get a closer look at it. The tattoo would settle the question.

Despite feeling a slight vertigo, Jane forced herself to her feet.

If it was Mark, he wasn't going to recognize her anyway. He wasn't expecting her. He had no reason to be suspicious or on his guard.

And this possible Mark, this *woman*, hadn't turned around in the ten full minutes Jane had been watching her. Why would she now?

Heart slamming in her chest, self-conscious to the point of psycho-sis, Jane edged forward. One foot in front of the other. As if in a trance.

Nearer and nearer, making her way among the tables and people.

The bartender glanced past the woman's shoulder, toward Jane. Like maybe Jane was approaching to order another diet cola, no ice. Seeing this, Jane cut left toward the rest rooms. She made a waving-off gesture. No thanks.

But in the same instant she turned to do this, she let her eyes flick to where the tattoo peeked out beneath the bottom of the blouse, trying for a clear, close-up look at it.

She got one.

It was a tiny baby rattlesnake. Yellow and coiled to strike. She'd seen it on Mark that night in her bed. In playfulness, she'd kissed it.

Taking a shivery breath, Jane kept moving.

Down the hallway, then left again into the ladies room.

At one of the sinks, she took off her sunglasses. She examined herself in the mirror, as if there were something to learn. What?

Grimacing, she put her glasses in her shoulder bag and stepped into one of the stalls. Shut and locked the door behind her. Sat down on the closed toilet seat. Then got out her phone.

"Kirbi," Jane said in a hushed voice, surprised when the call was answered after two rings, "This is Jane Bouchet."

"Hi, Jane."

"I've found Mark."

Silence for a moment. "Mark Hatcher?"

"Yes. You won't believe this but he's dressed in women's clothes."

"Does he know you've...*found* him?"

"No. I'm in a bar down in the Gaslamp. Called The Pub." Jane gave her the address. "I got a tip, but didn't really believe it would pan out." She heard herself utter a nervous laugh.

"Hold on a minute," Kirbi said. Then seemed to be speaking with someone on her end. "Okay, listen. Stay right where you are. I'll be there as soon as I can. Maybe ten or fifteen minutes."

"If he leaves, I'm going to follow him," Jane heard herself say.

"Janie, please don't. This guy is very dangerous. Let's just keep this call going until I get there, okay?"

This seemed like a good idea. "Okay," Jane told her.

THIRTY

When Mark first noticed Jane, all tricked out in her disguise, it'd set his mind reeling.

He'd wanted to bolt—to slip quickly away, unseen.

But that left too many questions unanswered.

Like how had she *gotten onto* him? Was she here by herself, or was law enforcement involved? Also, did she somehow know about his nearby hidey hole?

So despite the nuclear force of the methamphetamine raging in his bloodstream, Mark put his hands calmly flat on the bartop and closed his eyes for several seconds. This was no time for panic. Panic was not an option. He needed to find out what was going on.

Yes, find out what was going on.

Opening his eyes, Mark raised a forefinger, catching the attention of Davey the bartender. He pointed to his now empty glass. And when Davey nodded, said to him, "I'll be right back," and turned to walk away toward the rest rooms.

The two of them had a thing, Mark and Davey. Mark had been staying in the man's condo and sharing his bed since the night of the robbery. They got along well. Davey seemed to find Mark's occasional drag tripping amusing.

Nevertheless, Mark had made sure Davey knew as little as possible about him. Nothing about prison or the warrants out on him from Texas. Nothing about Harvey or Jane or RayBright or Seaport Village. A matter of compartmentalization.

At the door to the ladies room, Mark hesitated.

He put his hand into his bag and grasped the handle of the revolver. Drew it. Then with his other hand, opened the door.

Jane had just come out of the stall.

She had her sunglasses off, and he could see the terror and astonishment in her eyes.

Her fear of the gun gave him confidence.

"How did you find me?" he asked.

He liked the intimidating snarl that came out in his tone. Usually, when he had on women's clothes, he worked to keep his voice higher, sweeter.

Her eyes were fixed on the weapon in his hand.

She seemed too stunned to speak.

"What are you doing here?" he demanded, getting in her face.

"I had some pictures of you printed out from the parking garage surveillance. The woman who works there called me because she thought she'd recognized you here."

"Seems like a lot of coincidence."

Jane's face contorted. "I'm telling you the truth."

"Who else is here?"

"Nobody."

"Nobody. No cops? Feds?"

She shook her head. She was looking at him in a different way now.

Mark touched the muzzle of the revolver to her chest, meeting her eyes and boring his threat into them. "Walk away, *right now*. Out the front door and keep going. I don't want to shoot you, but I will."

"*Fine*," she said back, surprising him, coming up with some attitude.

He just stared at her for another long moment then turned to leave.

That was when something extraordinary happened.

Mark had just dropped the revolver into his bag. He was at the door—weight on his right foot as he pushed the swinging door outward into the hallway—when he heard a grunt. It was all the warning he got.

Because a half second later he was slammed hard from behind.

Jane, he realized.

She'd jumped up on his back and thrown an arm around his neck. In surprise and disbelief, he stumbled forward, awkward in his three-inch heels. He felt her yank back on his head as he collapsed to the floor outside in the hallway.

Though he scrambled to get free, the arm around his neck was tightening. She was on top of him. He bucked, trying to shake her off.

"How do you like that, fucker?" she said, her voice loud in his left ear. "Chick fight."

The absurdity of this added to the unreality of the situation. Mark fought to break her hold. He knew he was stronger. He dug his fingertips into her forearm, trying to inflict pain and make her release him.

The arm across his windpipe wasn't really *choking* him. She couldn't maintain pressure with his wild twisting and thrashing. But even the slight feeling of suffocation was having its effect.

"Hey!" somebody shouted. "Take that outside."

Mark recognized Davey's voice. Saw his feet. He could feel Jane shifting atop him. Maybe Davey was pulling her off. He hoped so.

Now came Jane's voice, muffled, calling out, her face compressed against his shoulder. "Leave me alone. Phone the police. They're looking for this guy."

"Let her go," Davey said now, meaning Mark. "Let her go now. Come on, break it up."

Then in an instant of abrupt relief Jane was off him.

For a frozen moment, Mark didn't move. He took a couple of deep breaths and rolled onto his back. He saw Davey had her under the armpits from behind. Still, somehow she managed to drag him forward so she could land a savage kick to Mark's thigh.

Mark winced at the pain. He'd lost his wig and his skirt was pulled up on one side.

"Call 911," Jane shouted, whipping back and forth, trying to break free. "This is a *guy*. He's a wanted criminal. Call 911. Help!"

A group of bar patrons had gathered, looking on, aghast and curious at the same time.

Mark got his feet under him and made an effort to stand.

He put the wig on and gave it a quick, practiced adjustment. Stepped into his other shoe. Straightened his skirt. And resituated the strap of his shoulder bag.

"She's crazy, Davey," he said in a woman's voice.

Davey made no reply, but continued to restrain the struggling Jane.

Mark put on a sad expression. He turned to slowly look at her, shaking his head as if in disappointment and disapproval. Then sought the eyes of Davey and those looking on, enlisting their sympathy.

As he left, Jane called something after him. He missed exactly what though. Because by the time she said it, he was already striding across to the front door, mentally—if not yet actually—gone.

Outside, he bore left up the sidewalk and made another left at the corner.

Halfway up the block, he jaywalked across the street on a diagonal. As he did so he peered back over his shoulder, but saw no one in pursuit. Neither Jane nor any obvious law enforcement.

Still, the smart move would be to get to Davey's place, grab his possessions, and set about making himself scarce. Maybe even bolt San Diego altogether. His van was in Spring Valley, getting a cheap paint job, but there was nothing in it he truly needed. If necessary, the vehicle could be abandoned.

Then there was his meet-up with the old man in El Cajon in a few hours. At which time Mark hoped to receive his one-third slice of the Merman pie. A lesser pie now, granted, since the arrangement with the original buyer had gone bust. Still, if he was going to be making his *get-away*, every dollar would help.

Ahead at the corner, a dozen people were clustered, waiting for the Walk signal.

He joined them. Jostled impatiently to the front. And found himself having to fight down the urge to dash across against traffic.

Easy, he told himself.

You're high and jacked-up on adrenaline.

This is no time for recklessness.

You give in to panic and you're going to end up back behind bars.

THIRTY-ONE

A mere block away, Jane now stood on another curb.

She'd been *running*—something she didn't do a lot of at her age. And as a result of this unaccustomed effort, her chest was heaving and her heart pounding.

She'd come out of the bar almost a full minute after Mark. Which meant she'd had to take a blind chance on the direction he'd gone. Had she chosen wrong? She was beginning to think so. Because for all her desperate scanning of the cityscape around her, she was not seeing the color combination yellow and white.

Her spirits sinking, she continued to peer left and right, finally stepping into the street to walk south along a row of parked cars.

"Damn!" she said aloud.

But in the instant of uttering the word, happened to notice something ahead.

At the next corner, the light had just changed. A group of people were using the crosswalk. Among them, Jane thought she was catching flashes of yellow.

Was it him? Or rather, *her?*

Over the last few days, Jane had finally managed get her head around the fact that the guy she'd known as Mark was gay. Or bisexual, or whatever he was. But she was still in the process of absorbing today's discovery—that he also seemed to be a cross-dresser.

Jane waited, transfixed, peering intently ahead at the group crossing the street.

After a few moments, a tall woman in a flowing yellow skirt broke free from the others and strode jauntily ahead, brown hair bouncing on her shoulders.

Gotcha, Jane told herself.

Then set off up the street in pursuit.

For some reason she thought about Norman as she ran. Poor Norman. Mark had played him to learn RayBright's secrets, just as he'd played her.

Kirbi had mentioned that they'd found a diary Norman kept. One which told the story of his affair with Mark. An affair that Norman had heartbreakingly described as his first experience of love.

Kirbi had also passed along to Jane the coroner's findings. That Norman had killed himself. And that tests showed the finger had been cut off *after* he was dead.

So while technically Mark had not murdered Norman, he might just as well have.

Jane liked Norman and missed him. He'd been a good boss. She may have speculated about his sexuality over the years, but it hadn't been in malicious fashion. She didn't care in the least where he or anyone got their jollies.

Thus, finding out he was gay came as no big surprise. But that he'd been embezzling and was a compulsive gambler did. Bigtime. For one thing, Norman personified *cheap*. He ate cheap food, wore cheap clothing, and drove a cheap car.

Was this, Jane wondered, because he'd always been frugal, or because the gambling losses forced him to be?

Ahead, Mark still had a half block on her, but she was gaining.

Suddenly though, she watched him veer right, off the sidewalk toward the entrance to a high-rise. She was already driving her middle-aged body hard. She tried for more speed, but there wasn't much umph left to tap.

If she lost sight of him, she knew she was screwed. The high-rise was huge, and God knew how many separate units it contained. Also, this being downtown San Diego, there might be a security gate.

Was there?

Damnit, there *was*.

But wait, a small balding guy with a gray goatee was just coming out through it.

"Could you hold that for me, please?" Jane called out.

She could see he'd heard her. But a hesitation had come into his manner and he wore a conflicted expression. A panting, disheveled, oddly dressed female was asking him to break the rules. What to do?

She watched his eyes dart nervously from hers. Then his fingers released the gate, and the rectangular metal frame began to arc shut on its spring hinge. With a wild jump forward, Jane managed to catch it at the last moment.

"I know," she said as she slipped past him. "I look like exactly the kind of person you're not supposed to let in."

Inside, as the gate clanged shut behind her, she headed up the walkway.

And at the building's entrance got another break. A trio of teenagers was exiting just as she arrived. And the last of the three, a young man, politely held the no-doubt-locked door for her.

Jane thanked him and stepped into a dim lobby.

At once she halted, and—above the rasping sound of her breathing—strained to listen.

No, nothing. No clopping of a woman's high heels.

She trotted forward around the corner and found a pair of elevators. The doors to both were shut. But above the elevator on the right, numbers were flashing sequentially. The car on the right was ascending.

284

She pushed the button to summon the other elevator, but did not take her eyes off the flashing numbers. Eight. Nine. Ten. *Eleven.* The other car had stopped at eleven.

When the doors to the second elevator opened, Jane jumped in and thumb-punched the button for the eleventh floor.

Nothing happened for a few frustrating seconds. Then the doors finally began to glide shut. As the car rose, she struggled to think of something productive to do. Patting her shift pockets, she found her phone.

The screen was dark. The open call to Kirbi had cut out.

Jane tried redialing a couple of times and realized it wasn't going to happen. The display showed no service bars whatsoever. Interference from the elevator?

When the car stopped on eleven and the doors opened, Jane stepped forward, but not fully out. Blocking the doors open with a foot, she slowly peeked down the hallway. Left, then right.

No one. And when she listened, no sounds.

Doubt niggled at her. What now? If it was in fact Mark who'd taken the elevator up, among all these closed doors, how was she now going to find the right one?

Jane stepped out of the elevator into the carpeted hallway.

Behind her she heard the doors close and the elevator's whir of descent.

She tried her phone. Service. She punched in Kirbi's number.

Two rings, then an excited, "Jane!"

Jane kept her voice low. "I followed him from the bar. We had a fight."

"I'm double-parked outside the bar now. Where are you?"

Jane exhaled. "I'm not sure. We went at least two and half blocks. It's a high rise apartment building or maybe condos. I'm on the eleventh floor."

"The outside of the building—what color is it?"

285

"Yellowish. Like twenty stories high." Jane tried to mentally retrace her pursuit of Mark. "It's more or less east of The Pub, maybe *south* east. The entrance has an alcove thing and a dark orange security gate."

"Okay, I'm coming."

Jane thought of something else. "There's a little mini-market right next door. I can't remember what the sign says but it's in big green letters."

"Good girl," Kirbi said. "I'm heading your way as we speak. Stay on the phone."

Voices to her right made Jane turn.

An elderly couple had appeared, coming around the corner, the man carrying a wrapped gift under his arm. Her mind raced. Knowing her appearance worked against her, Jane reached deep for maximum charm.

"Excuse me," she began carefully. "Maybe you can help me."

The woman smiled and looked at her with expectation. The man reached past her with his free hand and pushed the button that summoned the elevator.

"I'm looking for my friends, Mark and Mary Hatcher. They told me they were staying on the eleventh floor, but they're not answering their phone." Jane held out the phone in her hand. "I was supposed to follow them up but we got separated."

"Hatcher?" the woman asked. "I don't think I recall that name." She looked at her husband, who thought for a long moment, then shook his head.

"They're twins," Jane went on, undeterred. "They're both tall— " She made a gesture of extreme height with her hand "—with dark hair. In their late twenties. Always nicely dressed. They don't live here, but they're staying with someone."

Jane was just about to turn away when the woman said, "Wait, I think I know who you mean. I ran into the boy a couple of times. Curly hair and long eyelashes."

"Yes!"

"I don't know which number, but it's down that way, around the corner." She turned to the man. "Where the Hargroves live."

"It'd be…twenty-one through twenty-five," he said, looking off as he thought it through. "Eleven twenty-one through eleven twenty-five." He pointed, then crooked his finger, indicating it was around the corner.

The elevator arrived with an electronic dinging.

"Thank you so much," Jane gushed. "I'm so lucky to have run into you two. Have a wonderful day, okay?"

The woman gave her a concerned look. "You too, dear."

Jane set off down the hall to the right, checking the sequence of the numbers on the doors as she went. A noise from her phone brought her to a stop. She'd forgotten about Kirbi.

"Jane?"

"I'm here. Sorry. I think I know where he is."

"I overheard. I'm downstairs but I can't get in yet. Wait for me."

"Okay." Jane told her, but stayed in motion, watching the numbers on the doors.

Eleven fourteen. Eleven fifteen. Eleven sixteen.

Again, she focused on sound, listening for some telling clue.

Eleven nineteen. Eleven twenty.

She turned the corner. Five units. Five possibilities. Assuming the elderly woman knew what she was talking about.

Jane slowed her progress, hovering briefly at each door, ears pricked.

But nothing—no noises, no music, no voices.

At the last door, eleven twenty-five, she smelled garlic and onions. A fresh scent as opposed to something residual, she thought. She had her knuckle poised to knock when she heard a click to her left.

Glancing in that direction, she saw Mark coming out of eleven twenty-one. His back was to her. And he was wrestling a suitcase out the door into the hall.

Jane froze for several seconds, holding her breath.

She was almost tempted to leap on his back once more, as she had in the bar.

Instead, she spoke into her phone at normal, conversational volume. "Kirbi, I've just spotted him. The apartment number is eleven twenty-one."

Mark turned, face blanching.

Then awkwardly fumbled the suitcase back through the door.

Jane raced toward him. He'd almost closed the door after him when she launched herself into it, bashing inward, right shoulder and upper arm making contact. The door collided with something on the other side. Mark, she assumed.

Flexing at the knees now, she used her legs to drive, and for a short while, inch by inch, seemed to make progress. But then progress slowed, ceased, and the tide turned. He was successfully pushing back. She was going to be locked out.

At the last second, Jane jammed her left foot between door and frame.

Though an awkward move, it did the trick—the door couldn't be closed. This stalemate didn't last long, however. Mark began stomping down on the offending foot.

Despite the pain, which brought tears to her eyes, Jane forced herself not to pull back.

Not then, nor when he switched tactics, opening the door slightly and slamming it against *the side* of her foot.

She knew she should just wait for Kirbi and/or the police. But she couldn't.

Shifting her stance slightly, she lowered her shoulder and began pushing once more. Matching her efforts to the rhythm of the door's motion. Shoving inward with all her might when pressure on the door was eased in preparation for the next slam.

And on the fourth such on-the-off-beat shove, she got results.

Inside, she heard Mark cry out. Apparently he'd been struck by the door. And to her astonishment—it swung open, he stumbled back, and she lurched into the room.

For a long moment they just looked at each other.

His eyes were wide, and his expression a mixture of rage and alarm. Though dressed as a man now, Jane noticed he hadn't got around to removing the lip gloss or mascara.

Then he bent to a zippered side pouch on the suitcase. Drew out the same handgun she'd seen in The Pub's ladies room. And brandished it, arm extended, the barrel in her face.

"Get the fuck away from me!"

There was a lot of strain in his voice and his arm quivered. The muzzle moved in little circles. Jane was afraid, but also oddly detached from the feeling.

"Hold that thought," she heard herself say.

And watched herself turn, and calmly cross the tiled floor toward the kitchen area beyond. There was a magnetic knife holder there, attached to the wall above the counter. She examined her choices for a moment. Then, from among the six knives displayed, chose what seemed to be a boning knife.

When she turned back with it in her hand, Mark stared in disbelief. "You cunt!"

Apparently to his way of thinking, only one of them was supposed to be armed. Jane smiled.

He fired the gun.

Once. Twice. A third time.

Amazing herself, Jane advanced, the knife out before her in her right hand, her phone still clutched in her left.

In the meantime, Mark had not stopped rapidly pulling the handgun's trigger. This despite the fact that there were no further explosions. After maybe a dozen such pulls, he at last seemed to realize it was empty and his expression changed.

He lowered the weapon.

Jane watched his Adam's apple bob twice. And as if of their own accord, his feet begin moving backward in a nervous retreat. Step after step. Until, that is, one of his legs bumped the suitcase on the floor behind him.

He jumped in surprise.

Jane was still coming toward him.

Soon, when she got close, he made a wild swing at her with the gun, trying to hammer her over the head with it. Though he had a long reach, she twisted out of its path. In doing so, though, her phone slipped from her fingers and clattered to the tile floor.

She left it there, throwing herself toward him, making wild stabs at his torso.

Aghast, he danced back, untouched, but not escaping by much. She could see fear in his expression. Encouraged by this, Jane pressed on.

Years before, her ex-husband had taught her chess and described the concept of *tempo*. As long as you kept your opponent on the defense, he couldn't attack. Only react. Tempo equaled control.

If she kept Mark engaged, kept him from running away for long enough, the cavalry should arrive. Jane just needed to keep from getting hurt or killed in the meantime.

Continuing to shuffle slowly toward him, she examined his face. His cheeks were flushed pink. And his gaze flicked about in a frantic search for some way out of the situation.

Then, having taken several steps back, he suddenly reversed course and lunged at her. Once more, he tried to hit her with the gun. Again in a vicious, mostly overhand motion, aiming for her head.

Jane leaned away in time, but caught a glancing blow on the outside of her left shoulder. The pain was intense. She could feel her face contort and her vision mist over for a moment.

Thankfully, because the momentum of Mark's swing sent him staggering, she had a moment to recover. She scooted by and turned. Taking deep breaths, she watched him wheel around to face her.

Now it was he who seemed to have gained confidence.

Behind those eyes, his mind was working. She saw him look at his suitcase, then the door, then back at her. She advanced, holding the knife in both hands now. She waved it side to side as though to block his passage by her.

No—she would not let him simply get away.

Maybe Kirbi would come in time, maybe she wouldn't. It didn't matter. In the present moment, there were only two people in the universe. She and Mark.

"You're going right back to jail, McGarrity," she told him. "They got your fingerprints. You'll need a new arrest photo though."

Jane was heartened to see her knowledge of his real name register negatively in his expression.

But then without warning he made another attempt to hammer her with the pistol. This time she avoided the attack by stepping to her right. And as she did so, she extended her arms, poking the sharp narrow tip of the knife at him. It was more of a threatening move than a true counterattack.

So she was surprised when his forward motion brought him into forcible contract with the blade. She felt it break the skin. She jumped back, watching his mouth become an oval of shock.

He was wearing a white T-shirt bearing the face of Bob Marley, printed in black. Above the face it said *Freedom*. Below the face, *One Love*. Between the words *One* and *Love* a blotch of red had appeared.

"You fucking cunt," he spat out in a bitter tone.

291

"You don't have much of an insult repertoire do you, Martin?"

He scowled.

The two of them looked at each other. Several moments passed.

Jane knew time was on her side, just as he knew it wasn't on his.

He'd heard her on the phone to Kirbi in the hall. Plus, the red blotch on his shirt was growing.

Again, she could see by the movement of his eyes that he was thinking of making a try at getting by her and out the door. He looked desperate now. She stepped sideways to block his way.

She could feel her heart pounding in her chest. This was so crazy.

Then, abruptly he reached back and heaved the pistol at her.

Though she had no time to duck or dodge, he missed, and it sailed harmlessly by her head, thudding against the door behind.

Now Mark had nothing and she had the knife.

He backed up, groped to his left, and yanked a big cushion from the couch beside him.

He threw it at her, missed, and glanced about for other things to throw.

Jane didn't have a good feeling about how this might eventually play out. She liked things better when she was advancing and he was retreating. Tempo.

In the process of grabbing up another cushion, Mark's eyes widened when he saw that she was again closing on him, knife boldly out before her.

He looked afraid and she liked that. Or at least liked it better than being afraid, herself.

She saw his gaze drop to the bloody front of his shirt. Then watched him begin shying back again, step by step with her approach. Good.

Behind him, the sliding glass door to the balcony was open. His shoulder bumped its anodized metal frame. His eyes still locked on hers, he rolled his back around its edge as he moved outside into the open air and bright sunlight.

Later, Jane would consider this moment.

If she'd been thinking clearly, she might have simply closed and locked the sliding door. Maybe she could've imprisoned him out there on the balcony. Or at least forced him to take the time to somehow break the glass.

But it never occurred to her. All she knew was that she couldn't lose her momentum.

And so she followed him, menacing him with the knife, afraid to stop, lest he get the upper hand before help arrived.

Later that day, she would be asked about her intentions. Several times, in several ways, and by several people. Had she been trying to hurt him? Or kill him? Maybe, say, in order to get back at him for what he'd done to her?

Not really, she told them. She'd just been caught up in the moment. As had he.

And what happened, happened quickly.

Jane scuttled out through the doorway in a crouch, the blade before her in both hands.

And Mark kept backing up, looking more and more crazed somehow.

The railing would be measured later and found to be an OSHA-compliant four feet. The question of how he, at six-two, managed to lurch over and fall to his death came up, but Jane had no answer.

Out on the balcony, she hadn't touched him. With the knife or with her hands.

And it hadn't been intentional on his part. The fall. She'd seen his panicked face when he realized what was happening, and had tried to catch himself.

THIRTY-TWO

irbi didn't have much occasion to go to Poway. Another time, with less on her mind, she might have enjoyed the drive more. She got to Van Horne's place just before noon.

Though Monday, it was a holiday, Martin Luther King Day. And, as he'd warned her, he was having a family get-together. So when she reached the top of his drive she was not surprised to see a jumble of parked vehicles. Just not this many. Apparently he had a big family.

The house was a sprawling, two-story behemoth overlooking a golf course. Fleecy clouds hung in a startlingly blue sky above the hills. She found a place to park her Jag and climbed out.

Following the instructions Van Horne had given her on the phone, she ignored the front door and made for the wrought-iron gate on the far end. Then once through it, followed the sound of music and the odor of cooking meat around to the rear.

The party appeared to be catered. A small, open, tent-like structure had been erected next to the pool. Inside it, a woman in a red apron tended covered dishes laid out on a long serving table. While a man in a similar apron, fork in hand, poked what looked like chicken breasts on a charcoal grill.

Kirbi ball-parked the attendees at fifty people. She noticed many were small in stature like Van Horne. All seemed to be having a good time.

On the lawn beyond the pool a group of teenagers kicked around a soccer ball. Some younger kids gleefully played a game of chase-and-be-chased with a spotted puppy. A half dozen adults sat submerged to the neck in the frothy waters of an in-ground hot tub. And three times that number sat around two large circular tables, eating off paper plates.

Van Horne was among the group at the tables. Noticing Kirbi's arrival, he flashed her a toothy smile and got to his feet, glass of red wine in hand. Until now she'd seen him only in his usual white shirt, suit pants, and bow tie. Today he had on jeans and a pale blue guayabera.

"You hungry or thirsty?"

Kirbi shook her head. "I'm good."

"You sure? There's some killer flank steak over there."

"Thanks just the same."

Van Horne shrugged and gestured for her to follow him. "How's Jane holding up?" he said over his shoulder.

"I think she'll be okay."

"She won't face any legal trouble over what happened?"

"No. The police questioned both of us most of the afternoon, but seemed to accept what'd

happened as an accident."

"Good."

Van Horne in the lead, they were strolling down the back side of the house.

Kirbi registered the things they passed on the way. A lap pool. A section of lawn laid out

with wickets and posts for croquet. A tall vinyl-hooded item on a tripod that she concluded had to be a telescope. A tennis court. A row of small ornamental trees, pruned to topiary ovals.

Eventually, coming to a set of French doors on the far end, Van Horne stopped. Opened one. And bade Kirbi precede him.

Inside was a broad, high-ceilinged room with a slate floor and matching fireplace.

She trailed Van Horne across to an arrangement of wooden desks. Behind them were some built-in cabinets. She waited while he unlocked one of the cabinets with a key.

"You feel good about this buyback?"

Kirbi frowned. "More or less. But I'm wary of how *easily* he settled for the hundred K."

"Well, assuming the offer is real, John and I appreciate the hell out of your getting him down to that price."

"Not a problem," she told him in a properly modest tone.

As she looked on, he took an aluminum attaché case from the cabinet. Then laid it flat on the nearest desk and opened it. Kirbi saw that the case contained stacks of banded currency. But also a pen and piece of paper, both of which he passed her.

As he sipped wine from his wineglass, she scanned the paper. For the most part it was a receipt for one hundred thousand dollars in cash.

"Should I count it first?"

Van Horne gave her a baffled shrug.

Kirbi chuckled, signed the thing at the bottom, and handed it and the pen back to him.

"You think this guy's got in mind to try pull something?" he asked.

"Not necessarily. But I'm going to be armed and extra vigilant."

"David will be with you, right?" Meaning Martinez.

Kirbi nodded. "Yeah. Like I mentioned, I'm not sure how the arrangements will go. How this guy'll want to do the actual exchange."

"Just be careful, whatever happens."

"I will."

"With the money and with your own safety," Van Horne said, his expression serious.

"I'll do my best."

"And you've already got the packet, right?"

"Yeah."

The day after the robbery, as requested, she'd been given Merman photos and specs. Now that today she was finally going to see the thing, they should help to make sure she didn't buy some fake. It would be even better to also have along a RayBright employee from Project Sixteen. But for some reason Van Horne and the general had nixed this idea.

Next to her, Van Horne closed the aluminum case and snapped the latches shut. After which he turned to her with an odd look, put his hand on her shoulder, and leaned close enough for her to smell the wine on his breath. Their eyes met.

For an instant she was afraid he was coming on to her.

He wasn't.

"Please get that thing back." he said. "*Please.* Otherwise we're so eff-ing screwed."

Kirbi, at a loss for a reply that was both honest and reassuring, settled for a decisive nod. Then another.

* * *

The desk phone in the RayBright Security office sounded at exactly three.

"This is Kirbi," she said.

"You got the money?" The same deep-voiced older male. But speaking in a raspy whisper.

Kirbi glanced at Martinez, who was listening on the speaker. "Yes. And I take it you've got the device."

"I have."

"Okay then, let's do some business. When and where?"

"Why not right now—there at RayBright."

"Why not?" Kirbi agreed, making an effort to conceal her surprise.

"Here's the way it's going to happen then. In a few minutes, I'm sending someone over. He'll be driving a rented moving truck. What you want will be in the back of the truck. You give my guy the money and what's in the truck is yours. Okay?"

"Okay."

"Here's something else. While the transaction is going on, someone will be watching from a distance with a scoped rifle. If there's any monkey business—the money's not right, or you try to grab my guy—two things can happen. Are you listening, dear?"

"I am," Kirbi answered, her thoughts flying as she worked through what he'd said. The *dear* grated on her, but she figured it was probably meant to.

"One, a couple of high-velocity slugs can make a mess of all that wonderful foreign technology. You don't want it damaged. Two, a couple of slugs can also easily make a mess of the human anatomy. Do we understand each other?"

The sniper threat sounded bogus to Kirbi, but she didn't fully discount it. Maybe the guy was just that crazy. "We do."

"Good," the caller said and broke the connection.

She and Martinez exchanged a look. Then Martinez picked up the aluminum case of cash, and the two of them headed down the hall to the reception area.

When they got there, they got something of a shock.

Out the front windows, they could see that the rental truck was already present, up at the gate.

Kirbi and Martinez pushed through the front doors. It must have just come, because the gate guard was striding toward it from his shack. He had his hands on his hips in annoyance. Maybe because the vehicle was parked sideways across both entrance and exit lanes.

"Carmichael," Martinez called out from halfway up the sloping asphalt.

The guard turned and took note of his approaching boss. He glanced impatiently back at the truck, wanting to confront the driver. But waited, having picked up on something in Martinez's voice.

Kirbi kept her hand on the butt of her holstered Glock as she ran. She was also wearing a tactical vest over her long sleeved T-shirt. And on her belt, was carrying a can of Mace and one of RayBright Security's radios. She swung her head from side to side, trying to decide where a sniper might hide, if there indeed was one.

When they'd just passed the traffic barriers, Martinez said, "Jesus Fucking Christ."

Hearing this, she stopped quartering the area to look where he was looking.

Steven Stanko had appeared at the back of the truck. He had his arms turned out, palms up. And wore a grin that said he appreciated the irony of the moment as well.

Had they misread him? Was he in deep—part of the robbery all along?

"Hi, David," Stanko said. Then gave Kirbi a knowing smile. "And you're looking good, baby. Got that G.I. Jane thing going."

"Good to see you, too, Steve," she told him, coming to a halt. She fixed him with her gaze and returned his smile.

"Life is so unpredictable."

"Isn't it," she agreed.

Martinez was scowling at Stanko.

She touched his arm to break the spell. "*David*, let's look in the truck."

"While you're looking in the truck," Stanko said, "how about letting me see the money." He gestured toward the aluminum case.

Kirbi shook her head. "First we take a look at the merchandise."

Then breezed past Stanko to the rear of the truck, where Martinez joined her. After handing her the case, he released the truck's rear latch and raised the roll-up door.

Inside on a RayBright Labs pallet jack sat a long, metallic gray box.

"Carmichael," Martinez said, catching the gate guard's eye, and glancing meaningfully at the beaming Stanko. "Watch Judas, here."

Carmichael nodded.

Then Martinez climbed into the back of the truck to do the authentication.

Kirbi, for her part, wheeled about and began a continual visual sweep of the street in front of RayBright. She kept her right hand on her Glock. Be ready for anything, she told herself.

When perhaps a full minute had passed, she heard Martinez jump down to the pavement behind her. Turning, she watched him put a tape measure into his pocket. Followed by the plastic envelope of specs and photos.

When he looked up, she said, "What's the word?"

He shrugged. "It's either the real deal or one hell of a fake."

"Good enough," Kirbi told him.

She held the aluminum case out to Stanko, who immediately stepped forward to take it.

He laid it on the truck bed next to her and popped it open.

"Oo-la-la," he said, running his fingers over the money.

Then, as if performing a magic trick, produced a tightly folded white pillowcase from his back pocket. Shook it out. And began shoveling the money into it.

When the task was completed, he shot Kirbi a mock-wicked grin.

"Gotta go," he said with a laugh, darting around the side of the truck to disappear from view.

Kirbi, Martinez, and Carmichael exchanged stunned looks.

Finally she dashed around the back of the truck after the fleeing Stanko. The driver door was closed. She leapt up on the running board and peered into the open window, but the cab was empty. She'd feared Stanko had some wild plan to jump in and drive off before they could get the device out.

"Look," Martinez said, but Kirbi had already seen.

300

The running figure of Stanko was already well down the street. The white pillowcase swinging back and forth in his hand as his arms pumped.

Kirbi jumped down from the truck and watched, trying to think.

She turned to Martinez. "Listen, you stay with the device—priority one. The prime directive. Drive the truck down inside and secure it."

He nodded. "Yes."

"I'm going to go after Stanko."

"Why?"

"I'm not sure," she confessed. "But something's not right here."

Then grimaced, took a deep breath, and set off down the street at a run. Behind her she heard that cab door open and close, and the truck's engine start. She didn't look back.

For the first ten yards or so—despite giving little credence to the sniper threat—she could almost *feel* the cross hairs lined up on her. A vivid imagination wasn't always a blessing. However, when no actual bullets came, she soon relaxed and focused on the pursuit.

Ahead, Stanko had a strong pace going. But unless he was in *a lot* better shape than he appeared to be, he was hardly going to lose her. Regardless of the fact that she was running in boots. Regardless of all the equipment she was carrying.

And Kirbi was right.

She caught him in maybe four tenths of a mile.

Lost in his own world, he never looked back, nor gave any sign he heard her pounding steps closing on him. She considered tackling or tripping him. But ended up merely zooming up alongside of him, matching her speed to his, stride for stride.

"Hey, Steve," she announced in a jaunty tone.

He flinched in surprise, then rallied to offer a flirtatious look.

"You're pretty good," he told her in a strained voice, breathing hard.

"I usually run three or four times a week," she acknowledged.

301

"So it would seem."

"What I need you to do, Steve, is stop for a minute so we can talk."

She saw his eyes stray to her pistol.

"Okay," he said, chuckling and slowing to a halt.

Something was going on, but Kirbi couldn't figure what.

Part of the strangeness was Stanko, his personality. She didn't have an exact take on him somehow. His mixture of smarts and goofiness.

"Listen, would you have a cup of coffee with me sometime?"

Kirbi looked at him. What? "I don't think so. I don't feel any compatibility, Steve—no chemistry."

"Never say never," he insisted, giving her his I'm-so-wonderful grin.

"Where you going with the pillowcase, if you don't mind saying?"

"Nowhere in particular."

"Nowhere in particular?"

"Yeah," he said and handed it to her. "I was just running."

Kirbi held it for a moment, perplexed. Then opened the top and looked inside. It contained cut newspaper, bundled as the money had been bundled. She glanced up and saw Stanko's eyes lit with amusement.

That was why he'd been told to take it out of the briefcase. So a substitution could be made. It had taken place and she'd foolishly missed it.

"Where'd you do the switch?" she asked in her calmest tone. As if the answer didn't really matter to her. As if they were two professionals, analyzing some common bit of business.

"I'll tell you if you'll have that coffee with me."

She thought about it for a moment. "Fair enough."

They shook hands.

After which he just looked at her.

"So," she said, not bothering to hide her impatience.

"Uh, yeah, sorry. It was by the gate, right in front of the truck. He was in those oleanders."

"Who?"

"The guy from 'Homeland Security.'"

"Did you see him?"

Stanko shook his head. "Not really. Just his hand—and he was wearing gloves."

Kirbi pushed the pillowcase back into his reluctant grasp, and sprinted off in the direction she'd come.

Her boots slammed the pavement as she ran full-out now. Shit. Shit. Shit. How had she not seen it coming?

When she got to the gate, the truck was gone—down around the back of the building, she assumed. The guard, Carmichael, was at his post, though.

She gasped for oxygen. "Did you see anyone? Or any cars? After I left?"

He peered at her, agog, taken aback by her intensity. But after a moment, the question still hanging in the air, shook his head.

Kirbi walked over to check the bushes. Where the guy had supposedly been hiding. As she could have predicted, there was no sign of him. She got out her phone to call Van Horne about getting Merman back, but decided to wait until she'd stopped panting.

Before she made the call, Stanko arrived, pillowcase of fake money dangling from his hand.

The truck had been rented in his name, he explained. He needed it back. What had happened, he'd gotten a call, been given an address, and had driven there to find the device sitting on the loading dock of a warehouse.

"How much were you paid to do all this?" Kirbi asked.

Stanko gave her his trademark smirk. "Enough to buy you the cup of coffee of your dreams, baby."

Kirbi sighed.

(THIRTY-THREE)

A couple of days later, Harvey was out in his barn, mucking out one of the horse stalls. Though a hired man came regularly to help with such chores, Harvey sometimes like to do things himself. He couldn't have said exactly why.

Maybe it was to prove to himself that he still could.

In any event, he'd hadn't been at it long before his phone vibrated in his pocket. He paused to check it. He'd been expecting a callback and this was it: Luis Maldonado, who managed a small business for him. A business through which he occasionally laundered cash.

Harvey spoke to Luis for a few minutes, then went back to work.

He was just getting back into the rhythm of the task, when something drew his attention. A sound outside. Footsteps? He paused to listen and, a moment later, saw a backlit figure appear in the bright rectangle of the barn doorway.

"Harvey Grant?" a young female voice called out.

"Over here," he said.

Dorothy must have told her where he was.

He leaned his pitchfork against the stall. And stepping forward, examined his visitor. She was a small black woman with short natural hair. Maybe thirty years old. Wearing bluejeans, a blue top, and bright red running shoes.

But what was she? Not a salesperson. Dorothy knew better than to inflict anyone like that on him.

Accompanying her was Calhoun, his Australian shepherd, tail wagging and tongue lolling, everybody's instant friend. Harvey's trust was harder to earn. Getting a vague cop vibe from her, he wondered if she was maybe some kind of code-enforcement bureaucrat.

"What's up?" he asked.

She put her hand out in forthright fashion. "I'm Kirbi Mack."

They shook.

"I'm a security consultant working for RayBright Labs," she went on. "I believe we spoke on the phone."

Frowning, Harvey met her gaze. "Did we?"

"You're a hard guy to catch up with."

"Well here I am. What was it you wanted?"

"I'd kind of like to get back that hundred thousand dollars we gave you," she said, chuckling.

He chuckled along. But in the polite manner of one not quite getting the joke yet. Then waited, watching her, a smile on his face. Their eye-lock continued until at last she broke it off, turning away to glance out the barn door.

"You've got a beautiful place here. I hardly ever get out to the back country. I live in Normal Heights, over on the edge of Kennsington."

"That's a nice area," Harvey said.

"Yeah, it is. But we don't have the open spaces you do out here."

"We like it, my wife and I. It's quiet."

She nodded. "I notice you keep animals. Is that thing I passed out there in the pen—" She made a gesture toward the north side of the barn "—a donkey?"

"Pedro. He's a burro. A rescue animal."

"Like rescued from someone who abused or neglected him?"

Harvey shook his head. "He used to live in the wild. The BLM adopts them out to people who can give them a good home."

"Very cool."

Crossing to a metal potato chip canister, Harvey opened it, grabbed out three apples, and replaced the lid. "Come on," he said. And walked past her out the door.

Outside, Pedro either read Harvey's body language or smelled the apples. Because by the time he got to the fence, the animal was there to meet him.

"He likes fruits and vegetables. But when you feed him, you need to push it into his mouth with your palm arched. Like this. You don't want to lose a finger."

He demonstrated with the first apple as she looked on. Then passed her the other two.

"Can I rub his head?"

Harvey blew out a breath. "You know, I wouldn't. Horses like that sometimes, but he can be a little… cantankerous."

By now Pedro had stretched his neck over the top board, eyes bulging, wanting another apple. She gingerly fed him one. Grinned with delight as the animal noisily chomped it down. Then gave him the other.

"So what was it you said you did again?" Harvey asked.

"Security consultant. Working for RayBright Labs."

"And you mentioned you were trying to get some money back."

She nodded. "Right. You ever hear the name Mark Hatcher?"

By this time the two of them had turned away from Pedro the burro, and were strolling, side by side, back toward the front of the barn. After pretending to think for a moment, Harvey shook his head. "I don't think so."

"Dorothy didn't seem to recall the name either."

"Hmmm," Harvey said absently.

The night before, he'd made sure to prepare Dorothy for just this kind of question. Together they'd seen news reports of Mark's dramatic fall to his death. Harvey had suggested to her that it might have been a mistake taking him in, since he'd turned out to be some sort of unsavory character. Maybe it would be best if the two of them simply played dumb—should any investigation of him find its way to their doorstep.

Dorothy had agreed.

Then Harvey had gone up above the garage to clean for a couple of hours. After which he'd divided the things Mark had left there into three trash bags. And had driven the three bags to Santee, where he threw each away in a separate public trash can.

Beside him, the little black woman said, "Why I mention him is that he was implicated in a robbery."

"This Hatcher guy."

"Yeah. But there were two involved. It's the other one I'm after now."

"The other robber."

"Right."

"Well, I wish you luck," Harvey told her. "You seem like a real smart and determined little gal. I think you'll accomplish whatever you set your mind to." Then paused and gestured at a mound of horse droppings ahead on the asphalt. "Watch out for that, by the way."

She nodded and made a slight alteration in course. "Thanks."

"I didn't notice it earlier or I would have cleaned it up. I'll get it after you go."

"I'm not going yet."

"Okay," Harvey said equably.

They'd arrived back at the barn door, where the two of them halted.

Together they looked out across the canyon. A single-engine plane was visible, but because of the distance, the faint noise of its engine seemed to come from well behind it. Light and sound. Different speeds.

"Sometimes in life," Harvey said after a moment, "when you arrive at an impasse, you have to consider that it might be because you've been framing things the wrong way."

Though the little black woman made no reply to this, Harvey sensed he had her interest.

He went on. "Like if you're talking to somebody, and you're not getting what you want out of the conversation. Maybe you need to rethink what's going on."

Again, she said nothing.

"Maybe what's really taking place" Harvey continued, "is more a *negotiation*."

"Like two people making a deal," she said.

"Right. Where both parties benefit."

"For instance."

Harvey offered a careless shrug. "For instance, once in a while information is more important than money. Let's take, as an example, this guy you're after. But let's say he *knows* something this company you're working for would want to know. What was its name again?"

"RayBright."

"Right, RayBright. Let's say, just for the sake of discussion, there's more to the situation than RayBright imagines."

THIRTY-FOUR

That night, Kirbi called Van Horne and asked him his location. When he told her he was still at RayBright, working late, she drove there to speak with him in person. At the gate, the guard who'd been pepper sprayed during the robbery was on duty. He let her in, waited for her to park, then brought her into the building and up in the elevator to Van Horne's office.

Van Horne was behind his desk. Giving her his toothy smile, and tossing aside the paper he'd been reading, he beckoned her in. Kirbi took a seat across from him, and without preamble began telling him about Harvey Grant and what she'd learned from him.

Several times he stopped her to ask questions. Or get her to clarify something.

It wasn't a pleasant conversation, but she hadn't expected it to be.

He listened and took her seriously. She'd built up a lot of trust and credibility with him over the previous two weeks. But she could see he was having a hard time with what she now had to say. It wasn't hard to imagine why.

Finally, given the implications of this new information, he suggested they present it all to Shellhammer. Immediately. That night. Kirbi agreed with the idea, and they set off together in Van Horne's Lincoln Navigator for Shellhammer's house in Mission Hills.

The general, however, proved not to be home.

At the door, his wife explained that he was out walking the dog. Did the two of them want to come inside and await his return? Van Horne demurred.

"Is something wrong, Eric, you seem upset?"

"I'm fine, Abby, we just need to talk with him."

"You should call him on his cell and find out where he is in the neighborhood."

"That's a good idea," Van Horne told her as they left. "We'll do that."

But they didn't.

Instead, he and Kirbi drove around the area for several minutes until they spotted Shellhammer on a side street, half a dozen blocks west. He was standing under a streetlamp. A large hound-like dog on a leash was snuffling about at the base of a nearby palm tree. They parked across the street from him and got out.

The cool night air smelled faintly of irrigated vegetation.

Shellhammer seemed neither surprised nor unsurprised by their arrival.

Not for the first time, Kirbi was impressed by his self-possession. She wondered whether it came from some kind of native neurological wiring, or was a trait he'd cultivated over long years of military command.

Per prior agreement with Van Horne, she was to make the case.

"General," she began, "I've turned up something new and pretty startling, having to do with the Merman situation. I've already shared it with Eric. But we thought you should hear it, too, right away and first-hand."

Shellhammer glanced at Van Horne, then swung his attention back to Kirbi. "This doesn't sound good. What's going on?"

"Well, it has to do with the identity of the person who might've been behind the robbery itself. The buyer, so to speak. The person who commissioned the stealing of the device."

"I see."

"What I've learned is that this buyer may have sustained a gunshot wound in the melee that occurred when the thieves tried to actually turn over the device to him."

"Then you've found the second thief—the thickset one."

310

"Yes. His name is Harvey Grant, and he's a local. And unlike Mark Hatcher, he's alive and willing to talk to me."

Shellhammer's eyes went wide. "That's fantastic. Good work!"

Kirbi dipped her head in acknowledgement of the compliment, but continued. "If I remember right, general, the other day you mentioned you'd hurt your leg playing tennis. Is that correct?"

But before she could get an answer, Van Horne cut in.

"I'm sorry, John. This Grant guy claims it was *you* who hired him, which is of course preposterous …"

Her heart sank. Van Horne hadn't been able to contain himself.

She didn't doubt Shellhammer had intuited where she was going in her spiel. But that wasn't the point. The point was that she and Van Horne had settled on a *plan*. She was to logically lay out the evidence, the two of them would observe Shellhammer's reaction as she did so, then they'd give Shellhammer a chance to rebut the charge.

Which Van Horne hoped, if not expected, his partner could easily do.

So Kirbi waited now, disappointed, but with her gaze locked on Shellhammer.

She willed herself not to be distracted. The way Van Horne had made the accusation had been clumsy, but he'd made it. She was eager to see how Shellhammer handled it.

Though violence seemed a remote possibility, Kirbi had her Glock in the right-hand pocket of her coat, just in case. There was no point in being caught flat-footed if things turned weird.

And, for an instant at least—when Shellhammer took an alarming step forward—she almost thought they had.

His intention, however, was benign. He laid a comforting hand on the distressed Van Horne's shoulder. Then expelled a noisy breath which Kirbi only belatedly recognized as a chuckle. A confident and dismissive chuckle.

Listening to it, she felt a chill that had nothing to do with the night's brisk temperature.

Could she have been *wrong* about all of this?

Was it possible Harvey had duped her? Run a game on her?

Maybe he'd merely told a story designed to deflect from his own guilt and sow discord within RayBright. Fear and doubt stirred in her. Her mind raced.

She felt outside of herself, an observer.

She watched Shellhammer pass her the dog's leash, which she numbly accepted. The creature appeared as confused by the action as she was. It gazed up at her, sniffing her hand.

Meanwhile, Shellhammer, now bent forward from the waist, was grasping the bottom of a baggy woolen pant leg. And as Kirbi and Van Horne looked on, raised it. Up along a lean muscular ankle, to a bony knee, then beyond, almost to the crotch, where the fabric was bunching in a wrinkled wad.

"I twisted the hell out of it when I fell," he said. He moved a gentle palm along the outside of the knee. In the illumination from the streetlamp the exposed leg looked obscenely pale. "I probably should give it a rest, but Buddy—" He meant the dog "—won't let me. He's got to have his nightly turn around the neighborhood."

This said, he peered up at Kirbi and Van Horne, swiveling his head from one to the other. His eyes met theirs. His expression seemed to say, Was there anything else?

No, Kirbi thought. That pretty much does it.

Her stomach felt queasy. Her breathing and heart-rate had slowed. She felt momentarily unsteady on her feet.

Beside her, she heard Van Horne speak, as if from a distance. "Well, thanks for letting us interrupt your evening, John."

"Not at all."

"I'll see you tomorrow then."

"Good."

"At least we got the device back in time, didn't we?"

"That we did," Shellhammer agreed.

Then reached to take the leash back from Kirbi.

She felt her limp fingers release it. Saw the dog tip its head back, giving its master an eager look.

When Van Horne headed across the street for his car, Kirbi followed wordlessly behind.

Hands thrust deep in the pockets of her coat, she moved with a lethargic step, her thoughts bleak. She waited for Van Horne to zap her door open. Then slid in.

"Well, we got that settled," he said off-handedly.

Kirbi grunted, not trusting her voice yet. Then turned to look out the back window at the general's retreating figure.

"I'm afraid this Harvey buckaroo was bullshitting you."

"Maybe," Kirbi managed after a long moment, going for blandness but not getting it right.

"You still don't think so?"

"I didn't say that."

"Then what?"

He'd started the engine and put his hand on the shift lever. But hesitated, peering over at her for several seconds, his expression unreadable. "What?" he repeated.

Kirbi knew there was still time to play it off. To just say to him, *No, forget it. Let's go.* To allow Van Horne to drive her back to her car at Ray-Bright.

She was all too aware she'd already lost big points this night. She'd essentially accused one of her employers, a multimillionaire retired army general, of conspiracy and theft and whatever else that all implied. And she'd been made a fool of.

The humiliation stung.

When you bet and lost, it was best to take stock. You didn't throw *everything* away. You didn't double down on error and make a bigger fool of yourself, did you?

No.

But somehow she couldn't get Harvey out of her head. She'd sensed in him an unexpected integrity. And what he'd told her made a kind of twisted sense. The information fitted together with other things she knew.

Van Horne was still expectantly looking over at her. She sucked in a deep breath, and felt her chest rise as the air rushed in though her nostrils.

"Would you humor me in something?"

He looked as if he wanted to say something else, but forced a reluctant, "Okay."

"I'd like to drive around the block, or even a couple of blocks. I'd like to come up on him from another direction. I want to see him when he doesn't see us."

"John?"

She nodded, holding his gaze.

"What for?"

"As I said, just to humor me."

He made a face. "What are you looking for?"

"I don't want to say yet."

"You don't want to say yet," he drawled, his tone skeptical but not unkind.

He put the Navigator in gear and eased out into the street.

Though ready to tell him what to do, she didn't appear to need to.

314

At the corner he made a right, drove a block, and made another right. Advanced three blocks in that direction. Circled back with two more rights. Then pulled to the curb, and shut off the lights and engine.

Ahead, out the windshield in the distance, a tall indistinct silhouette could be seen. A smaller, four-legged silhouette trotted along beside it. Kirbi and Van Horne observed the duo's slow approach without speaking.

"You think he showed us the wrong leg," Van Horne said after a while. "The one *without* the wound."

"No wonder you got the Nobel Prize."

He gave a soft laugh at the gibe. "So, he should be limping on his *left*."

"I could very well be wrong."

"Let's see if you are."

They waited some more.

Soon the two silhouettes came more clearly into view. Yes, Kirbi thought. The human one walked with a definite limp. The guy has a *hitch in his gait,* as her Mississippi grandmother might have put it.

Next to her, Kirbi heard Van Horne sigh.

"No, you're right," he said.

She shrugged. "He almost had us."

"No, he almost had *me*."

"You wanted to believe. I wouldn't have minded being wrong, but I had less at stake in the matter."

Van Horned sighed again. "Yeah," he acknowledged.

"He is a bold one though, isn't he? Brazening it out with that leg charade."

"He is," Van Horne agreed in the same grudging tone. "He's always been a kind of larger-than-life character."

"I read he was captured by the Viet Cong in Vietnam."

315

"He was. He doesn't like to talk about it much, but one time he told me he spent two months in a four-by-four-by-four bamboo cage."

"But then managed to escape. And make it back to American lines, traveling at night and living off the land."

Van Horne nodded, giving her an odd look. Maybe surprised at the depth of her research. "Right. Amazing, isn't it?"

Then the two of them turned back to stare out the windshield once more. Shellhammer was still a block and a half away, his pace unhurried. Half a minute passed.

"I guess I'm having a hard time make sense of this whole thing."

Kirbi glanced over at him, and saw his round cheeks slick with tears. "Of course."

"I don't know what to feel."

"It's understandable. This has to be a big shock."

"We worked together for ten years, building a business, dealing with crises, putting in these incredible hours. And now, it's like he just spit on all that—on our unquestioned trust in each other."

Kirbi nodded in helpless sympathy, but then saw Van Horne abruptly reach for the door handle, about to get out of the vehicle. She grasped his opposite forearm. He wrenched around to look at her.

"Wait," she said.

"I'm going to—"

"Of course, but listen. We know, but he doesn't know we know."

His expression remained confused.

"Here's my professional advice," she went on. "Don't give away this advantage."

"Why?"

"Because confronting him isn't going to help anything. All it will do is allow him to cover his tracks further, maybe even pull something else. Let's get out of here before he sees us, okay?"

He continued to look at her for several seconds, then dropped his eyes and nodded. She took her hand off his arm. As he started the engine, Kirbi sagged back in her seat and took a last look at Shellhammer.

Though his deviousness and double-dealing disturbed her, it somehow didn't fully tarnish her admiration for him. For one thing she was a sucker for good manners, and Shellhammer had them. He was a classy guy. That shouldn't count, but somehow it did.

She knew it wouldn't count with her older relatives on her mother's side.

Immigrant Jews from Eastern Europe, they'd associate Shellhammer with the era of housing covenants and academic quotas. To them he'd be just another entitled WASP. An arrogant vanilla guy used to running things with his arrogant vanilla buddies.

But if nothing else, Kirbi had been in the military long enough to respect the acquisition of rank. She knew you didn't make two-star general just by knowing the right people, or which fork to use for which course. It came to down to hard work and grit. Both of which she approved of, wherever she encountered them.

Van Horne made a U-turn.

She peered idly out the side widow at the houses. People lived in them. People she didn't know. People with needs and wants, hopes and plans.

What had Shellhammer been up to? Was it simply money? Or did he have some less obvious, but equally human, motivation?

The whole thing seemed strange and counterintuitive.

On the eve of an Initial Public Offering of stock, you stole something from your own company, the loss of which would very likely damage that company's reputation and therefore the price of the stock?

Whatever the answer, Kirbi felt good in having come as far as she had. Buoyant even.

She'd not only successfully gotten the Merman device back, she'd tracked down Harvey.

Stanko's number for him had turned out to be a disposable. It hadn't gotten her anywhere. But in *Mark's* smartphone—which she'd swiped from his luggage before the police came that day, downtown—she'd found a number that had.

And Harvey had been the key. Because he was able put her onto Shellhammer's role in the crime. Shellhammer, who might've buffaloed her, if she hadn't trusted her instincts.

Outside, Kirbi watched the dim residential streets whiz by. Followed by the various stores and restaurants along a more brightly lit commercial boulevard. Then finally the freeway leading down to Mission Valley.

Lost in her thoughts, she was slightly startled when Van Horne spoke.

"So what do you think my next step should be?"

Kirbi took a breath. "My recommendation would be you get a lawyer, you personally, and examine your options. It's a complicated situation. You need to protect yourself and your company."

"You think Harvey would testify?"

"Not a chance."

"Why not?" Van Horne asked, surprised.

"There's nothing in it for him. And he knows you can't really do anything to him without making things worse for RayBright."

"Like bad publicity."

"Exactly."

Van Horne shook his head. "You know, it's funny. John was the one who brought you in." Meaning Shellhammer had been the one to suggest hiring Kirbi in the first place.

"He probably figured I'd be just small-time enough and incompetent enough not to be a threat."

"Ah. I hadn't thought of that."

"That day Baines and I delivered our recommendations, let me guess, was it the general who pushed hard for paying me off? Like everything was all fine, and the problem was solved?"

Van Horne shot her a look, acknowledging the accuracy of her prediction. "Because you were proving *too* competent. If you'd kept on it, you might have stopped the robbery."

"And he couldn't have that."

"Right."

"But then, the irony is," Kirbi said, "by getting greedy and trying to screw Harvey and Mark, he ended up bringing about circumstances that allowed RayBright to recover the device."

"You're right. Thank you, by the way, for handling that, as well as everything else."

"You're quite welcome."

He signaled, checked his mirrors, and changed lanes. "I'm assuming most of your other jobs aren't quite as…drama-laden as this one."

Kirbi chuckled. "It *has* been an adventure."

"Would you be willing to stay on the case a little longer."

She looked over at him. "Let me guess, reporting only to you."

"Yes, reporting only to me."

"You'd like to know *why* you were stabbed in the back."

"That's precisely what I'd like to know," Van Horne said.

319

⬭ THANKS ⬭

Tiffany King, Clydette Herrier,
Dan Bacal, Gloria Martin, Gary Johnson,
Kate Marshall, Tom Chambers, and Paul Patino.
Also, of course, Marie, Bill, Doug, Leigh, and Pat!

Made in the USA
Monee, IL
27 April 2023

32485124R00194